Dear
Emmie Blue

Dear Emmie Blue

LIA LOUIS

EMILY BESTLER BOOKS
—
ATRIA

New York   London   Toronto   Sydney   New Delhi

EMILY
BESTLER
BOOKS

ATRIA

An Imprint of Simon & Schuster, Inc.
1230 Avenue of the Americas
New York, NY 10020

First Emily Bestler Books/Atria Books hardcover edition July 2020

EMILY BESTLER BOOKS / ATRIA BOOKS and colophon are trademarks of Simon & Schuster, Inc.

For information about special discounts for bulk purchases, please contact Simon & Schuster Special Sales at 1-866-506-1949 or business@simonandschuster.com.

The Simon & Schuster Speakers Bureau can bring authors to your live event. For more information or to book an event, contact the Simon & Schuster Speakers Bureau at 1-866-248-3049 or visit our website at www.simonspeakers.com.

Interior design by Erika Genova

Manufactured in the United States of America

1   3   5   7   9   10   8   6   4   2

Library of Congress Cataloging-in-Publication Data has been applied for.

ISBN 978-1-9821-3591-1
ISBN 978-1-9821-3593-5 (ebook)

For Juliet.
This book could be for nobody else.

The Fortescue Lane Balloon Release 2004:
celebrating 50 years of excellence in education!

Emmie Blue, age 16, Class 11R

Fortescue Lane Secondary School, Ramsgate, Kent, United Kingdom
Emmeline.Blue.1999@fortescue.kent.sch.uk

July 1, 2004

If this balloon is ever found, you'll be the only one in
the world who knows. It was me. I am the girl from the
Summer Ball. And I was telling the truth.

I was ready; so ready for him to ask me. So ready, I was practically beaming, and I imagine so red in the cheeks, I probably looked ruddy, like streetwise children do in Charles Dickens novels—a tomato with a beating heart. Only five minutes ago, everything was perfect, and I don't often use that word because nothing, however wonderful—people, kisses, bacon sandwiches—ever truly is. But it was. The restaurant, the candlelit table, the beach beyond the decking with its soft-sounding waves, and the wine, which tasted so close to what we'd had nine years ago, on the eve of our twenty-first birthdays, and hadn't been able to remember the name of since. The fairy lights, spiraling the pillars of the wooden gazebo we sat beneath. The sea breeze. Even my hair had gone just right for the first time since, well, probably that one, singular time it *did*, and that was likely back when I listened to a Walkman and was convinced Jon Bon Jovi would somehow find himself on a mini-break in Ramsgate, bump into me, and ask me out to the Wimpy for a burger and chips. And Lucas. Of course, Lucas, but then, he always looks as close to perfect as you can get. I close my eyes now, palm pressed against my forehead, knees bent on the tiles of this cold bathroom floor, and I think of him in the next room. Handsome, in that

English, waspy way of his. Skin slightly bronzed from the French sun. That crisp white shirt pressed and open at the collar. When we'd first arrived, just a couple of hours ago, swiftly ordering wine, and sharing two appetizers, I looked across at him and wondered dreamily about how we looked to other diners, against the setting sun. Who were we, to the silhouettes of strangers, ambling along the sand and past the veranda on which we sat, their shoes dangling from their fingers at their sides? We'd looked meant to be, I reckon. We'd looked like a happy couple out for dinner by the beach. An anniversary, maybe. A celebration for something. A date night, even, away from the kids at home. Two. One boy, one girl.

"I'm nervous here, Em," Lucas had begun with a chuckle, hands fidgeting on the table, fingers twisting the ring on his index finger, "to ask you." And in that moment, at that table, in that restaurant—the bathroom of which I'm hiding in now—I think I'd felt more ready, more sure, than I have ever been of anything. Ready and waiting to say yes. I'd even planned how I would say it, although Rosie said that if I rehearsed it too much, I'd sound constipated and give the impression I actually didn't want to say yes, and "tonight is not the night to do that thing where you talk like you've got the barrel of some maniac's gun shoved into your back, Emmie, 'cause you do that sometimes, don't you, when you're nervy?" But I did rehearse it in my head, ever so slightly, on the ferry over this morning. I'd say something sweet, something clever, like, "What took you so long, Lucas Moreau? I'd love nothing more." And he would squeeze my hand across the table— across the same, scallop-edged tablecloths Le Rivage has had draped on every one of their little round tables for as long as we have been coming here, and outside, on our way home, we'd walk along the beach, Lucas pausing, as always, to show me where he'd found my balloon all those years ago. He'd kiss me, too, I was sure. At his car, he would probably stop and bend, slowly, hesitatingly, to kiss me, a finger and thumb at my chin. Lucas would kiss me for the first time in fourteen years, both of us tasting of moules marinière and the gold-wrapped peppermints left on the dish with the bill, and at long last, I would be able to breathe. Because all of it would have been worth it. Fourteen years of friendship, and six years of swallowing down the urge to tell him how I really feel, would come full circle tonight.

At least, that's what I'd expected. Not this. Not me, here, crumpled in this bathroom, on a perfect night, in *our* perfect restaurant, on *our* perfect beach, after a perfect dinner, which now stares back at me, chewed and regurgitated in the restaurant's toilet bowl, an artist's impression of "utter fucking soul-destroying disaster." I was expecting to say yes. Minutes ago, I was expecting—practiced, perfect line on the tip of my tongue, back straight, and eyes full of stars—to say *yes*, to going from best and longest friends, to boyfriend and girlfriend. To a couple. On the eve of our thirtieth birthdays. Because what else could Lucas have to ask me that he couldn't possibly ask me over the phone?

I think I hid it well, the shock I felt, like a hard slap, at the sound of the question, and the nauseous, long ache that passed across my gut as his words sunk in slowly, like sickly syrup on a cake. I'd gawped. I must have, because his smile faded, his eyes narrowing the way they have always done when he's starting to worry.

"Emmie?"

Then I'd said it. Because I knew, looking at him across that table, I could say nothing else.

"Yes."

"Yes?" he repeated, sandy brows raised, broad shoulders relaxing with relief.

"Yes," I'd told him again, and before I could manage another word, tears came. Tears, I have to say, I recycled masterfully. To Lucas, in that moment, they weren't tears of devastation, of heartbreak, of fear. They were happy tears. Overjoyed tears, because I was proud of my best friend and this momentous decision he'd made; touched to be a part of it. That's why he'd grinned with relief. That is why he stood from his chair, circled the round, candlelit table, crouched by my side, and put his strong arms around me.

"Ah, come on, Em." He'd laughed into my ear. "Don't grizzle too much. The other diners'll think I'm some dickhead breaking a girl's heart over dinner or something."

Funny. Because that's exactly how it felt.

Then it had come: that hot rising from my stomach, to my chest. "I need the loo."

Lucas drew back, still crouched, and I willed him to not question it, to not look me in the eyes. He'd know. He'd be able to tell.

"Bit of a funny head since this morning," I lied. "Bit migraine-y, you know what I'm like. Need to take some painkillers, splash some water on my face..." *As if.* As if I'd smudge my makeup. But it's what they say in films, isn't it? And it didn't feel at all like real life, that moment. It still doesn't, as I hug this public—albeit sparkling—toilet, the bowl splatted with the dinner and wine we'd ordered, all beaming grins and excitement, a mere hour ago.

Married. Lucas is getting *married.*

In nine months, my best friend of fourteen years, the man I am in love with, is getting married to a woman he loves. A woman who isn't me. And I am to stand right there, at the altar, beside him, as his best woman.

T here is a knock at the cubicle door.

"Excusez-moi? Ça va?"

I have always been a loud vomiter; the sort who retches so loudly it sounds like I'm being beaten up from the inside out by the spirit of a professional wrestler, and I'm guessing this person—this concerned-sounding do-gooder on the other side of the door—wants to confirm that's not what's occurring as she washes her hands.

"Yes," I call out. "I—I'm okay. I'm just, uh . . . I'm sick—*malade*. Yes. Er, je suis malade."

The woman asks me something in French that I don't understand, but I pick up the words "partner" and "restaurant." Then she pauses, and I hear her shoes scuff on the tiles, the locked door creaking ever so slightly as if she's moved closer to press an ear to it. "Should I fetch someone? Are you okay in there?" She sounds young. Calmly concerned. One of life's helpers, probably, like Marie. Marie is always the person who stops to help the stumbling street-drunk most would be too wary to approach, talking in calm, warm tones, with no fear, no "this person could have *a goddamn knife*, and I would very much like to live until at least pension age, thank you" running through her wholly good brain. It's no wonder, really, is it? No wonder he's marrying her.

"Hello?" she says again.

"Oh. Oh no, I'm fine," I reply, my voice tight and high-pitched. "Nothing to worry about. I'm okay. Merci. Merci beaucoup."

She hesitates. "You are sure?"

"Yes. But thank you. Very much."

She says something else I don't catch, then I hear the squeak of a hinge, and the door banging softly under the romantic notes of classical music, which floats from the bathroom's speaker. I flush and get to my feet slowly, my knees tingling with the blood that trickles back in, the ends of a loose curl at my chin, damp. I can't believe I was sick. So suddenly. So forcefully. Just like they do on *Emmerdale*, throwing themselves over to the kitchen sink after shocking news, and staring down into the plughole for a moment afterward. How *dramatic*, how over the top and unlike real life, I'd think now, if this were a character on a soap. But it seems I've just made it almost thirty years without feeling gut-punched enough.

I pull out my phone, unlock it, and find our window in WhatsApp. An instinct my fingers obey before my brain can intervene. A habit. My first port of call, always. *Lucas Moreau, last online at 6:57 p.m.* Offline. Of course he's offline. He's sitting on the other side of the bathroom door, on the fairy-lit, beachside veranda, opposite an empty chair and a half-eaten bowl of garlic mussels, waiting for me. I stare at our last messages, just seven hours ago.

Me:

> There is a man sitting next to me on the ferry who is eating squid from a freezer bag. WTF???? HELP ME!

Lucas:

> Hahaha, seriously?

Me:

I'm gonna pass out.

Lucas:

I'll be waiting at the other end with smelling salts. You can do this Emmie Blue! You are made of strong stuff.

He always says that. It's Lucas's answer to so many of my doubts, my worries. When I was seventeen and alone for Christmas and I called him from the landline in my tiny flat, praying he'd pick up just so I could hear someone's voice, those were the words he'd spoken through the line. When I left Ramsgate and moved two towns over to escape every whisper, every nudge and stare in college corridors. Four years ago, when my ex, Adam, left me as well as the little flat we'd started renting. The last time he'd said it—the squid-in-freezer-bag moment aside—was almost eighteen months ago, when I moved the contents of that little flat I'd tried so hard to hold on to, into one small, roasting-hot-in-all-weathers double room, with a slightly grumpy, reclusive landlady downstairs. "You can get through this," he'd said from his bed to mine, via FaceTime. "You are made of strong stuff, Emmie Blue. Remember it." I wonder what he'd say now, if it weren't him that had caused me to flee to a toilet cubicle, mid–main course. He'd laugh, probably, say, "Christ, Em, how did that come about?" Then, "But listen, the joke's on him, you know. If he can't see how brilliant you are . . ."

I slide my phone back into my bag, wash my hands with plenty of soap that smells like fabric softener, and straighten in front of the stretch of mirrors. You'd never know. I look nothing like I feel—nauseous and shaky.

Heartbroken. I appear as preened and as glowing as when I'd left Lucas's parents' house two hours ago, bar a smudge of mascara at the corner of my eye that I dab away. Good. He can't know. Especially not now.

I swing open the bathroom door, stopping for a second to let two smiling, perfumed women pass me to the inside, and walk—slow, steady, and as tall as I can pull myself. Low, chattering voices swarm to mix with the clinking of glasses, the scrapes of cutlery on plates, and the lost notes of too-quiet music. The air is thick as it always is at Le Rivage, with the smell of garlic and lemons and the salt of the sea from outside. This is one of my favorite places. Has always been. Memories are ingrained in the walls here, in the wood of the planks of the decking. So many endless summer days and aimless beach walks over the last thirteen years have ended here. Those "Dream House Drives," where we'd drive for miles, Lucas fresh out of uni, me, newly permanent at my admin temp job, slowing as we passed huge châteaus and ramshackle four-hundred-year-old cottages, pointing out our future homes, what we'd change, what we'd keep when they were ours. Of course, every single time, almost as tradition, Lucas would get us so lost in Honfleur, he'd have to pull over and ask farmers for directions, and it was here, among the sizzle of the grill in the open kitchen and the calm rumble of the waves, that we'd refuel. With multiple appetizers, bowls of salty, rosemary-sprinkled chips, and sometimes, nothing but beer. We talked about everything on those drives and within these walls. But mainly the future, and all the things that waited for us in the sprawling years ahead. I wonder if we ever imagined this. Not so much Lucas getting married, but . . . this. Did we ever think *this* was a possibility? Something finally coming between us and changing the landscape of everything. Of us.

I step through the open glass doors of the outside dining area and see Lucas before he sees me. It's quieter out here, the gentle silk of the sea, the beautiful, now darkening view. That's where Lucas's eyes are, on the violet horizon, his elbow on the table, hand rubbing at his chin. Then he turns and sees me, his face breaking into a huge white smile. Worry. I see it, just a glimmer.

"Hey," he says. "Are you okay?"

I stand behind my chair, gripping the curved wood of its backrest. I nod at him, plaster on a smile, but I don't think I can bring myself to sit down at this unfinished meal, across from him. I thought I could, but I can't. My throat is raw. My mouth tastes of bile. And looking at him, like this, here, in this restaurant, with those slate-gray eyes, those freckles I know the exact constellation of, I might burst into tears. A disaster. Unbeknownst to Lucas, this is what tonight is. An utter disaster. The opposite of everything I planned on the dreamy, packed, squid-y ferry trip over.

"Would you mind if I head back?"

He stands then, like me, a tanned hand smoothing down the front of his white shirt. "No. No, of course I don't mind. Seriously, Em, are you all right?"

"I just feel really sick. I think I probably need to go to bed, if I'm honest. Sleep it off. Classic bloody migraine!" The chuckle I force sounds part-motorcycle.

"You haven't had one of those in a while," he says. "The last time was in London, at the cinema, wasn't it? Do you have your stuff with you? Your tablets?"

I stare at him and feel my heart lurch as if someone just slammed the brakes on. Two years ago, Lucas had come over to London for work—some architectural conference—and I'd met him in the July sunshine, on the Southbank; but in the queue for the cinema, those zigzagging dancing lights at the edge of my vision began, and like clockwork, so did the dull ache behind my eyes. We dropped out of the queue and went back to Lucas's tenth-floor hotel room, where I took the gale-force painkillers I always carry in my bag, and slept, drapes blocking out the sun, Lucas working silently, face lit blue by his laptop, beside me. He ran me a bath when I woke hours later, called quiz show questions through the door as I soaked and shouted back my answers. And after, a room service tray between us, no light but the television, I told him, there, on that bed, watching nineties quiz shows, that I felt closer than I'd ever been to that "home" feeling I've searched my whole life for. And he remembers. He remembers that night, like I do—like so many of our times together—and yet, here we stand.

"I have my tablets back at the guest cottage," I say now. "I probably just need some rest."

Lucas nods, eyes softening with concern. "Let's get the bill. Ah—" He softly takes the arm of a passing waiter, apologizes, asks if he can pay. In French, of course. Perfect French he has tried forever to teach me, laughingly, as I pronounced things—as he's often said—"like a smashed Paul McCartney lost in Marseille." Over the years I have learned only the basics. Nothing more ever stuck.

"Luke, I could just get a taxi."

Lucas's brow furrows as if I have suggested something ridiculous. "Are you joking? Don't be silly, we'll just head home. We have all weekend."

"But . . . Marie," I say. "Y-You said she would meet us after for dessert, to celebrate."

"It's no big deal, Em." He smiles, hand delving into his back pocket. "I can call her."

The bill arrives, and Lucas hands over a fan of notes, telling the waiter to keep the change. For twelve years we've taken it in turns to pay for our birthday meals, and tonight, it's Lucas's. I ignore the little voice that tells me, sadly, that my turn—now weddings, now a new wife, and a broken heart is in the mix—may never come again.

"Right." Lucas pulls on his navy-blue blazer, straightening the lapels. "Good to go?"

I nod, and with his eyebrows raised, and his mouth curved in a tiny smile, he holds out his hand. And, heart sinking all over again, I take it. Because what else is there to do right now? I love him. I have said yes to being his best woman because I love him. My best friend. My *only* friend, once upon a time. The boy who found my balloon fourteen years ago, and against all odds, through rain and storms and across miles and miles of ocean, found me.

3

WhatsApp from Rosie Kalwar:

This is exactly how it
happened, isn't it? This (or
so I hear) is how the French
ask people to go steady with
them.

WhatsApp from Rosie Kalwar:

Yep. I said "go steady."
Whaddya gonna do?

WhatsApp from Rosie Kalwar:

PS: I hope everything went
perfectly!

WhatsApp from Rosie Kalwar:

PPS: Are you shagging now?

I hold my phone high above my face, swollen, gritty eyes squinting at the
screen's bright light. Rosie has sent a photo with her four messages, and despite myself and everything I'm feeling, I laugh. In the photo, Rosie stands

on the clinical white tiles of the hotel's kitchen floor, hands to her mouth
in mock-shock, and Fox is in front of her, long suit-trousered legs bent on
one knee, holding out a croissant the way someone would proffer an en-
gagement ring. Ironically, it's sort of close. Lucas proposed to Marie over
breakfast in bed, apparently. "With a ring, across about seventeen pastries,"
he'd laughed.

I lock my phone. I can't bring myself to respond yet. I'll do it tomorrow or explain when I see them on Tuesday when I'm back at work. I'd
have made some sense of it by then, found the meaning. Because everything happens for a reason, doesn't it? Even if at first it all seems hopeless,
or wrong, or bloody disastrous. This is the headway I have made in three
hours, since leaving the restaurant and trying desperately to claw myself
out of the quicksand I feel I'm standing in: *There is a reason for this. I just
can't see it yet.*

The car journey to Lucas's parents' house from the restaurant seemed
to take longer than usual, and Lucas had chatted breezily the whole way
as I nodded and made all the right noises, the familiar leafy fields and
teeny, cobbled French villages whisking by the window. He'd walked with
me, from the driveway of his parents' ivy-blanketed house, through the
side gate, and down to the bottom of their vast, neat garden, to the farm-
house door of the guest cottage. I'd unlocked it quickly, racing against
the tears I'd worked my arse off to keep dammed during the car journey,
the key Amanda, Lucas's mum, has always handed to me in a white A5
envelope on arrival as if I'm the guest at a country B&B, clammy in my
hand. He wanted to come in. I could tell as I stood in the doorway, facing him—the way his hands were in his pockets, his shoulders rigid, one
foot on the doorstep, looking past me into the little kitchenette. Lucas
was expecting to come inside with me, like he usually does. To throw
himself on the bed, to kick off his shoes, to flick through the TV chan-
nels, listening, as I put on my pajamas in the bathroom and update him

on quirky customers at work, the door pushed to, but not shut. Instead I thanked him for dinner, apologized for cutting it short, and waffled about migraines again.

"Well, rest up, Em," he'd said. "And call me if you need me, yeah? I'm only in the house, upstairs. I can be like room service."

"I'll be fine."

"I mean it," he'd said, then he leaned forward and put his warm cheek to mine. "Happy last-day-of-being-twenty-nine to us. Been waiting years to wake up as thirty-year-olds who know *exactly* what we're doing with our lives, haven't we?"

"Sure have," I'd said with a wide smile, then I closed the door, turned my back to it, and burst into hot, silent tears in the empty darkness. That's all I've been doing. Crying. It's what I'm doing now, wrapped in this thick, feather duvet, my cheeks stinging, eyes swollen, a lap of crumbs from the scrunched, crumbling tissue I've been swiping under my nose for the last few hours.

Best woman. *Best woman.* What even *is* a best woman? Best men, sure. Maids of honor, of course. But a best woman? A "no-brainer" Lucas had called it in the red-cheeked, slightly disjointed lead-up to the question. "Because nobody—seriously, not *a soul,* knows me like you do, Emmie. It could be no one else." Ugh. I was so poised. So sure—so much so I bloody rehearsed my reply.

"We're getting married, Em." He'd beamed as he spoke. "Marie and I. And I'd . . . love for you to be my best woman. More than anything. You. Standing up there. With me. What do you say?" *You. Standing up there. With me.* I shudder so hard now, my teeth chatter, and I pull the duvet over my head. Vomiting. Uncontrollable sobbing. Swollen features. And now shivering. Nobody warns you about this in love songs, do they? Dr. Hook didn't sing about this. There are no NHS web pages for heartbreak like there are for whitlows and UTIs, but there should be.

WHEN TO SEEK MEDICAL HELP:

- *When you have cried so much that your eyes become so small and bulbous, they disappear into your face.*
- *When tears persist so much that your voice morphs into that of Barry White.*
- *When signs of insanity are demonstrated, i.e., gracefully accepting being a best woman to the person who caused the above symptoms.*

On the other side of the duvet, the air-conditioning unit rumbles on the wall like a boiling kettle, the sticky summer heat wave shut outside. My musty room back at home in Fishers Way is a tiny furnace in comparison. So hot that the second the temperature tips past the seventy-three-degree mark, I go to bed convinced that by morning I'll be found shriveled by my landlady, like a raisin in a nightie. No risk of that happening here, staying with the Moreaus, though. So I suppose there is always that. Even in the darkest of times, it is always important to focus, if you can, on the positives. No matter how small. No matter how few.

I pull back the duvet and sit up in bed, pressing the heel of my hand to my forehead, which, ironically, is beginning to throb with the beginnings of a real headache, and click on the bedside lamp. I calculated on the ferry over, and counting on my fingers, that I have spent thirteen of my birthdays here—our birthdays—in the Moreaus' back garden. My first was when Lucas and I turned seventeen. The ninth of June 2005. It was the first time I had ever stayed here, and only our second ever face-to-face meeting, but Lucas's parents treated me like a family member who'd visited a thousand times before. "Lucas speaks only of you," Jean had said as he'd shown me around the guest cottage, and then he'd brought his shoulders to his ears and smiled, almost defeatedly, as if to say, "And if you're important to my son, you're important to us." That weekend, Lucas's parents bought us a birthday cake each and took us to dinner at Le Rivage—newly opened at the time, smelling of fresh paint and freshly sawed wood. It was one of the first restaurants I'd ever been in, although I was way too embarrassed to admit it to them. The next day, Lucas and I went with his older brother, Eliot, and a group of their friends to a gig, and although I definitely didn't dance, not once, it was one of the best nights I'd ever had. Not because it was fun. But because of how they all saw me. As one of *them*. As a regular seventeen-year-old, world at her feet. Not "that girl from Fortescue Lane." Just Emmie Blue, cocktail in hand, out for a good time before she finally escaped school and started college. And tomorrow, on our fourteenth birthday together, we will be thirty. *Thirty years old.* The age I've kept my eye on over the years, like a prize in the distance, like a safe haven, a warm light in the dark on the horizon. Because everyone is settled at thirty, aren't they? You're an adult at thirty—fully fledged—and everyone knows who they are. Or at least, everyone knows exactly where they are going, even if they haven't quite made it there yet.

I stretch over to the side of the bed now and pull my suitcase onto the bed. I unzip it. Everything is still folded neatly inside from when I packed it last night, excitement fizzing in my stomach, imagining exactly what would happen after he asked me. After Balloon Girl looked across that table, on the beach that brought them together, and said yes to Balloon Boy, fourteen years later.

I take out the black gift box nestled in among my clothes and remove the lid.

"So, hang about, this was New Year's Eve? As in New Year's just gone?" Rosie had asked last week. It's how we've learned about each other over the last two years, Rosie and I. Condensed histories, anecdotes, worries, hopes, and memories in tiny, thirty-minute digestible capsules on our lunch breaks.

"Yeah, he'd had a shit night and got in at just past midnight, French time, and I was already at home in my room, watching Jools Holland, so we FaceTimed. From our beds."

Rosie had stared, wide-eyed, smiling. "*So hot*. And you said one of your resolutions was to meet someone?"

"Fall in love," I'd said, and she'd fluttered her eyelashes and said, "Tell me what Lucas said again."

"He called me bold," I'd said, laughing. "Said, *fuck, Em, that's bold*. And then he was sort of falling asleep, 'cause he'd had like a million whiskey sours, but he said—he said that had I ever stopped to think about why we were so hopeless when it came to love. Because he had a theory. It was us. We were probably always meant to be together."

Rosie had squealed then, grabbing my wrists. "Oh god, Emmie, he's going to ask you, you do know that, don't you?" she'd said. "*That's* why he said he can't ask you on the phone, in case you hang up or freak out or something. It's beautiful, isn't it? Like, totally. After all these years . . ."

I look at the open gift box now, in front of me on the bed. The bespoke leather sketchbook I'd bought a few weeks ago, his initials embossed on the front and on the corner of every blank page inside, didn't feel like enough after that conversation with Rosie at work. She was right. It *was* beautiful—would have been. Two people who met against all odds, just when they needed each other. Same age, same birthdays, same obsession with Marmite and *Footballers' Wives*. By chance, some might say, but I don't. And I wanted to mark it with more than just a nice birthday gift. That's when I'd decided to buy the gift box in front of me, excitedly making a list on the back of a napkin in the kitchen at work, of the important things that needed to go inside. I take an envelope out of it now, containing the first ever email Lucas sent me, when we were strangers. *Subject: I found ur balloon!* I take out the jar of Marmite too. Newly purchased, but a double of the first thing I ever sent Lucas (along with my French oral tape for him to listen to and check for accuracy before I handed it in to my languages teacher). I sent it because he said along with *EastEnders* and chip shop mushy peas, it was something he missed from home, which was London before France. That was when the mix CDs started. He'd sent the first one in exchange for the Marmite—a little thank-you that grew into something that became a ritual; a lifeline. I'd send him something from home, and in return, he'd send a mix CD, which were like little letters in themselves. Eight in total. He still owes me the ninth. It's the final thing in the box, the first CD. And although there is a single crack across the plastic casing, the card inside curling at one of the edges, it's still perfect. The ink of Lucas's handwriting navy blue and unsmudged. All straight capital letters, written calmly, confidently, slowly. Not like Lucas now, his handwriting flighty and energetic, as he is, always with something bigger, better to be doing.

I can't. I can't hand these things over tomorrow—a history of us, of how we got here, to this moment, in objects, across the usual breakfast table on Amanda and Jean Moreau's picture-perfect patio. So I put everything but the CD in my suitcase, and replace the gift box lid on the single, benign, *friendly* thing inside—the sketchbook. I put it on the bedside cabinet, ready for the morning, and snuggle down into bed.

My phone lights up with a football news notification I wish I knew how to switch off, and I check the time. 12:33 a.m. Well. There it is. I am officially thirty. I'm *thirty years old*, and it's safe to say that at this precise moment, I definitely do not know where I am going.

I close my eyes, pull my knees to my tummy. I never thought this would be how I'd begin my thirtieth year. Feeling tiny. Pathetic. Insignificant. Because I know, deep down, I *am* made of strong stuff. Rebuilt with it, at least, the way we all are, over the years, with age and experience, skin thickening, heart softening, patched up double in the places prone to breakage. A sum of all the things that have hurt us, scared us, sheltered and delighted us.

And that's what Lucas is to me, I suppose. Delight, yes, of course. But shelter. *Safety.* I rebuilt a new Emmeline—a new Emmie—after that Summer Ball, aged sixteen, painstakingly. But from that very first email, he was the one who helped me do it. Supported every decision, applauded every tiny step I took as if they were giant leaps.

Tears sting behind my eyelids now. Because I know, in that certain way you only do when your gut has taken charge, that I have to support him. I know I have to applaud this step Lucas is taking—this huge, giant leap—regardless of how much it hurts. I owe him that. That's what a best friend does. A best woman.

I hold the CD in my hand. The final track listing the last thing I see before my eyes close and I fall asleep.

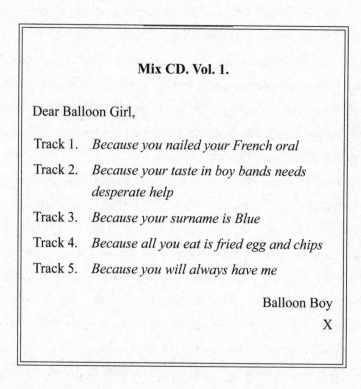

Mix CD. Vol. 1.

Dear Balloon Girl,

Track 1.   *Because you nailed your French oral*

Track 2.   *Because your taste in boy bands needs desperate help*

Track 3.   *Because your surname is Blue*

Track 4.   *Because all you eat is fried egg and chips*

Track 5.   *Because you will always have me*

Balloon Boy

X

The Moreaus' long, parasol-shaded patio table looks like something from *House & Garden* magazine, this morning. Its crisp, white tablecloth is weighed down with plates of warm golden pastries, coffeepots, bowls of ruby-red strawberries and dewy blueberries—and of course, in keeping with tradition, two birthday cakes, sitting high and proud on ceramic cake stands. One at each end. One for Lucas. One for me. Each one, like every year, with a story.

"I know a black cake isn't exactly cheering." Amanda, Lucas's mum, smiles, adjusting the tower of croissants so they're all in perfect Jenga-like alignment. "But all I hear about at the moment is your bloody car's new leather interior and I thought, well, if fondant was my thing, I might make Lucas a car. You know, actually carve the car out of sponge . . ."

"No, no, no," mutters Jean over his espresso, eyes over the top of his glasses. "I would not have survived the stress of living with you during such a thing, my love."

Amanda rolls her eyes but smiles, her thin lips, as ever, painted the color of pink pearls. "But I thought, this was the next best thing. And I thought, if I do it *quilted*, you'll know it isn't just—"

"A jet-black cake," chuckles Lucas.

"And not a representation of your soul," I add. Amanda stops, a hand coming up to her mouth, and laughs; the laugh she does that's a yelp before it's a giggle, and Jean, who has only laughed a maximum of twice in his whole life, and both times accidentally, smirks from behind his tiny white espresso cup.

"Oi, it's my birthday." Lucas leans to nudge me. "You've got to be nice to the middle-aged."

"*Says you*," I say. "You greeted me this morning by calling me Moon Face."

"Moon Face." Amanda laughs again, a bitten strawberry between her fingers. "It was that photo of the pair of you, wasn't it? That we took in . . . was it Honfleur, for your brother's birthday? Where the flash turned you both white as corpses."

Lucas nods. "Eliot's twenty-first. Years ago, now."

"And my face was just *so* round and *so* white," I say, and Lucas laughs.

"Like I was having lunch with the actual moon in a denim jacket."

I scowl at him, and he grins.

"I can't believe you still call her that." Amanda smiles, sitting down, fanning a napkin out on her lap.

Lucas laughs, "Only on special occasions."

"Like thirtieth birthdays," I add.

"Exactly." Lucas nods. "Now, would you pass me that thing of jam, please, Moon Face? *What?* I'm making the most of being able to say it. I won't use it again until you turn forty or get married or pregnant, or something equally as big."

I had felt sick at the thought of walking out here this morning. The dread of opening my eyes to see the sun peeping from behind the heavy cream curtains of the bedroom, and knowing it was morning, knowing it was our birthday, was so heavy last night that it pinned me to the mattress. If I woke up here, in Le Touquet, in this bedroom, on the ninth of June, my eyes swollen, surrounded by scrunched tissues, it meant it happened. It was real. The man I love told me he wanted to spend forever with someone else and wanted me to be there, right next to him, in the spotlight, as he told the world.

Rosie's voice swirled through my brain, as if she were on the phone, when I lay in bed first thing this morning, staring with gritty eyes at the ceiling. I hadn't texted her back last night—as far as the real Rosie is concerned, Lucas and I are tangled up in white sheets right now, fingers laced, all sleepy smiles and morning plans. Boyfriend and girlfriend. But I knew what Rosie would say if she knew what had actually happened last night: "Arse up, Em. In that shower. Go in Mopey, Heartbroken Emmie Blue, but come out the Strong, Independent Woman you are. I mean it. Like you're on *Stars in Their Eyes*, and the Moreaus are your gullible bloody audience." And that is what I did. Hoisted myself up and showered for twenty minutes solid, washing my hair, shaving my legs, and even exfoliating using one of the glass, gold-lidded products Amanda always leaves me in the bathroom. I blow-dried, I moisturized, and even tried out contouring using a tutorial Rosie had hammered out and saved in the notes app on my phone, and then I walked down the path to the Moreaus' picture-perfect, lush green back garden like my heart was full, and not aching. Like I was thirty years old, with everything figured out, and not lost. Not alone.

"Emmie?"

I look up to see Amanda angling the plate of pastries toward me.

"Almond, darling? I always get the almond ones for you."

I take one. "Thanks, Amanda." My appetite is nonexistent, my stomach in a constant churn, but if I don't eat, not only will I feel sick, but Lucas might notice and ask if I'm all right, and I don't want that Lucas today. Kind, hand-on-my-arm, concerned Lucas. That Lucas might tip me back into the melted puddle of tears I was last night.

"This smells amazing," I say to Amanda, tearing off the end of the warm croissant.

"Doesn't it? I'm just glad you're not on some silly regime, like this one," she says, her eyes sliding toward Lucas. "There's nothing to him, and he lives at that gym."

"It's called keeping fit, Mum," Lucas says with a smile, sitting back in his chair, coffee cup in his tanned hand, his other arm across his chest, hand on his bicep. "It's called keeping *healthy*."

"Yes," says Jean simply, in approval.

"He doesn't eat anything I make anymore, Emmie," she carries on, cutting a muffin in half. "Did I tell you we did bain-marie in my class, and he refused to try my crème brûlée?"

"It was super high in sugar—"

"A tiny bit, is all I asked. A bite. Not like our Luke, is it, Emmie, to turn down something sweet?"

"No—"

"And I said to him, I said, when have you ever met someone who got heart disease from one—"

"I have a suit to fit into, Mum." Lucas sits forward then, cocks his head, smiles at his mum, who stops talking and looks at him. Her eyes widen to full circles.

"*Did you . . .*" Her face breaks into a smile, then she looks at me. "He's told you?" I stare at her, but Lucas nods proudly beside me. Even Jean looks up from his plate, eyes unblinking.

"Oh, Emmie!" Amanda whoops, a hand flying across the table to land on mine, her mouth stretching into a watery smile. "Can you believe it? Can you actually *believe* it? Married! Oh, tell me, what did you say?"

Ah. They thought I didn't know yet. I swallow, a chunk of pastry disintegrating in my mouth. I look up at them, my gullible, on-the-edge-of-their-seats audience, and force a smile. "I couldn't believe it," I tell them. "I really couldn't believe it."

"I didn't know you knew! I've been dying for him to tell you. Haven't I, Jean?" Amanda beams, looking around the table to her calmly nodding husband, then to Lucas, then to me. She's wide and glittery-eyed, squirming in her seat like an impatient toddler.

"I told her last night." Lucas smiles at me, his hand reaching out to touch my arm. "She was so shocked, she went and had a migraine. Didn't you, Em?"

Even Jean laughs at that, and says in his deep, broken English, "She is not the only one. My migraine of shock has only just dispersed."

Amanda is not listening, though; she's gazing at Lucas, freckly, gold-ringed hand at her chest, the nails painted pink. "Oh, I'm so glad you told her," she sighs dreamily, then she looks at me. "I hate having secrets, especially from family. You can help us plan now, Emmie. Talk him out of wearing those horrible tight trousers all the youngsters are wearing these days—"

"Actually," says Lucas, setting down his coffee cup, elbow on the table. "There's one more secret."

Then he looks at me and smiles. And then I realize, they don't know. They don't know what he asked me. "Last night," says Lucas, "I asked Emmie . . ."

Amanda gasps, puts down the jar of lemon curd she had just picked up. It thumps on the tablecloth.

Lucas looks at me, nods his head encouragingly. I clear my throat, my smile unwavering.

"Luke asked me to be his best woman," I say.

Amanda brings her hands to her mouth. "Oh!" she squeals. "Oh! Oh, Jean!"

Jean smiles, closed mouth, ever sensible, ever rock-steady. "And?" he says. "And did you say yes?"

Lucas laughs at that, as if the thought of me saying anything else is hilarious.

"Of course," I say, and Amanda yelps again, standing up and gesturing for me to stand too, so she can wrap her arms around me, the chiffon of her blouse swooping over the plate of muffins on the table. "Oh, my darling," she says into my ear, squeezing me close, all warmth and soft skin and floral perfume. "Nobody deserves the job more than you. He loves you," she says. "He loves you so much. We all do." And I don't let her go. I hold on to her, this woman, the closest thing I've had in the last few years to a mother, as if she's the only thing keeping me upright. My nostrils tingle, a prologue to the tears that are desperate to come now, but I sniff, blink them away, plaster back on that smile.

"Oh, it's enough to make you weep, isn't it?" chuckles Amanda as we pull away. She sits back down, draping the napkin across her lap. She busies herself with her breakfast, and Lucas reaches for a bowl of berries, still smiling over at his mum. Jean, opposite, sips his coffee silently, but his eyes are on me, serious and watchful. I'm glad when he looks away. It's just in time to miss my smile slip.

5

"What?"

"He's getting married. Lucas is getting married."

Rosie stares at me, deep-red hair wild, coffee cup in hand. "What? To who?" And before I can reply, her glossy red mouth breaks into a huge grin. "Oh my shit, it's you, isn't it? Oh my God, it's—"

"It's not me."

"Oh."

"It's Marie," I tell her. Rosie looks at me blankly. "Ex-girlfriend Marie."

"Avocado Marie?" Rosie's mouth is open, her top lip in a confused snarl. "As in organic-deli-owner Marie? I thought she dumped him after she thought he was texting that girl. The Aussie."

"Ivy." I nod. "And Lucas didn't text her. She texted *him.* But yeah. *That* Marie. They patched stuff up a couple of months ago, apparently. I didn't even know. He said it was all really quick."

"And what, then they got engaged immediately?" says Rosie, face crumpling. "Who does that?"

I shrug. "Happy people?" I offer. "In love people."

Rosie's brow furrows under her blunt, red fringe and she shakes her head. "So why the desperate need to talk to you? To summon you—"

"Rosie, he didn't summon me; I was already going—"

"But he made it a big thing, didn't he? That he *had* to ask you something and it *had* to be face-to-face. Then there's the thing he said on New Year's . . ."

I was waiting for this—braced for it. And as much as I wish I hadn't told her about Lucas's text, telling me he had something to ask me, or about that drunken comment he made about us being meant to be together, it's not like *not* telling Rosie was even an option. I can't keep anything from her. She sees right through me; through anyone.

"I can always sniff out the little shits before I've even handed over their room keys," she'd told me on my first day here, at the Clarice, two years ago. "The ones cheating on their wives, the ones filming porn in the rooms, the ones who're *so* leaving with a cleaning bill because they eat shellfish from that dodgy bloke on the pier and can't make it to the loo in time. Yup. Can't hide jack from me."

"So, when you say engaged," Rosie carries on now, "do you mean he and Avocado Marie just *talked* about it? Because anyone can make big, bold promises. I dated that bloke from Slough, you remember, the one with the eyebrows, and he promised me he'd take me to Montenegro, to Bali, to—"

"He proposed."

"What, actually?"

"Actually."

"Hm." Rosie pulls her mouth into a grimace, as if she's considering the validity of what I've just said; as if at any moment she's going to stroke her chin and say "interesting." A stark comparison to the Rosie of last week, who was squealing, rosy-cheeked, and dancing about so much that she sent two confit duck legs flying off the kitchen pass and skittering to the floor out of excitement. And that's why I'd told her, I suppose. I was excited, and I knew she would feel the same. Fox was excited, too, in his own weird, measured Fox way, listening as he always does, quietly in the background, before appearing and delivering the sort of calm, timely, fatherly advice or opinion you'd expect from someone double his age. "Don't overthink it," he'd said this time. "Yield and breathe and hold no expectations." And Rosie had tutted and said, "I've got expectations, all right. He's gonna be *bomb* in the sack, that's what I expect. All those years of unrequited love, all that repressed sexual energy . . ."

Rosie is staring at me now across the shiny, freshly scrubbed kitchen counter as I fill tiny, fancy butter dishes from a giant pot of cheap margarine for the lunch service.

"So, what was it all about, then, Em? That's what I wanna know," she says. "What did he need to ask you?"

I look up at her, spoon hovering over the margarine tub. "He asked me if I would be best woman, for the wedding. That was the question."

"Fuck me, you are kidding?" breathes Rosie. "You didn't say yes, did you?"

I say nothing.

"God. You did. You said yes."

"Yes I did," I tell her as Rosie makes a groaning noise into her coffee mug and downs the last drop, throwing her head right back, as if it's vodka and she needs it to numb the agony. "Then, of course, I threw up. Puked."

Rosie drops the mug from her face. "On him?"

"*No,*" I laugh. "After he asked me. Immediately after. I couldn't help it; I felt sick to my stomach. I panicked, I think."

"Poor you, of course you did."

"And I made my excuses, ran to the loo, and chundered it all. My appetizer. My wine. My dinner. My dignity. Well, most of it. I have a small shred left, I think, if I look hard enough."

"Oh, Emmie."

"It was the way he was looking at me, Rosie. It—I thought he was going to ask me to—well, you know what I thought he was going to ask me."

Rosie reaches across the counter and touches my hand; the one holding a spoon loaded with yellow marg. She looks at me with huge brown eyes. "So, what happens now?"

I give a theatrical shrug. "I guess I'm going to be the best best woman to be found this side of the universe," I say with a sigh. "That's what happens now. Because what else am I supposed to do? Say no? Pull out? Risk ruining the only long-standing relationship of any kind in my entire life?"

"Er, yeah?" Rosie cocks a perfect, auburn-penciled eyebrow. Her makeup is always incredible. Porcelain-smooth cheeks, dewy skin shimmering gold every time the light catches the tip of her pixie-like nose or the Cupid's bow of her mouth. "You love the bloke, Emmie. Nobody in their right mind would put themselves through this. Jack it in."

"But I can't," I say. "He'll know if I pull out."

"Good," says Rosie, folding her arms. "Maybe he needs to."

"Maybe who needs to what?" Fox, immaculate in shining suit and hideous paisley shirt, appears from the tiny office off the kitchen and squashes himself next to Rosie. Fox is the Clarice's hospitality manager, and perhaps the poshest person I think I have ever met. He went to boarding school; some private establishment he'd said all the politicians went to, and who hoped photographic evidence of their drunk days there miraculously disappeared before they gained a seat in Parliament. But then his dad went bankrupt. "I think it was the happiest day of my life when he told me I had to drop out," Fox told me once. He'd moved out of London the second he could and has been here for nine years. He lives on-site, upstairs, in one of the suites. "Like the bloke in *The Shining*," Rosie says at least once a day. "Just a matter of time before he bludgeons us all."

Fox leans across the counter now, clean, slim hands clasped together. "So, how did he ask? Are you *going steady*?" He laughs and leans closer to me. "I admit, I have absolutely no idea what that means."

"Oh, yet you knew that other word," tuts Rosie. "Whatever it was.

Fust—fast . . . fastidious, that's it! That's what he called me, Emmie. Fastidious. I had to google it. I thought he'd made it up. Pulled it out his arsehole."

I burst out laughing, bringing the cuff of my blouse to my mouth. "Well, that's a compliment, isn't it?"

"Actually," Fox says with a smile, "I said she could try and *be more* fastidious. The reception desk is like the bottom of a swamp. Mugs with dregs of coffee inside so old, they have pensions. Disgusting."

Rosie nudges Fox in the side with her elbow.

"Ow."

"I hate cleaning. It's for bores. Anyway, shut up, Fox, we've got a crisis here."

"It isn't so much a crisis . . . ," I start, but Rosie butts in.

"That knob-end in France took her to that restaurant and asked her to be his best woman." I love how Rosie makes "asked" sound like "arsed."

Fox screws up his pale face, his nose wrinkling. "Sorry, what?"

"That's what I said," says Rosie.

I shrug, unable to bear to look up from the lines and lines of butter dishes. "He's getting married," I say again. "I—I got it wrong."

"Married to whom, for Christ's sake?"

"That's what I said," says Rosie again. "Well, without the posh *whom* bit, obviously."

"Marie."

"His ex," cuts in Rosie. "On-off girlfriend. Patched stuff up. Emmie didn't even know."

Fox makes a sound; a loud inward draw of breath; a cross between a gasp and a growl. "Gosh," he says, wincing. "And he took you to a restaurant to ask you this?"

"Yep," says Rosie. "Their restaurant. The one they always go to. It's on the beach. The beach he found Emmie's balloon on when they were sixteen."

I look at Rosie and a smile blooms across my face. "Thank you, Wikipedia page," I say, and she laughs, reaching to touch the side of my face. "Sorry, Emmie," she says sweetly. "I'm just absolutely fuming on your behalf."

"But he hasn't really done anything wrong, has he?" I tell them. "We're best friends. He asked me to be his best woman, over his brother, over all his mates, even his friend Tom, who he's known since nursery. That isn't nasty behavior. It's . . . nice behavior. It's—"

"Knob-end behavior," Rosie stampedes in, leaning forward and mirroring Fox, lacing her fingers together and budging up next to him. Her long nails are silver and yellow this week, the index ones with tiny painted daisies on them. "You forget what he said to you New Year's Eve. He can't say that shit, then take you to a restaurant and ask you to be his best woman without being branded a raging knob—"

"Do you think we could use another word?" Fox asks. "Like—"

"Oh God, what, I suppose you want me to say *nincompoop*? Well, this isn't the sixties, Fox," says Rosie, looking at her watch, then standing up straight and reaching over for a bread roll from one of the baskets beside me. "So knob-end is staying."

Fox smirks as Rosie bites into the roll and walks backward, slowly, to the kitchen exit. "Coming out your wages, then, is it, this stolen granary roll?"

"Emmie." She chews, ignoring Fox. "Come and see me on your break, yeah? Mum made honey cake and I've got you some."

"Deal," I say, and she gives a smile and blows a kiss before sashaying out of the kitchen. I know of nobody else on this earth who moves as sexily and as confidently as Rosie does. It's as if there isn't a space on this earth that's out of bounds to her. Even on my third ever shift here, she'd come galloping toward me on my lunch break in a bright green sundress, lips the color of mahogany, her receptionist uniform nowhere to be seen, and said breathlessly, "I've got ten minutes. How are you with a camera? Any good?" Before I could reply, I was clicking away on a digital camera I had no idea how to use, while she sprawled across the sandstone steps of the hotel, posing like the models on the pages of *Vogue*, saying, "Hurry up, Emmie. They'll string us up if they catch us. I'm supposed to be a dedicated hotel receptionist, remember, not a plus-sized blogger."

Fox straightens. "Right, let's give you a hand." He pulls a spoon from the drawer beneath the counter and starts scooping up perfect ovals of butter. Fox knows every inch of this hotel. From knowing the exact amount of butter needed to fill one dish in one drag of a spoon, to knowing the time Sol, the chef, prefers the mint to be added to the home-churned ice cream, to how to operate the ancient, round-the-houses reception system on Rosie's computer. I long to be as at home, somewhere, as Fox is at the Clarice. To feel like yes, this is exactly where I belong.

"Thanks, Fox," I say.

He looks up at me and smiles. "So, are you still needing to leave at five today?"

"Yeah," I say, "if that's okay."

"Sure." Fox nods. "Off anywhere nice?"

"Meeting a friend. She travels a lot and she's local."

"Ah. Sounds grand."

It's easier to lie, I've found. If I'd said that I was going to visit my mum, someone I have barely mentioned the entire time I've worked here, in the many coffee and lunch breaks I've spent with Fox, questions would have come, and I'm never comfortable answering them. Plus, the dread I feel before seeing her, that breaks out of my stomach now, like weighted butterflies, as I stand here, hours from it, can usually be read on my face. I'm not sure what I dread exactly, but I always make my way to see Mum with a churning stomach and stiff shoulders. "What happened, love? World that terrible and ugly, is it?" a passing man had chuckled the last time I stood at the bus stop on my way to meet her, and when I'd texted Lucas and told him, he'd said, "You should have said, 'It is with you in it, mate, yeah.'"

"You seem all right, you know, about this wedding business," Fox says now. "Considering."

"I'm not," I say. "I wish I could say I was, but I'm not."

Fox nods wordlessly, hands all the time spooning and pressing. "Anyone would find something like this tough, Emmie. And everything else aside: your best friend is getting married. It's hard enough when there are no feelings like yours, believe me."

"Really?"

Fox's eyes widen and he nods rapidly. "God, yes. Nobody says it, of course, it's all 'I'm so excited; I'm so happy for you!' But deep down, every friend is thinking 'Shit. Everything's changing. I'm going to lose my mate to this person who could absolutely be a total and utter bastard. And I've got to smile throughout it while I let them go into the arms of a potential monster. And what does that mean for *us*?' Poke writing a speech, I would actually like to spend my time having an existential crisis in peace, thank you very much."

I look up at him and laugh. And it feels nice to smile; really smile. "Thank you, Fox. That helps. It really does."

"I'm glad," he says.

"And you're right," I tell him, my voice rising to be heard over the loud clatter of plates being removed from the dishwasher on the other side of the kitchen. "It's just that it feels . . . *wrong*. Like, this isn't how it was meant to be. That something somewhere missed the boat. Forgot."

"What, like fate? The *universe*?"

Heat creeps up my neck at those words, but still I shrug, give a weak nod. "I guess. I don't know. Because at the same time, I feel like I've been delusional. Stupid. For even thinking for a moment that he could see me like that." I stop. A lump has gathered in my throat. I can't bring myself to voice another word. I don't want to cry at work. The last time someone did, it was gossiped about so much that it may as well have been added to the staff newsletter, along with the bulletin about the misuse of sanitary waste bins and Chef Sam's Custard Bathtub Charity Fund-Raiser.

"Look," says Fox simply, his hands stopping to rest on the counter. "You both met in such a grandiose, serendipitous way. You let go of a balloon and he found it, an ocean away. It's *exceptional*. And I defy anyone to meet someone in that way and not attach meaning to it."

I nod, eyes on the counter.

"So do not feel stupid for a second." There's a pause as Fox pushes the lid on the giant pot of margarine. "Emmie? Are you okay?"

I look up to meet his eyes. Soft, the color of chestnuts. "Not really," I tell him. "But I will be. Plus," I say, "Rosie feels sorry for me, which means I'll probably get cake from her mum for at least a week. There's always a silver lining."

Fox gives a chuckle, stands tall. "One day *I'll* get honey cake."

I smile at him. "You know she loves you."

"Yes," says Fox, folding his arms across his chest. "In a way you love that grumpy grandfather you only wish would ask you to euthanize him."

"Oh, Fox, don't be daft," I say. "An *uncle*. I see you as more of an uncle."

The last time I went inside Mum's camper van was over fourteen years ago. It was the September after the Summer Ball, and the day after it broke out that it was me—that I was the girl that got Mr. Morgan suspended. Mum was due to leave for Edinburgh for a festival, then to Skye to meet a friend, and after school I'd walked in on her packing in the tiny lounge of our flat, and collapsed in the doorway, hysterically whimpering and shuddering in a heap, too far gone for a single tear to come. She hadn't moved, told me coldly to pack a bag, and the next day I'd gone to Edinburgh with her, in her van, where I spent the whole time feeling like an inconvenience—like an old relative who had nowhere else to go. Three weeks later, Lucas's first email finally found me, like a searchlight in a storm. *I found your balloon on a beach near Boulogne-sur-Mer yesterday*, it said. *It made it one ocean and over 100 miles!*

Tonight, I find the van parked up at the far end of the Maypole Folk Festival, beside a small white gazebo, shrouded in the thick, warm smell of hot dogs and incense. There is rust around the wheel arches now, and the seal around the window dangles loosely, unstuck with age, but like seventies wedding presents, like elderly neighbors, the van is one of those things that just keeps going. I'm not sure Mum would ever get rid of it unless it conked out altogether. She's like that. Not so much a hoarder, but someone who frowns upon buying new things where it isn't warranted (cigarettes being an exception, of course). Even the ex-pub chalkboard is the same one she has always had, cloudy with how many times it's been written on and erased. Today there are fresh looping letters scrawled upon it in yellow chalk: Katherine Blue at the The Maypole Festival. Tarot Card Reading: £15.00.

"Mum?" I tap on the van's window. A strip of yellow light seeps through a tiny crack in the drawn curtains—beige, covered in painted pink roses.

I knock again, twice, when the rusty door clicks and slides across. Mum sits there, tea in her lap, book over her knee, marking her place, and her arm stretched across the seat, fingers on the door handle. "Oh," she says, the smile on her pale lips there, but only just. "Emmeline."

"Hi," I say. She is the only person who calls me Emmeline now, but it no longer makes me wince. "Taking a tea break?"

She looks down at the china cup in her hand. "Yes, I suppose. It's been a long day. Thought I'd recharge."

"Good timing by me, then," I say, and like a reluctant, awkward stranger making space on a park bench, she moves over.

The van is stuffy and smells sweet, like warm fruit, and I'm glad when she doesn't ask me to pull the door to, to shut out the fresh sea air. It reminds me of that trip to Edinburgh, that smell. The way I'd told her, in the silence of the tiny van, parked in a pitch-black campsite, that I hadn't slept for weeks. That every time I closed my eyes, my dreams would take me to that classroom at Fortescue Lane, with him, and it would be so vivid, so real, that I swore I could smell his aftershave on my neck, like I still could that night when I got home. She sipped. That's all she did. I wanted her to hold me, to cradle me, to tell me she wouldn't let him hurt me again. But instead she'd said, "You know dreams aren't real at your age, Emmeline," as if a bad dream is all it ever was, and once again, brought the cup to her lips.

"Do you want something to drink?" she asks now.

"I was actually thinking maybe we could have dinner or something." I hate the way my skin prickles with embarrassment at such a simple, normal suggestion. "I thought you might be working, but if you're taking a break—"

"I actually have plans shortly."

"Oh. Do you?" What I want to say is, why would you email me, then? Why would you send me a message, telling me you're here, at this festival, in the next town, if you didn't want to spend time with me? "It's just, well, it's been a few months and I thought we could spend some time together. Have a drink? Take a walk? Have an ice cream to celebrate?"

"Celebrate?" Mum stops, tea at her lips. "What is there to celebrate?"

My heart sinks, as if it is a rock dropped into a tank of water. "My birthday, Mum. My thirtieth." And I know. I know from the way her hazel eyes glint, the way they widen, just a little, that she had forgotten. That her emailing me a couple of weeks ago, to "check in," to tell me she'd be here, saying she'd "hoped" to see me when I said I was working but would ask for time off, was just a coincidence.

"Oh, Emmeline, stop it," she says, clattering down the cup and saucer on the wooden counter behind her. "Don't insult me."

"I wasn't—"

"I *know* it was your birthday. I didn't forget. How could I?"

I nod. "Well. That's what I meant by celebrate. Thirty. It's kind of a big deal."

"Is it?" she asks. "It is but a number, sweetheart, you know that. People place too much meaning on age."

"Maybe," I say, and then I change the subject, because I can feel her gearing up for a debate, about age, about *people*, as if she isn't one of us. "So, how is everything? Have you been traveling a lot?" Most might ask about business, but I know better. I'll be accused of caring too much about money if I do that.

She settles in the seat beside me, leg inches from mine, but never touching, and begins to list the places she and Jim have been since January. I have never heard of Jim before, but she talks as if I have known him all my life. Mum has always done this with boyfriends. One minute she doesn't know them, the next minute they're talked about as if they have been part of the furniture since day one. When I was seven, it felt like Den had been in my life all along because of this—because of Mum and her routine of jumping feetfirst, introducing me to them quickly, bypassing "dating" and going straight to meals at home and eating in front of the telly together, them helping me with my homework, putting me to bed. Mum and Den, someone I called my stepdad, were actually only together for three years, yet I don't remember a time before him. He and Mum got together when I was five, and he'd left when I was eight, almost nine. It went from him hiding sweets in his jacket for me to find, picking me up from school, and reading bedtime stories, to waiting for his key in the door and to looking for him in every red car that drove by, for however long it took me to realize he wasn't coming back.

"We went to Cornwall last weekend, for a festival in Bude," Mum says, brightening.

I nod enthusiastically.

"And before that, we actually went to Guernsey, which was glorious. There's something special about it. The air . . ." Mum pauses and looks skyward, as if she can see the sort of air she's referring to, around us. "It feels clean. Welcoming. A little bubble all its own, you know?"

"Like Skye," I say, and she nods, eyes lighting up as if something has ignited.

"*Yes*, Emmeline," she says, "*exactly* like Skye," and I curse myself that my stomach sparks with something. Validation. For pleasing my mum, for getting something right for her, as if I am three, and a "good girl," and not a grown thirty-year-old woman.

"And what about you?" she asks, smiling thinly. "I said to Jim just a few nights ago, that for all I know, you could be on the other side of the world. That's why I emailed. What have you been doing with yourself?"

It's times like these that I wish I had the relationship with my mum that my school friends had—that Rosie has with hers. I'd love to confide in her about Lucas. About the wedding, about Fishers Way and my roasting-hot room, and how much I worry sometimes, that I'm so off track, so "off plan" from where I thought I would be at this time of my life that it fills me with panic. That I'm scared of the loneliness that swamps me sometimes, so much I feel like I can't breathe. That despite it being fourteen years ago, while I no longer dream of Mr. Morgan, his hot, wet voice in my ear, his hand bruising my thigh, I often feel *guilt*, of all things, about him, about telling someone what he did to me that night. Because he was suspended while it was "looked into." He moved away alone, for a while, away from his wife and children—one of whom was my best school friend, Georgia. So many people hurt—so many people I cared about, and because of me. "Because of *him*, Emmie. Not you. It was all him," Lucas would say, like he has so many times before, if he were here now. But I don't tell Mum this stuff. It has never been that way for us.

"I haven't been up to much," I say to Mum, pausing to look around the tiny, musty space. I can hear a band—electric guitars, a fast, jolly violin— just beyond the van and its little cubbyhole on the field. "I'm still renting the place on Fishers Way."

"Not the flat?"

"No," I say. "I told you, I rent a room now. I left the flat eighteen months ago. I just couldn't afford it anymore."

"Well, I told you that a long time ago, Emmeline, but you refused to listen to me. You should have never tried to keep it on once, you know, erm, the police officer up and left you."

"Adam," I say, and I ignore the little jab in my stomach at the "up and left" part of her sentence. As if it was nothing. It was a long time ago now, yes—four years—but Adam, my first serious boyfriend, leaving the flat we'd moved into together, planned futures in, picked out furniture for, certainly didn't feel like nothing back then. But then, Mum had "up and left" me all over the place when I was just fourteen, and she's had more boyfriends and breakups than I could ever count. "We are meant to be babied *only* when we are babies," she used to say, when I'd show heartache, show fear, or simply ask her to come with me to the dentist, or to miss a trip to help me study, like Georgia's mum did, with flash cards and timers and plates of cookies. Of course it is nothing to her.

"How's the photo studio?" she asks.

"I lost that job, remember?" I tell her now. "Laid off. I did tell you."

"I don't think you did."

"I did," I jump in, despite my best efforts to stay calm, stay neutral. This is all it ever is. A cold questionnaire of recycled questions she feels obliged to ask. "I've been at the hotel for two years now."

"Hm." Mum nods, eyes sliding to the side as if she's considering whether I've told her the truth or not. "Well, forgive me, Emmeline, but it's a blessing, if you ask me."

I say nothing and avert my eyes to the torn, shabby linoleum at my feet.

"I mean it. The way they preyed on parents. I don't know how you did it."

"Preyed?" I say, my face crumpling. "It was a photo studio, Mum. For families. For children."

"But the *prices*." She shakes her head. "All those photos they'd take, knowing no parent would ever in their right mind turn any of them down." Parent. She says that like she isn't one herself too. "What?" she presses. "What is it?"

I pause, consider saying nothing at all. "I just . . . I was made redundant, Mum. I enjoyed it, I worked with families, with kids, and I miss it. You could be a bit more sympathetic."

"Well, I won't apologize, Emmeline," says Mum curtly. "I am not ashamed that I am pleased you're out of a job for an organization in a line of work I don't agree with."

From beside me, Mum huffs, then sips her tea, which is the color of ripe raspberries, and I hear Lucas chime in, in my mind, a smirk in his voice: "So, hang on, your mum doesn't agree with meat, religion, and . . . *photography?* Nice one, Kath."

Nobody speaks for a while, and chin resting in my hand, I watch the night outside closing in on me and Mum, a dimming bulb. I wonder what we look like up here, on the hill. A tiny, cozy orange light in the distance, by the sea. Two silhouettes squashed together, catching up on forgotten news, reminiscing about old times. Nothing, I suppose, that is close to what it really is: a stifling tin can with an atmosphere so thick inside, it feels as though I'm inhaling smoke.

"I saw Lucas last weekend," I say finally. "We talked about going to Brittany again for a few nights." I almost do it deliberately, mention it to see her jaw tighten, as it usually does, but instead she just nods. "I was talking to Lucas and—was it in Saint-Malo you said my dad—" I stop. "Peter lived."

Mum looks up at me, eyes narrowing, shoulders stiffening now she knows where this is going. "Sorry?" I find it hard to believe sometimes that Mum was ever that carefree, free spirit she painted herself as. That twenty-two-year-old with the world at her feet, and a passport to anywhere she wanted. Before she had me, and I ruined it.

"You always said Peter lived somewhere by the beach, and that he worked in Saint-Malo in between touring with his band. And I was talking to Luke about it and he said he would take me there if I found out exactly—"

"For goodness' sake, Emmeline, why would you want to go there?"

I swallow. "To see—"

"Don't waste your time," she says dismissively, words clipped. "It's a seaside town, like here, like Ramsgate, like bloody Southend. Except full of the French."

"I just wondered if you could tell me where. I'd like to see. Get some sort of idea where I'm from—"

Mum huffs, bored with my insistence, as if the years of my pushing for information is wearing her down. "I don't know how many times I have had to say this, but you are from *me*, Emmeline, and all the places we have lived," she says shortly. "You really must stop dragging up dead bodies."

"I want to know who he is."

"Am I not enough?" she snaps, and my stomach turns at the sharp spite in the words. "I brought you up, Emmeline. I looked after you and he was nowhere to be seen. You wanting to find him tells me you're not content with the parent you *do* have. How do you think that makes me feel?"

I don't respond. Her. Everything is about *her*. Everything I say, or do, every decision I have ever made is how it makes *Katherine* feel, what people must think about *her*. And no. The truth is, as much as it hurts to admit it, she isn't enough. Nowhere near. She never has been.

Mum clears her throat, sniffs deeply, straightens, stroking a hand down her cardigan as if composing herself.

"It's unnecessary," she says. "You have other more important things to focus on than *that*. People get so hung up on genes. It makes me laugh." People, again. People like me, like everyone else out there. Not her. Not whoever she calls her boyfriend at the moment, I bet. They are better than us. Us clueless sheep.

There is more silence, and Mum finishes her tea. I want to run back to Fishers Way, climb into bed, and pull my duvet over my head until the sun comes back up. I want to call Lucas. I want him to make me laugh through the tears, say, "So you've had the Wrath of Kath, have you, Emmie Blue?"

He understands Mum. He knows how exhausting, how much like hard work she is, how I spent my whole childhood on eggshells.

"I'm not trying to upset anyone," I say eventually into the silence. Mum stares straight ahead, her nostrils flaring. "I would just like to know who my dad is."

I wait for her to say what she normally does: "Well, I don't know anything more than what I've told you, Emmeline." But she doesn't. Instead, she looks down at her hands. "I couldn't see you," she says.

"Sorry?"

"If you and he . . . started to have a relationship." A muscle in her jaw pulses. "I couldn't bear to see you."

I open my mouth to speak, but I can find no words. It's an ultimatum. It's a toxic, controlling ultimatum, hanging in the air between us. *Find your dad, and our relationship is over.* My stomach bubbles. Rage. Utter, plummeting sadness and rage, but . . . hope. The tiniest speck, glittering among the black. She always said she never knew where he was. I'm not sure I ever believed her, but now she speaks like she might. That a relationship between us both could be possible.

"Okay," I say eventually.

"*Okay?*" Her eyes are wide, like saucers.

"Okay," I say again. "If that's how you feel, then . . . okay."

There is silence as Mum stares at me, clears her throat as if snapping herself out of a trance. She fiddles with a box of tea bags, trying to make it so the lid, which is bent, covers the opening, and I sit beside her, staring around the tiny van that took her away from me so many times when I needed her most. Age fourteen when I'd gotten my first-ever painful, heavy period and panicked and called Georgia. Georgia's mum came rushing around with a hot water bottle and nighttime sanitary pads and ran me a bath. Age fifteen when I'd failed my mock Maths GCSE, when I had my first kiss, when the neighbor downstairs had a screaming argument with her boyfriend, who threatened to "torch the place," and I waited, for the sound of fire alarms or the smell of smoke, alone in bed, unable to sleep for weeks after that. The Summer Ball. The migraines that had started soon after, and the nightmares. So many, many times I had watched this tiny van disappear down the road, from my bedroom window.

"I should get back to it, actually," says Mum. "There will be people out there wanting readings, and it isn't fair if I sit in here, letting it pass them by."

I don't want to, but I hug Mum goodbye outside the van, her body rigid— sharp bones and cold necklace chains—and as we part, I think I know. This is the last time I put myself through these meetings I expect nothing from. Over the years, I have hoped for more, of course, the way someone hopes to fall in love, to see the northern lights one day, but I don't expect it. It's why I came tonight. It's why I asked her to dinner. Because I have always hoped that one day she will say yes. That we'll sit at a little round table, eating together, a bottle of wine between us, and she will tell me about when she was happy, and about the words I'd pronounced wrong when I was a toddler, with chubby hands and dimples for knuckles. And maybe, I always hope to myself, she will tell me how I would make her clay lumps in the first year of kindergarten, painted red and speckled with glitter, or how after bedtime stories she would smell the soapy crown of my hair as I'd fallen asleep beside her.

I walk to the bus stop, my eyes on the horizon, the darkening sky the shade of blossom, the sea like blue ink. I think of my hot but safe room at Fishers Way. I think of the hotel, and Rosie and Fox. And I think of Lucas. Of my balloon, and how far it traveled to him, across those inky waves. I think of the wide world out there and all its possibilities.

Maybe one day I'll see the northern lights.

And someday I'll fall in love.

You might think being a best man simply means organizing the stag, carrying the rings, and making one hell of a speech to remember, but you can elevate yourself to Best Man God by helping in other ways, too, my dude! Have you thought about arranging accommodations for the groomsmen, or asking the happy couple if they need help with the guest list? And, of course, there is the important subject of the outfit. It's down to you, Best Man Boss, and official right-hand man, to help your groom look his dapper best on the day he ties the knot, so get comfortable in those changing rooms. It's time for Chapter Seven: Let's talk about suits . . .

"I look a twat."

I stare at Lucas, who stands under the harsh spotlights of a changing room cubicle, the heavy curtain pulled to one side, in a brilliant-white tuxedo. He looks like someone made of fondant icing.

"Oh god, I *do* look a twat, don't I?"

"No, no, not at all."

"Emmie, your face says it all."

"No, I was just . . . well, I wasn't expecting—it's very *white*, isn't it?"

Lucas looks down at the suit as if he's only just realized he's wearing one, and looks back up at me and laughs. "I look like . . . I dunno, a—" He stops, catching a look at me, with my hand at my mouth, my lips pressed together, and goes wide-eyed. "*What?*"

"Nothing."

"No, come on," he laughs. "What do I look like?"

I pause, a smile breaking out across my face. "You just for a minute reminded me of when little curly-haired Screech from *Saved by the Bell* went to prom."

Lucas gawps at that, gray eyes widening. "*Wounded,*" he laughs. "But that's settled it then, hasn't it? I cannot in any way, shape, or form, wear a fucking white suit."

"I didn't say that."

"Screech, Emmie. You said *little curly-haired Screech.* That's all any prospective groom needs to hear." Lucas throws his head back, sighs, then with one swift movement draws the curtain to closed. A moment later I hear laughter from behind the drape.

We have been here in the changing rooms of a high street menswear chain in Berck-sur-Mer for the last half an hour, mostly laughing, as Lucas tries on suits and blazers in an array of different styles and colors; some that make him look like a Hugo Boss model, and others, part–Willy Wonka, part–varicose vein. He'll be using a bespoke tailor whom Jean has used for many years for his actual wedding suit, apparently, but he wanted to come here to get a "feel" for the sort of style he likes. So far, he likes only the dark shades of blue best. The only color Marie told him she *didn't* want.

"Marie wants me to try powder blue and *white,*" he'd said on the phone, the day after I saw Mum at the Maypole Festival. "White, Em. Like a member of bloody *NSYNC or something. I need your eyes. I know you won't let me look like a loser. When's good for you? Can you come for a week-end?"

I was nervous, I admit, coming here to do this. I think that's why I immediately, despite having no shifts, told him I was busy last weekend. I'd give myself a week, I thought, before I'd come back here. A week to strengthen my resolve. Allow my heart, and my head, a breather, some time to heal. I did some more crying in bed, some rewatching of my favorite Hallmark straight-to-television films full of meant-to-be's and men in plaid shirts, and had many pull-my-shit-together chats with Rosie over packed lunches at work. I'm far from enthused, far from excited, but it's like Rosie said: chance, meant-to-be's—they cannot be rushed or planned. And if it's meant to be, I have to trust it will be.

The next morning, I'd sat at the kitchen table beside my quiet landlady, Louise, with her mint tea and golden pen, poised on another crossword puzzle, and I started a Pinterest board called "Lucas's Wedding" and or-dered a book. "Threw myself into this best-woman business," as Fox had put it. *Eased in*, is probably more accurate, the way you do into a too-hot bath.

"A book?" Lucas had picked it up last night off the coffee table and set-tled back down on the sofa. "*You the (Best) Man!* Wow. Clever."

"It had the strongest reviews. Shockingly."

Lucas had looked at me then and smiled lazily, head against the back of the sofa. "I love you for buying a book."

"Well, I'm a rookie at this," I told him. "I've got to start somewhere, haven't I?"

It was like old times last night: his parents in the main house, reading, cooking, listening to classical music; Marie miles away with her dad, for business; and just Lucas and me, with a takeaway pizza and a bottle of rosé, in the living room of the guest cottage. It felt normal, like it's always been, and my stomach had settled, the way it does after the first slice of toast and cup of tea post–tummy bug.

"And you've marked all these pages." Lucas smiled, opening the book and tugging at a pink sticky tag. "Where Emmie Blue goes, so do the Post-its, eh?"

"Naturally."

Then he'd stretched his strong arm around me and pulled me toward him, my head on his shoulder. "And you're . . . cool with this," he'd said softly, over the mumble of the TV. It wasn't a question, but I nodded.

"And . . . you are?" I asked.

He'd sighed then, and when I looked up at him, he nodded too, robotically, mimicking the way I had, and chuckled.

"And remember, Marie said the dress is up to you."

"I know," I said.

"And you don't have to worry about the stag stuff either. Tom said he'll sort the party and only involve you on the little details, so don't feel like you have to do everything and—"

"I know, Luke."

I felt him nod again, his chin brushing the side of my head. Then there was quiet again, and I could feel them, the way you feel a storm before the first thunderclap: so many unsaid words, swelling, multiplying, hanging above us like fog. "Em?" he said, lips against my hair, and I braced myself.

"Yeah?"

Could I? I thought, squashed into him. Could I lie if he asked me outright, right now? If he asked me how I felt about him doing this?

He hesitated, cleared his throat. "You the man," he simply said, then laughed, and so did I, with relief as the fog slowly dispersed. And that's where we'd stayed—there, against the soft cotton of the button-studded sofa, watching a film—one of Lucas's many "oh my God, how have you *not* seen it?" choices we've been working our way through for years.

"Seriously," he says now from behind the changing room curtain, which juts and judders with his movement. "Couldn't you have lied and said I looked like Chris Evans?"

"God, you're not *still* going on about it," I say from the padded cube I'm sitting on outside the dressing room.

"I definitely am."

"You wanted me here for honesty," I call out. "Let it go, Moreau."

The curtain is drawn back. "*No.*" He grins. He's in only jeans, muscular and bare-chested, and I don't know why, because during the fourteen years we have known each other, I have seen Lucas in all different stages of undress—albeit mostly drunken, him sobbing into various vessels as he pukes (toilets, jumbo crisp packets, hats, his mum's mop bucket)—but today, my face is instantly aflame at the sight of him.

"Jesus," he says. "How roasting is it in here?" He reaches inside the cubicle and pulls on his shirt and starts buttoning it up.

"Are you not . . . trying any more on?" I look away, pretending to take great interest in the characterless changing room, the fluorescent lights, the carpet, and oh, are those *beams*?

"I think we've seen quite enough," says Lucas. "Plus, Marie wanted me to try the white, didn't she, see how I felt about it . . ."

"And how *did* you feel about it?"

Lucas looks at me, smiling, fingers fastening a button at his chest. "I don't know," he says, "but we all know how *you* felt about it, don't we?"

Moments later we walk through the sliding doors of the shopping center and out to the warm, salty breeze of Berck, a seaside town with the biggest stretch of beach I think I have ever seen. I've lost count of the amount of times we have come here. Dinners and lunches and paper bag wrapped sandwiches on the beach, and shopping trips where we've whiled away the day, talking, with Lucas stopping every now and then to point things out—the use of a certain material on a villa, the fifteenth-century carvings on the stone corbel of a church. Tiny snippets of beauty in buildings the rest of us would walk by and miss.

"Architects aren't real people, are they?" Rosie said last week. "I mean, they're in all the films and ITV dramas and that, but I don't think anyone in real life actually does that job."

"Oh, interesting take," Fox had said.

"Why is it?"

"Just interesting. But then you do only date mechanics and people that emerge from a day's work coated in a greasy residue, so I must say I'm unsurprised."

"Er, what?" she'd said, then looked at me and said with a smirk, "I can't be sure, Emmie, but I think he's speaking Latin again."

Lucas's dad is an architect, and I often wonder if Lucas actually really *wanted* to be the same, or whether it was instilled in him, this love for design, for structure, so long ago, that it's impossible to know whether it's a natural part of him or something planted and now fully grown. Jean had decided Lucas was going to university long before Lucas knew he definitely wanted to go; decided *which* and what modules and "if you can be only one thing, you two, be driven." Jean is like that. People are mostly their successes, and although I have frequently worried about what he thinks of me—working class, single-parented, someone who only managed one year of college and goes into Waitrose for no more than a scotch egg to eat on the bus—it has helped me in the past, having Lucas beside me, his dad snapping at his heels. I may not have quite managed to finish the full two years at college in the end, but I found the strength to keep studying because he did. Despite the loneliness, despite Georgia, despite the rumors about me and Mr. Morgan, because he told me it would be worth it, that I was bigger than it. Having someone who could see their future so clearly, with so much excitement, helped disperse the smoke distorting my own.

"Where you at, Emmie Blue?" Lucas looks down at me now as we walk slowly in the sunshine. He asks this a lot, texts it sometimes, in horrendous on-purpose shorthand text: *emmie blue whr u @?* It can mean where am I physically sometimes, yes, when I haven't answered my phone for a while or if it's been a day or two since hearing from me, but he asks me mostly when I'm quiet, when my brain is spiraling off somewhere, and he can somehow tell, and wants to help pull it back to land.

"Food," I say with a smile. "I'm thinking about food."

"Then you're going to love this new place we're going to for lunch. Plus," he says, "they do chips that taste like the ones we used to eat in your flat. When you'd use your old-lady fryer. That's why we're going."

"God, I miss my old-lady fryer," I sigh.

"*I* miss your old-lady fryer. And your chips, actually."

"Me too. Why *haven't* we had them for ages?"

Lucas gives a little shrug. "I dunno, Em," he says. "I guess I haven't been over in a while. Life, work, the promotion, all that. Bit shit growing up and being an adult sometimes, isn't it?"

I look up at him, the sun turning his hair the color of spun sugar. I'd style it when we were younger. I'd sit on the sofa and he'd sit on the floor, between my legs, his back against the couch, and I'd plait chunks of hair, spray punky spikes bolt upright on his head as he watched TV and said, "Make me look beautiful, Emmie Blue. I'll accept nothing less." His brother Eliot and I straightened it once. "You look like our old neighbor. Leticia," Eliot had said, and Lucas had grabbed a mirror and said, "Fuck, I *do*. Why hello, Leticia. Fancy a shag?" Even though I know it wasn't, the sky is always blue, the sun always shining, in those memories.

I look up at Lucas now, the sky cloudless and azure behind him. "Eating chips from my eighties chip pan is not a reason to not grow up, Luke," I tell him.

"Yeah, I know, it's just . . ." He takes a hand out of his pocket and runs it through his hair. "I miss it sometimes, I suppose, don't you? Being young and silly and drunk, and you waking me up on your sofa with fried eggs and chips and that thick white bread you used to get from that weird bakery-slash-cab-office by your flat."

"Ned's."

"*Ned's*," laughs Lucas. "Good old Ned and his inability to choose between careers."

"And do you remember the ketchup we'd have? That cheap, radioactive ketchup."

"*Yes*." Lucas grins. "Basically vinegar. Sublime shit, that stuff."

"We get it at the hotel."

Lucas's head swings round, his eyes just visible over the tops of his sunglasses. "Seriously? I thought it was a five-star place."

"Four," I say. "But the ketchup is still as cheap as they can get it. Two years and it just gets more neon as the weeks go by."

Lucas laughs, hand outstretching to land on the small of my back so to weave me around a group of teenagers, windsurfing boards under their arms, walking toward us on the pavement. It's moments like this that I understand why people in the past have mistaken us for a couple. Lucas always plays up to it when it happens.

"Two years have *flown*," says Lucas. "Is it totally shit?" He drops his hand again as they pass. "I mean, are you bored?"

"Of the job?" I ask. "No, it's good. I mean, I definitely didn't expect to be there two years later, but the people are really nice. I did sign up to an agency last month, though."

"That's great," says Lucas.

"It's not that I don't enjoy it. But it's just—"

"It's *waitressing* at a hotel?"

And I don't know why, but the way he says it feels like a punch to the chest. It makes me feel shrunken down, like a speck, here in this beautiful place, next to Lucas in his designer shirt, he newly engaged, weeks past signing one of the biggest projects his firm has ever signed.

"No," I say shortly. "I was actually going to say, I'd like a little more money. I'd like to be able to afford my own flat again."

"Ah. 'Course," he says, nodding, eyes to the floor. "But you'll get something better, Em. You've got loads of experience in admin after all your years at the photo studio. And I can always talk to Dad."

"About what?"

Lucas shrugs, hands back in his pockets. "Well, he has tons of friends in London who have their own firms. I'm sure if I sent your CV to Dad, he could make some calls."

"I don't really want to go into London, Luke."

Lucas's brow crumples. "*Why?*"

"I don't think I'd be able to hack commuting every day," I say. "I'm not sure that's me."

"So waitressing at a hotel is you, then, or—"

"Oh my god." I stop on the pavement outside an open-fronted busy café, and freeze. "Listen."

"What? What's wrong?"

I gesture with a hand. "This song. I don't think I've ever heard this in public *anywhere*. Don't you remember?"

I do. I remember exactly where I was when I heard it for the first time. The CD arrived one morning before I left for college (in exchange for the six bags of Milky Way Magic Stars I'd posted to Lucas a fortnight before), and I listened to it on the bus there, on my Discman, the sun beating through the murky window, heating my skin. I had two classes that day with Georgia and her friends—the girl and the constantly smirking two boys—but I listened to it on repeat all day. That CD carried me through. Like arms around me, like a hand squeezing mine, reminding me I wasn't alone in the world.

Lucas smiles at me, puzzled, and slowly shakes his head. "You've lost me, Em."

"Seriously? You put it on one of the CDs. The *Dear Balloon Girl* CDs."

"*Oh.* God, 'course. Yeah," he laughs, then he taps his finger to my forehead. "You and your elephant memory. No doubt you know the—"

"Volume two, track five," I say, and Lucas smiles. "Knew it," he says.

> **Mix CD. Vol 2.**
>
> Dear Balloon Girl,
>
> Track 1. *Because your dad was probably in Whitesnake*
>
> Track 2. *Because you snort when you laugh*
>
> Track 3. *Because you said you'd never heard of this one*
>
> Track 4. *Because none of what happened to you is your fault*
>
> Track 5. *Because I should have asked you to dance in Berck*
>
> > Balloon Boy
> >
> > X

It was here, in Amanda and Jean Moreau's kitchen, that I realized I was in love with Lucas. It was six years ago, two weeks before Christmas, and we had been out for dinner and drinks with Lucas's friend from work. The friend was leaving to start his own business and had found out after years of IVF that he and his wife were expecting a baby. He gave a speech in a private room he'd hired out in a local bar and Lucas had translated parts of it for me afterward, saying, "Listen up, Paul McCartney, you might learn something here."

We'd taken a taxi home, giggly but not drunk, and there was a thunderstorm so bad, we let ourselves into his parents' house, not wanting to stay out in it a minute longer to walk the tiny but torrential distance to the bottom of the garden to the guest cottage. We whispered, tiptoed our way around the huge, dimly lit kitchen like teenagers home too late, laughing, shushing each other, making coffee, and trying not to rustle the packets of cookies Lucas pulled from the cupboard in case we woke his parents.

At the black marble of the breakfast bar, we'd hunched, opposite each other, hair wet, cheeks flushed with cold, and I watched him sip, and eat, and look over at me, gray eyes and golden lashes, the spattering of freckles across his nose and cheeks, and I felt it. This tug. This sickening pull in my stomach, like nausea, like excitement and fear all balled into one fizzing, burning orb in my gut. And it threw me. I was standing right there, opposite him, in the calm of the kitchen, rain battering the windows, but the realization felt like I'd been flung across the room. I knew. I knew right then.

He smiled at me, powder-blue shirt speckled with raindrops. "Where you at, Emmie Blue?"

"Nowhere." I swallowed, the dead silence of the house intimidating, goading me to tell him. "Nothing."

"You sure?"

I nodded once, hesitated. "That . . . speech," I'd said instead, hands cradling my mug. "Patrice's wife, when she cried. I keep thinking about it."

Lucas put his coffee mug down, forearms leaning on the counter, hands balled together, the silver watch at his wrist tapping on the marble. "The poetic, soppy bit. About how they met?"

"Yeah," I said. "About how they knew each other as kids yet it took them twenty years to find each other again."

"Yep." Lucas smiled warmly, light catching in his eyes. "And two marriages. Imagine that. You've already met the person you're meant to be with by the time you're twelve, but it takes you twenty years to realize it. Depressing in a way."

"But worth the wait."

He'd nodded, eyes fixed on me. And in that moment, for the first time in our whole friendship—of sleeping beside each other, of passing towels through ajar bathroom doors, of meeting my boyfriends and his girlfriends—opposite him on that counter, I felt too close to him to bear. Because I knew I loved him; had always loved him. And there was no way I could tell him.

Seven weeks later I met Adam, who quickly became my boyfriend, and three weeks after that, Lucas had started dating a woman at work. And I was relieved, really. It was an excuse to say nothing. To push it down, as if it were something shoved to the back of a wardrobe, closing the door quickly, before it had a chance to jump back out at me again. And it worked, at least for a little while. Adam numbed the longing; distracted me from having to look properly at the feelings that tumbled free from somewhere inside me, that rainy night at the kitchen counter.

Tonight, that same kitchen counter I leaned across six years ago is laden with platters and cake stands of exquisite-looking desserts, each handmade by Lucas's mum, who's just finished her first year at a renowned French cookery school. She's hosting a dessert party—something that sounded flippant and casual, but actually looks more like a home-hosted black-tie event.

"It's the caramel I keep tripping up on," says Amanda to Ian and Athena—the Moreaus' expat neighbors, and the final guests to arrive tonight. "It's one of those things, I think, Athena, you take your eye off it and poof, it's ruined. Like jam. Like a béchamel."

"Well, I think you are a talent," says Athena, tiny white plate in mani-cured hand. "I wouldn't know where to begin. Would you, Ian?"

"Oh, I am but a mere apprentice," Amanda laughs, and her eyes scrunch up the same as Lucas's when she smiles. "And have you ever tried these? These are made with *rose* water, Ian. Now, even if you're not a rose water fan, I have to insist you try. Go on. Pop it in. That's it."

I stand a few feet away, by the sink, a glass of wine in my hand. There are far more people here than I expected—although I don't know why I'm so surprised. The Moreaus bloody *love* a party—always have—and every one they throw, even the casual-sounding ones, look like the sort of parties I had only ever saw on TV as a child. Plates of canapés, olives, and people in shirts and heels and proffering gifts at the door that wouldn't look out of place at a wedding gift table. There are even cocktails being made by a man hired from a local catering firm.

"I was going to wear a T-shirt," I'd whispered to Lucas earlier. "I only went for this blouse in the end because I realized my T-shirt had a smudge of Nutella on it and it looked proper dodgy."

Lucas laughed. "You know what Mum and Dad are like."

"That woman over there is in *pearls*."

"She's a mayor."

"Of course she is."

"What?" Lucas chuckled.

"'Just the family and a few friends,' your mum said. A *little get-together*. Rosie had one of those last month and we were beside ourselves because we had the posh dips from Marks & Spencer and her neighbor with the mustache actually came."

Lucas had laughed into his glass of orange juice. "I'm going to insist you give me more on the neighbor with the mustache later, please," he said, "but now I've got to go and get Marie."

And I've been standing here, waiting for Lucas to return ever since. I don't know anyone else well enough (besides Jean and Amanda) to elbow my way into the conversation, and the only person who's spoken to me is the mayor, and when I tried to tell her—in terrible, loud, exaggerated English that resembled Neanderthal dialect—that I didn't understand, she laughed confusedly and walked off, looking over her shoulder to check, I suppose, that I wasn't about to jump her with a club. But despite not knowing anybody, I feel comfortable here. It's like a second home in a way; more constant than any other home I've had, actually. My room at Fishers Way doesn't really feel like home just yet, and the flat in which I lived with Adam never really got there either, somehow, although it had all the ingredients for it. But here, I can help myself. Here, I am looked after. And maybe that is why it feels more like home than anywhere else has ever felt. Maybe home isn't a place. It's a feeling. Of being looked after and understood. Of being loved.

"So, have we got to just stare at it, or are we allowed to actually eat it?"

I know the voice before I turn around, and it's like my body does, too, because I feel my shoulders stiffen, my skin prickle. I turn around. Eliot. A hand in his pocket, another holding a green bottle of beer to his chest, token teasing smile on his face.

"Oh. Hi."

"It *is* a dessert party, right? Nobody's touched anything yet."

I nod, and gesture with my glass to the table on the other side of the kitchen. "I think everyone seems to be on the canapés at the moment. There're salads over there too—"

"Yeah, sorry, no, I am not about *leaves* tonight. Pastry, though. Different story." Eliot smiles, dark eyebrows lifting along with his bottle of beer as if to toast. "It's good to see you, Emmie. How're things?"

I find it hard sometimes to believe that Lucas, Eliot, and I were once so close. I remember the day Lucas told me about Eliot. It was during one of our first phone conversations, just a few weeks after that first email.

"Yeah, I've got a brother. Eliot," he'd said. "Almost three years older than me."

"I always wanted a brother or a sister," I'd told him, and Lucas had told me they had different fathers. Jean and Amanda got together a year after Eliot's father, John, passed away—Jean and Amanda worked together—and got pregnant with Lucas, a surprise, quickly. "I forget he's a half brother," he'd said down the line, proudly. "He's my best mate."

And that's how it was. They did everything together back then, and when I'd visit, we'd go almost everywhere as a threesome, with Eliot, being the older brother and the owner of a driving license before either of us, driving us for miles—to the beach, to the park, to parties, and to pick us up from the cinema after he'd finished work.

"I'm all right, thanks," I say to Eliot now. "How about you? Did you come on your own?"

"I'm good." He nods, hand at the dark stubble on his chin. "And no. My girlfriend Ana's here." He cranes his neck, scanning the room for her. "Somewhere."

Ah yes. Ana. The new girlfriend. Eliot got divorced a couple of years ago, and apparently Ana was his divorce counselor.

"Imagine that," said Lucas a few weeks ago. "Showing someone the darkest recesses of your mind, probably crying like a twat and snotting into tissues because of your failed relationship, and someone falls in love with *that*."

"The dream, surely," I said. "Someone loving you despite and because of all the flaws and shit in your life."

Lucas shook his head. "Well, *yeah*, but shagging your therapist? No thanks."

"So, where's Luke?" Eliot asks, shoulders back, hand shoved back in his jeans pocket. Scruffy. That's what Lucas calls Eliot, and although I'm not sure I would go with that term, compared to Lucas, I suppose he is. Where Lucas always looks waspy—smart, clean-shaven, his hair styled—Eliot is never without a smattering of stubble, and looks as though he's always on his way to watch a band in Camden town. Jeans, T-shirt, Converse, sometimes a hat. Tonight he looks very much the same, less the hat, and plus the dark-blue blazer he wears over the top of it.

"He went to pick up Marie," I say. "She doesn't have a car today or something."

"Ah. The fiancée."

I say nothing, just smile and nod, and neither does he, but he watches me, waiting for a response.

"Yep," I say. "It's exciting, isn't it?"

"Yeah?" he asks, eyebrows raising in surprise, as if he was expecting me to say something else. "Mum says you're best woman."

"Yes," I say. "I am. And you're . . ."

"Brother of the groom?" A smirk tugs at the corner of his mouth.

"Right," I say. "Exciting."

The smirk is still on his face. "Yeah. You said."

We both drink, silence stretching between us. It ate me up, once upon a time, that Eliot and I went from friends to people who could barely hold a conversation. I'd lie awake at night, torturing myself by replaying memories, like film clips in my mind: Eliot and I laughing hysterically at the dining table after Jean would scold Lucas over dinner for swearing; Eliot holding a tissue to his nose, clutching his chest, mock-crying as he waved me off on the ferry, as Lucas pretended to console him, the pair of them holding on to each other like they were waving their husbands off to war. The times I couldn't sleep and would creep out into in the garden for fresh air, at midnight, to find Eliot out there too, hunched over his phone, texting a girlfriend, or with his earphones in, singing softly to himself. "Welcome to the insomni-club," he'd always joke. "Pick a life crisis to mull over and take a seat." I missed Eliot desperately for a while. But I had to remind myself that it was on him why more memories ceased to be made. And that turned the missing into anger, which eventually fermented into a sort of indifference. I didn't have Eliot anymore, but I had Lucas. And he was the only friend I needed.

"A bit mad, though," says Eliot now. "Not that I can judge—but, I dunno, it's . . ."

"Quick?" I suggest, and he bows his head in a nod.

"Yeah, I guess that's what I meant. But then that's Luke, isn't it? Mr. Haphazard. Thinks it's something he should be doing 'cause everyone else is doing it." I say nothing. "I mean, come on," Eliot carries on, leaning in. "We've been here before. He got engaged to that poor girl at uni. Holly."

"He was a kid then, though."

Eliot cocks his head as if to say, "Yeah, but still."

I look around to check nobody is listening, but I don't react. I want to.

I want to agree and add loads of other things to the list too—like when he went backpacking because a few friends at university did and came home after four weeks because he "couldn't hack hostels"; like the time Lucas moved in with Joanna, the ten-years-his-senior barrister, after knowing her six weeks, only to move out five weeks later—but I don't, because Lucas is my friend, and Eliot, divorced at almost thirty-three, is probably jealous. I might be too, if I were him. And the truth is, I don't trust Eliot. I can't. Yes, it was eleven years ago now, the night of Lucas's and my nineteenth birthday, but he has never apologized for what he did. He was why the three of us never had a single car ride together again, or bundled under one blanket for films and drinking Jean's beer concealed in coffee mugs. He broke the trust we spent two years weaving between the three of us.

"Yeah, well, Marie is different," I say. "She's lovely. Truly." And she is. Despite everything, despite myself, and the heart in my chest that's barely holding it together, it's impossible to call her anything else.

"Yeah, no, don't get me wrong," says Eliot. "I just—well, put it this way, I don't think I'll be buying my suit just yet. I mean—"

"Canada." I swoop in changing the subject. "Lucas says you lived in Canada for a year. Working. How was that?"

Eliot pauses, eyes narrowing just slightly at the sudden change of topic, but he goes with it. "Y-Yeah, with a friend. Mark. He's a joiner, in the same game as me, and he had loads of work over there. And to be honest, I needed to get away."

"Your divorce," I say.

"Yeah," he says matter-of-factly. "Perfect place, really, for pulling your head out your arse. It's beautiful where he lives. Quiet. Far enough to feel like you've actually *got* away."

"Do you miss it?" I ask, and he nods.

"Yeah," he says. "Thinking of going back soon, to be honest. Mark's starting up his own business—" And at that exact moment, Ana appears. I recognize her from a photo Amanda uploaded to Facebook last year of the whole family out for Jean's sixtieth. Tall, heart-shaped face, and a wide, glittering smile. One that fades quickly at the sight of me.

"Hey," says Eliot as Ana's hand snakes over his shoulder and rests flat on his broad chest. "Ana, this is Emmie."

"Emmie?" says Ana, stone-faced. "Lucas's Emmie?"

"Yes," I say, smiling wider than usual, as if to coax one onto her lips, but she gives me nothing. I hold out my hand. She takes it weakly, barely shaking it, then drops it.

"Nice to meet you," I say, and she says simply, "Yes," then turns and says something to Eliot in whispered French. His cheeks flush, and he looks at me with a flash of embarrassment.

"Emmie, we just have to go and say hi to some friends, but—"

Ana cuts in again with something I don't understand, pulling at his shoulder, and as Eliot opens his mouth to speak again, I put him out of his misery.

"See you later," I say. "Think I'll go and . . . eat some *leaves*," and I whisk off in the opposite direction. You are the company you keep; that's what they say, don't they? I'm not sure I ever expected Lucas's brother to date a bitch, but Cold Ana and Jealous Eliot belong with each other, I am sure.

I meander through guests to the kitchen, and stand eating a little square plate of balsamic vinegar–soaked tomatoes. I watch Eliot and Ana, all hand-holding and big grins, and then Jean, marveling proudly to anyone who will listen, about Amanda's dedication and incredible pastry skills, and I scan the room, from happy couple to happy couple to happy couple, and . . . *I can do this, can't I?* Can I be the *best* best woman for Lucas, stay positive, and trust it'll work out how it is meant to? They may even get married. God. *They might.* But I suppose I just have to keep trusting. Maybe we'll end up like Patrice and his wife. Maybe it'll take us twenty years and two marriages for us—well, him—to realize it. That it's me. That it's us.

I place my empty plate in the sink and move into the hallway, heading to the little cubby of an under-stairs loo, when the front door clicks and opens. Lucas and Marie appear in the doorway, Lucas wrangling free his key from the door with one hand, the other holding on to hers. The ring on Marie's finger glitters like the hallway's chandelier.

"Emmie!" She grins, dropping Lucas's hand and holding her slender, brown arms wide. "You're here! Shall we sit? We have so much to speak about. Oh, you look so *beautiful!*"

"And so do you," I say as her arms envelop me, her warm, perfumed cheek to mine. "You look lovely. Truly."

Impossible. Impossible to call her anything else.

To: Emmie.Blue@gmail.co.uk
From: Hina@recruitment1.com
Date: June 25, 2018
Subject: School Counselor Services Administrator position

Dear Emmie,

I wondered if you would be interested in a position that has become available at a local secondary school. I know you said you would prefer not to work in a school environment, but it seems a shame to not pass on a position like this to you, considering your certificates in education and training, and your experience in admin. The salary is also very competitive.

Would you like me to organize an interview?

Kind regards,
Hina Alvi
Recruitment Consultant

Laughter is universal. To understand laughter, you do not need to be multilingual. Half an hour I was waiting at the bus stop, bus after bus passing by without Calais on the front of it, or anywhere I had even heard of, actually, and eventually, after thirty minutes of countless buses and countless passengers filing off and on, I got onto the next bus I could see, and told the driver in the best French I could muster that I needed to get to Calais.

He laughed. *For ages.* As if he was auditioning for a rerecording of *The Laughing Policeman.* "It does not exist," he told me from under his thick black mustache. "No more."

"But I—I looked on Google," I said pathetically, and he lifted his chubby hands at his side, as if to say, "What do you want me to do, lady?"

"It is old," he grumbled. "Last December, service stop. No more. You get taxi to Boulogne, and then bus. Or train. But . . ." He tapped the glass face of his watch and shrugged. "No time."

I panicked then; stood flapping for a moment, face dewy with sweat, before realizing a busload of people were staring at me as if they'd all quite like to disembowel me. I got off and watched defeatedly as the doors slammed, and the bus whirred away.

It's never happened before, Lucas letting me down for a lift to the port. *Didn't want to wake you, Em, but I've had to come into work,* his text said. I read it through bleary eyes, having just woken. *Fucking Frederic AGAIN. Guy's a prick. You'll have to make your own way to Calais. Is that okay? I've left a taxi card in the kitchen next to the coffee machine. They're local. Reliable. So so sorry to do this. Text me!!!*

And although it's nothing, really—it's work, it can't be helped—I still had to graft hard at ignoring the swirling in my stomach when I read his text. The churn that said, *Everything is changing now he's engaged, Emmie. He doesn't even have time to take you to your ferry, like he always has.*

It was a good ten minutes before I admitted defeat on the side of the road and trudged back to the Moreaus' under the blistering sun, where now I find the side gate to the back garden wide open. I can hear the distant sound of Eliot sawing and a radio blasting, and I wish there was a way I could call that taxi number and pay whatever the fare is, make it so I don't have to see Eliot's smug "I told you so" face. He stayed the night, after the dessert party, without Cold Ana, thankfully. Eliot is a carpenter. A cabinetmaker, actually, something he corrected me on every time, back then, when he was working as an apprentice for a local furniture designer. And he's working at the house today, making a start on a decked bandstand for Amanda and Jean's garden. We barely spoke as we drank coffee on the patio this morning, and he'd simply looked up as I'd left for the bus stop, pulling down his dust mask just in time to tell me that he didn't think any sort of bus service existed anymore.

"There's a bus in fifteen minutes, actually," I'd announced proudly as I passed him in the garden, sunglasses on, my case in hand.

"You're sure?" he'd asked.

"Yup," I'd sung. "Good old Google; a fine invention." And Eliot had shrugged and said, "Cool. See you later, then."

Now Eliot looks up at me, unsurprised, as I slump down onto a deck chair on the Moreaus' lawn. He pauses, saw in hand, then straightens. I can hardly breathe with the heat, but Eliot looks completely at ease, in nothing but a pair of jeans, his chest golden, dots of sawdust clinging to the hair on his forearms. He pulls the mask down and looks at me.

"No buses," I pant, cheeks pounding with sunburn. "Old service."

"Yeah," he says. "I think I did say."

I nod breathlessly. It's eighty-seven degrees today here in Le Touquet, and the air is stifling and thick. There is not a wisp of breeze to be found. I feel like I'm suffocating.

"You need a lift to the station," says Eliot, swiping a forearm across his forehead.

I hesitate, fan my face pointlessly. "Yes."

"No worries. What time's your ferry?"

"Three?"

He looks at a thick brown leather watch at his wrist. "Right. I'll finish up here and then we can jump in the van. Good?"

I nod, feel something like shame prickle up my back. Maybe it's being unable to afford the taxi. Maybe it's at having to rely on Eliot. "Yeah," I say. "Thanks, Eliot."

He shrugs, stretches the mask back over his face, and continues sawing.

"So, Lucas left getting to the station to you," Eliot says, adjusting his backward red baseball cap, tufts of dark hair sprigging from the sides.

"It wouldn't have been an issue had the buses been running."

Eliot drops a hand to his lap, the other holding the steering wheel. "Lucas drops everything for that boss. Whatshisname. Dude with the eyebrows."

"Frederic."

Eliot nods. "That's it."

"Well, he left me details of a taxi service and texted me to—"

"And why didn't you get a taxi?"

I look over at him. He says nothing more, just looks at me, then back at the road, and lifts his shoulders as if to say, "Well?"

"You, um, said you didn't mind—"

"I don't," he jumps in. "Not at all, actually. It was just a question." He laughs and holds a hand to his chest as if in surrender.

"Right," I say, and Eliot reaches to turn up the radio louder than it was.

The van rattles as it turns a corner, and the smell of creosote and the sweetness of wood reminds me of when I'd first begun visiting Lucas and the Moreaus. The way Eliot would come in from work at his apprenticeship, hair full of dust, smudges of varnish on his T-shirt, and smile a hello before going upstairs and joining us for dinner, hair wet, and freshly showered.

"Nice wheels," Lucas would laugh, gesturing to the truck on the gravel drive through the dining room window, and Eliot would say, "Least I've got wheels, dude."

"Least I don't sound like a rag-and-bone man." Lucas would grin back, nudging me, and Eliot would lean in across the table and say, "Ask Luke about his wheels, Emmie. His little BMX out front. How far's he going to take you on that, eh?"

I'd giggle behind my glass and Jean would look sternly over his spectacles. "Stop now, boys. Eat your mother's dinner, will you, please. And Emmie, don't engage them."

I loved those evenings around the table. It felt like being part of a family. The sort of families I'd see through windows around dinner tables or in front of televisions when I'd walk home in the dark in the winter, the edges steamed up with cooking. How easy my life would be, I'd think, if Amanda was my mum, and Jean was my dad. If this was what I came home to, every day.

"Sorry," says Eliot now, over the music. "Didn't mean to pry. You can get to the station however you like. Taxi, dragon, hang gliding." He looks over at me and smirks. "Bloke with a van . . ."

I give a reluctant smile. "I can't afford it right now," I admit. "I have thirteen quid in my bank, all of which I'm hoping to spend on food on the way home for the fridge, and I thought the bus would be far cheaper."

Eliot nods. "Well, Lucas should've left you some money if—"

"He didn't know," I cut in. "I know he'd feel bad that he asked me to come out here with so little, but I wanted to. He needed me. And I don't want charity or to borrow, so . . ." I trail off, catch a look outside the passenger window. The sky is so blue, it's as if we've been tipped upside down, and the ocean is now high above us. No clouds, not even a tuft. Just endless, still blue. The sort of sky, I imagine, that helped my balloon make it all this way, intact.

"Sorry to hear that, Emmie," says Eliot. "Is it . . . work troubles?"

"It's not really work troubles," I say. "Just . . . life stuff, really. I got in a little debt a couple of years ago, trying to keep a flat I couldn't afford. But I moved into a cheaper place, which really helps, and my job at the hotel doesn't exactly pay well, but there're always extra shifts, so I've gradually been able to get back on my feet. I'm just not left with much at the end of the month. But it's fine. Much better than it was."

"Well, that's good," Eliot says gently. "Life's a dick sometimes. Creeps up on us while we're not looking. Throws us a curveball, chucks us off track . . ."

"Sounds about right." I smile. "But I think that happens for a reason."

"Seriously?"

I pause, raise my eyebrows with surprise. "*Yeah.* Don't you?"

Eliot laughs, rubs the stubble on his chin with his hand. "Um, no. Definitely not," he says, his smile lopsided. "It's all just—life, isn't it? Disordered and chaotic and out-of-nowhere, and we have to plan and navigate our way around it the best we can."

I look at Eliot over my sunglasses. "So you don't believe in chance, then? At all?"

"Oh God, no," he says, pulling a face, pink lips stretched into a grimace. "I mean, maybe I used to. When I was young, a kid. But . . . life happens, and you learn you sort of just have to roll with it, right? Make the best of it. That's all we can do, really. Thinking some divine power has our back. I mean, seriously, how stupid do you have to be to—*what?*"

"How do you know there's no divine power?" I ask.

Eliot gives a heavy shrug, hand on the wheel, forearm resting on the open car window. "I'm just saying, I think if you don't take charge of your own stuff and instead, sit back and wait for someone—*something*—to handle it for you, you're sort of doomed."

I stare at him. "So it's all on us. All of it."

"I reckon so," he says confidently. Then he looks at me, a little smirk on his face, and says, "Mind you, I'm not sure I'd fancy having you in charge of my stuff. You planned your way to Calais, and look what happened there. You planned your bus route, too. I saw the little Post-it you were carrying . . ." Eliot laughs, biting his lip, and it surprises me that my back goes up, defenses clinking into gear. "Faith didn't make the buses run, did it, Emmie B—"

"I suppose your life is perfect, then," I barge in.

Eliot hesitates. "No. Not really," he says. "But it's nice, yeah."

"Well," I say, giving a harsh nod. "Good. Good for you."

Eliot opens his mouth, pink lips parted, and gives me a double take, as if he can't quite work out if I'm joking or actually offended, but he thinks better of speaking any more on the subject.

"Let's, er, have some more music," he says, then he turns up the radio once again.

I lean my head against the window and watch greens drift by in all the colors of the ocean, and will for the journey to speed by. "It must be nice to be you," I want to say to Eliot. But faith is how I got to be sitting right here. If I hadn't believed better things were coming, that all that pain would be for a reason, to make me stronger, I would have disappeared the night of the Summer Ball. Mr. Morgan would have won, after what he did to me that night in the IT room. Georgia and all her friends would have won—pushed me out of college before the first year was out, with their stories about me lying and home-wrecking, about me crying assault—and then where would I have been? Faith kept me going—probably kept me alive. And *silly old chance* dropped my balloon in Lucas's path. Chance brought me my best friend.

"Food?"

"Sorry?"

"Are you hungry?" asks Eliot. "We could stop here. We have plenty of time." He motions with a quick, lazy hand to a string of shops, a café, and a KFC. "Coffee? Almond croissant? You still like those, right?" Then he lowers his voice and says, "A *bargain bucket*?"

"I'm fine, thanks," I say, despite the hunger bubbling in my stomach. "I'll eat on the ferry."

"Sure? Jean did say the food was comparable to eating human flesh, this morning, remember?" Eliot pulls the handle of the driver's door. It clicks open. "But then again, he said that about the one and only Beefeater restaurant we ever visited."

"I'm sure I'll survive. My expectations are far lower than Jean's. I like a ferry sandwich."

"Suit yourself," Eliot says, and slides out of the car, shutting the door behind him.

Twenty minutes later we are pulling up at Calais, in a busy taxi rank. Eliot keeps the engine running and circles the van to retrieve my bag from the back as I unbuckle my seat belt.

"Have a safe journey, Emmie," he says, handing it over, and jumps back into the driver's seat. A taxi driver presses hard on his horn as Eliot pulls away, and I hold my hand in a wave as he drives off.

On the ferry, I text Lucas.

Me: This is a message for Curly-Haired Screech: I am about to get on the ferry!

Lucas: Hey! Good!

Lucas: Curly-Haired Screech is really sorry he couldn't take you himself.

Me: I accept his apology (but never his suit).

Lucas: hahahaha

Lucas: Text when you're home safe, Em.

Me: I will x

Lucas: xxx

The ferry judders as it pulls away from the port, and in almost-synchronization, my stomach rumbles with hunger. I unzip the side pocket of my bag for my purse. Sitting on the top is a white paper bag, folded at the top like a seam. Inside: two still-warm almond croissants.

10

There is one lovely thing about living here, at Two Fishers Way, with Louise, my of-few-words landlady. It's waking to the comforting sound of a day that has already begun. I am in no way a late riser, but Louise is always up at six, or before, and I wake most mornings to the chink of cutlery, the scrape of a broom against the patio, the muffled sounds of the radio from the kitchen—BBC Radio 4 usually, sometimes Magic FM— or the smell of warm food. Louise cooks a lot of soups and marmalades. Things in big pots with handles, which she stands by, unmoving except for her skinny hand, which stirs. After Adam moved out, the last place I'd wanted to end up was in a rented room in an old, cluttered, dusty house like this, but most things in life have their plus points, and waking up in Shire Sand, this close to the beach, knowing I'm not alone, is one for living here.

This morning when I open my bedroom door to go downstairs, the radio is on—Radio 4 today. A poet talking about the Industrial Revolution— and I am expecting to find Louise, as usual, at the padded bottle-green cushioned chair at the head of the kitchen table, where she sits with murky cups of mint tea and giant crossword books. But as I turn to descend the stairs, I see the silvery top of her head, the ball of her neat bun at the nape of her neck. She's sitting on the second-from-last step, her hands on her knees.

"Louise? Louise, are you okay?"

Louise turns to look over her shoulder, the skin of her face pale.

"I, uh, I dropped the vase. Lost my balance. I was emptying the old flowers." Louise's voice is strong and clear as it always is, but I can't help but notice the wobbles at the edges of her words. I trot to the bottom of the stairs, and bend to pick up the vase. I place it on the wooden radiator cover where she always keeps a spray of fresh lavender. There is a puddle of water by her feet, staining the brown carpet black.

"Let me get some cloths."

Louise nods. "In the top cupboard. Next to the sink."

I go through to the kitchen—clean but cluttered, and straight from the seventies, with pale yellow units, and a lino floor in brown and mink squares and circles—and return to the hallway with a roll of paper towels. Louise is trying to pull herself up on the banister, but groans, then sighs, and stays where she is, on the steps. I wonder, crouched down onto the wet carpet, how long she's been sitting there.

"Are you all right?" I ask.

Louise sighs raggedly. "Fine. I just lost my balance, as I said. Almost fell. Grabbed on to the banister, dropped the bloody vase."

I nod and carry on, pressing squares of paper towels onto the puddle of water. "Well, better it be the vase and not you."

She makes a sound in her throat; an amused scoff, as if to say, "Is that so?" and says nothing else as I blot up the water. In the eighteen months I've lived here, Louise and I have probably only had two conversations that have lasted longer than a few minutes. She isn't rude, but abrupt. That's the word for her. I imagine she was once the head teacher for an all-girls' school, or a matron in a hospital. She says what needs to be said, with no filler whatsoever, because filler would just waste everybody's time. No "Did you sleep well?" No "They say we're going to have an Indian summer, don't you know." Just "This is what needs to be done" and "Oh, stop sniffling, it's only your spine that's utterly irreparable. Accept it and move swiftly on."

"You didn't eat dinner," she says.

"Sorry?"

"Last night. You came in, went straight up to bed, and I didn't see hide nor hair of you until just now." Louise watches me, her breath slowing, her thumb and finger twiddling the rings on her hand, all large colored stones and pewter.

"I was really tired." I stand and slot the scattered lavender back into the vase. "Got into bed and fell straight to sleep," I lie. The truth is that I got home from Lucas's yesterday, got into bed, and couldn't face food, or even seeing a single face. Something about Eliot and what he'd said about chance, how he laughed at me. Something about Lucas letting me down with the lift to the port. Something about not being able to afford the taxi. Last night, I felt like I was sixteen again. *Alone.*

"And how was it?"

I look at Louise blankly.

"France," she says shortly.

"Oh." I ball the wet tissue in my fist. "It was nice. We went suit shopping. Lucas tried white."

"*White?*" Her mousy eyebrows raise, her mouth downturned at the corners as if to say, "So that's what the youth of today think looks good, then, is it?"

"It looked terrible," I say, and Louise gives an exasperated sigh, as if despairing of the world, and says, "Of course it did. What was he thinking?"

I don't know, I want to say. I wish I knew. And a part of me wants to pour everything out to her, tell her I think he's making a mistake, tell her I feel like he's rushing this, that it'll be just like backpacking, like so many things and relationships before, and that I have never felt so close to telling him how I feel. But the built-in, fourteen-year-long best-friend loyalty stops me. Because how *dare* I make this about me, when this should only be about him. About Marie. So I don't. As much as Louise watches me now, wise, her eyes serious; eyes that have seen so many things in her seventy years that nothing much would faze her, I say nothing, and instead look around at the room—the vase with its flowers sitting neatly on the radiator cover, the carpet's water stain now barely visible. "Well, the good news is your vase appears completely unscathed."

Louise gives a weak nod. "Suppose that's something."

I look down at her on the step. "Do you need a hand?"

"No. I'll be fine."

I want to ask her if she's sure, but I don't press. I just tell her if she needs me, I'm home until eleven, then leaving for work. She gives a nod, and I go into the kitchen, make a cup of tea and two slices of toast. I think about the double shift ahead of me tonight as I set a tray—the lunch shift, followed by dinner—and plan a treat for tonight, for when I get back. It's the only thing that gets me through some days, when the balls of my feet are burning, my back throbbing, and I know there is nobody to return home to. Small things. Ever-attainable things. They help. A bowl of soup in bed with a comfort-watch on the TV. *The Leading Man*, perhaps. A movie nobody has ever heard of, of course, starring Jon Bon Jovi, but a DVD I got for 99p when I was sixteen, from the Blockbuster bargain bin. It's the only way I could afford to buy DVDs back then. It's why most of my favorite films are those nobody has ever heard of.

"The Leading Shat," Lucas calls it, and of course I've told him that doesn't even make any sense. It doesn't even rhyme. "I tell you what else doesn't make any sense," he'd say.

"That it didn't win several Academy Awards?"

"No, Em. The fact you voluntarily watch it over and over again."

I wash up the knife now, wipe down the counter, and tray in hands, on my way into the hallway, I find Louise still there. Not on the bottom step, but on the floor now, sitting with her back against the stairs. She looks up at me, then her papery eyelids close.

"Would you like a hand up?"

Louise pauses, then sighs raspily. "Please."

I place the tray behind me on the floor. "How is best for me to—"

"Emmie, just give me your hands, please."

I widen my feet on the carpet and hold out my hands as I'm told. She takes them. Her hands are warm and dry, and she squeezes them so tightly as I pull, that her rings pinch my skin. Twice, Louise almost gets to standing, before she sits back down again, her poor face contorted, a dapple of sweat above her lip. On the third try she stands properly, letting go of one of my hands the second she's up, and steadies herself holding on to the banister.

"Do you need help getting to a seat or to the kitchen?"

"I'm fine from here, thank you."

"Are you sure?"

"Quite."

"Okay," I say. "I'm upstairs if you need me."

I pick up my tray from the floor behind me as Louise shuffles off, purple velvet skirt skimming the carpet.

"And Emmie?" she calls out.

I stop on the stairs. "Yes?"

"You have a package in the porch."

"Emmie! Oh, Emmie, how are you?"

Marie's smiling, beautiful face fills the screen, the phone shaking in my hand. "Oh. Hi, Marie."

"Luke is in the shower. He is just coming out!" Then her face leans from the shot, and I hear her call out something to him in French. "Emmie is on the phone, my love." She looks back at the screen, at me, white, straight-toothed smile ever fixed. "He will not be long. Are you okay?"

I remember when I met Marie for the first time. It was in the winter of 2014, at a wine bar—all exposed brick and low lighting—and I remember how badly Lucas had wanted me to like her. "She's seriously great," he kept saying in the taxi on the way there. "I think you'll really get on. She's bubbly, you know? Really laid-back, really warm." Lucas had had many girlfriends, most of which were so short-lived I'd never met them. I was sure I'd dislike her. I was living with Adam at the time, happy, I thought, but I know now, living in total denial. Denial of the butterflies I'd get every time Lucas would put his arm around me, talk into my ear over the loud music of a bar, breath against my neck, every time he'd fall drunkenly asleep beside me, and I'd wake and watch his eyelashes flicker against his cheeks. But he was right. She was great. We got on instantly. We clicked, as they say. And I'd thought, *Well, that's that, then, isn't it?* and I ignored those butterflies so expertly, they almost disappeared altogether. Lucas and Marie broke up four times in an on-off, disjointed three and a half years, after that. The final time because Marie was sure he had cheated with Australian Ivy on the business trip after she texted him something flirty, and Lucas was tired of the accusations.

Marie gazes back at me now, smiling, but the corners of her brown eyes crinkle ever so slightly with puzzlement.

"Yes, I'm fine," I tell her. "Look, if it's a bad time, I can call again later—"

"No, no, absolutely not. It is fine. We can chat until he's out, no? Tell me all about this book you have bought. Luke tells me you are the *perfect* best woman already."

"B-Book?" My mouth is dry, my hands still shaking, the parcel from Louise's porch spilled out beside me on the bed.

"He said you have a book you are using to help with suits and speeches and—"

"Oh. Oh yes, my best man book."

"Yes!" Marie smiles a beaming smile and nods into the camera, and I can see from my face in the tiny postage stamp of a window above her bright eyes and smooth skin, that I look ashen and drained. It's like Beyoncé is FaceTiming Marley's Ghost. "Did I tell you, Emmie," Marie says, "that my girlfriend is taking a bridesmaid *class*? Can you believe there is such a thing?"

I'm not sure what I was expecting there to be in the parcel. Something I forgot I won on eBay. Perhaps a redirection from the flat or the old landlord, a collection of old posts or something. But I wasn't expecting this— *these*. Seven of them. Marie chatters away, and I catch a glimpse of one of the envelopes in my lap, and my stomach lurches all over again, the way it does when you're teetering at the top of a roller coaster. His writing. This is *his writing*. I know now that he writes his *E*s like back to front threes, in mixed capital letters and lowercase. I brush a finger over one. France. To think these came all the way from France, somewhere. Saint-Malo, maybe. I wonder if he looks like Jean. I wonder if he leaves the letter *H* off the beginning of English words in his French accent, like Jean does. '*Oliday*. '*Orrible*.

"Oh! I leave you now," says Marie, her gaze fixed off camera. "My turn to shower." She turns back to the screen and smiles widely. "So lovely to speak to you, Emmie."

"You too," I say quickly, desperate for the sight of Lucas to slide onto the screen. He'll make sense of it. He'll help, as he always does, to settle the dread, the unease in my stomach.

He appears, shiny-skinned, wet-headed. "Hey," he says, swiping a hand through his hair, screen wobbling as he settles on the sofa. "Sorry. I was in the shower."

"That's okay."

Lucas stops, takes in my face. "Em, what's wrong?"

I hesitate, look down at the fan of envelopes in my lap. I look back up at him, an ocean away, and I wish so much he was right here, in this room, beside me.

"I got a parcel today," I tell him, my voice tiny. "And . . . it was full of cards. Birthday cards. To me."

Lucas stares into the screen, his eyebrows knitted together. "Right? Who from?"

"My dad."

Lucas doesn't react straightaway. He just stares into the screen, frozen, a bit like I was when I opened the first one. Unmoving. Not breathing. "Y-Your . . . *dad?*"

I look down into my lap at the scatter of them. Seven. Seven children's birthday cards, every envelope opened, no address on the front, just my name. I hold one up to the camera. There's a pink elephant on the front of this one, its trunk curling into a number two.

"There're seven of them, Luke. And the handwriting on the parcel; it's Mum's."

Lucas brings a hand to his forehead, lips parted. "Shit, so . . . she's had these, what, all along?"

"I don't know."

"And decides to send them to you now? *Why?*"

I think back to what she said at the festival. The sharpness to her words, the finality of them. That if it was what I wanted—finding my dad—then she knew I no longer needed her. "Okay," I told her. "Okay."

My hands, clammy and cold, tremble, and my throat constricts as if it's being squeezed. I can't speak. I look down into my lap. "Daughter. You are 7 today!" stares back at me, and a picture of my seven-year-old self, obsessed with rabbits and hair clips and collecting key rings, flickers into my mind, like a video springing to life. She wanted her dad so desperately, that little girl. She dreamed of him, drew pictures of him, pretended men who smiled at her and her mum in supermarkets were him.

"Shit, Em. I'm—are you okay?"

"I don't know," I manage, my words mere squeaks, and the tears come easily. No warning. "She said he didn't know about me, Luke. For my whole life, she told me he . . . She . . ." I bring my hands to my forehead, cold palms cooling my hot skin. I open my mouth to speak, but Lucas is nodding. He already knows everything I want to say. "I know," he says softly. "I know, Emmie."

Tears keep coming, and I hide my face in my hands as they fall. All I can hear is his voice from my phone propped up in front of me in the folds of my duvet, the whooshing of blood in my ears.

"I'm sorry, Em. It's such a lot to take in. But listen, this could be the start of something, couldn't it? We know now that your mum knows more than she let on. Em? Em, are you okay?" And when I look up again, I see Lucas, those familiar, soft gray eyes on me, narrowing with worry. Then I see Marie in the background, frozen, a thick, burgundy dressing gown tied at the waist. The three of us, staring back at one another.

"I'm going to go," I say.

"Are you sure?"

I nod.

"Emmie, I think you need to talk to your mum," says Lucas, and I nod again, quickly, finger already hovering over the button to hang up.

"I'll be okay," I tell him. "I'll text you."

I watch Lucas and Marie disappear to black on my screen and curl up into bed, pulling the sheets to my neck. Thirty whole years of wondering, hours of searching, dead ends, barking up wrong trees. Lucas is right. These prove Mum knows more than she said she did. These prove my dad knew about me. *Thought of me.* These seven cards—the seven messages inside, exactly the same—tell me my dad cared. About me.

Dearest Emmeline,

Happy Birthday.
Thinking of you always.

Love,
Dad

11

WhatsApp from 073622819199 in group "OPERATION STEN!!!!":

Hi guys and gals! It's Tom Boding here. Luke gave me your numbers, so thought I'd start a group for operation STEN party. Stag/hen. Get it?! We've got best woman (hi Ems ;)), maid of honor (hi Lucille, stop us if you need to Google Translate lol!!!), brother of the groom (hi Eliot m8), and me, usher and legend :P

WhatsApp from 073622819199 in group "OPERATION STEN!!!!":

Just thought it would be cool to have a place we can discuss ideas and touch base on this party shiz. Thoughts?

WhatsApp from Eliot Barnes:
STEN.

WhatsApp from Eliot Barnes:
legend.

WhatsApp from Eliot Barnes:
shiz.

WhatsApp from Eliot Barnes:
Who knew it could take only three words to make me hope for death?

"Right, I have an idea, Emmie. Lay down."

"What?"

"Well, you're always taking photos of me from above, so maybe you could lie down beside me and get some close-up, same-perspective—"

"But isn't the sand . . . *wet?*"

Rosie tuts and pauses, splayed out on the sand at my feet. "Well, a bit but—"

"You have to suffer for art?"

"I was going to say a bit of wet sand is nothing when the end result is me looking like a frigging betty, actually."

I look down at Rosie sprawled out elegantly on the beach like a 1950s movie star, her sunglasses huge, her white kaftan fanning out around her on the ground, the pop of pink of her bikini shorts.

"Fine," I say. "But if Fox finds any sand on my back and makes me wear one of those smelly spare blouses again from Lost Property, I am coming straight for you."

Rosie laughs, the apples of her cheeks glittering with bubble gum–pink blush. "Come on down, baby."

I do as I am told, and crouch to lie beside Rosie on the cushiony, wet sand. Spots of water pierce my shirt. "Terrific." I grimace, and Rosie grins at me, a dimple in each cheek.

"This is a bit cozy, isn't it, Emmie Blue?" she says.

"Most romantic position I've been in for ages, to be honest."

"Can you imagine Fox's face if he was here?" Rosie says. "*You do realize that the precipitation has rendered the sand utterly unfavorable for a photographic shoot, you fools.*"

"You *unfastidious* fools."

We both laugh, there on the wet beach, the summer sun high in the sky, Rosie in her new "gifted" kaftan from an Instagram-famous, plus-size fashion brand, and me in my hotel uniform of white blouse, name badge, and drab black trousers I often hope find their way to Lost Property, to never return. A man walks by us, a border collie trotting at his side, and he slows, staring at us as if we have just squatted naked in the street. I often find myself in these positions with Rosie.

Rosie is a fashion and beauty blogger, and almost every lunchtime it's her blog she works on, either writing posts at her desk littered with coffee mugs and empty sandwich wrappers, or taking photos in various outfits I wouldn't have the first clue how to put together. The only time Rosie doesn't spend them working on her blog is when the builders are back working on the hotel, when she will invite me to have lunch in the courtyard behind the kitchen, where she will admire with wonder the worker with all the tattoos, the way Attenborough admires mating seals. Last time they were here, we watched them over sandwiches and tea, and when Fox approached and asked how long we'd be sitting there "wondering which poor bugger is single," Rosie said, "Actually, Fox, I'm wondering how good the one who looks like Bradley Cooper is at giving head." Rosie is smart and bold and has a confidence that rubs off and makes those around her walk a bit taller. Rosie is how confident I aspire to be.

"Get the bracelets in," she says now as I snap away at her with her new iPhone.

"I'm trying."

"Try and get the light reflecting off the topaz one."

I stop and look over the phone at her. "Rosie, I'm a waitress with a fucking iPhone. I am not David Bailey."

After a few moments, Rosie rolls over onto her front and I hand back her phone. "Thank you." She smiles at me, unscrewing the top to a bright pink smoothie. The beach may be damp from a night of summer rainfall, but the air is warm and smells like deep-fried doughnuts and seaweed, and there isn't a cloud to be seen in the sky. It is on days like these that I love Shire Sands. The novelty of living here, with its small, sandy beach, its orange-bricked Victorian houses, the chintz of the arcades, has never truly worn off. I knew I wanted to live here the second I stepped off the train. I'd made the decision to move after that first year of college finished, and Lucas and Amanda had come with me, helping me move two towns over from Ramsgate.

"A new start," Amanda had said, positioning daffodils in the windows of the tiny studio flat I'd started renting. "You deserve that, my darling. You'll be happy here." And she was right.

Rosie sips at her smoothie. "Talk to me, Blue."

"What about?"

She leans and touches her arm to mine. "Whatever's been giving you that face all week. The constipated face. Where you look like you have a small village jammed up your arse."

I laugh, picking out a petrol-blue mussel shell wedged in the sand. "I do not have that face."

"You do. You always do when you're thinking too hard about something. What is it? Is it the Frenchman?"

No, I want to say. Today there is something overriding Lucas: the seven birthday cards. From my dad. I can't get them out of my head, and it has put my stomach into a constant churn ever since. I have spent a week with a ball of nerves, of sadness, and even a shred of excitement, in my chest. Excitement because I know I am closer to finding him, closer to the day I look my dad in the face. The man I am half of.

Rosie pulls her sunglasses down to look at me with big brown eyes. "Well?"

I look over at her. "It isn't the Frenchman."

"Okay," says Rosie. "Wanna talk about it?"

I shake my head, but she watches me, allowing a warm space to expand between us, encouraging me to fill it. "Do you remember when I told you about my dad? That I didn't know who he was."

Rosie nods, fiddling with the label on the bottle in her hands. "Yeah," she says. "French, wasn't he? A sexy musician."

"You may have added the sexy bit."

"Except, all musicians are sexy," says Rosie. "Even the ugly ones. Anyway, go on."

"Well, my mum has always told me she doesn't know anything about him," I tell Rosie. "Just that he was in a band and she was working at the same festival as him, and they had a couple of days together. His name was Peter and he lived in Brittany, that's all she'd told me. And that he doesn't know I exist."

"I remember." Rosie nods gently. "You said you never believed her. Not really."

"Yeah," I say, and pull my handbag toward me, the brown leather speckled with sand. I hand her the jiffy bag from inside. "She sent me these last Tuesday."

Rosie pulls the cards out in a pile, taking the first out of its pink envelope. Like the rest of them, they're scrawled with our old address. She's silent for a moment, then she looks at me, mouth open.

"Oh my God." She gawps at me, flinging the sunglasses to the top of her head. "This is . . . this is *huge*, Em." I love the way her face has lit up, the way there are tears in her eyes now, glittering at the edges. The way she holds my arm and says, "He knows about you, Emmie. He cares. He's always cared. This is proof."

Rosie pulls her glasses back down, fingers swiping her eyes for stray tears under the dark lenses. "So, she's had these all along, your mum?"

A swoop of seagulls crow low overhead. A family behind us, from behind a blue-and-pink striped windbreak, throw a scatter of chips in their direction.

"I guess so," I say. "But I don't know, Rosie. I can't get through to her." I don't add that I'm not sure I will again.

"Shit." Rosie's phone vibrates and she taps a finger hard at the screen. "That's my alarm, Em. We've got to get back to work. Why does it always go so bloody *quick*. Shall we walk?"

Rosie and I amble along the beach, empty boxes from our chicken wraps in our hands, the sun in our eyes. Rosie walks close to me, looking every so often at me at her side, watchful and careful, as if she wants to speak but doesn't for fear of pressing me too much. We come to the steps leading up to the pavement, and Rosie sits on the edge of the wall, dusting sand from her bare feet with her hands. I sit beside her and look out to the beach. Children jump over waves at the sea's edge, parents struggle swiping sun cream on tiny arms and faces, people lay still, facedown, milky legs under the sun.

"So, the cards—that's the reason for the village," says Rosie, slipping on a shoe. "The one jammed up your arse."

I nod and tell her it's not so much a village but a small hamlet.

"I searched for him so many times," I tell her. "But I haven't really tried since that last time. In school." Words dry in my mouth.

"The teacher. Morgan," Rosie says carefully, and I nod again. Rosie and Fox, apart from the Moreaus, are the only people who know about Robert

Morgan. About the night of the Summer Ball. That he, an IT teaching assistant, was helping me find my dad on the computers in the IT block. The night of the Summer Ball was when he'd told me he found something. And I believed him. Went back to the empty, silent IT room with him, while the rest of year eleven danced, to mark the end of childhood, of school as we knew it. I didn't even tell Adam, or the colleague or two I grew close to at the photo studio. Every time I tried, it felt so alien, to be saying those words out loud about something that actually happened to *me*, that I'd stop. For a time, every time I talked about it, it felt like I was exposing too much of myself, that if I told them, they might shrink away, recoil, leave. I'm getting better at that part—saying it out loud—but only very slowly.

"That address," says Rosie, feet dusted, shoes back on, legs dangling over the wall. "On the back of the cards. Did you see it? You need to go there. Or at least get yourself on Google Maps."

"I did. It's my old town. I just don't recognize the road."

I didn't recognize it at all as somewhere we lived, or anybody we knew back then. I've listed them over the last fortnight, the people we knew when we lived in Ramsgate for the first time. Mum's cousin Sheila, but she lived in London. And sometimes we visited Den's mum, but she lived in a high-rise flat, a train ride away. And Marv, Den's friend. Kind Marv with the Scottish accent who would pop in when Mum was at work, take me for rides on my bike, buy me an ice cream, balance piles of shells I'd collect, in his large hands. But he was from Aberdeen, I'm sure. The list of people is short. We kept ourselves to ourselves. Mum made sure of it.

"You could go there, then," says Rosie. "Someone might know something. He might have lived there or maybe he has a sister or relative or *anyone* who lives over here."

"I don't know," I say. "I haven't been back to my old town for a really long time," I say. "It all feels a bit scary. And I *am* scared, Rosie."

"Listen, Emmie," says Rosie, putting an arm around me. "I get scared. I went to a school full of arseholes who bullied me to the brink. Yet look at me. I was just on my back on a wet beach in nothing but a kaftan, while dudes with their dogs looked at me like I had two fuckin' heads."

I laugh, and Rosie squeezes her arm around me tighter as we walk, hip to hip.

"You know what you need to do?" she says.

"What?"

"What I do. I think about the Rosie Kalwar who *isn't* afraid, the one that thinks nothing of posing in a bikini on a beach, or doing an Instagram Live with a massive pimple and no makeup, and I just pretend I'm her. Every damn day."

Rosie swipes her security pass to unlock the side gate of the Clarice, and together we walk through the back entrance to the hotel, down the cracked concrete path, past the hot waft of the recycling bins.

"*That* Emmie Blue—that's who you need to find," she says. "The one who arrives in her old town like Miranda Priestly just fucking landed. Pretend you're her. What would *she* do in this situation?"

I smile up at her. "You're smart," I say, and she leans in and kisses my cheek at the same time Fox appears in the courtyard through the kitchen door, a cigarette in his hand. He gawps at Rosie in her kaftan and cerise-pink bikini bottoms. "Emmie took about seven hundred photos if you're interested, Fox." Rosie grins and makes for the door. "Collect 'em all. I'm gonna go get changed."

Fox, pale cheeks blotching pink, looks down at his unlit cigarette and then at me. "You two have been lying on the sand again, haven't you?" he says. "I'll, er, get you a spare blouse, shall I?"

———

Me:

Guess who has just said yes to a job interview at a school next Friday?

WhatsApp from Lucas Moreau:

SERIOUSLY?!

Me:

Yep! Totally terrified but feeling like it might be time to face it. It's working with the school counselors!

WhatsApp from Lucas Moreau:

EM!!!!!!!! This is fucking incredible.

WhatsApp from Lucas Moreau:

I'm so proud of you.

Me:

Thank you Luke xxx

Me:

Can't even believe I've said yes.

WhatsApp from Lucas
Moreau:

I can. You'll smash it.

Me:

Might need you to come and instill that confidence in me on Friday.

Me:

If I don't poo myself on the bus there, obv.

WhatsApp from Lucas
Moreau:

You won't. Even if I have to sit on the phone with you on the bus.

Me:

Ha. Like old times!

WhatsApp from Lucas
Moreau:

Yep. Leave it to me. I'll get you there in one piece.

Tuesday, December 14, 2004

"I still don't think your voice matches your face."

Lucas laughs down the line. "I still don't know how to take that comment."

"It's nothing *bad*," I say. The bus veers a corner, and I shoot a hand out to hold on to the seat in front of me. "I just think you look a tiny bit like Richard Gere."

"Emmie, I am sixteen."

"A *young* Richard Gere."

"Which is still old, man," laughs Lucas. "He's been, like, forty forever, hasn't he?"

I burst out laughing, a hand instinctively flying up to cover my mouth. I look over my shoulder. The top deck is empty, save for one other student: a girl I recognize from two years below. She's reading from a Latin book—something they teach at an after-school club that goes on until four thirty—and she looks up at me, our eyes meeting. I sweep around to face the front before I see even a glimmer of anything. I bet she knows too. She might be quiet, mousy, hardworking, but they all know. The whole school knows it was me now, who wrote that anonymous letter about what Mr. Morgan did. The whole school knows I am the reason he moved away, that Georgia doesn't speak to me now and instead cries in class, kids flocking around her. She'll tell her, I bet, this mousy girl.

"She doesn't even care. She was *laughing* on the bus. Like, proper full-blown laughing."

And they'll whisper about it in English class, loud enough for me to hear, like they did today. "Did you hear she and Zack Aylott in the year above shagged last year? They'd been going out like a *week*." "She blatantly fancied Morgan. You could tell." "Georgia said she's a proper liar. Always has been."

"Hey. You still there?"

I close my eyes, lean my head against the bus window. "Yeah," I say. I hate how wobbly my voice always is lately. "Still on the bus. Are you sure about this phone call, Lucas?"

"'Course. Dad gets free minutes on his business phone."

"And he doesn't mind?"

"He doesn't *know*," laughs Lucas. "But nah, he probably wouldn't care. Think he's just happy not to see me moping about or hearing me bang on about missing London and saying *I wish I was back in England*. Even though I really, really do."

"I wish you were too."

"Be cool, wouldn't it?" says Lucas. I love the way he speaks. He sounds older than the boys at school. Smarter. Cooler. "You could come and help me and my brother eat this weird-as-shit dinner my mum has made. Chicken. With orange things in it. Apricots, I think. Even if we don't like it, my dad is a total demon headmaster about it and makes us eat it. I could make you eat mine. Then you could show me one of your crap films."

I can't help but smile at that. "I wish I could."

"Same," Lucas says, and my stomach bubbles with longing, because I want that more than anything. I want dinner made for me. I want to be in a busy family home, with the clink of washing up, and bloated, full, warm tummies, I want to sit under a blanket watching films, chatting during the quiet bits. I want a friend. I miss so much having a friend.

"You all right?" asks Lucas.

"Yeah. Just tired."

"Another day done, though," says Lucas.

"And it was a hard day," I say. "Every class, I had with Georgia."

"But you did it," says Lucas. "You did it, and you're on the bus home to watch *EastEnders* and eat cheese-and-pickle sandwiches."

"Lucas, I told you, I hate pickles."

"You will eat Branston pickles for your poor homesick mate, and like it." He laughs. Mate. I love that he said he's my mate.

I push the bell on the bus. "I'll compromise with you and have Marmite on toast," I say.

"This is basically phone sex now you've mentioned Marmite, Emmie."

I laugh again, not caring about the girl behind me, or what she might report back. I'm allowed to laugh. I am allowed to live my life, go to school, and learn. Lucas is right. I haven't done anything wrong. "You're the weirdest person I have ever met," I tell him as the bus slows, and I stand up.

"Except we haven't met," says Lucas. "Lived an hour from each other our whole lives and only found out each other existed the month I moved countries. Mental, eh?"

"So mental," I say. "That balloon was a sadist, really."

"And a genius," adds Lucas.

13

Voice mail.

Again, straight to voice mail. Lucas's phone never goes to voice mail. Ever. Why today? Why now, when I really need him? I stare up at the school gates, the huge square windows looming, the tops of many heads at an upstairs classroom window, the lines and lines of bikes chained up at the entrance, the edges of computer screens through the windows of another room, and I feel my stomach lurch. I can't. I thought I could, but I can't do this.

I back away, my legs shaking, feet tripping down the curb. And that is when my phone bursts into song in my hand. Without even glancing at the screen, I rush it to my ear. It'll be Lucas. It'll be Lucas full of apologies that he wasn't there, on the phone, like he said he would be.

"Hello?"

"Hey, it's me."

I freeze in the street, the sky darkening with rain clouds above. "Me? W-Who . . . is this?"

There is a sigh and a familiar warm laugh on the line. "Do you really not have my number saved yet?"

"Um . . ."

"*Jesus.* It's me. Eliot."

"Oh. Sorry. Hi." I take a breath and start walking now, bag over my shoulder, picking up speed. That's it, then, I suppose. I'm not going to do it, am I? I'm not going to walk through those gates. I thought I could. I really thought I was going to do this, but I can't. "I, er, forgot to save your number, after your texts. Sorry."

"Emmie, are you okay?" Eliot asks. "You sound a bit . . . weird."

What is it about someone asking if you're okay? Even if you think you're holding it together, all it takes is someone asking if you're all right to completely melt away your resolve and bring that lump bobbing straight into your throat. "I just—I had a job interview and I couldn't go in. Just now. When you rang."

Eliot hesitates on the line. "Okay?" he says slowly. "Is there a reason you couldn't?"

I get to the bus stop, my chest is tight, my feet—in heels I borrowed from Rosie—are unsteady, scuffing on the pavement as I sit down clumsily. A man looks over his phone at me, eyeing me as if he disapproves of my sitting beside him. "It w-was in a school," I tell Eliot, my voice wobbly, disjointed. "I really liked the sound of it, and the money was—but you know, I just took one look at it and—I couldn't go in. I was . . . overwhelmed or . . . something."

I don't know why I'm telling him, but his voice is warm and it's so nice to have someone in this moment, listening. Right here, as black clouds swell and hang above my head.

"Right," says Eliot calmly. "Well, look, it's no big deal, Emmie. I'm sure people get waylaid and even sick on the day of job interviews, so, you could always reschedule?"

I shake my head, swallow, trying desperately to slow my racing heart. Hina. What will I tell Hina at the agency?

"No," I say. "No, I don't think it's right for me." I look down at the black court shoes I meticulously picked out of Rosie's wardrobe yesterday, at the A-line, midi skirt I'd bought specially, at the nails I painted last night, sure I was ready to face it. Finally. And feel my eyes well with tears. I lift my hand to my mouth. A waste of money. A waste of time.

"Well, that's good," says Eliot obliviously. "Sometimes we need to be face-to-face with these things before we realize it's something we don't want."

And I nod, pointlessly. Pointless because he can't see me. Pointless because it simply isn't true. It's not that I don't want it. My excitement of getting the interview, of getting my outfit ready, of thinking far ahead, at all the good I could do in this job, shows me that I do. I am just too scared. *Still* too scared to step back into a school. I am thirty. I am thirty years old and I still can't do it. Anger surges through my veins, my skin tingling.

"Emmie? Emmie, are you still there?"

I swallow, dab away roughly at the tears running down my cheeks, with the pads of my fingers. "Yes," I say. "S-Sorry, I'm here."

"Look, if you need someone to talk to, I—"

"Why did you call?" I cut in.

Eliot clears his throat. "Oh. About the hotel. The place my brother's getting married. The drinks we're having there in a few weeks, so we can all see the venue. You're going too?"

"Yeah." I sniff. "Yeah, I am."

"Yeah, so am I. And I'm driving. Ana's back from her conference, so I'll be staying there with her, but I don't mind driving you to Le Touquet if you want a ride. I have to pass you on the way, pretty much, anyway."

I pause, using the sleeve of my cardigan to dry my cheeks. "Do you?"

Eliot chuckles. "You have no idea where I live, do you?"

"No," I say with a grimace, and he laughs again.

"I'm in Hastings."

"Really? I didn't realize you were that close."

"Yup. Neighbors. Anyway, I just thought it saves you the buses, saves you the ferry ticket, the hassle . . ."

I think of those things. And I wonder what the sense would be in saying no. I might not really want to travel with Eliot, but it would be rude to decline. Awkward. He's Lucas's brother. He's helping with this STEN party that I am supposed to be organizing with "legend" Tom, and Lucille, the maid of honor who speaks only in emojis and lols. And he saved me buying an awful ferry sandwich, with those two gorgeous almond croissants he'd left in my bag, which was sweet, really. It was.

"Yes," I tell him. "Thanks, that'd be really helpful."

"Cool," says Eliot. "Text me your address, yeah? And I'll be in touch soon with times and all that."

On the bus home, I check my phone. Lucas has read my messages and not replied, and when I check his Instagram, he and Marie have checked into a hotel in Honfleur, a photo of them holding two cold misty glasses of white wine. "When you both finish work early and ur wife-to-be suggests a spontaneous night away! #itswhyimmarryingher is the caption, followed by ten grinning emojis in a row. I try to ignore the sinking heart in my chest. He's too busy to talk me down from the panic, from sadness, because he's with his fiancée. His *wife-to-be*. Of course she comes first—before me.

The bus winds through town, getting closer to my stop. I see lovers, hand in hand, parents dashing after toddlers. I see the building that used to be Moments—the children's photo studio I worked at for six years before it closed. A signless office now. I see the flat in which I lived with Adam, then alone, until Fishers Way. The old single-glazed windows that seeped heat in the winter, have been replaced, the doors of the Juliet balcony, white now, with blinds at the windows.

Change.

Everything is changing. Except for me.

Mix CD. Vol. 3.

Dear Balloon Girl,

Track 1. *Because I taught you to swim in the sea (do not listen to my brother, it was definitely me)*

Track 2. *Because Bon Jovi. They need no reason.*

Track 3. *Because there are only 120 miles between us and that really isn't that long*

Track 4. *Because you aren't what happened to you*

Track 5. *Because you've never seen a shooting star*

Balloon Boy

X

14

Eliot is early on Friday. A whole half an hour early. I don't even realize he's arrived until I lug my case downstairs and hear his voice. I find him in the kitchen, standing in the doorway, talking to Louise, who is, as ever, stirring something on the hob.

"I used to use Shelby's all the time. It was the only place to go," she is saying. "When that closed, I didn't really have any reason to go to Hastings anymore, which I suppose is a shame."

Eliot is nodding, waffling about a man with a "bad hip" and a pawn-broker's, and Louise is saying, "Oh yes, Clint's owned that shop since he was twenty-one." I have never heard her talk so much, and she sounds awake, bright. It hardly sounds like the Louise Dutch I know.

"Hey," I say from the hallway, and Eliot turns to face me. He's in jeans and a white T-shirt—the logo of a band I've never heard of on the chest—and it makes his tan seem even more golden. "You are really early."

"Nice to see you too." He smiles, and then with a shrug says, "I heard there was traffic. Left early. Clear roads, so here I am. Yours for a whole extra half hour."

Louise looks past him, her mouth twitching a small smile at me, before looking back at the pan on the stove. It smells of garlic and woodsmoke down here. She'll be making vegetable chili again, I bet, or a spiced chutney from all the tomatoes she grows in the conservatory.

"I see," I say. "Well, I'm ready to go when you are."

"Okay." Eliot nods, a hand in his pocket. "Well, Louise, it was really nice to meet you."

"Oh, you too," she replies. "Bye, Emmie. A safe journey." I don't think she has ever wished me a safe journey before. It's not that Louise is rude, but she is standoffish most of the time. Reluctant, I guess is the word, to engage or give too much away.

"Louise seems nice," says Eliot as we buckle our seat belts in the front of his truck.

"She is. Quiet."

He raises a dark eyebrow, throwing a look over his shoulder to the rear window. "Yeah?" he says. "She didn't seem too quiet in there."

"Well, maybe she likes you more than me," I say with a smile.

"Hard not to," Eliot laughs.

"I think maybe she thinks I'm a bit of a wet blanket," I tell him. "She can't understand why I go to France all the time, when Luke rarely comes here. Tells me I use the ferry more than I use the bus, and *What's wrong with his legs?* She's always asking me if I've seen certain jobs in the local paper too."

Eliot frowns. "Maybe she's looking out for you."

"Maybe," I say. "But I also think she believes I'm some sort of weird dreamy damsel with my head up my arsehole."

Eliot chuckles. "And you aren't."

"I'm a lot of things." I smile. "But I'm not that."

"Good to know." Eliot starts the engine, his arm coming round to hold the back of my seat as he reverses off the drive, gravel crunching under the wheels. "Emmie is no dreamy damsel," he says.

"With her head up her arsehole," I add.

"*With her head up her arsehole.* Noted."

We start driving, winding past the coast, the sun reflecting on the water in silver sheets, and I tell Eliot to nudge me if he needs me.

He turns down the radio, which is loud and blaring a classic rock song that sounds as though it's being sung by a man who is standing a country mile away from the microphone. "What?"

"Do you mind if I put my earphones in? I'm listening to this podcast. About being a best man . . . or woman, in my case."

His mouth lifts at the corner. "Interesting."

"It's just, I won't hear you if you speak to me."

"That's all right," he says. "I'll tap instead. Bit of Morse code." Then he carries on singing quietly along to the radio. I look out the passenger window, trying hard to hold on to the words being spoken in my ear, about best man speeches, about stag dos, but they merge together, become a swirl of background chatter, and my mind wanders. I used to look across this same ocean we drive by now, when I was a child, and I'd think about my dad over there, somewhere, traveling around with his band, handsome and strong, adoring fans waiting by the tour bus, or outside the large iron gates of his rock-star mansion, hundreds of hands holding concert programs and marker pens in the air, like flags.

"I used to listen to rock bands on the radio and imagine their drummers were my dad," I'd told Lucas once. "I used to think my dad was in Bon Jovi until I was about twelve."

"Until you realized Tico Torres wasn't from Brittany?" he laughed. "Or called Peter."

"Well, I'm glad you find it funny, because I was heartbroken when I realized there was no way my dad could've been their drummer."

"Why?"

"Because that meant I had no *in* to Jon. No way of meeting him, no way of having him stare angstily across at me backstage, pretend he can't stand me, that he doesn't even see me, because he's a rock star and rock stars don't fall in love. No way of him inviting me to a party, despite himself, and rescuing me from a drunk . . . and then kissing me in the rain, in the dark, before falling in love with me."

Lucas had laughed, slung his arm over my shoulder, and said, "You've been reading fan fiction again, haven't you?" Then, "And there is still time, Emmie Blue. Jon Bon would be insane not to drop everything the second he lays eyes you."

Eliot taps my leg. I pull out an earphone, look at him.

"Any requests?" He gestures out of the window. I hadn't even noticed we'd stopped, the engine killed, the radio off. "I've got to get some petrol. Chocolate? Sweets? Bag of charcoal?"

"I'm okay, thanks."

Eliot nods and gets out of the car. My phone vibrates on my lap. A message from Lucas.

Lucas Moreau: So are you with the
rag n bone man then?

I lean forward to catch a look in the side mirror at Eliot slumped against the truck, one hand under his armpit, another on the pump, brown eyes on the ever-moving dial of the petrol gauge. I look for shreds of evidence, like I used to when I was a teenager, that Lucas and Eliot share a gene pool. They have the same shoulders. Broad, rounded. And their lips. Their coral-pink lips, and the way they chew them when they're bored or concentrating. Eliot's doing that now.

Me: Safely on board. Just
    stopped for petrol!

                    Lucas Moreau: Can't wait to see you :)

Me: Same :*

                    Lucas: PS. Good luck with
                    Smeliot. Don't be bored
                    to death. I need you in
                    one piece.

Moments later, Eliot slides into the driver's seat. He chucks a chocolate bar in my lap.

"Picnic still your favorite?" he says, turning the key in the ignition.

"*Yeah*, wow. Well remembered. Thank you."

"No worries." Eliot gives a wry smile as we pull away. "You can stick your earphones back in now. I'll nudge you when I think of something else to say."

"It's okay." I pause the podcast and wrap my earphones around my phone. "It's finished anyway."

Eliot nods, a hand on the wheel, the other holding a sport-bottle of water to his lips. "Right," he says, sipping. "So, what're we doing, then? Operation STEN-ing as we drive?"

I shake my head. "Not sure the *legend* would be happy that we were organizing things without his priceless input."

"Ah shit, very true," he says. "Okay. How do you fancy telling me about this interview I caught you walking out on?"

I look at him, shake my head. "Not really. If you don't mind."

"Nope. Definitely don't," he says. "All right, how about *you* choose the next topic of conversation? Just, uh, don't choose fate again. Or chance. If you don't mind." He looks at me and gives a grin that makes his eyes glint. Despite myself, I smile.

"If it wasn't for the Picnic, I'd have called you a dickhead just then."

"Ah." Eliot smiles. "See, that's why I gave you the Picnic before I made the joke."

We drive—clear traffic, smooth tarmac, blue skies—and Eliot clicks arrowed buttons on the stereo, flicking through stations. He settles on one, and it hums quietly. A soft, slow Beatles song that he taps along with, his fingers on the steering wheel.

And I don't know if it's the sea air, the calm quiet between Eliot and me that waits to be filled, or if it's being right beside someone I could once be my whole self with, but I tell him. "I got a package the other day," I tell Eliot. "Birthday cards. From my dad. For when I was a kid. And there's this address on the back . . ."

15

Friday, June 9, 2006

"You can't choose Maltesers, Luke."

"Why can't I?"

"Because Maltesers aren't chocolate bars, and the whole point of choosing one chocolate bar for the rest of your life, is choosing a chocolate bar."

"Well, that's bullshit." Lucas pushes his sunglasses up his nose with one finger and turns his face to the sky. "And I am sticking with it."

"Fine." Eliot looks over at me and shakes his head, smiles. "And you're sticking with a Picnic?"

"Hell would have to freeze over before I chose another."

"But with all those raisins, it's pretty much fruit."

"Picnic, and that's my final answer, Eliot."

"All right. And I'll stick with Dairy Milk."

"And *that's* because you're a boring bastard," says Lucas groggily beside me on a sun lounger. "Come on, then, what's next? Potatoes? Choose one sort of potato to eat for the rest of your life. Me first. Mash."

"*Mash?*" Eliot grimaces and pulls his aviators down over his eyes. "I may be boring, dude, but you are disgusting."

It's a sunny, cloudless day, and we are sitting in the Moreaus' back garden, Lucas and I on the bed-like sun loungers at the bottom of the garden, while Eliot slumps on a navy-blue old-style deck chair. Jean and Amanda have gone out to buy things for a barbecue for mine and Lucas's birthday tonight, and like always when I'm here, I've had the most wonderful day, so far. Which means I feel a bit uneasy. It's weird, but in moments like this, with Lucas and Eliot, our cheeks aching from laughing, with nothing to do but to make up silly games to pass the time, with cold lemonades at our feet, the sun in the sky, and nothing but lovely plans for the next few days, it feels almost risky to be this happy. It feels like I am goading all the things that could go wrong, to happen. Because everything was so awful, so hopeless, before Luke. I lost my best friend because she believed her dad over me. That I was a silly teenager with a crush. That the only assault was on her family with my lies. A family I'd known and trusted and idolized for five years—her sister, Megan, Georgia's mum, and Georgia's father, Robert, too, of course. Even Georgia's grandmother, who'd pop in on Friday nights for a takeaway when I'd stay the night, with pajamas and popcorn, and Robert always so funny, so interested in Georgia and me. And I lost them. In one blink. Classmates who'd lend me pens, laugh at my jokes, compliment my new bag, now laughed at me, snarled at me, called me awful things I can barely think about, let alone say aloud. Even the teachers. Most were kind, but I'd often catch a couple of them looking at me out the corner of their eye. I was a mystery, I suppose, with missing school trip admission slips, a mum like mine, mostly absent, but who wrote long complaint letters about the pointlessness of subjects I was learning, as if she was anything but. My life lost all warmth, all love, after the night of the Summer Ball. And friends like Lucas and Eliot—a family like this. A *life* like this, all this acceptance. This love. It feels too good to be true. For me, at least.

"Go on then, Em," says Lucas, nudging my knee with his hand, across the small gap between the loungers. "Spuds. Go."

I hesitate. "It's got to be chips."

"*Yes*," says Eliot, clapping slowly, as Lucas groans. "Homemade chips, that's what I said."

"Chip shop chips or homemade, nothing else," I say.

"Ah yeah, shit, those ones you make are *good*," says Lucas, hand behind his head. "But I still think I'm sticking with mash, you know."

"Mash is shit," says Eliot. "Sorry, dude, but it's school dinners to me."

"So? School dinners were the bollocks, what're you even talking about, El?"

"Get rid of the *the* and you'll be spot on. Our school dinners *were* bollocks." Eliot sips his lemonade and gives me a lazy smile. "Your turn, Em. Choose the next question."

I pause, my head to one side. "Um. Celebrity crushes? You can only have one for the rest of your life."

"Deal." Lucas yawns.

"I'll go first," I say. "Jo—"

"*Jon Bon Jovi*," say Eliot and Lucas at the same time, and the three of us look at one another and burst out laughing. The boys stretch over and slap each other's hand in a high five. "Nice one," says Lucas, and then he looks at me and grins. "Too easy," he says. "It's always Jon."

I can't believe now that I reached out to Georgia last week. It was a weak moment, I suppose. I was alone in the college cafeteria, and so was she. I looked at her across the room and saw a thousand memories play out in front of my eyes in a moment. When we were in year seven and we'd do each other's hair. When we were fourteen and her mum took us to see Busted and bought us a poster each and we were so excited, we cried when they came onstage. Sleepovers, where we'd shared a bed, a pillow at each end. Baking. Makeup. Sunday roasts. And I felt desperately sad, thinking that we had shared all of that, and now we couldn't even say hello. It wasn't her fault. It was his. Not hers. Not mine. His. But I had barely opened my mouth, barely got to her table before she had stood and said, "Don't you dare, Emmie. Don't you fucking dare."

"You like blondes, don't you?" Lucas cuts through my thoughts. "I mean, you say you don't have a type, but you do."

"I guess," says Eliot, then looks at me. "Whereas he just likes them with eyes, a nose, and a mouth, right?" he says to me, and Luke bursts out laughing.

"Hey, fuck you," he says. "I am not that bad, am I, Em?"

"You are," I tell Lucas. "I'm sorry, and I love you, but you do fancy *every-one.*"

"And you don't?"

Eliot shrugs. "I dunno," he says. "I tend to only fancy one person at a time."

"Anyway," says Lucas, turning over on his side and nodding at me. "Next one. Movies. And you better not say any of those train wrecks you make me watch, Em. They're barred."

I don't need Georgia. I have Lucas. I have Eliot. That will always be enough.

M arie holds a powder-blue dress next to me and smiles.

"This color and your blond hair," she beams, "is a dream come true."

"I do love the blue," I say, and she puts the dress back on the rack, her brown eyes not leaving the line of dresses, plumes of creams and blues and yellows. She grabs at another.

"Oh! This would work too, no?" A dress swings in her hand from a padded pale-pink hanger.

"Oh, definitely," I say, reaching and running a hand over the fabric in her hands. Jean, Lucas, and Tom have gone to Jean's tailor, and when I woke up this morning, within minutes of rubbing my eyes and sitting up in bed, I was surprised to find Marie knocking on the door, and not Lucas. I answered it looking like something from a swamp, to find her hair glossy and blow-dried, face made up, and top to toe in perfect but casual Parisian fashion, keys in her hands.

"No rushing," said Marie, "but the boys are already up, and I thought us girls deserved some proper time too. There is a boutique near Lucas's office that has beautiful dresses and ball gowns. I thought we could take a look?"

Half an hour later, we were in Marie's pristine car, winding our way through the leafy country lanes as she talked nonstop about her business—a new deli she's opening soon—and I listened, but mind wandering the whole time to Lucas's face as he had waved us off. It's the same face I'm sure he'd wear waving off his two children to school for the first day. A proud face. That "and there they go" smile. And why wouldn't he? It's a dream situation, isn't it? Your fiancée getting along with your best friend.

"Any dress you see that you enjoy the style of, just let me know. If it isn't perfect, it doesn't matter, because my, er . . . er . . ." Marie pauses, eyes skyward, searching for the English word. "Dressmaker?"

I nod.

"Yes, well, she said she can make anything that we please, adjust, change . . ."

Marie's English is practically perfect in that husky, sexy French accent that melts many a person. She went to university in London, and her mother was born in Cornwall. Like Lucas, her dad is French, and he and Marie own a deli together. One that sells things to gym-goers and the health conscious. Protein shakes, juices, "clean" salads and faux brownies and so many things made from avocados. It's how she and Lucas met. The deli had just opened, and Lucas had gone in for lunch after a gym session, and he and Marie had ended up talking so much, they had lunch together.

"It was avocados, wasn't it?" I'd asked Marie on our first meeting. "It's all Lucas eats. I think he goes to bed with them. Kisses them good night. Gives them massages. Listens to their problems."

Marie had giggled madly and held my arm. "It *was*. We ate *two* avocado dishes. I eat so many of them too. I even make *hair conditioner* from it."

"A match made in heaven," I'd said, and ever since, avocados have been a little "in" joke of ours.

I nudge Marie's arm now. "What would you think," I say, lowering my voice, "if I insisted on that," and I point to a tiny red minidress only Rosie and Cher would be able to pull off.

"Oh," Marie laughs. "But if that is what you want, Emmie, I would be happy for you to wear it."

We wander through the shop, hardly able to hear each other over the blasting dance music booming from the shop's stereo, but both of us talking all the time nonetheless, and I am struck with a pang of something that feels like guilt and heartbreak all at once as Marie turns to me and says, "I'm so excited, Emmie." It's the shame, I suppose, of wishing deep down that this wasn't happening, and I imagine for one painful, stomach-churning moment as Marie takes a photo of a dress on a mannequin and looks down at her phone, punching away on the keyboard in WhatsApp, sending it excitedly to her bridesmaids to add to their shared Pinterest board, what she would do if she knew—if suddenly I told her, right here, what I had expected Lucas to ask me that night at Le Rivage.

"Emmie." Marie links her slender arm through mine. "What do you say? Shall we eat?"

"Sure. I could definitely eat. And escape this music."

"My treat," she says. "For our best woman. And considering I woke you up too early."

"Oh, I'm glad you did," I laugh. "When I don't have an alarm, I could be out for a good thirteen hours."

Marie squeezes into me and gives a warm giggle. "Luke said you are an *epic sleeper.* Now, come on, I know this beautiful little place. You'll love it."

Marie takes us to a small but higgledy café down a cobbled alleyway, with round, rustic tables and empty tin cans holding cutlery in the center. It smells like strong coffee and garlic, and we take a seat at one of the outdoor tables.

It's only eleven, so we are handed a breakfast menu—paper clipped to a small wooden clipboard, the text small, spaced and neat, as if it's been written on a typewriter. Marie leans in. "The waffles and chocolate, oh my goodness."

"Good?" I ask, and she sighs and says, "Like heaven, Emmeline." Then she freezes. "Gosh. I never say Emmeline. Sorry. I don't know why I said that. You don't like being called it, do you?"

Heat passes over my cheeks. "Nobody really calls me Emmeline," I say. "But don't be sorry. At all."

"No, I should be. I think a person's preferred name should be respected," she says, and I just want to reach out and hold her face and tell her I'm sorry, because she is so bloody *nice*.

"My mum calls me Emmeline. Jean used to too, actually. He doesn't believe in shortening names."

Marie rolls her eyes, an elbow coming up to rest on the table. She leans her face on her hand. "How shocking it is that it's *a man* who ignores a woman's preferences," she says quietly. "So, you were baptized Emmeline?"

"Oh no," I say, "I've never been christened or baptized. My mum never really believed in any of that. But it's on my birth certificate. My mum loved the name. Plus, my dad is from France." My mouth feels dry as I speak those last words. "It's been years since I've gone by Emmeline, that's all."

She nods, almond eyes serious, and doesn't press, which tells me she either knows more than I have told her, or that she can tell I don't really want to give her any more than that. Robert called me Emmeline; used my name so many times, in such short conversations, that it felt weird sometimes, and purposeful. He called me Emmeline that night. Hot and wet against my neck and my ear, the back of my head pressed hard against the door. I couldn't bear hearing it after that.

"So, Emmie, shall we order?" Marie smiles warmly, clearing her throat. A waiter hovers by the door, waiting, his eyes flitting from us, to the two couples eating, chattering quietly at neighboring tables. "Are you ready? I know I am off caffeine, but surely *one* Americano can't harm me?"

We order our food—both of us go for the waffles with chocolate sauce—and Marie tells me about the bad wedding dreams she keeps having despite it still being eight months before she marries Lucas. She asks me about my journey here, with Eliot, too, and I tell her it was nice. "'Smooth, no traffic.'" I don't tell her that we talked for an hour, solidly, about my dad and the birthday cards, and even about Mum, too, or how much telling him has helped. I feel lighter after talking to Eliot. Like he's taken some of the weight that was dragging me down. A smiling waiter brings our food over, and we sit in the shade, watch the world amble by beneath the sun, and swap stories and anecdotes, the rich smell of coffee and cigarette smoke from a man at the next table swirling around us. Mum's ex Den used to smoke roll-ups, standing by the front door, blowing the smoke into the outside, as I hung off the handle and gave him an hour-by-hour account of my school day. I love the smell, and I feel a warm settling, as if there's a cat curled up, snuggled on my lap.

"I still cannot believe how you and Lucas came to meet," says Marie, adjusting the napkin on her lap. "So . . . *serendipitous.*"

"I know. I still find it so difficult to believe that he found it, all those weeks later."

"Your balloon?" She says balloon in the French way—*ballon*—and I love the way it sounds.

"Yes." I smile. "I still remember where I was when I received that first email."

Marie beams at me, brown skin smooth, a line above her top lip appearing as she smiles. "What did he say?"

I remember every word, and of course, have it printed out and in an envelope, which is now safely back in a shoebox under my bed.

Hi Emmeline,

My name is Lucas Moreau. I'm 16 and I live in Le Touquet, France. I found your balloon on a beach near Boulogne-sur-Mer yesterday. It made it over one ocean and over 100 miles!

I'm from London. We just moved here.

Hope me finding this means you win some sort of prize!!!

Well done to you and ur balloon.

                                        Lucas x

PS: I hope you're okay.

"Just that he'd found my balloon in Boulogne-sur-Mer," I tell Marie, "and that he'd just moved there. I was so excited when I got that email. Honestly. Having French roots and everything. I couldn't believe it." I don't say anything else, or how I clicked on it on a computer in Mrs. Beech's geography class while hiding from the other kids at lunchtime, tears streaking my cheeks. And I don't tell her that Lucas's P.S. was like a gentle, wordless hug that morning when I opened my inbox. In that moment, this stranger across the ocean—Balloon Boy as he jokingly called himself after that—was the only person who cared in the whole world.

"It's amazing," Marie sighs dreamily. "He told me you sent him DVDs and jars of food."

I laugh. "Yes. Marmite. Tesco's own brand of fizzy sweets. Anything he missed from home."

"And did he send you French food back?"

"No," I say. "No, he actually sent CDs back."

"CDs?"

"Mix CDs that he'd make. Music."

"Oh *God*." Marie laughs, hand touching my forearm on the table. "You poor thing. My fiancé's taste in music leaves a lot to be desired, do you not think?"

"Really? Well, maybe he's lost his talent," I say. "Okay, occasionally the odd Jason Donovan slipped through the net, but his choices were not bad at all back then. He introduced me to loads of songs and bands I'd never heard of."

Marie laughs again. "I *dread* our wedding playlist."

"Oh, well, I'll keep him reeled in," I tell her, and she leans across the little round table, her eyes on mine. "I know you will," she says sweetly, then she pauses, her eyes still on mine, her smile fading slightly. "He seems happy. Do you think?"

It makes me swallow, the way she asks me. I recognize something in her eyes. Worry. Unease. "Yes," I say. "Of course."

"You know him more than anyone; he tells me that. And . . ." Marie reaches for her coffee but doesn't drink. A prop, I think, for her nervous hands. I feel my heart start to thump in my chest. Is she going to ask me? Is she going to ask me if I have feelings for him, if I think he has feelings for me? "I have had no luck, Emmie," she says eventually. "I am thirty-four and I have had my heart broken enough for you, me, and everyone in this café." She smiles at me sadly, eyes shining. "And Lucas. Well, with Lucas, I know we have stopped and started a lot, our silly arguments, distrust, but I feel like it is different this time. And I know that's cliché, that everyone probably says that . . ." She pauses, looks up at me, and for a moment I think she's going to tell me she can hear the loud drumming of my heart; ask me why it's beating so hard. But instead she says, "I am so happy. I'm *engaged*. Lucas wants to marry me. *Me*. He has chosen no other person ever in his life to propose to. To marry. And . . . it feels . . ."

"Too good to be true," I say. I hardly realize there are tears in my eyes until I speak, and my words are thick, wobbly. Holly, Lucas's ex-girlfriend, flashes into my mind too, momentarily. Lucas was engaged to her when he was twenty. But they were kids then. It lasted mere moments, really. But I do wonder if Marie knows.

"Yes," says Marie. "That is it, Emmie. You understand. I am so happy that I am terrified."

It isn't a question, but I nod. "I do get it," I say quietly. "I really do."

Marie looks at me, laughs, brings a knuckle to her eye. "Gosh, I am sorry. I cry at everything, my father says. Do not let that rub off on you."

I smile, tell her not to apologize, and although my appetite is now non-existent, chased away by the heart that plummeted moments ago and now sits heavy and sad in my gut, we begin eating again.

"I cannot wait for you to see the hotel tonight, Emmie," says Marie after a while. "And their bar; the best cocktails. The *best* dancing. It won awards, you know, for the music, the ambience . . ."

"The best dancing," I repeat. "You do realize Tom is going? I'm afraid after tonight, it may be stripped of its awards."

Marie bursts out laughing, neat, manicured hand at her mouth, and says, "Have you *seen* him do the hips?"

"Yes," I say. "Many times. And he hasn't even improved. I first saw Tom dance when Lucas and I turned eighteen, and I swear, it's gotten worse since then, if that's possible. I hope he leaves his hips safely in his hotel room tonight."

Marie leans in and whispers, "And the rest of him."

I feel out of place. I am in a dress I've had for five years that's been sewn twice at the armpit, and I have thirty euros in my purse; the price of one of the most expensive cocktails on the menu. I couldn't help but notice the wedge of notes in Lucas's wallet when he got the first round in, and I had tried not to be a part of it. To accept a drink is to owe a drink, and I doubt a soul in our group is on tap water.

We have commandeered a booth with velvet seats and a hanging orb of a lamp in the center of the table. Eliot and Ana (who has yet to say a word to me since we arrived at the hotel's bar) sit snuggled in the corner, his arm around her, and I sit in the opposite corner beside Lucas, with Marie on his other side, who is in a fast and smiling conversation with Tom, who is sweaty from the dance floor.

Lucas throws his arm around me and squeezes me against him. He can always tell when I feel uneasy, or nervous, because every time, along comes that strong arm and that squeeze. The arm, protection, the squeeze, a wordless *Everything's okay. I'm here, right next to you.* It was mostly after our nineteenth birthday when I needed it the most. A night Lucas, Eliot, and I had looked forward to for weeks—a house party. A huge inflatable swimming pool. A barbecue. Cocktails made at Jean's bar. A night we counted down to. A night that ended up driving a wedge between me, Lucas, and Eliot. The two people that knew everything about me, because I trusted them with it. And I shouldn't have. Eliot betrayed it. In one stupid moment that ended up throwing me miles backward, sent me toppling. I dropped out of college, moved to Shire Sands, into a new flat in a new town that felt alien, but at least it was far from everything and everyone I knew. And I'd get through it, I was sure, because of Lucas. His arm around me. My head against his chest, his lips against my hair, listening to the strong, dependable beats of his heart.

"Hey," he speaks into my ear now, whiskey on his breath. "Where you at, Emmie Blue?"

I look up at him. "In a bar," I say over the music. "With Tom's offensive hips."

Lucas laughs, crinkles at the corners of his eyes.

The bar is heaving. When Lucas mentioned the bar of the five-star Le Touquet hotel he is to be married in, I expected a tinkling piano and 1920s light shades. I didn't expect this. It reminds me of a London bar on a Saturday night. Ears ringing from the layers and layers of music and chatter of hundreds of voices dying to be heard above it, the clinking glasses and bottles. The lights are low, and behind the bar are glowing blue panels, casting the white-shirt-wearing bar staff deep lilac, as if they're standing under UV lights. It's dark and the air smells like perfume and wine. People are dancing, too, on the minuscule dance floor, and Tom is getting up from beside Marie now and heading back there, to where he's been most of the night, dancing as if he has a family of live eels trapped in his underpants.

"It is quite extraordinary," laughs Marie to me now, leaning over Lucas, her hand resting on his thigh.

I nod. "He has only one move."

"Sorry?"

"He only has one move!" I shout above the ever-increasing-in-volume music, and she laughs and takes a sip of her cocktail. Ana, opposite, explodes into laughter, and I catch Eliot's eye, who smiles at me and sips at his beer, Ana's arm around him, her free hand on her chest. Lucille is beside her, Marie's maid of honor who hasn't looked up once from a smiley conversation she's been having with a handsome man who wouldn't look out of place in an aftershave ad. He sidled up to her at the bar within about ten minutes of us getting here, and joined us pretty much straightaway, transfixed with Lucille. But it's no surprise, really. Lucille is beautiful. Like a 1950s movie star or something. The pair of them look like a moving GIF from a black-and-white film. He even floated over as if there were a stage cue.

"Don't fancy joining him?" Eliot leans toward me as Ana's long fingers pummel her phone's screen, beside him.

"Who, Tom?" I shout.

Eliot smiles, nods.

I shake my head. "I think it's law to avoid people that dance like that."

"Ah, I dunno, you might learn a thing or two." Eliot grins and starts mimicking Tom popping his shoulders. I laugh. Eliot always did make me laugh. I missed that, once upon a time. Ana, brow furrowed, looks at him now, as if he is far from the apparent comedic genius she thought he was only a moment ago. She looks at me. I smile—an "isn't your boyfriend funny?" smile. Her face doesn't move. She looks back down at her phone.

"Won't learn that on any podcast," says Eliot over the music, and puts his lips to his beer again, acting as though he hasn't noticed Ana's face, her coldness toward me, but I see his eyes, just slightly, shift to the side to her as he drinks. I fix a smile on my face to mask the awkwardness I'm feeling, too, pretending to not even care, or notice that beside me, Lucas's face is buried in Marie's neck—they're talking, laughing about something, and as I drink, I notice Ana is staring at me. I smile again. This time so does she; all teeth.

"Your dress," she says.

Instinctively I look down at it, then back at her. "Yes?"

She says something, smile fixed, and her words are lost over the music.

"Sorry? I can't hear you."

Ana laughs, large, round eyes rolling, then motions with a hand for me to lean in closer. Eliot watches us. "I said," she says, "you should have pressed it."

"*Pressed* it?"

"*Yes.* Pressed it. Ironed it. It is very creased."

I am thankful for the dark lighting, because my neck, my ears, my whole face beams red-hot at those words. *Creased?* What sort of person leans forward in a loud bar and tells someone—and tells them *twice*—that their dress should have been ironed because it's creased?

"Oh," I say as breezily as I can muster. "It's been in a suitcase."

She nods, a smile still on her face, but it's changed from friendly and engaging, to almost mocking. She turns and says something to Lucille now, and I am left with Eliot's eyes burning into me. I pretend I don't notice, and instead avert my gaze to Tom on the dance floor. My cheeks are burning, my throat is dry. And now I feel a centimeter tall. Out of place was something I thought I just felt. I didn't think it was something I looked. I lean across to Lucas. "I'm going to get another drink."

"I'll get it," says Lucas, scrambling to stand. Eliot looks up.

"No, no, Luke," I mouth, expression overanimated as you do when being drowned out by music.

"No, let me."

"It's fine; I want to," I say loudly, and I scoot out from the booth before he can say anything else. I don't have the money, not really, but I have my credit card on me if worse comes to worst, so I hold my almost-empty glass up to the table and mouth "drink?"

Lucas and Marie shake their heads, smiling, raising their full glasses, and Eliot smiles and says, "I'm good, thanks," while Lucille and Mr. Aftershave don't look up, enrapt in each other. Ana ignores me. Good. I was worried for a moment she might present me with a catalog of ironing boards.

I cross the floor to the blue-lit bar. I don't really want another drink. I want something to do. Because as I sat there at the table, I felt myself lift from my body and view myself from a distance. Squashed there, beside my best friend—the man I am secretly in love with—and his beautiful and kind wife-to-be. Opposite Eliot, someone who was once one of my closest friends, and his stony-faced girlfriend, who won't stop touching him, looking at him as if she can hardly believe he is hers. Lucille, who was falling in effortless love with a man she'd met an hour ago. Tom, all flaccid arms and cocky grins, yes, but happy, content, confident. And then there was me. *Me.* The girl in the old creased dress. The girl who loves someone she shouldn't. A third wheel. A *fifth wheel.*

At the bar I order lemonade. I cannot afford the cocktail Lucas has shoved in front of me twice now, and I don't want my head to get any lighter.

"Surely that's exactly what you want," Rosie would say if she was here, and I wish so much I was back at the hotel now, out the back, in the courtyard, chatting to her as she talks about her blog and why men should never wear espadrilles, while Fox smokes and Rosie pokes fun at his long words. I don't want to be here. I don't want to watch Marie, with her arm around

Lucas's neck, kissing the side of his face. He whispers to her, eyes drooping with too much whiskey, biting the side of his lip, smiling as he talks. The sight of it makes my stomach ache. I push my glass toward the bartender and ask for vodka to be added to my lemonade, but an arm is slung over my shoulder.

"Heeeeeeeey, Emsie."

"Hi, Tom," I say, shrugging out from under his heavy arm. He stands back, leans clumsily on the bar and grins at me.

"How're we doing?"

I nod. "Fine."

"Getting yourself a drink there?"

I nod again. "I am. Had enough of dancing?"

He laughs, throwing back his head, all white teeth and oval, flared nostrils. He's Rosie's type. Square-jawed and beardy, loud, "cheeky." The type to come on cocky and strong in a club, but weeps on you the second you get him home and the time comes for entering you. "Maybe just for a minute. Can I get you a wee tipple?" He tries a mock Scottish accent.

"I already have something," I say, holding up the tall glass just placed in front of me, and he laughs, nudging me with his shoulder. "I see that, Emsie. I just meant something else. Shots?"

I shake my head. "No, no thank you."

"Suit yourself." He leans against the bar, and I turn around, drink in hand, and freeze when I see Lucas and Marie kissing. Softly. Gently. Slow. Eyes closed. Tiny flashes of tongues touching. He *hates* PDA. Lucas has always said he hated it, and yet here he is, kissing, lips, tongues, arm pulling her tightly into him, no shame, no embarrassment whatsoever. Eliot turns, and I don't look away in time, and he sees me watching. He tries a smile, closemouthed, almost regretful, and goes back to his drink. God, it's like he knows and feels sorry for me. I wonder if he does know. And if he does, does that mean Lucas might know? No. No, surely not.

"So, what do we think?" The arm comes down upon my shoulders again, hot and heavy. "Best woman, eh, Emsie, and me. A fucking *usher*."

I step to the side, but there is no escaping him, so I just stiffen and lean as far away from his hot, slurring breath as I can. I try to take a deep breath, to slow my racing heart. Because he's just drunk. And it's just Tom. It's Lucas's Tom. Present at so many of the birthday get-togethers we'd have as teenagers. Friendly, funny, cheesy Tom. Always too loud, too clumsy after too much to drink. Big, idiot Tom. That's all. Nothing to panic about.

"I'm—I'm honored," I say.

"Nah, nah, me too, babes, me too, I swear. I mean, I'd have loved to have been best man, but seriously, you and him . . ." His heavy eyelids close. "You're fucking *family*, you know? The man adores you, and that's . . . that's sayin' something."

"And I adore him," I say, attempting to free myself from him but failing.

"What?" he shouts into my ear.

"I said *and I adore him!*" I shout, leaning to move away from his hot breath, his arm like a heavy weight, and I can feel I'm starting to sweat, starting to fluster.

"Hard not to," he says, then he pulls me tighter to him and shouts across the bar, "Eh? Eh, Luke? Ain't that right, baby? We love you!"

He bellows so loudly that, even over the loud music, people hear, stopping what they're doing and turn to look at us, at me, stuck to his side, his other arm flung into the air. Our booth sees us too—Lucas, Marie, Eliot, and Ana. Even Lucille and Mr. Aftershave Ad turn. Lucas's face explodes into a grin and he holds his arm in the air, with his thumb up. "Love ya, Tom!"

And with that, Tom cheers, then squashes his sweaty, stubbly cheek to mine. Breath hot, aftershave-soaked skin pressing into mine. Panic. It rises like water in a hose. I pull away from him.

"Come on, you," he laughs, oblivious, pulling me clumsily into him again, and I can feel it. Hot, raw panic, the thumping of my heart in my ears, in my throat, hands and feet tingling. I stumble away as he goes to put his arm around me, the way someone might duck at an incoming Frisbee.

"Don't," I say, and I can feel them all looking at me, and the music feels too loud, and the air too thick with alcohol and the smell of other people's bodies. He puts his arm out again, grinning, as if this is all one big game, and as I stride back, he puts his arm out, like a barrier, trapping me between him and the shining, black bar. Then, grinning, he says, "What're you doing, Emsie? Come here, talk to me. Plus, you know what they say, me the usher, you the—" And before I have even thought about it, my instincts, my fear, my panic, act on my behalf. As he moves toward me, I shove him. I put out two hands, one still holding my lemonade, and shove him hard in his hard, broad chest. He stumbles back, grabbing on to the bar to steady himself but knocks a number of drinks onto the floor with his arm. His hand grips the bar, hairy knuckles white, and two strangers help him stand again. And Tom is livid. His face fallen, eyes as wide as orbs, and his mouth open. He can't believe it. He is in total shock that I have reacted in this way. I can barely get my breath, my head rushing with blood.

"I'm . . . I—I told you not to . . . ," I start, but my voice is lost in the music, and I see then that Eliot is there, looking at me, brow furrowed, standing behind me.

"Emmie?"

"What the *fuck* was that?" says Tom, and he steps forward. Eliot puts a large hand flat on Tom's chest.

"Dude," he says, "let's just go back to the table, yeah?"

"She fucking *hit* me, man, did you not see?"

I can't listen to any more. I can't bear to stand here, knowing he can see me. That Lucas watched that. That Ana saw. That Eliot and Marie saw. So many people are watching me, so they must have, too, and I cannot bear to turn around and see their faces, so I turn and walk away. I walk at speed, an almost-run, crashing into the one of the double doors that I push to open, but it's bolted closed, and a woman touches my arm.

"Are you okay?" she asks me, and I ignore her, pulling the heavy door open, tearing outside, and stumbling onto the street.

Why did he do that? Why didn't he listen to me? I had to, didn't I? I had to push him away. I don't even remember when it was that I lashed out, but it was the arm across the bar. It was the arm, the wristwatch, the not being able to get away, the hot breath, the sweaty skin pressed against mine. It felt like back then, for a second. Like being trapped in that classroom with Robert Morgan, his rough, sweaty hand squeezing my thigh, his fingers grazing the edge of my knickers, his words in my ear. "Come on, Emmeline. You think about this, don't you? Don't you? I do."

"Emmie."

I jump, look up, my chest rising and falling, my cheeks pounding with heat. Eliot. Eliot and his serious, judgmental face. Eliot, asking Tom to go back to the booth with him, as if I was some wild animal who needed to be restrained. His face. It's the same face as that night of our nineteenth. He'd told his girlfriend. The girl with the ponytail and the drunken, spiteful smile. Eliot had told her about what happened to me. Everything. And she had let me know. The face he had in the bar—confusion, disappointment, judgment—was the face he wore back then as she told the whole party.

"Emmie, are you all right?" He steps forward now, ducking to look into my eyes, and I step back. "You're shaking."

"I'm fine. I know I shouldn't have—I shouldn't have pushed him, I know that. But—"

Eliot scoffs. "You should have. I wish I had. The man's a dick. He was being a heavy-handed, inconsiderate *dick.*"

I look up at him and I want to cry because someone is being nice to me; is on my side.

"I panicked, Eliot. I know it's just Tom, and he would never, but I—I just panicked."

"Yeah well, he was fucking out of order, Emmie. Look, do you want to sit down? You look like you need to." Eliot looks around quickly, at the length of tables—all full—lined up outside the hotel entrance, hand at his chin, as if working out a conundrum.

"I'm okay. I think I just want to head back."

Eliot nods, dark brown eyes on mine, the lashes thick and jet black. "Well, Ana and I were thinking of going too, to be honest. I can call us a taxi. You can jump in with us."

"Yeah, thanks. That'd be good." I stare past him to the door, willing Tom to stay inside. I don't want to look at him. Embarrassment surges through my bloodstream. Lucas. I want Lucas. I want to be back at the guest cottage like we used to. Like the night we went to a bar not far from here and sang karaoke—two days after Adam broke up with me. I sang a Bon Jovi ballad that I cried into the microphone. I want to go back and lie beside Lucas and watch quiz shows. The French ones I don't understand a word of, Lucas translating them, tipsy, working his way through a pile of toast, and laughing every time I answer "Jason Donovan"—our default answer when we don't know the correct one.

"We can walk, if you like, while we wait. I know with me, sometimes walking can help calm me down, and you must feel—"

"Eliot?" Ana, voice frosty, with the face of a disapproving police officer, appears, the doors of the bar closing behind her, a square fawn-colored handbag swinging from her shoulder. She asks him something in French. He gestures to me, then says, and only for my benefit, "Emmie just wants to go home now. I thought we could share the taxi, see her home safe . . ."

Then she speaks fast, sternly, eyes on Eliot the whole time, never once even acknowledging me, the heathen in the unpressed dress, and then Tom appears behind her, red blotches on his cheeks, shirt open down to the chest. He sees me but looks away, at his phone in his hand, and begins to walk away. Ana follows. Eliot calls after them in French, but she doesn't react, walking straight and tall beside Tom, like a teacher who has just broken up a fight.

Eliot puts his hand on my arm. "Ana has said it's best Tom leaves. *He's* sharing our taxi." He bites his lip, nostrils flaring. "It's fucking bullshit, I know, but . . . look, I'm happy to come with you to the taxi rank and walk with you, see you home safe—"

"Em?" Lucas appears now, skin flushed, and when he sees me he speeds up, shoes scraping on the pavement. "God, are you okay?" He puts his arms around me, tight and safe and strong, smelling of aftershave and whiskey sours. I scrunch my eyes closed, hold him close, and when I open my eyes, fleetingly, a moment later, I see Eliot walking slowly away after Ana, hands in pockets.

"I'm sorry," I say. "I overreacted, I know."

"No," he says. "He overstepped the line and you . . . you just *reacted.*"

"It—it was the way he stopped me. He—"

"I know," he says. "Em, you don't need to explain. You don't need to say a word."

He looks down at me, waits, but I can say nothing else. The adrenaline leaves my body as fast as it came, and then it all catches up with me. I cry into his shirt. And yes, I am crying because I'm embarrassed and I am crying because I'm shaken up, my whole body surging with the shame and guilt I thought was long-buried. But mostly I'm crying because my heart is aching, like a wide-open wound behind my ribs.

Because I am alone, and I am scared. And I want to tell him I am, like I do everything else. But I can't. With this, *I can't*, and that's what's so hard.

Lucas looks down at me, pushes the hair out of my face, spidery strands sticking to the tears on my cheeks, and I see him swallow, Adam's apple contracting in his neck. He stares at me, sadness clouding his eyes, and I feel it between us. Heavy. Like static. Neither one of us moves. Tell me, I think. Tell me you've made a mistake.

"Emmie," he says. His lips remain parted, as if words are there, queueing up. But nothing comes.

"You're—you're getting married," I say, my words barely there.

"I know," he whispers. And for a moment I tense, because I really think he's going to kiss me. I don't want him to. But I do. All at the same time. But then he takes a deep breath and says, "God," and takes a step back, as if he's just been shaken awake. "D-Do you want—another drink, or . . . sh-shall we go back to the cottage?"

I will him to step back toward me, to tell me he doesn't want this. To tell me he feels it too. But he runs a hand through his hair, straightens his shirt at the neck, and I see it happen, as if a button has been pressed. Confident Lucas is back. Knows-it-all, content-with-exactly-where-he-is Lucas.

"You stay," I say to Lucas. "I'll go back."

He'd usually fight me on it, usually insist on coming with me, but he glances behind him, to the sounds emanating from the bar, and nods.

"You're sure?"

"Positive," I tell him, and after saying goodbye, I head in the direction I saw Eliot and Ana take earlier. I walk and walk, aimless, stopping only once to look up at the sky, stars like a spray of white paint on black silk, and want to ask it why? *Why* did you pull me toward him, for miles and miles, if this is how it ends up?

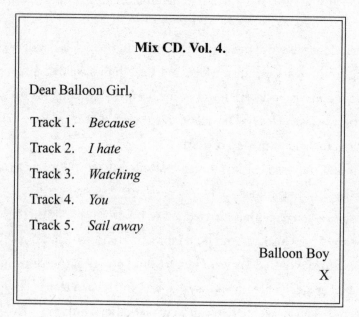

Mix CD. Vol. 4.

Dear Balloon Girl,

Track 1. *Because*

Track 2. *I hate*

Track 3. *Watching*

Track 4. *You*

Track 5. *Sail away*

Balloon Boy

X

17

"So, is this the bloke with the beard?"

Rosie scrunches up her nose. "Beard? Emmie, he never had a beard. Didn't even have an ounce of stubble. Dunno what I was thinking, to be honest."

I furrow my brow. "But I'm sure you said he was really hairy. Mike. Mike with the bike. And . . . beard."

Rosie, mid prawn sandwich, bursts out laughing. "It wasn't a beard, you wally."

"Oh, you *thought* it was a beard, but it turned out to be . . . dirt?" asks Fox as I push my finger through the tiny gap in my bag of Maltesers for the last one.

"*No.* God, you two are shit. Mike was the one with the pubes."

"Ah. That's the one. Easy mistake to make." I crunch and look over at Fox, who is wearing the expression someone might wear when they have just heard someone say the moon landing wasn't real and conducted in a studio.

"Um. Sorry?"

Rosie looks at him, pulling off a crust. "He had loads, Fox," she says with a shrug, and stuffs the bread in her mouth. "Like loads. Like . . ." She looks around her, mouth full, as if searching for the perfect word to pluck from the sky. "A disco wig down a pair of trousers."

I burst out laughing, watching Fox grimace as if trying to work out an algebra equation, before he says, "Well. I'm sure Mike would be thrilled to hear his crotch described in such a way," and Rosie laughs.

"*Thrilled*," she says. "Only my nan says that."

"Only your nan and *me*," Fox says, leaning into her, and sitting here in the sunshine on the beach with the both of them heals me like chicken broth does, like medicine. It was all I wanted to do when I got home from France last week; come to work and see them both, talk about dating and busy lunch shifts and Fox's new paisley trousers. And pubes, apparently. I needed distance. Just a few days to gather my thoughts, to get back on track. It's knocked me a little, that night at the bar, the same way hearing a song that was played at the Summer Ball used to, the way seeing a man in the street who looked like him—like Robert Morgan did. And it's that weird little moment between Lucas and me on the street too; the hesitation. I have since put it down to drunkenness. Lucas is an affectionate drunk. New Year's Eve is one of the examples, I see now. Our twenty-fifth birthday, when he pecked me on the lips and stayed there longer than he should have, and said, "I just really fucking love you, Em," before puking onto the pavement. But the whole night made me crave Shire Sands. A quiet tea with Louise in the morning, Radio 4 mumbling in the background. Rosie and Fox. Toast in bed, a Hallmark movie. Some quiet time at home, to digest it all.

"I'm not sure Emmie could deal with another wedding this soon," says Fox now. "Isn't that right?"

I look up, blinking, eyes glazed, fixed on the horizon. "What's that?"

"Me," says Rosie. "This bloke I'm going on a date with tonight. *Ravi.* We have the same star sign, *and* his mum is from Pakistan, like my pops. I said to Fox, it probably means it's fate and we'll get married."

"It definitely sounds like fate." I smile. "Does Fox need to borrow my best man book? Oh, I can send you my spreadsheet!"

Fox folds his arms and raises his eyebrows. "You have a *spreadsheet?* And also, absolutely not."

"She does." Rosie nods. "She studies hard, does Emmie. She has these Pinterest boards, too, and it's like a fucking library of its own. There are brides everywhere that would hire you on the spot through those alone, Em, you do realize that, don't you?"

I shake my head and sip from my can of 7UP.

"Mhmm," says Rosie.

I shake my head again. "Maybe until they found out the last and only wedding I did, I spent most of it staring at the groom, wanting to scream *why isn't it me?* Then I'm pretty sure I'd be blacklisted and written about, like a cautionary tale, like that psychopath husband-stealer from *The Hand That Rocks the Cradle.*"

"Oh!" says Rosie, flinging her arms in the air. "As if that's what you are. That is the *furthest* from what you are."

Fox unfolds his arms and pulls out his cigarettes. "Agreed," he says, then getting one out, he asks, "What's brought this on?"

I scrunch up the empty bag of Maltesers. "What do you mean?"

"Well, not that I'm stripping you of your right to be pessimistic or self-loathing, but . . . well, you've been fiercely determined and positive about this whole wedding and best woman business and now you sit here, in front of us—"

"He said *before us* this morning," adds Rosie with a smirk, but Fox's voice overlaps hers.

"And you seem different about it. Has something happened?"

They both look at me. I don't want to tell them about my dad's cards, which is starting to seep and swirl, like ink in water, into my every thought, and I don't want to talk about Tom and the bar, and the school I couldn't walk into. I've gone over it all so much in my head over the last few days. So instead I shrug and tell them the thing that's on the surface. I miss Lucas. And looking at him outside that bar, I realized just how much, and how much I will miss him after he says "I do." I tell them everything is changing. Yet I feel like I'm standing still. And they listen, eyes narrowed, nodding, all sympathetic sighs and hand-squeezes. Rosie cuddles me and says, "I still think you should talk to him," and Fox leans back on the bench, blows out a stream of smoke, and finishes his cigarette.

"You know what I think, Emmie?" he says. "I think you put too much onus on this man. You don't give yourself enough credit. Who you are on your own."

We walk back to the hotel, all three of us in a line, arms around one another, regardless of how reluctant Fox was to let Rosie's hand hold on to his waist. And deep down, I know he is right.

But it's hard for them to realize, I suppose—Rosie with her large and warm and loving family; Fox with his dad who visits, and his postcard-sending mother—that over the last fourteen years, Lucas has been my only constant. And when I had nobody, he was right there.

It isn't very often that I enter Fishers Way and hear voices, besides the radio. Louise doesn't really ever talk on the phone, and she never has visitors. When I walk through the hallway door today, just to say hello, Louise is talking quickly, smile on her face, old hands cradling a cup of mint tea at the kitchen table, her crossword book closed, her golden pen retracted and on the cover. Eliot, from his seat at the table, looks up at me, mug in hand. "Hey," he says with a smile.

I stop, feet on the carpet. "Um. Hi," I say, and Louise looks at me, the whites of her eyes bright and twinkly, color in her cheeks. She smiles, and it's nothing like her usual polite smile. The one reserved for postmen and passing neighbors in the street, so to not appear completely without a heart. "Sorry, I just—I didn't screw up and forget we had plans, did I?"

Eliot shakes his head. "No, no, not at all, I was just passing through. Thought I'd stop by. Plus, I wanted to run something by you." *God.* The STEN party, I bet. I really can't think of anything I want to do less right now, feet throbbing, cheeks red, hair stuck fast with the smell of cooking, than sit and talk about the bloody STEN party. Tom has booked the venue— something he announced excitedly in the group chat. A ballroom not far from Le Touquet that's been featured in a number of films I've never heard of, which I know will be right up Lucas's street. It has shocked me, actually, because I'd expected the French equivalent of Stringfellows or something; a roast dinner served on some poor woman's oiled-up buttocks.

I nod at Eliot. "Sure," I say.

Louise is already getting up, putting her mug in the sink and shuffling past the table to the conservatory out the back, where she waters her tomato plants and sits among shelves of books I never see her read.

"I made a vegetable curry," she says, her woolly-cardiganed back to me. "It's on the stove. There's plenty for you, Emmie, to eat for your dinner, if you'd like."

"Oh," I say, surprised. "Thank you, Louise. That's really kind."

"You can't keep living on toast. It's empty calories." Then she stops, glances over her shoulder. "You're welcome to some too, Eliot."

Eliot smiles, looks at me. "Thanks, Louise. Smells really good."

"I'm still good at some things," she says, the corner of her mouth lifting, and walks away.

I take a seat at the table. Eliot balls his hands together in front of him and looks up at me, brown eyes, long eyelashes. He looks like his dad. And this is something I only know from the photos Eliot used to keep of him in his bedroom, when we were young. He's dark, like him, tall, sharp jaw always peppered with stubble, his hair always "just" on his head, hand raked through it. He reminds me of the men Georgia would crush on when we were fifteen and we'd wander around smoky Camden Market buying posters, and jeans from Punkyfish.

"How are you doing?" asks Eliot, and I know what he's referring to. The last time he saw me. Shaking and wobbly, outside that bar, the anger in his voice at Ana helping Tom over me, obvious as he spoke.

"I'm fine," I say.

"Luke got pretty wasted after we left, I hear," he says, eyes on me.

"Did he?" I lift my shoulders to my ears. "I wouldn't know. I left. We've not really spoken much since then, actually."

Eliot hesitates, raises his eyebrows, gives a nod; one singular nod. "And how's work?"

"It's okay," I say. "Tiring. I did a double shift today and I cannot feel my feet."

"Do you want tea?" Eliot asks, brows raised, already getting up. "I'll make it. Kettle should still be hot."

I go to say no, but then I nod because I can't remember the last time I got home from work and someone made me a hot drink. "Yes. Please."

It's weird watching Eliot in Louise's kitchen, opening cupboards, pulling open drawers, making tea as I sit here at the table exhausted and sweaty after a long shift. If someone had told me this would be happening one day, I'm not sure I would have believed them. Even when I see Eliot at the Moreaus', at a family barbecue, we chat, but only ever strictly small talk, the way you do with someone at the till in Sainsbury's—to pass the time, to fill an awkward silence. But I feel like something has shifted, just slightly. The gap between us that was left that night; that sudden, harsh, irreparable-seeming tear, doesn't seem so huge. And I am glad.

"It's nice of you to sit with Louise," I say as he busies himself at the hot kettle, dropping a tea bag into a cup.

"She's cool," he says. "Knows a lot of shit, eh?"

I shrug. "I guess so." I drop my voice to a whisper. "She doesn't really speak to me some weeks."

He pours water in, a tiny smile on his lips. "Or you don't speak to her, more like. Still one sugar?"

"What do you mean? And yes. Still one."

Eliot gives a shrug. "I'm just saying, you're quite *tough* sometimes, and I don't mean that in a bad way. I just mean that you're . . ." Eliot stands back, folding his arms, waiting for the tea bag to brew. "Well, you're a bit of a closed book, aren't you?"

"Am I?"

"And so is she." He simply nods. "So, two closed books living together." He closes his hands together, a teaspoon in one, and smiles. "Voilà. A house of no words."

I stifle a laugh, pressing my lips together as he squeezes the tea bag, adds milk, and looks at me, eyebrows raising as if to say, "See? I'm right, aren't I?"

He places the tea in front of me and sits back down where he was. "So, I've been thinking about what we talked about on the car ride up to Mum's."

"About the live band? For the STEN?"

Eliot stops and shakes his head. "No. Well, yeah, I have been thinking about that, too, but that's not what I was going to say."

"Oh. Right."

"I was thinking more about what you told me, about the cards." He leans forward slightly. "About your dad. I've been thinking a lot about it, actually."

I nod, feel warmth tingle across my skin at those words. There's something about the way he says them that makes me trust him, and although a tiny voice asks if I should, I shake it away.

"Me too," I say. "I tried calling my mum again last night. Nothing. Not a single call or text or even *email* back."

Eliot grimaces, hand at the dark stubble of his chin. "I'm sorry."

"Don't be. It's how it's always been."

The clock on the wall above the cooker ticks, and Eliot looks at me. "So, I was thinking we should go," says Eliot. "To the address."

"To the one on the cards?" I ask pointlessly, feeling my heart plummet with dread.

Eliot nods. "I think if we do, maybe something might make sense, someone might know something . . ."

My hands tighten around my mug. "Eliot, I—I don't know."

"It's fifteen minutes away. I'm happy to knock if you don't want to. But . . . I dunno, with these things, I find it's better just to say fuck it, and face it, you know?" He's leaned back in his chair, elbow bent resting on the back, slouching. I don't think I have ever in my life seen Eliot panicked or worried. "What's the worst that can happen?"

"Everything," I say across the table. "I—I don't know." I place the mug down, suddenly going off the steaming cup of tea in my hands—and a *good* tea, made just how I like it, with a mere swirl of milk. He needed no reminder.

Eliot waits, watching me, his face soft, sympathetic. The calm of the kitchen, and of him, relaxed, no pressure, helps settle my nerves. I remember Lucas calling me, three or four years ago, to say Eliot and his wife, Pippa, had divorced. "He's a mess, Em," he'd said. "Stayed up till two this morning with him, just talking. He's not sleeping, not eating, and God—he looks ill." I try to muster that image of Eliot as I look at him now. I can't.

"When?" I ask him.

Eliot shrugs, and gestures with a hand to the sun streaming through the kitchen window. "Now looks good?"

"*No*," I say, without even thinking, and Eliot laughs. I look up at him, his eyebrows raised, a warm smile tugging at the corner of his lips, and I take a breath.

"I mean . . . I need to shower first," I say. "Then maybe we can go."

Where we are doesn't look like the Ramsgate I remember, the streets I'd walk to school, to Georgia's house, to the train station, to college. The houses are terraced and small in this little cul-de-sac. Sixties-built, with neat lawns and bushes. And I recognize it from Google Maps. There are rosebushes by the front door and a single potted lollipop of a bay tree in a terra-cotta pot. I sit in Eliot's truck, beside him, the engine off.

"I don't recognize this street at all," I say into the still silence of the truck.

"So, it's not where you might've once lived. A friend of your mum? A family member?"

I shake my head. "No. We lived in Cheshire from when I was about nine, after Den left. Then we moved back before I started secondary school. Into a flat. Maisonette. A different one from the one we lived in with Den. I've never lived in a house. Not somewhere like this."

Eliot nods. "Maybe it's worth asking," he says gently. "Ask them if they know your mum. They might even know your dad."

"But my dad lived in France. In Brittany." The nerves rattle through me as I say those words, and Eliot nods slowly. "Well, still," he says, "worth an ask, right?"

I look up at the house. Small. A little shabby, but neat. Cream roller-blinds at the windows at half-mast, large, mustard-yellow sunflowers in a vase on the windowsill downstairs. "Do you think I should . . . just knock?"

Eliot nods once enthusiastically. "Definitely. And in my experience, people are mostly nice and want to help." And it's that thought, that ideal, many, I'm sure, would counter, that gives me the courage to pull open the truck's passenger-door handle. The door squeaks as I push it open. I look at the house, then look over my shoulder at Eliot, who watches me calmly, one hand on the wheel.

"Eliot? Would you . . ."

"Come with?"

I nod.

Eliot smiles. "Sure."

Together we walk up the path, Eliot a step ahead, hands in his pockets, walking as though he's bowling up to a bar in a pub he's been in hundreds of times before. Before I can talk myself out of it, I press hard on the bell on the door frame, and it rings, like an old-school telephone. Inside, a dog barks. And now I realize I don't know what to say. I don't know how to word it. I don't know how to ask, and I feel my hands begin to sweat.

"All right, all right, you silly old mutt," says a man behind the door. There's a jangling of keys. By the sound of his voice, I'd hazard a guess at midfifties, maybe older. And Scottish. A strong accent.

The door swings open. A man fills the frame. And it falls out of my mouth before the memory of his face has even properly registered. "M-Marv."

Scottish Marv stares at me, his blond hair now white, and tummy rounder, but still, the same as the smiling, patient man who would bring comic books and chocolate coins over when Den had to pop out to work. The one who'd sit and play Snakes and Ladders with me, and balance shells in his shovel-hands on the beach. Marv looks at Eliot, then to me.

"Yes?" he says. "I'm Marv."

"I—I . . ." A smile breaks out on my face. "It's me."

Marv stares, and I realize, stupidly, that although he has barely altered, the last time this man saw me, I was eight years old.

I laugh, embarrassed. "Sorry, it's been years, I . . ." Eliot is staring at me, brow furrowed. "I'm Emmie. *Emmeline.*"

Marv stares at me again, mouth agape, eyes fixed.

"Emmeline Blue?" I say again. "*Katherine's Emmie.*" He keeps staring, so I keep talking, but I know he knows who I am. It's the way he swallows.

The way his cheeks flush. Yet the words just keep coming. "Den's Katherine. Den Walsh. Twenty years . . . twenty-two now, would it be?"

His face. Marv's face doesn't break into a smile, or anything that even resembles surprised, or confused. He just stares at me, the flushed color in his face now draining, second by second, from his ruddy face. Trouble. Maybe he thinks—true of my mum and Den's relationship in those final months—that I'm here to stir up trouble. Their split was sudden and volatile, Mum always screaming at him, Den, gritted teeth, storming out. Marv, as one of Den's friend's, is on guard, most likely. He doesn't want to be dragged into Katherine Blue's drama, and doesn't want his friend to be either.

"I'm not here for Mum," I rush out. "I don't want any trouble at all. I just want to show you something, and I hope you can help somehow."

A nod. Once. That's all I get from him, his mouth still agape as I pull the jiffy bag of cards from my bag.

"Mum sent me these."

Eliot watches Marv, and shifts beside me, folds his arms across his chest, straightens, stands taller. Reluctantly, Marv takes them.

"They're cards," I say. "Birthday cards, with . . ." He's just looking at me now, eyes downturned at the corners. "With y-your address . . ." And it's as if my heart knows before my head. Because I feel the sting across my chest. I feel the words dry up in my mouth. Why hasn't he spoken? Why hasn't he said a *single* thing?

He swallows. "I'm sorry," he says.

"S-Sorry?"

Marv looks at me, his breath ragged, his chest rising and falling as if he's been jogging, then at Eliot, as if for help. Eliot watches me, calm, steady. Waiting.

"I'm sorry," Marv says again. "I am. But . . ." He clears his throat, swallows. "But I can't do this now. I really can't. I . . . I have a family. They don't—they don't know . . ." And I already know, as I look at him, his eyes watery, hesitating, hands open in front of him as if he plans to reach out and touch me but decides against it.

"No," he says. "I can't. I'm sorry." Marv closes the door quickly. I hear the clatter of the latch, locking us out.

I look up at Eliot. "Emmie," he begins. "Are you—"

I turn. I can't stand here. I cannot stand here on his path. I cannot be here.

I run to Eliot's truck. I hear the dog barking again from behind the locked door, and I hear Eliot's feet pounding the concrete behind me. And I don't cry until I'm in the truck, bent into myself, arms shielding my face. I wonder if he's watching, from inside the house. I wonder if he's desperate for us to drive away before his family gets back.

I hear the driver's door close beside me, feel Eliot's hand softly land on top of mine. I try to speak, to tell Eliot to drive, but tears soak up my words.

"It's okay," Eliot says softly. "It's okay, Emmie."

But it's not. It's not okay. It can never be.

My dad. I've found my dad. And my dad is Marv. Marv, who made me laugh so much I cried when he made my Barbie dolls dance along to the adverts on TV. Marv, who took me to the beach on my bike. Marv, who disappeared when Den did. Marv, who only turned up when Mum was out. He isn't in Brittany. He never was. And every day I dreamed about finding him, about having him to talk to, to tell him things I'd done and achieved, he's been right here. Fifteen minutes away. Around the corner. And he doesn't want me. He shut a door in my face. I am half of him, and he *shut a door in my face.*

Eliot's hand squeezes mine. I hold it.

After a while the tears stop and we sit in silence, the only sound in the truck was of someone's lawn mower outside, and the hiccups in my throat as I try to catch my breath.

After a while, Eliot brushes his thumb over my knuckles and draws back.

"Let's go," he says. And he starts the engine, and we drive away.

I should have stayed in the cubicle. But I thought they'd gone. I had knelt on the toilet seat, my knees under me, my mouth closed, eyes closed, trying so hard to concentrate on my breath, and on not making a sound. I could hear them laughing, swapping lip glosses, Georgia's voice saying, "She's fucking pathetic," and another girl saying, "She's a joke, mate. *Desperate.*" I waited, hands sweating, bones shaking beneath my skin. I thought it was best I kept going to school—so nobody would talk, or believe the anonymous letter left in Ms. Spark's pigeon-hole was mine. They'd suspect the girl who was suddenly off school, she said. But they know anyway. I should have never written that it happened in the IT block, because that's what did it and gave me away. As soon as the school told Mr. Morgan they'd had a report that something happened there, the night of the ball, Georgia knew it had to be me who wrote the letter. Her mum too. Because they all knew he was helping me find my dad. And that's why they say I accused him—Georgia's amazing, strong, loving dad—of those awful things. Because I'm jealous. Because I'm lonely and desperate for attention. But they're true. As much as they think I'm making it up, that Mr. Morgan is too cool, too funny, to do something like that, it is true. And I wish so much that it wasn't.

I heard the knock of the bathroom door as it closed, and their voices fade and disappear. That's why I opened the cubicle door and stopped hiding. But as soon as I did, I regretted it. Georgia was standing there, with Ashley, from the other form. A girl Georgia and I once chatted with in PE, who told us her boyfriend was a drug dealer, and Georgia had said as we walked away, "Her boyfriend probably works in Burger King, Em. She lies. Wouldn't mess with her, though. I like my teeth too much." And we'd laughed, arm in arm, through the leafy school grounds. But it's seemed to have made Georgia more coveted, this whole thing. Students that barely spoke to us before, now flock to Georgia as if she is a celebrity, all of them leaning across dining tables, listening to her, holding her arm, rubbing her back; so many faces staring at me, with hooded eyes and smirks.

"What're you doing in here?" Georgia says now, lip curled.

"Yeah," laughs Ashley. "You hiding in here, *Emmeline?*" She says Emmeline as if it's amusing.

"No," I say, shaking my head. I walk, to try and get past them, and Ashley pushes my shoulder.

"You not even washing your hands?" She laughs, looking back at Georgia, who stares at me, nostrils flared, the skin of her cheeks red. "Dirty skank."

"Please let me past," I say, voice tiny, and I wish so much that it wasn't, but I can't help it. I am shaking from head to toe. I am trying so hard to pull strength from within me, but I can't stop trembling.

"Nah," says Ashley.

"Please." I look at Georgia pleadingly. My best friend of five years. The girl I'd spend every evening on the phone to. The girl whose family

I holidayed with in caravans, went to pantomimes with, stayed with, ate breakfast with. "*Please*, Georgia."

"My dad has moved away because of you," she says, voice tight, wobbling. "My mum is *ill* because of you."

"Georgia, I never ever wanted—"

"What, you didn't want to hurt me? Is that what you were going to say?" Her teeth are gritted, and instincts from so many years of friendship make it so hard to not reach for her, to hold her. Ashley steps back, scowls at me, puts her arm around Georgia. "You fucking *lied*."

"Georgia, I didn't, I—"

"And I feel sorry for you," she carries on. "Because no wonder you lie about my dad, when your own doesn't even know you exist. Your mum doesn't even give a shit about you. Where is she now, then, Em? *Where?*"

Ashley laughs, a snort in her nose, as if she's pretending to try and conceal it, and my chest aches. I wish I'd never gone to the Summer Ball. I wish I'd never trusted him to help me find my dad. I wish I'd never written that letter.

"It's pathetic," says Georgia, her eyes watery now. "*You're* pathetic. And well done. Now you've got no one."

Georgia turns, pushing the bathroom door and whisking out.

Ashley looks me up and down. "Slut," she says.

19

My phone wakes me up. A FaceTime call, from Lucas, the beep like a soft alarm clock nudging me gently awake. I open my eyes and it takes me just a second to remember. The sight of my sandals, tossed on the floor next to my bed, and my handbag beside them, on its side, its contents spilled out remind me of when I got home yesterday and crumpled into bed. Marv. My dad. Eliot. God, Eliot. Poor Eliot. I couldn't speak, and he didn't pry, didn't push me for anything. He just drove and drove as I stared out the passenger window, and as he turned into Fishers Way, I said croakily, "I can't go home. Don't drop me home." "Okay," he said. "Let's take a drive." I don't know where we went, just that we drove for ages, windows down, hot August air lapping in, Eliot's radio playing Bowie, him drumming his hands softly on the steering wheel. And I'd felt physically sick. I kept replaying his face. Replaying his name. *Marv.* Not Peter. Not a drummer in France. Scottish Marv.

Eliot had pulled up in a car park after a while, wheels crunching on gravel. I don't know where we were, but we were surrounded by thick forest and shade. A pay and display machine sat among the wildness of the trees. He killed the engine.

"It's always quiet here," he said. "I need to make a phone call, but sit, or if you like, we could walk afterward."

I sat, staring, my heart still hammering, my stomach nauseated. I could hear Eliot as he spoke on the phone, but not loud enough to hear the words, his hand rubbing the back of his head, squinting up at the sky. Ana, I bet.

When he got back into the car, I looked up at him for the first time.

Silence. Eliot grappling with the words to say to me, and me, scared for any of it to be said out loud. To be made true.

"I'm sorry, Emmie," he said. "I really am."

"All along" is all I could say, and Eliot put his hand on mine again, and I held on to it, across the handbrake, and I was grateful that he was there with me. Because the devastation was waging a storm through me, and not because it was Marv who is my dad. But because I was looking for Peter. I was looking on those computers at school, every night for weeks, on Friends Reunited, sending messages to strangers, to Peters in Brittany, going onto Ask Jeeves, searching for the festival where Mum met my dad. This Peter guy that she, what? Made up? To stop me ever discovering that my dad lived around the corner from us? And that is why *he*, Robert Morgan, Georgia's dad, sat with me at that computer desk. Helping me. My dad Peter was why I went to the IT room, why I turned to him. He kept finding things—clues, people, not a drummer but a guitarist in a jazz band, who often played the festival my mum worked at. But all along I was searching for an imaginary person. If I'd known Marv was my dad . . . what happened, would have never happened.

I hold the phone in my hand now, Lucas's name above "accept" and "decline." I accept the call. Lucas's smiling, handsome face springs onto the screen, and I could cry at the sight of him. We haven't spoken much since the bar. I can see he's in his car now, vest on, hair wet. He's been to the gym.

"Fuck. Did I wake you?"

"It's fine," I say groggily. "I need to get up anyway."

"Hate to sound like my dad, but I've been up half the day. Been to the gym, been for breakfast . . ."

"What did you eat?" I yawn. "Go on. Tell me. Make me jealous."

"Ah," laughs Lucas. "There's no way you'll be jealous. Avocado toast. Shitload of eggs. Chili flakes. Pumpernickel bread."

I screw my face up. "Ugh. Lucas Moreau, what's happened to you?"

Lucas laughs. "Hey look, if I could eat sausage McMuffins and get all my protein, I would." Then he fixes his hair in the screen, pouts ever so slightly, the way he always does when checking himself in a mirror, and says, "So I'm going suit shopping again, for Dad and El. Mum's coming. So's Eliot, obviously. If he ever gets here. He was meant to come last night, but said he'd leave first thing. Where were you last night, by the way?"

The phone call, by the woods. I bet he canceled because of me. Because of me crying on him twice on the way home. Because he walked me to my room and asked if I needed him to sit with me. It was kind. I almost wanted him to. Tall Eliot with his kind brown eyes. But I just couldn't shake the thought. I should have never been in that room. That room that made me "that girl." The girl they said probably deserved it, brought it on herself, his heavy body, the tear he made in my dress as I managed to wriggle away. Then my brain whispered memories of my nineteenth party. And I just wanted to be alone. Without anyone. Without even Eliot, because he had thought the same as all those others, once upon a time. What was said at the party, by his girlfriend, proved it. He had been one of the voices that had almost destroyed me, even if he hadn't meant to be.

"Hey," says Lucas now. "Are you all right, Em?"

"Fine. Just tired." Lucas knows. He knows every time I yank out a stock answer to that question.

"Look." He swallows. "I'm so sorry about the other night at the bar. Tom said he'd text you—"

Tom. He thinks it's Tom. He thinks it's the bar. And I wish now that it was.

"And he's called," I say. "He apologized, more than once. It's fine. Water under the bridge."

Lucas nods. "Marie said you sent her some photos of some light arrangements for the top table that you found on Pinterest."

"Yeah, I saw them as I was browsing best woman, stag stuff, you know—"

Lucas smiles, and hesitates. "Thanks, Emmie. I mean that. You are—I dunno, a *dream* at this. I couldn't do this without you. I have total imposter syndrome with this whole deal, but you're this . . . pillar. As always."

"Someone's gotta keep you in check," I say, and I feel like a fraud, because a pillar I am certainly not. Not today. Not after last night. I think of Louise's face when we walked in. She'd looked at Eliot quizzically, as if ready to blame him for my tears, yet she asked nothing. Just watched, like a minder, as we trod up the stairs, Eliot lifting a heavy hand to her in a wave. I shook beneath the duvet last night. I used to shake back then, in bed by myself, Mum, miles away, and that feeling of being totally alone enveloping me. Nothing helped stop it. I couldn't even bear to listen to a CD last night, to help me to sleep. It just reminded me of the rock ballads Lucas would put on there. "Because your dad was probably in Kiss."

Lucas is waffling about work now, and how a guy who never speaks to him is suddenly all over him now he knows the STEN party is being held in the ballroom, and how Marie's parents are "shitting checks."

"Luke?" I cut in.

He stops, eyebrows raised. "Yeah?"

I stare at him, the words in my throat stuck. Why can't I tell him? Why can't I bring myself to confide in him as I always have?

"I . . . last night . . ."

Then his head turns swiftly, to the passenger window. I hear the knocking too, knuckles against a window. His face breaks into a smile. "Hey!" he laughs, then he looks back at the screen. "Sorry, Marie's just got here. What were you saying?"

I shake my head. "Nothing. I'm going to go, Luke, okay? I've got work. I need to shower and—"

"Are you sure you're all right?"

I nod. "Just tired. I haven't stopped working. Loads of overtime and double shifts."

"Well, take it easy. Take some holiday, a break. They're taking advantage, that hotel."

I swallow down the urge to say, "Normal people can't just do that, Lucas," but he carries on. "See, this is why you need to let Dad have your CV, Em. Nine to five. You'd get your weekends."

"I'll be fine," I tell him.

"Promise me, yeah?" he asks. "That everything's all right?"

"Everything's all right," I say, and hearing that out loud is a weird comfort, because I pretend for a second that the words are true.

A moment later Lucas is gone, and I am left in the silence of my hot bedroom.

WhatsApp from Eliot Barnes:

Hi closed book. How are things looking this morning? Brighter, I hope. I'm in France for the next fortnight. Ana's sister's wedding & I've got to press on with Mum and Jean's bandstand while they're away. Hopefully see you soon. E, x

Fishers Way is silent. In the eighteen months I have lived here, I have never known to wake up to no sound at all. There is always the rumbling of a kettle, of a distant radio presenter, the clanging of pots, or of Louise, humming a song. It's 10:30 a.m. Louise is an early riser. I am not. So there hasn't been a time, I don't think, that I have woken to no Louise. She doesn't really go out either. "A bit of a recluse, then," as Lucas once suggested, and I suppose he is right.

I go down to the kitchen and make a cup of tea, and realize before I switch it on that the kettle is stone cold. The air is silent, unnervingly so. Before the kettle has finished rumbling, I duck my head through to the conservatory and then to Louise's large, cluttered lounge. *Nothing.* I tread the stairs, heart pounding a little now with anxiety. I remember waking up to a silent home so many times, and sometimes, I would feel so alone that I would go straight to a window to see a car drive by, or a person stroll past, just so I knew I hadn't slept through the end of the world and woken as the only human left.

I find Louise in her bedroom, in bed. She is sitting up, the silver, tripod-legged walking stick flat on the floor, out of reach. Her hair, which she always keeps up in a loose teacher's bun, is long and frizzy, and flowing over the shoulders of her button-down pajama top.

"Sorry," I say from the doorway, ready to duck back out again. "I just wanted to check you were okay. When I saw you weren't up, I was worried."

Louise swallows. "I can't get up," she says.

"Do you need me to pass you your stick?"

She shakes her head. "No. No, that won't be much use. I just . . ." She stops herself, then sighs. "Some days I just can't get up. Vertigo."

"God, I'm sorry, Louise." I edge into the room a little more. It smells of patchouli and fabric softener. "Can I get you anything?"

She grimaces, as if it is paining her to tell me all this, and says, "I've been here five hours, since I got up and just about made it to the en suite. Could you get me something to eat and drink please, Emmie? Toast would be fine."

"Of course. Tea too?"

She nods, smiling weakly. "Please."

Downstairs, I set a tray of two slices of buttered toast with marmalade—her own homemade, from a Kilner jar—a banana, a couple of napkins, and a cup of mint tea. She thanks me and, taking in the silent, cluttered bedroom, I offer her my television.

"I don't care for television," she says, "but thank you."

"How about some books?"

"I struggle nowadays," she says, "to read. My eyesight."

"Is this to do with the vertigo?" I ask, standing next to her bed, wanting to sit at the bottom of it but feeling that would be way too overfamiliar, especially with someone like Louise.

"No," she says, shaking her head. "I have macular degeneration. Common. Eyesight has been slowly worsening since I turned sixty. Partial blindness, but I'm fine. It doesn't hinder me really. Well, just with the books, which is a shame, I have to admit."

"Audio books could help? I see them at the library. They do these USB sticks and these machines that play them, like a radio . . ."

She smiles. "I find with the audiotapes and things that I always lose my place. But thank you. I'm quite all right. When the vertigo stops, I'll try my crosswords. They'll keep me company." The huge, oversized crossword books make sense now, and the way they always seem to take her a while, as she sits there at the kitchen table, glasses on the end of her nose, roller-ball pen poised over the page, the clock ticking, the radio mumbling.

"Do you need anything else?" I ask her, and she shakes her head.

"No, no," she says, smiling, and I get the impression she wants me out of her space.

I lied to Lucas this morning, telling him I had back-to-back shifts all weekend so wouldn't be able to talk much. But today is a totally free Sunday. I have no plans, no shifts at work, and as I switch on the radio downstairs in the kitchen and make myself some toast, I think about why. Why didn't I tell him the truth? Why didn't I feel I could tell Lucas about Marv? About going there with Eliot? I wash up the plates in the sink and take out the rubbish and recycling. I even run the vacuum around the house and put on a load of my washing—putting two of Louise's dresses in there with it. For an August afternoon, it's windy, so I hang it out on the rotary line in the garden and watch it through the window in the conservatory with a smug satisfaction of how quick it'll dry. I dreamed of having a house with a garden and a washing line when I was a kid. Still do, as simple and as sad as that may sound to some. A string of clothes—large trousers, tiny socks—spelling a family, blowing gently in a breeze.

I polish and clean the windows, and I water the tomato plants, running a finger along the stalk of one, and smelling the deep, viney smell on my fingertips. I wouldn't usually touch them, Louise's pride and joy, but the summer sun burning through the windows of the conservatory is drying out the soil. I stand among the books and the plants afterward. I've never really been out here. It's Louise's room, and as a lodger, I only need to use the bathroom and kitchen. There are hundreds of books out here, and I feel sad that she can no longer read the words. I run a hand along them, stopping when I come to the many weird ornaments between and in front of them, and photos too. Mostly of scenic beaches and mountains, but some of people. Two are black and white. Three are color. And all feature a woman with short, bobbed, shiny hair, standing beside someone who is undoubtedly a young Louise, age twenty-five to thirty, I'd say. In all of them they are smiling, widely, holding on to each other, shrouded in happiness and sunshine. There are yellowing postcards propped against things, too, and ceramic bottles painted in tribal patterns, and plates with country names painted on them by hand. A display of a life lived. Not of a recluse. And I wonder here, among it all, when she stopped taking adventures.

I take tea up to Louise, in between dwindling the day away, sitting in the conservatory in the sunshine and reading the best man book, my legs bent under me, a cup of coffee on the windowsill, but my mind wanders. To Marv. To his face, drained of color. To Eliot. And I can hardly bear it. I'm nauseous when I replay yesterday, when it swirls through my mind, a mess of emotions and memories and shocked faces on doorsteps. I have to state it to myself, to tune it all up, like an old radio. Marv. Marv has been my dad all along. Marv is my father.

At four, I set a tray of biscuits and two satsumas, and two cups of mint tea not just for Louise, but for me. "Good for the stomach," she always says as she pours it, and today, I could do with something to help settle it. Before I take the tray up, though, I take a book from Louise's shelf. There is a butterfly breaking out of its cocoon on the cover. I don't know what it's about, but it looks dog-eared, read more than once.

She brightens, unmistakably, as I appear in the doorway, looking away from the window she was staring through.

"I've brought supplies for you." I smile, placing the tray across her lap. "And for me too. I thought I could read to you," I say. "If you'd like."

Louise's cheeks flush, her mouth open, as if searching for the right thing to say. "I, uh . . . I'm sure you have better things to do . . ."

I shake my head. "I'd love to. This one caught my eye, actually." And I see the glimmer in her eyes, of excitement at the sight of the book in my hand.

"Ah. Have you read it?"

"No," I say.

"Do you like love stories?" she asks, and I lower myself to sit at the foot of Louise's soft, creaking bed.

"I do," I tell her. "They're my downfall, actually."

WhatsApp from Lucas Moreau:

Hey Em, was thinking . . .

WhatsApp from Lucas Moreau:

Mum and Dad are away for the next couple of weeks and, not this weekend but next, it's Marie's birthday. The bridesmaids and her mum have arranged a thing at her place and Marie would love you there. But I thought we could go to the beach too? Say hi to our spot, have some time together, chill, just us, like old illuminous ketchup times!

WhatsApp from Lucas Moreau:

I'll even let you choose the movies. (I just ask that it isn't that fucking Vanilla Ice film.) Let me know.

21

Marie's parents' house is huge. The sort of house painted on the labels of wine bottles. I am greeted by her mother, who is the loveliest and most glamorous woman I have ever seen. She is fanning her face when she answers the door, her blond hair, in Marilyn Monroe–style curls, bounce as she moves.

"Salut!" she says, and I tell her I'm Emmie, Lucas's friend, and without hesitation, she squeezes me.

"Oh! The best woman," she says in a posh English accent. "I have heard so much about you from Marie and from Lucas. Please, come, upstairs. You are just in time for nails!"

She leads me up a huge spiral staircase, the carpet springy like sponge cake, and into a room with a baby grand piano and opened double oak doors. There must be ten guests arranged in the room on sofas and armchairs, all female, and three smiling women at their feet and hands, painting and filing and fussing. Everything here is dripping with class and money, and I instantly feel like a stray cat, lost in Buckingham Palace. Marie looks delighted to see me and comes bouncing across the thick beige carpet toward me.

"Darling Emmie!" she says. "Thank you so much for coming. It is so lovely to see you."

"Happy birthday, Marie. I got you, er . . . a little something." I eye the top of the baby grand, lined with square, rope-handled gift bags, designer names on the side of them, and instantly wish I'd left my gift on the backseat of the taxi Lucas put me in. I almost forgot it. The cab driver called me back and handed it to me. A box of handmade vegan bath bombs and a recipe book on avocados.

"Merci, mon amour, you did not need to," she says, putting my gold-wrapped gift among the towers of gift bags. "And are you okay now? Really?"

I blink. "Um. Yes?"

"Lucas told me all about it," she says, and I feel all eyes on me—pairs and pairs of strangers' eyes. "About your mother and the cards that arrived from your father and how you thought he knew nothing of you and . . . gosh, I was so worried, you seemed so sad on the screen and Lucas said—"

"I'm fine," I cut in. "It's all fine. So, are these your friends?"

Every one of Marie's friends is lovely and welcoming. They smile, break out of their fast, French conversations to talk to me—well, as much as the language barrier allows—and to get me champagne. They keep my glass filled up, pass around the canapés, all colors of the rainbow, and nudge me, smilingly, to tell me I *have* to take more than one. And after a while, after I switch off from playing a scene in my head of Lucas and Marie over glasses of wine, over an elegant, grown-up dinner, discussing my car crash of a life as if it's something to be dissected and analyzed, in the style of a book club meeting, I'm having a nice time. I'm having a really nice time here, actually, in this beautiful house, with gorgeous food and crisp, cold champagne. Maybe I needed this. An ocean away from my normal life, from Marv, and the sleepless nights that taunt me at the moment. Pure escapism, that's what this is; face glowing with the warmth of champagne and laughter, and my hands, like silk now, and glistening with sparkly red polish.

The doorbell sounds, and Lucille, maid of honor, jumps up to get it at the same time as Marie's mother does.

"No, no, sit," Lucille says, waggling her dry nails.

"I think you should open gifts," says a woman who introduced herself, in a London accent, as Marie's roommate from uni. Isabelle. She passes a light blue Tiffany bag to Marie. "This is from me and Ben." Marie's hands press into her chest and she cocks her head to one side. "You spoil me," she says, and pulls out a box. It's a beautiful bracelet, with Marie's birthstone hanging from the chain. We all lean in to get a closer look, and it's passed around, held high, admired like a new baby.

"Latecomer!" Lucille giggles from the doorway, and beside her is Ana. Eliot's Ana, a cream pencil dress hugging her tall, willowy frame, a wide, shimmering smile on her face. The smile she seems to use for everyone else, bar me. I'm surprised to see her here, really. I didn't think Ana and Marie were friends, but then again, Marie is marrying her boyfriend's brother. They'll be a hop, skip, and jump from in-laws soon.

Ana launches into a gushy, fast French frenzy, standing back and taking in Marie and the beautiful chiffon floral dress she's wearing, and Marie does the same to her. They kiss each other twice, once on each cheek, and Ana takes a seat beside me, on a gray, arch-backed armchair.

"Hello." She nods to me, and I lean forward, almost too hastily, to grab a champagne flute for her. As if to impress her. The way someone does in secondary school, to the cool girl in sixth form who looks at everyone as if they are shit on her shoe. She shakes her head at me, nostrils practically flaring.

"I do not drink."

"Oh," I say. "Right. Well, that's good. More brain cells." I don't know why I say that, but it may be because I have murdered several of mine in just under two hours.

Marie opens all her gifts and acts as if I have given her the Hope diamond when she opens mine. She passes around the bath bombs, and the girls smell them, talking in fast French I don't understand. Ana doesn't take one when they make their way to her. She just studies the back and front of the avocado recipe book and says to Marie, in English of course, "But you hate cooking." My heart sinks.

Marie ignores her and says, "But I *like* avocados." Then she leans and kisses me on the cheek. "Baths and avocados. You know me better than Lucas does." I see Ana smirk. I look at her and force a huge, glittering smile. You will not ruin my afternoon, super bitch, and I will not let this urge to run from this room and from this house, into the French countryside, win. I knock back another mouthful of champagne.

The nail technicians leave, and the natural sunlight of the room dims as thick, smoky rain clouds drift in front of the huge bay window. Ana talks constantly, and I pick up random words to hazard a guess that she's talking about a new home she "can't wait" to move into. "Bravo, Paul McCartney," Lucas would be saying now. "Nice work."

Eliot's name is mentioned several times, too, and it's strange, but I can hardly imagine it's the same person. The Eliot who is with this cold, smirking woman. The Eliot who held my hand outside Marv's. Who saw me up to my room, who drew the curtains as I collapsed into bed.

Desserts are handed out—tiny little mousses and parfaits—and there is a conversation sweeping the room, commandeered by Ana, who seems to be quickly, huskily, questioning people one by one. I can't quite grasp what with my Paul McCartney French. She talks a lot. Probably because she does nothing but listen in her job. I can't imagine feeling comfortable enough to air a grievance about a below-par appetizer with Ana, let alone air the things that frighten me the most.

"And you?" she suddenly says, turning to Isabelle, Marie's uni roommate. "Are you married?"

"Yes. I'm married," she says with a smile. "Ben. We met when we were eighteen. We have a son. He's two."

"Ohhh, I remember so well," says Marie, giggling, tiny parfait spoon at her lips. "He was best friends with this guy who was in our shared house, and she used to wait every day, hoping he would come over."

Isabelle laughs, tucking mousy hair behind her ear, and nods. "It's true," she says as Marie chatters in French, translating to a friend at her side.

"And I would say to her, *ask him,*" Marie carries on, to us. "The guy we live with. *Ask* who his friend is, but she wouldn't."

"So I just waited, and then when he did appear—"

"She would rush to my room and steal all of my makeup," laughs Marie, reaching across and grabbing Isabelle's hand. "It took her such a long time to even *speak* to him."

"I just used to swish about, hoping he'd say hi."

"Full face of makeup on a Sunday morning," giggles Marie, and Isabelle laughs. "Yep. Now, poor soul gets this face," she says, gesticulating with a hand at her pretty, pale face, "with no makeup, baby puke in my hair—"

"And he still is hopelessly in love," adds Marie.

The girls aww and coo, even Ana, which is almost like seeing your teacher in the supermarket. It looks completely weird and wrong.

"This is like Eliot and me," says Ana, and I can't help but freeze at the mention of him again. "It took us such a long time," she says, "to finally admit how we felt. He started staying later and later after sessions, and I would hate him leaving."

"Ana is a psychotherapist," says Marie to Isabelle, who says, "Oh wow, and Eliot was a client?"

"He came to me with a broken heart." Ana smiles, as if she has rehearsed this before, and if this were a film I was watching, even I, a romantic, would definitely pretend to be sick at that line. "And I fixed it," Ana says. "Romantic, no?"

No, I want to say. No, it isn't actually, Ana, because he is lovely, and you are not.

"We of course waited until his therapy ended until we began anything.

And then there were a lot of texts, and a lot of coffees *as friends.*" She rolls her eyes and titters a laugh. "But it was obvious. He was besotted."

"Really? *Why?*" I want to ask, but instead I knock back my champagne and realize that perhaps I should stop, as that "why" was mere centimeters from spilling from my mouth.

"Oh, how *lovely,*" says Marie's mum. "I've not spent much time with Eliot, but he seems just as lovely as our Lucas."

Marie smiles over at her mum, dreamy-eyed, and Ana nods.

"Oh yes. My Eliot is," she says, looking out the side of her eyes at me. "So loyal. And *romantic.*"

"Same as Luke." Marie beams, and the girls melt into smiles and giggles.

I knock back the rest of my champagne. I top it up.

———

The girls chatter among themselves. About boyfriends and girlfriends and husbands doing the most wonderful things—the real things, like pulling up their knickers when they were so drunk on drugs post–wisdom teeth removal, like baths run, like journeys to the middle of nowhere to pick them up, post–pub crawl. Of proposals. Of romantic dates and funny anecdotes, and I sit nodding, cheeks aching with the amount of grins and smiles I am dishing out. Even Lucille is joining in, telling everyone how she and Mr. Aftershave Ad from the bar are on their third date and she feels "different" with him. And I am trying hard to ignore it. This empty pit in my stomach. Loneliness. That's what it is. I recognize it, with a sinking heart, like an old symptom you thought was cured.

"You, Emmie?"

I look up. All eyes are on me. Ana stares over from beside me, her question hanging in midair.

"Me?"

"Yes. Are you married?" asks Isabelle hopefully.

"Nope," I say. "No, I am not."

"Boyfriend?" asks Ana, her eyes hooded and head to one side, as if she is enjoying this, and it's weird, because she knows the answer. We had this discussion on the way to the bar, in the back of a taxi. It was the only thing we did talk about that night. Well, that and the joys of a trouser press.

"No," I say. "Still single, from the last time you asked me. But happy with that."

"You're one of the lucky ones," says one of the women, and everyone laughs, and thankfully, the conversation moves on. Nails are shown off, drinks are drunk, and desserts turn into tiny cheeses and fruit.

"Oh!" I hear Marie say from behind me as I reach for my champagne. It's my fourth, I think. Maybe fifth. "I'm going to show you girls the montage."

"Montage?" asks her mother. "Of bridesmaid dresses?"

"No, no, of Lucas and me. Photos that are going to be on a, er . . . er . . ." Marie hesitates.

"Projector screen," Isabelle says, and Marie nods.

"Yes. Oh, I was *crying* when my brother showed me. I know it's early, that there are still months to go, but I want to be organized. I show you sneak peek."

And I know, filled champagne glass in my hand, stomach nauseated, that I can't stay here for this. I have to leave. So as everyone chats, and as Marie ducks off for her laptop, her mother switching on the television above the fireplace, I slink off to the bathroom, two doors down. I breathe in deep breaths, hunched over the glistening countertop basin, panic heaving in my chest, my head swirling with what feels like multiple golf balls rolling. I can't sit through that montage. I can't sit beside Ana any longer, either. I'll make up an emergency. Leave. I need to leave.

With my phone in hand—a Rosie tip when faking an emergency phone call, for it to appear more authentic—I go back into the room and find

Marie and tell her I've had a wonderful time but I have to go. "My friend Rosie has just called me crying, and I need to go back to the cottage and talk to her." It sounds fake to me, my words too matter-of-fact, too wooden, but Marie, barefooted and clumsy with champagne-consumption, doesn't press for me to stay, or pry. She does insist on calling me a taxi, though.

"No. It's okay. Lucas gave me a number, so I can do it."

"No, no, I insist."

Her friend tugs on her arm, a laptop open in her lap, and before she can say another word, I hug her and walk away, at the exact moment a photograph of Lucas and Marie appears on the TV screen, his nose nuzzled into her neck, Marie's face glowing with happiness. There is a chorus of coos and happy cheering as I descend the stairs and leave.

I am lost. I am completely and utterly lost. I left Marie's parents' house so quickly, taking a left and walking purposefully, my mind racing, my body sighing with relief at being out of there, of feeling so lonely, so tiny, so insignificant, with nothing to offer a room full of people with vibrant, wholesome stories of love and family. No heartwarming anecdotes about my mother, no partner in crime to speak of who would pull my knickers up for me, or still find me completely lovable and attractive mid-winter-vomiting-bug. No stories about my dad. Nothing. Lonely. Small. That's exactly how I felt, and so I kept walking, as if to walk it off, the way you do a stiff muscle in the morning, hoping that shortly I would come to the town or even village of this leafy, hill-bordered area in which Marie's family lives. But after twenty minutes of aimless walking in one direction, I find myself completely and utterly lost in the wilderness, trudging on and on, and seeing only one house, set back, gated, quiet, to every seven thousand bloody trees. And now it is raining. The thick smoke of the clouds have given way, and my sandals squeak with water every time I walk.

"Rain is forecasted for later," Lucas had said earlier, fishing his black, fitted rain mac from the cupboard. "You might want a jacket."

"Oh, it's fine," I told him. "It's not like I'll be going on a country *hike* or anything. I'll be at Marie's. Inside."

And I should have brought a coat; shouldn't have been fooled by the late August sunshine. I don't know where I am, and now I have absolutely no idea where Marie's house is either. I have no internet signal on my phone to google anything, and if I call Marie, she is going to think I am a colossal dickhead for leaving her house with nowhere to go, no car to get into, and walking miles uphill, instead of just waiting safely in her home for a taxi. She will know something is wrong.

Lucas. Could I call Lucas? I stand beneath a tree, which slows the rain pitter-pattering down on my head to slow, steady, fat droplets, and hover my thumb over Lucas's name. I can't. I can't call him and interrupt the open house he's having to attend today—a ten-million-euro condo in Brittany he worked on—to tell him I walked out of his fiancée's party because I felt insignificant in a room full of together, on-track adults, and wanted to head for wetter, greener, and what is looking increasingly like Missing Persons pastures. Plus, he's hours away. I stand, the rain coming thick and fast, and say, absolutely pointlessly, "Fuuuck!" into the air and stamp a squeaky foot.

I wait. I listen for the sounds of a car, so I can hail it down, ask the name of the area, of the road, for a taxi number. Anything. But, nothing. Nothing but the sounds of pouring rain and the tweeting of birds. I want to cry. I could crumple into tears now, not stop. But I don't. If I do, I know I'll lose the quiet, sensible voice that is keeping me from panicking, here, in the middle of nowhere, miles from home.

I unlock my phone and stare at the names of my recently dialed list.

Lucas. Rosie. Louise Home. Eliot.

I look above me at the angry gray sky, and around me, to nothing but green, wild countryside I'm sure I would marvel at if I were seeing it from the safety of a car window.

I take a breath and push a wet thumb on his name.

"Hello."

"Eliot. It's me. I'm lost. I'm lost and it's pouring with rain and I have no—"

"Lost?"

"I—I was at Marie's mum and dad's . . . and I left and started walking, and everywhere I go, there are just trees and fields and burnt-out barns and so many bloody *cows*, and I just keep walking and walking, but—"

"Okay, okay, hold up. You went to Marie's parents'?"

"Yes. For a party. Marie's birthday."

"Okay, and did you turn left or right when you came out of there?"

"Left. Definitely left."

"Okay, and when did you leave?"

"I don't know, about twenty minutes ago? Half an hour? I know I'm an idiot, Eliot, but I thought I'd find a little village or town or a bus stop or something and . . . *oh my god.* Lightning. Fucking lightning. Like . . . Scooby-Doo fork lightning. *Shit.*"

I am sure I hear Eliot laugh, but the rain is so loud and the line so tinny that I say nothing besides, "Can you come and get me?"

"Already in the truck, Emmie," he says. "Can you see anything where you are?"

I swing around. "No. No. Just trees and bushes and fields and . . ."

"Cows. Yeah, you said. Anything else? Remember seeing anything of interest on your walk down, so I know roughly where you are?"

I look up and down the winding country lane. "No," I say. "Just trees and—"

"Don't tell me about the cows again," laughs Eliot. "Look, I'll be there soon, okay? Just don't move, no more walking, stay back from the road—"

"Turbine!"

"What?"

"A-About five minutes ago I walked past a massive wind turbine. Three of them. Massive, fuck-off wind turbines, and they were on my . . . my left. Yes, my left."

"Okay, stay put. I'll be as fast as I can. Put your phone away. It'll get wet."

Only two cars pass me in the twenty minutes it takes Eliot to get to me. I could have sunk to my knees with relief at the sight of his truck speeding down the narrow country lane, if I wasn't so soaked to the bone, my legs shaking. He pulls up, braking sharply, and leans to throw open the passenger door. I jump in, sinking against the seat. Warm air that smells of old dust, like the old electric fire Mum would put on in the winter, pumps through the fans on the dash, and an Oasis song hums softly through the radio. I look up at Eliot. He pulls his face into a sad grimace, deep brown eyes on me. "What're we going to do with you, eh, Emmie Blue?"

I lift my shoulders weakly to my ears. "Put me in the dryer?" I sniff, my voice tiny and pathetic. Eliot smiles, leans down, and pulls two fluffy white towels from a gym bag at my feet.

"The next best thing," he says, unfolding them with one hand and gesturing for me to lean forward. I do. He tucks one around me and wraps it around my shoulders.

"Get as dry as you can," he says, and I simply nod as he begins to drive.

Neither of us says much for a good ten minutes. Eliot fiddles with the heaters in the car, placing his hand over them to test the temperature, and sings softly along to the radio, not breaking out of the song even when waving to give way to people, fingers tapping the wheel. I am enveloped in towels, my head leaning back on the truck's soft, sawdust-speckled seat. I like Eliot's truck. It reminds me of Den's jumpers. Always dotted with crusts of wood and debris from work. The jumpers he'd lift at the hem to put his hand in his pocket and pull out a Picnic bar or a seaside fudge.

Eliot drives and drives, and I warm, quickly, beside him on the passenger seat. I'm exhausted, and my head doesn't feel as light now that the cold and rainy light of day has sobered me up.

"Thank you for coming to get me," I say into the quiet of the truck. We are pulled up in a car park now, a takeaway coffee thawing my hands, the rain still pinging against the glass of the windshield.

Eliot nods slowly. "Anytime."

"Were you busy?"

He shrugs and gives a smile, a flash of straight teeth. "I was only at Mum's. Working on the bandstand."

"God, I'm sorry."

"No, don't be. It started raining anyway, so your timing was actually on the nose." He turns to me. "What happened? Shit party?"

I give a laugh, look down at my lap. "No. No, it wasn't a shit party. It just . . . I dunno . . ." I trail off, remembering Ana. *Eliot's* Ana. And I look at him. His handsome face, those confident brown eyes, the towel at my shoulders he wrapped around me caringly, and I can't help but feel bafflement that they are together. Ana, so cold, so unfriendly. And Eliot . . . he's kind. He's funny. Warm. *Safe.* One of those people who would be really nice to have around if the world suddenly got the news of an imminent apocalypse. I trust him. I do. I suppose I'd have to, at least a little, to call him, to ask him to come and pick me up today, over Lucas.

"Do you ever feel like—like everyone else has it figured out and you don't?"

Eliot hesitates, thinks, tapping the wheel with the heel of his hand.

"Do you mean Luke?" he asks.

"No," I say, shaking my head. "Why would I mean Lucas?"

He gives a gentle shrug, looks down at his hands on the wheel. "I guess because you two are so close, and, well, he's getting married. That must be . . . hard for you."

I say nothing, lift a shoulder to my ear.

Eliot takes a deep breath. "Look, I remember I used to be one of those people. That appeared to have it all. Perfect life, perfect wife, perfect *plans*." He looks at me then, a little smirk. "And I didn't actually have any of that. Sure looked like it, though. But all of it—it was over in a heartbeat. Shit, I even had to piss off to Canada to sort my life out. Shut off. Heal."

"Pull your head out of your arse," I say, remembering the conversation we had at the dessert party, and he smiles. "Yeah," he says. "And that's what a lot of it is. How it *appears*. They're probably just as lost as everyone else is behind closed doors."

I look at him. "I wish I could feel sure about that."

"Take it from me, Emmie," he says softly.

I look at him, and he starts to laugh. "What?"

Eliot stretches to pull down my sun visor, to reveal a tiny, blurred mirror with a little pointless light above it. I look into it. There are black smudges all over my eyes, and little dots of mascara hanging off my lashes. "Oh my *God*. I look like Ozzy Osbourne."

Eliot laughs, elbow resting on the armrest between us, hand at his chin. "I mean, I'm not one to usually agree with you on this stuff, but you actually do. Feeling a bit starstruck here."

"Shut up."

Eliot hesitates, looks at me. There's a beat of silence. "Sort of wanna ask you where you came up with the concept for the *Technical Ecstasy* album—hey!"

"Shut up or I'll hit you again," I laugh, wetting my finger and smudging it under my eyes. It does nothing but make it worse. I stare at my reflection. "Oh, I give up," I say, pushing the sun visor back up and slouching back in my chair, the side of my face resting on the fabric of the headrest. "God," I sigh, looking at him. "If the girls in that room could see me now, they would be thinking *what the fuck*."

Eliot smiles gently, eyelids closing momentarily, then opening. "Who cares?"

"And then I'm sure someone would chime in about how that was when her boyfriend first knew he was in love with her. When she had makeup smudged all over her face like Ozzy Osbourne and looked like a wet spaniel after fleeing a birthday party."

Eliot's dark eyebrows knit together. "Is that the sort of stuff that's discussed at parties these days, then?"

"It was at this one," I say, sniffing, nose still running from the cold, wet weather I was caught in. "Your Ana was there. She instigated it actually, that conversation, so she is clearly very happy with you. Nice work on the candles and the bath last Sunday, by the way. Very eighties music video." Even I am shocked by the bitter twang in my voice.

"Well," Eliot says, ever cool, ever calm, his mouth opening as if to speak, but instead, his lips turning into a smile of disbelief. "Not sure I remember this romantic, eighties-music-video bath, but do go on. The party sounds like a fuckin' *hoot*."

I laugh, groan into my hands. "Oh, dunno," I sigh. "I just felt . . . *lonely*. That's what it was. Among all those people, those happy, together women, with these full lives and anecdotes and stories and . . . the fucking people behind them, you know? The wonderful people who love them unconditionally, who just take their faults and accept them. *Love* them, even. And I suddenly realized . . . I had absolutely nothing to add."

Eliot pauses, as if considering my words, eyes narrowed. "But nobody, regardless of what they say, has a totally full and perfect, flawless life, Emmie."

"No?" I look down, away from his unwavering gaze, conversations from that room with the baby grand echoing through my mind, fit to burst. "Helen back there, said she quit her job," I tell Eliot, "without even consulting her husband because she was so miserable, and they had *no* money and she just quit, and Alan, well, she was really nervous about telling him because of all the debt they had, but he said, *my flower*—she said he actually said *flower*—"

"Right . . ."

"He said, you go for it. It'll be hard but I will make it work, and I will sell my *balls* to make sure you're achieving your dreams."

Eliot bursts out laughing, his mouth open, like a goldfish, trying to find the words to interrupt, but I carry on, to desperately make my point. "And then Beatrice—Beatrice said she had a terrible fear of heights but climbed Snowdonia with her girlfriend anyway, because she knew how much her girlfriend wanted to do it. She even proposed at the top."

"I see, but—"

"She shook the entire way up, Eliot, like a dog on firework night, and had to have beta blockers and everything. But she did it and, God, imagine! Imagine having someone that *does that* for you. I can't even comprehend it."

Eliot folds his strong forearms at his chest, stretching his legs forward, and looks at me, head resting back on the seat. "Emmie, there are plenty of people who—"

"And Amy," I carry on, light-headed from the champagne and woozy from the exhaustion of walking for miles in the rain. Eliot's eyes lift to the ceiling, and he smiles to himself as if he's given up. "She broke her nose and damaged her back coming down some stairs at a train station. She couldn't even shit unaided. Her nose . . . it looked like a fucking tomato. A blighted tomato, Eliot. I saw the photographs."

"Jesus Christ," Eliot laughs. "Well, it could've been worse, I suppose."

"Could it?" I ask.

"A celeriac," he muses. "A butternut squash . . ."

"And do you know," I laugh but carry on, ignoring him, "what her boyfriend did? He *kissed* her nose. Her blighted tomato nose, and helped her wipe her arse. Several times, for weeks."

Eliot lets out a noisy breath, his dark hair bristling. "Fucking hell, Emmie," he says. "I thought you were meant to be going to a party. Are you absolutely sure you didn't walk onto the set of the *Sally Jessy Raphael Show*?"

I laugh, snottily, from a million swallowed-down tears, and look over at him in the driver's seat. "You're so nineties. They don't make Sally anymore," I tell him.

"Probably why people are sharing their sob stories at parties instead."

I smile at him weakly. "I dunno," I sigh. "Just all of them had these people behind them. These people who are saying, *flower*, I support you and accept you, and even though you're a wreck, I'm here, through it all." I pause, swallowing down a lump in my throat. "And what have I got? A job I'm too scared to go for. A dad that's lived under my nose all my life and yet, doesn't want to know me. And it hurts. And Lucas. Well, that's just . . ." I stop then, look up at him, and he waits, watching me.

"That's what?" he asks, words barely there.

And I want to. I want to talk to him about it, because if I am a closed book, unreadable as Rosie says sometimes, then Eliot is an open book. Not so much that he gives everything away, it's more in the way he is, the way he carries himself. Eye contact. Arms open. Shoulders relaxed. As if nobody and nothing can faze him and he has nothing to hide, and it's infectious. It is. It makes me want to tell him everything. But I can't bring myself to.

"I guess I just felt out of place there, today, that's all," I say instead. "I looked at everyone in that room, with families and partners and plans and good jobs and houses and kids, these nice, designer dresses and gifts—" I look down at my wet jeans, the old, squelching sandals, the towel around me, and bring a knuckle to my eye, crusted with dry-again mascara. "*God.* Look at me," I say, voice cracking. "Just look at me."

Eliot stares at me. And softly, into the silence of the car, he says, "I am."

The rain slows, and Eliot takes a breath, brings his hand to his mouth. "I'm thirty-three next week, Emmie," he says. "My dad was thirty-three when he died, and from what people have told me, the dude spent every waking moment working his arse off to fit in. To pay off the mortgage. To get the next best car. Holidays. Loft extensions. Worked to the bone, to have everything he thought he should have. Probably because he was looking at people like you are, thinking they had it all compared to him."

I stare at Eliot, my heart thumping.

"And at thirty-three, that was it. Heart gave out, all over. And nobody once talked about the money he'd saved, the car he had, the holidays he took. They just talked about him, Emmie. Missed *him*. For what he was. Because that was enough."

A lump sits in my throat, my nostrils sting with tears that fall, heavy, and slow, drop by drop into my lap.

"And you're enough, Emmie, without all that. Trust me."

After a while, the pair of us in silence, listening to the steady, slowing raindrops, the rumbling of passing cars, Eliot starts the engine.

"Come on then, flower," he says, clearing his throat. "Let's get you back."

Mix CD. Vol. 5.

Dear Balloon Girl,

Track 1. *Because you see the good in people*

Track 2. *Because I will always find it hilarious that you fancy seventy-year-old Dick Van Dyke*

Track 3. *Because you said you'd never heard of Eva Cassidy*

Track 4. *Because one Eva is never enough*

Track 5. *Because one day, I will tell you*

Balloon Boy

X

22

I feel as though I have been yanked out of 2018 and been plonked back into 2006. Lucas and I are on the sofa of his mum and dad's large, modern lounge, and he is flicking through the hundreds of movies on Netflix, as we fail to agree on a single one. The pillar candles in the fireplace are lit, the main lights off, and the two lamps on either side of the sofa both burn a soft amber light. Between us is a bowl of popcorn, and another big mixing bowl of random bags of chocolate and sweets. Whereas in 2006 it would have likely been glasses of Coke—or beer, if his parents were out—tonight we have lime-green cocktails Lucas rustled up at the bar in Jean's study, and covering us is a gray, heavy, faux-fur blanket. Just like we used to. The nostalgia is intensified even more by the sounds of Eliot's music in the kitchen, too, and him passing the living room door every now and then, phone in his hand, eyes lifting from the screen to eye us both, as he used to back then, as if he couldn't quite work us out, and was always expecting to catch us up to something. He'd always join us, though, lifting the blanket and slumping on the end, putting his arm around us and saying jokingly, "Don't mind me. Just pass the food this way." I missed it when Eliot stopped coming in to sit with us. When he stopped coming over to visit with the Moreaus, or when he stopped jumping in the car to wave me off at the ferry. It's nice to have him back.

"Why does everything you want to watch have a photo of a man in sunglasses or a random moored boat on a misty dock?" I say, looking up at the screen.

Lucas laughs. "And why has everything you want to watch never been released at the cinema?"

"Mm-mm." I shake my head, swallowing a mouthful of drink. "Not true."

"Is," says Lucas, leg bent on the sofa, wrist resting on his knee, remote in his other hand. "Case in point, *The Leading Man.*"

I laugh. "You only ever bring that one up. Plus, Thandie Newton was in that, and you love her."

"Well, she was dicked over with that one. A movie starring Bon Jovi—"

"*Jon* Bon Jovi."

"And all he does is hide in the streets like a shit Columbo, shagging people's wives."

"Sounds like a dream, to be honest," I say. "You've sold it to me. Let's watch it again."

"No."

"*Please.*"

"Twice was enough," Lucas laughs, then selects a film with Tom Cruise, and before he can say anything, I am shaking my head.

"No," I say.

"Fucking hell, we're going to be here all day."

Eliot pokes his head around the door, leaning against the white, glossed frame, a smile on his face. He looks at me from under dark lashes, then the TV screen above the fireplace, and says, "And why is there not a Jon Bon Jovi movie playing on that screen?"

Lucas turns at the sound of his brother's voice and says, "Because I'd like to watch something that was released this decade, El." Lucas and Eliot have grown closer again since Eliot's divorce and he moved back in with

Lucas and their parents for a while a couple of years ago, before he went to work with his friend Mark, in Canada. And while I'm not sure it's what it used to be when we were kids, it's nice to see them together again, around the house, laughing, stupid in-jokes and brotherly piss-taking.

Eliot looks at me and smiles. He lifts his chin. "Did you ever see *U-571*?"

I tut. "Of *course*. He played Pete Emmett *finely*."

"*Lieutenant* Pete Emmett, I think you'll find," corrects Eliot, and I laugh. "Okay, how about *Pucked*? Did you see that?"

"*Pucked*? No?"

"Sounds *fucked*," Lucas mumbles beside me, and when I turn to look at him, he's staring at the television screen, straight-ahead, eyes narrowed in concentration as if he said nothing at all.

"Yep," says Eliot folding his arms. "He's the lead. Plays the bad boy. Hair's wild and all rock star-y. Totally your sort of thing."

"Seriously?" I laugh. "And I haven't seen it?"

"Seems not," laughs Eliot. "Call yourself a fan, Emmie."

"Well, I guess I know what I'm ordering on Amazon when I get home— oh!" I turn to Lucas, beside me on the sofa. "Unless it's on Netflix."

"Nope," says Lucas, still not looking away from the screen. "No results for . . . *Pucked*." He says "Pucked" as if he's making fun of it, as if he doesn't quite believe that's its name, but he doesn't smile.

"It might be under National Lampoon—" starts Eliot, before Lucas looks at him, shrugs, and says, "No results." Then turns back to the screen. Eliot raises his eyebrows at me, and I smile, stifle laughter behind the blanket over my knees. It reminds me of the times Lucas would get in a mood, and Eliot and I would share secret awkward smiles, wondering which girl had dumped him this week, or what menial thing Jean had pulled him up on: dirty towels in the bathroom, an A grade instead of an A-plus.

"Well, I suppose I'll be making tracks now," Eliot says, pushing off from the doorframe. "You kids have fun."

"Making tracks," I repeat, and Eliot laughs, folding his arms. Rosie is right. Eliot *does* have really nice arms. She used my phone to scroll through his Instagram last week. "Fit," she'd said, scrolling. "Super fit. Hot. *So god-damn tall.*"

"What?" asks Eliot. "Is that *so nineties* too?"

"Making tracks." I nod. "A bit."

"See you then, mate," cuts in Lucas with a wave and a tight, close-mouthed smile, his eyes widening for a second as if to say, "We're actually really busy here, sort of in the middle of something." "Enjoy your dinner," he carries on. "Say hi to Ana for us."

Eliot smiles, amused. "I'm not going with Ana, actually, but . . . thanks." Then he nods at me. "Have a good evening, Ozzy—I mean Emmie."

Moments later, as I am drinking my cocktail, I realize Lucas is staring at me, eyes burning into me.

"What?"

He gives a tight shrug. "El was a bit . . . overfriendly."

"Was he?" I laugh. My ears burn as they always do, preblush, and I'm glad my hair is long enough now to hide them. "What do you mean?"

"I mean, joking about with you, stampeding in on our conversation, going on about Bon Jovi being in all those films and *ha-ha, you haven't seen that one, oh dear, Emmie, maybe we should watch it together sometime . . .*"

"*Jon* Bon Jovi." I nudge him. "And he wasn't being overfriendly, he was just being Eliot, he was being—"

"Emmie, my brother has barely spoken to you in years and suddenly you're what, *best mates?*"

It would be obvious to anyone with even a single drunken, dancing brain cell that he's jealous. Lucas would get like this sometimes, and admittedly, so did I. Territorial in our friendship, especially if one of us made a new friend. "I've heard a lot about this *Fox*. You trading me up?" Lucas's jealousy is partly protective, though, I think, and with Eliot, I understand why.

"We're just catching up," I say. "And to be fair, I haven't really seen *that* much of him. Yes, he gave me a lift today from Marie's, but only because the taxi didn't show up and I knew you were at work—" That was the lie I had told Lucas, about what happened after leaving Marie's party, and he'd annoyedly told me to call him next time.

"And he took you to your dad's too."

I look at him. I'd told Luke about Marv on the journey up from Calais, when he picked me up from the ferry. I hadn't said anything about Eliot being the one that took me.

Lucas nods once. "So, I'm right."

"Did he tell you?"

"No. He canceled suit shopping, and I couldn't get hold of you. And after that"—he points at the doorway, and then to me—"I guessed."

I feel oddly attacked. As if I'm being accused of something. My cheeks are burning now, as well as my ears, and my shoulders are tense, up by the side of my face. "But what does it matter?" I say. "He offered. He knew about the cards and he knew how much it was playing on my mind, and—I said yes. So I didn't have to go alone." What I want to say is, "Well, you didn't offer, did you, like you would have done once upon a time? You haven't been over once in seven months, to see where I work those ten-hour shifts, the burns on my fingers, to see how much I've changed the sweltering, dusty room I live in since I moved in. To go to the pub with me, the beach for a day, wander around my little town, like we do yours."

Lucas draws in a deep breath, hangs his head, and covers his face with a hand. "Maybe I'm being a dick," he says.

"A bit of a jealous dick, yeah."

He looks up at me between his fingers. I smile, and so does he. "I've got ye olde friendship jealousy, haven't I?"

"You do. Do you need me to tell you that you're still my best friend? Make you a little friendship bracelet?"

Lucas laughs, groans into his hand. "God, I'm sorry, Em." He looks up, dropping the hand from his face. His hand lands on mine. "I am. And I know I haven't really been there like I should, lately. And I wish I'd been there today. To put Ana in her place. Uptight bitch." I spun Lucas an enhanced truth; told him it was Ana that made me feel uncomfortable yesterday. I didn't mention anything else. The montage. The feeling empty and lonely.

Lucas pauses, eyes on mine. A silver pendulum clock ticks on the mantelpiece, the TV screen dims from inactivity. "I'm sorry if I've been too wrapped up in the wedding stuff," he says quietly. "But it's mammoth, you know, Em. It's all this pressure and it feels fucking *massive*."

"I know, Luke."

"But I'm here right now. Me, you, sitting here, films, blankets, your obscure, weird suggestions . . ." He laughs, gray eyes scrunching, his hand drifting up to touch my arm, then higher, thumb brushing my cheek. "It's like it's always been."

I look at him. I say nothing.

"I'm scared shit's changing," he says quietly, hand drifting from my face.

"It *is* changing, Luke," I say gently. "You're getting married. You're—"

"But it doesn't have to. Not completely. Not totally." He's looking at me now, and it feels just like it did outside the bar. That heavy, almost tangible pull, the swelling clouds of unsaid things bowing, sagging above us, threatening to spill out.

"I've missed you."

"I've not gone anywhere, Lucas," I say, and he says, "I know."

I put my arms around him before anything else spills free, and when usually I feel like he's holding me up, this time, I feel like it's me holding him.

We choose a film, something neither of us have heard of, and before it starts, Lucas says he'll go and refill our drinks. At the doorway on his way out, he stops.

"I'm glad we talked," he says. "And you know I'm just looking out for you, don't you?"

When he leaves the room, I think about Eliot. And I think about the night that it changed between us three.

Had I forgotten? Had I forgotten just how much that night hurt me? How tall I was standing, after all those months of hard work, until that night where Eliot told my biggest and most soul-destroying secret to his girlfriend, who used it as a disgusting, cheap laugh? He's never said sorry, has he? He's never once brought it up, the night everything changed. Never ever said sorry. Maybe I'd feel better if he did. Or maybe, to him, it was nothing. "No big deal" as he always says. "Life's too short, Em."

Lucas returns, two lime-green cocktails refilled.

"Shift over," he says. "You're hogging the blanket."

23

The movie credits roll, the black screen with white text darkening the lightless room. I look to my left. Yep. He's asleep. Lucas is out for the count, head lolled to one side, his breathing slow and deep.

Eliot, squished next to me, whispers, "He asleep?"

I nod. "Out like a light."

"Ah," he says, smile in his voice. "Wore himself out. Little love."

I giggle, turn to look at him, but can just about make out Eliot's face, his head leaned lazily back on the sofa, smirk on his lips, his long legs straight out in front of him, the blanket only covering him up to the knees.

"What's the time?"

Eliot shrugs. "Late."

"Unhelpful," I whisper, pulling my legs up to my chest and the blanket to my neck. The thought of moving from beneath this warm, cozy nook on the sofa, beside softly sleeping Luke, the lights out, and walking to the bottom of the dark garden to the guest cottage, is totally unappealing.

"So, I guess we're all sleeping here, then," says Eliot with a yawn, flicking the TV off.

"Mhmm. Can't be arsed to move."

"Ditto."

"Just don't snore," I say, and lean my head against the sofa. We're face-to-face, inches apart, but I can hardly see him in the darkness, just the peak of his nose, the edges of his eyelashes, caught in the light of a glass candle on the coffee table.

"I don't snore, cheers," says Eliot, voice low. "I'm an elegant sleeper. Like a little wood sprite."

I laugh, blanket over my mouth. I'm so tired and so sleepy that I feel drunk. My eyes adjust, and I can just see Eliot's mouth, a lazy smile at one edge, his eyes sleepy slits.

"You look weird in the dark," I whisper.

"Thanks, Em."

"You don't have a nose."

"I assure you I do."

I laugh again, and Eliot takes my hand under the blanket. "What are you—" He brings my hand up to his face.

"See," he says, pressing my fingers to his warm face. "Nose."

"Ah yes," I whisper. "A fine, functional, if slightly oversized feature."

"You still talking about my nose?"

I explode into stupid, sleep-drunk giggles under the blanket, and Eliot laughs deeply, quietly, and says, "Shhhhh."

There's silence then, and I close my eyes. Eliot still has my hand. Safe. Warm.

I don't realize I've begun floating off, into sleep, until I keep coming to, as if on a merry-go-round, passing consciousness every few moments, and it's then that I'm aware of Eliot's thumb stroking my knuckles. I'm woken awhile later, to silence, to Lucas's leg, hot and heavy against mine, to Eliot kissing my forehead, and leaving the room.

L ouise lies back, her eyes closed, as if she's listening to a beautiful piece of music and not me, reading from a book with old pages the color of hay.

"What do you think?" asks Louise, her fingers laced together in her lap, a ring on every knuckle. "Will she go back for him?"

"The dressmaker?"

Louise nods, eyes still closed, head tilted back on the velvet of her armchair.

"Yes," I say. "I think she will. I think she'll realize that although she wanted this job in Germany, she isn't happy without him and . . . what?" I stop, book in my lap. "I'm wrong, aren't I?"

Louise smirks. "I'm not saying a word about whether you're wrong or right, Emmie, but I'm just wondering why you don't think *he* will come and find *her*."

I pause, and smile. She's good at this, Louise. At asking questions you've never considered. "I don't know. Good question."

"Why should she leave her dream job," she says, "to go after him? Why can't he go after her?"

"Consider me told."

Louise smiles, brown eyes glittering. "Do you have time to read to the end of the chapter?"

"I do," I tell her. "There'll even be time for a cup of tea before my shift too."

Louise nods happily, and I carry on. This is something we have been doing ever since that day I found Louise in bed unable to get up, which have multiplied over the last few weeks. Those days, where she can only get downstairs to the sofa, or the conservatory, where she stays most of the day, or worse, when she stays in bed, seem to be ever-increasing, and when they arise, I do what I can for her. She is fiercely independent, though, preferring to do something that may take someone able like me only five seconds, even if it takes her hours. But I like that about her. She's strong. She needs no validation.

"I don't need company," she once said to me, but I think that is a belief she is slowly shedding. We talk now. Nonstop, actually, and even eat dinner together most nights. The gap in the bridge between us is closing, and I like the way it feels. I never thought I cared, but it's so nice coming home to someone who wants to hear about your day. It throws me, though, and Louise has made me promise that I will no longer apologize for simply speaking. So many times I have found myself going off on a tangent, telling her about a funny customer at work, or something hilarious Fox and Rosie argued about, or about France, and then stopping and saying, "Sorry. I know this is probably really boring for you."

"Boring?"

"Yes. Me, harping on about things that don't really matter, people you don't really know."

And Louise has looked at me every time, her wrinkled brow furrowing, and said, "That is called a conversation, is it not, Emmie? How relationships are made, slowly sharing pieces of yourself, in turn?"

And I try to remember that. That Mum and her rolling eyes and sighing when I would come home from school, desperate to tell her about my day, my new friend, the funny thing that happened in PE, or the band Georgia's mum was taking us to see, anything I'd seen or experienced that felt important enough to say aloud, was not how any person, especially not a mother, should react to another human being doing what Louise called it—sharing a piece of themselves. It was heartless, really, I know that now. And sad more than anything. But I wonder, even now, after sitting here with Louise for almost two hours, if I will ever shake the feeling that I am sharing too much of myself, boring the other person to tears, so in turn, draw back. Close my book, as Eliot would rightly say.

Eliot. I haven't seen him since that night I sat with Lucas and watched movies, like old times. It's been about four weeks now. We've texted a few times, but there's something about what Lucas said that night about looking out for me—that reminder of what happened on our nineteenth birthday—that has sent my barriers up again, like the sides of a cage.

I click on the kettle, the book on the kitchen counter beside me, the place in it marked with a pointed plant label stick.

The doorbell sounds.

"I'll get it," I call out to Louise, and when I pass the lounge, I see that despite being in a lot of pain today, with her back and legs, she was shuffling back into her seat where she had tried to get up and see to it herself.

I swing open the door of Two Fishers Way, the dust of the porch dances in the sunlight that floods in.

"Emmeline," Marv says from the doorstep, the jiffy bag of cards in his hand. "I was wondering if we could have a chat."

I make Marv wait outside while I make a tea for Louise, and make sure that there is a sandwich in the fridge for her, covered in foil, ready for her lunch, later. I get changed into my work uniform, my hands shaking with nerves, and when I go outside, I tell Marv I have only fifteen minutes.

"You can walk with me to work," I tell him, and as much as I will my voice to sound strong, it wobbles.

He smiles at me, sadly, almost embarrassed, and nods. "I'd like that."

We walk, both of us avoiding each other's gaze, and instead looking at the houses that line Fishers Way—large and Victorian, bay windows, gravel drives—and the knobbly oak trees that border the street. A mother wanders by, holding a waddling toddler's hand. Marv smiles at her, and it's then that I catch a look at him. A proper look, looking with the eyes of someone who is trying to recognize themselves in something. When he smiles, his eyes crinkle, the eyelashes fanning together, crisscrossing. In photos that have caught me mid-laugh, my fair eyelashes look exactly the same.

"I'm really sorry about what happened, Emmeline," he says, "when you stopped by."

"Emmie," I say.

"Ah. You prefer Emmie."

I nod. "I do. Insist on it, really. Without sounding too much like an idiot."

"No, I think that's fair. If you want to be called something, then that is your right." He nods, slotting his hands in the pockets of his jeans. He talks like a teacher. Well-spoken, authoritative. "Plus, Emmie is nice. I like it."

I don't say anything, steeling myself. I am ready. I am ready for an explanation of why he can't see me. I don't want one. The fact he doesn't is enough for me, and no explanation he pulls from the recesses of his brain to justify it will make it better. I'm his child. What excuse could there be?

"I was—I think I was in shock the other day, when you turned up with your pal."

"I was too," I say. "Even more so. You knew. I never did."

"I can imagine, sweetheart," he says warmly, and I feel shame at the way my heart twangs. *Sweetheart.* I have a dad and he's calling me "sweetheart," like all the dads do in books and on the TV shows I used to watch as a teenager. "I—see, I have a wife. Carol. We've been together for thirty-one years. Married for twenty-eight."

"You and Mum had an affair."

His eyes close momentarily. "I don't want to hurt anyone's feelings here, but I think it's best I'm honest." He takes a deep breath. "But I wouldn't even call it that. Sorry, Emmie. Well, I'm not of course, for me, but for you, a . . . *one off* doesn't sound very nice."

"I always knew I was the result of a one off," I tell him. "Well. That's what Mum told me. It was one romantic night—"

I see his eyes lift at that and he says, "It was one night. I was in the pub with a few mates. She was there. Katherine. I don't remember much about it. I'm . . . so sorry, that sounds dreadful, but well, that's how it was."

I pause, adjust the bag on my shoulder and look up, to the sea that appears in the distance as we round the leafy corner of Fishers Way.

"It's fine," I say. "I didn't expect candlelight and music." Except, I did. I would dream up the night they met sometimes. Dad, with his drumsticks, hair sweaty from the stage, him locking eyes with my beautiful mother across the sludgy grass of the festival, drawn to her, and unbeknownst to him, for a special reason. *For me.* So I could be born. A miracle result of timing and genetics and science in a tiny window of time, that resulted in my life. Not a local pub. Not a spoken-for man.

"Carol and I had been together over a year, and—it wasn't really serious, but it was getting that way, and . . ." Marv shakes his head. "Aye, I was just young and bloody stupid, that's what I was."

We walk for a while, and I ask him about his family. He has Carol. They struggled to conceive for years, but he tells me they had a daughter eventually, and that is when I stop in the street, feet frozen to the spot. "I have a sister," I say. "A half sister. I actually have a—" I can't speak.

"Yes," says Marv, his eyes shining. "Cadie. She's eighteen. At university."

"Studying?"

"Law."

I blow out a breath. "God. Wow," I say, voice breaking. "I have a sister who is studying law at university."

Marv chuckles.

We walk down to the seafront, ambling along slowly, past the sand, and moored up paddleboats on the beach, and shuttered ice cream kiosks, their stickered menus, discolored and sun-bleached.

"I remember," I tell him, "that you'd pick me up and we'd walk like this, but I wasn't allowed to mention it to Mum, or it'd make her jealous she'd missed it. That's what Den would tell me. And I only ever wanted to keep her happy."

"I knew about you, Emmie," he says. "I wanted immediately to be involved, to be a father to you. But Katherine—your mother—she shut me out. As soon as I told her about Carol and that it was a mistake, she shut me out completely. I came to find you when I knew you'd been born. News traveled fast in that pub. Not there anymore. The George it was called. And she refused to let me in. I tried all the time, I really did. And one day, Den answered the door." He smiles when he mentions Den, his eyes cloudy, and I feel my heart lift at the sound of his name coming from someone else's lips. "He let me in. He didn't agree with what your mother was doing. And as much as he loved her, he also loved you. He felt you needed your father, and mostly, I think he felt I should know you too. He came on every outing, though, the man. Hovering in the background, keeping an eye on you . . ."

"He left us," I say, and my throat swells as I hear the words.

"No, darling," says Marv. "He left your mum. Not you."

"But he never came back to see me. Neither did you."

"He tried," Marv says pleadingly. "He really did. But what right did he have? An ex of your mum's wasn't exactly going to get him access, was it, to a seven-, eight-year-old girl who wasn't his own?"

I can feel it now, anger rumbling beneath the surface of my skin. Mum. Mum stopped me being loved. She *made* me lonely. I could have had Den in my life. I could have had a father in my life. But instead I had nobody. I had her, but I didn't, not really. She left. Every month she'd leave for a weekend, and as I got older, turned fourteen, then fifteen, they increased, until weeks would go by until I'd see her again. Off touring. Off pretending as though she didn't have a child that needed her at home. I had Georgia, too, of course, and her family. I had him. Robert. The person I held as Dream Father in my mind. I shudder and gulp down tears and anger about it all, and I feel Marv's hand touch my arm. When I don't move, he moves, hesitantly, to put his arm around me, and we stand looking out to sea for a while. I enjoy the weight of his arm. I enjoy the warmth. "My dad," I want to say to passersby. "This is my dad."

"Your mum never forgave me," says Marv, "for never telling her about Carol. But it was a mistake. I messed up, aye, like all human beings do. I was a young lad, really. But that doesn't mean you should be defined by that mistake for your whole life, Emmie."

I nod, and I let those words stay there, in the air, to sink into me slowly. "I know," I say. "I know."

"And I'd like to see you," he says. "I know I've missed a lot, but . . . I'd like to build . . . *something.*"

"Me too," I say.

"But you need to give me some time, Emmie. I need to speak with Carol; with Cadie."

I look to my side at him, spidery veins broken beneath the skin of his face, lips purply, quivering ever so slightly, and I nod. "Time," I say. "Okay. I understand."

We say nothing more for a while, walking slowly, side by side to the

Clarice. I know, for the first time in my whole life, that I am late, but I don't care.

At the foot of the stairs of the Clarice's entrance, I give Marv my phone number, and he says he will call me.

"Fancy place, this, isn't it?" He looks up at the grand entrance of the hotel, his eyes squinting in the autumnal sun. "They treat you well?"

"They do. Money isn't great but . . ."

"They treat you well." He smiles.

"Exactly."

"Well, that's all that matters."

Marv puts his arms around me again when we say goodbye, his body warm under the shirt and thick fleece he wears, and he pats my back twice with his hand.

When I get into the Clarice, Fox doesn't mention the fact I am ten minutes late, and instead, puts his arm around me and leads me outside. "Nonsmoking fag break before we do anything, Ms. Emmie Blue. You *have* to hear about Rosie's date. You'll be laughing for the next seven centuries."

And as I stand listening to Rosie's horror story of a date gone bad, and Fox shoots me knowing looks over his cigarette, and Rosie holds on to my arm, laughter doubling her over, I think of Marv. My dad. And I realize I don't feel lonely. In this moment, the empty loneliness that has always followed me around like a chasm, ready to eat me whole, is simply not there.

I feel loved.

25

I have never seen Louise laugh as much as she is laughing tonight. Her cheeks are red and her eyes are slits and she keeps holding her chest, as if it's hurting her too much. She's eaten really well, too, and I only say that because the last couple of weeks I have noticed that half of the sandwiches I make her end up in the food waste box, curling at the edges, and the soup she makes herself sits mostly uneaten in a bowl, the foil never removed. She says her appetite suffers some days, but other times she's ravenous. This condition she has—one she refuses to talk about really—is erratic with its symptoms. Good days and bad days.

Eliot, beside me, holds the bowing aluminum case of cheesecake, its creamy topping slopped across the base, and rogue biscuit crumbs, rolling. "More for you, Louise?"

Louise shakes her head. "Absolutely not. But thank you."

"I might have to," he says, looking at me. "How about you? It was bangin', wasn't it?"

"Bangin'," I repeat.

"What?" he laughs.

"Nothing." I smile. "Just *bangin'*. Haven't heard that in a while. And yes. Do it. Ladle me up."

Eliot laughs and scoops us both a messy spoonful of cheesecake, then pours on more cream than I would have poured myself. He hands me the bowl with a smile.

"Gosh, I miss being your age," says Louise, opposite us, across the oil-clothed table. "Being young. Being able to eat whatever I wanted without being up half the night with a box of antacids. Being, oh, I don't know." She looks at me, her index finger and thumb pinching the stem of her wine-glass. "Young and beautiful."

"I don't know about that," I laugh.

"I do," says Louise, and she holds my gaze. Eliot looks to his side at me, then at Louise, and laughs. "Ah, come on, I'm waiting."

"For?"

"For you to tell me how beautiful *I* am, Louise. How young and handsome . . ."

Louise lifts her glass with a skinny, veiny hand and, before sipping, says, "You aren't too bad. Although you need a haircut."

"And to stop wearing Justin Timberlake's hats," I tease, and he laughs and says, "It was *one time*. It was hot. It was *sunny*."

This is the fifth time we've done this in two months, Eliot joining Louise and me for dinner. Things have been settled—cozy—for the last few weeks. Quiet, even. Lucas has been working a lot but has decided on a suit. Marie's been away on business with her dad, and has found her dress (and so have I). I've booked a pop-punk band for the STEN party, and its group chat has fizzled to only the odd weekly text. I've been working a lot at the Clarice, too, the shifts busier than ever before now that we're a few weeks from Christmas. And every break I take has been spent helping Rosie take photos, as her Instagram following multiplies by the second. Eliot coming for dinner has become part of Louise's and my weekly routine. And it's the time I look forward to every week. The first time he came over was the evening after Marv and I walked to the Clarice together. I'd called Eliot and invited him over for pizza, with Louise and me, and he had come over that night brandishing a bottle of white wine, a four-pack of beer, and a giant chocolate gateau. Every time he comes, it's the sort of evening that whisks by, the hours flowing, disappearing like water, and every time he leaves, I instantly think about when I can ask him to come next. Eliot is *easy*. He likes simple things. The pressure is off completely when he's here. And I've even enjoyed the start of winter. It single-handedly whittles me down, the dreaded countdown to Christmas Day, when the Moreaus go skiing, everyone squirrels away with their family, and I sit, as usual, alone, as if it's another day, sure, this time, that I'm the only human being left in the world.

"I feel like cheesecake is in my bloodstream," says Eliot now. "But then, it's Christmas soon. It's practically law to turn your insides to lard, right?"

Eliot stands on Louise's doorstep, empty-handed, the wine and dessert he brought over now devoured and drunk by us three, more wine than Louise is used to, as she's already gone up to bed. Last time he visited, we sat watching *Pucked*, the Jon Bon Jovi movie I'd somehow missed, and he stayed until well after midnight, his hand under the blanket occasionally brushing my leg, and even that hadn't felt long enough. But I'm glad. I'm glad I've let that gap between us continue to be slowly bridged, because it feels so much more natural, so much easier to let it. I keep thinking about what Marv said, and it has stuck. That someone shouldn't be defined by one mistake for the rest of their lives.

"Do you have to go? It's only nine thirty," I say.

He steps back onto the gravel of the driveway, hands in pockets, and says, "I don't want to. But I've got a lot of road to cover tomorrow, haven't I?"

I nod, try to stay poker-faced, but I've been dreading saying goodbye to him this time. Because I won't see Eliot until after Christmas now. He's working on a building site in Northumberland—a run-down country estate—for the next fortnight. And then he's away with Ana. With her family for Christmas. He never talks about her. But then, I avoid bringing her up.

"Well, enjoy sawing wood in Wrexham," I say.

"*Hexham.*" Eliot smiles.

"Ah," I laugh. "And Luxembourg after that. It is Luxembourg, isn't it?"

"It is," he says, nodding, and I cannot ignore this sinking heart in my chest. Lucas and Marie are counting down to their skiing trip in Austria with Jean and Amanda. Rosie is off, too, for Christmas week, going to Nottingham with her parents to stay with her sister and her husband until New Year's. Even Fox won't be at the hotel for the Christmas dinner shift, like me, on Christmas Day, because he'll be in London with his dad. And Eliot. Eliot will be hundreds of miles away. In Luxembourg. With Ana. (Or psychothera-bitch as Rosie calls her.) And me. I'll be right here, pretending it isn't happening.

"So, will you be seeing Lucas over Christmas at all, before skiing, or after, or . . ." Eliot trails off.

"No," I say, arms hugging my body from the cold. "He hasn't really mentioned it, and I know he's super busy with work so . . ."

"Right." Eliot nods. "And you. Any Christmas plans?"

"Work on Christmas Day, most of the day," I say with a small smile. "Louise has been invited somewhere. An old lodger of hers. Steve or something. She said she doesn't fancy it, though."

Eliot nods again. "So you won't be alone?"

"Definitely not," I say. "I'll be with one hundred Christmas-hat-wearing dinner guests and three hotheaded chefs."

Eliot smiles, standing tall opposite me. He hesitates, looks over the shoulder of his thick, black wool jacket, and I will for this to fizzle; this awkward, crackling atmosphere between us. "Your neighbors," he says eventually. "They know how to party with the ol' decorations, don't they?"

I smile. "I know. There's a rivalry. See who can cover their house in as many tacky lights as possible and get in the local papers."

Eliot raises an eyebrow. "Well, I think number Two Fishers Way could do with an injection of *tacky lights*, actually."

I shake my head.

"I dare you," he says, "to stick a few lights up. Buy a turkey. Stick a Christmas film on. Eat a *mince pie* by the fire in front of the *EastEnders* Christmas special, even if you've never seen an episode in your entire life."

I narrow my eyes. "Sounds . . . interesting."

"It's a sort of magic, actually, Emmie Blue," he says, smiling, his words making clouds in the icy November air. "So, listen. I got you something." He rubs his hands together, striding over to his truck, opening the door. "I didn't want to give it in front of Louise. Thought I'd wait," he says, leaning into the truck. "I know you get all embarrassed and hate opening things in front of people . . ."

"You didn't need to get me anything," I say, surprised.

Eliot closes the door, walks across the gravel toward me. "I know I didn't." He smiles. "But I saw it and immediately thought of you. It's no big deal."

He hands me a beautiful tissue paper–wrapped rectangle. The paper is gold, flecked with stars, and it's tied with black, sparkly ribbon. "The dude in the shop wrapped it. Don't give me any of the credit."

I look down at it in my hands and feel something tug in my stomach. A gift. I don't really get gifts at Christmas. Lucas and I have never really done presents, and probably because he knows I don't "do" Christmas, and have never done it.

"Thank you, Eliot," I say.

"Don't open it now," he says. "Save it. To open with your mince pie and *EastEnders* special."

"I will."

"Promise me you'll do it in that order?" says Eliot, stepping forward.

"I'll try it," I laugh, and reach up on tiptoes and put my arms around his neck, my hand still grasping the gift in one hand. His arms envelop me, his warm hands brushing the bare back peeping from under my jumper. Goose bumps prickle my skin. I kiss him on the cheek as we draw back, and say thank you again, but Eliot doesn't release his arms from around me, and I don't either. Our faces are close. Our breath making clouds in the air between our mouths.

"I don't have to go," says Eliot quietly. "I can stay."

I swallow, stare at him. Frozen. "Y-You have to work."

"I don't have to go," he repeats, whispering. "To Luxembourg."

"Eliot—"

"I won't go if you want me to stay."

I look up at him—the fan of dark lashes; his brown eyes, wide and almond-shaped; and his mouth, pink, the top lip a perfect bow. Like his brother's. Like Lucas's. *Lucas.* I step back.

"Go," I say, clearing my throat. "Don't be daft. It's Christmas. You—you have places to be, people to see."

Eliot pauses, says nothing, then throws an arm behind him, to scratch the back of his neck. "Right, then," he says. "I guess . . . Happy Christmas, Emmie."

"You too, Eliot," I say, the gift in my hand, the cold night air stinging my face.

Eliot gets into the truck and starts the engine. He holds his hand in a wave and I watch him drive away.

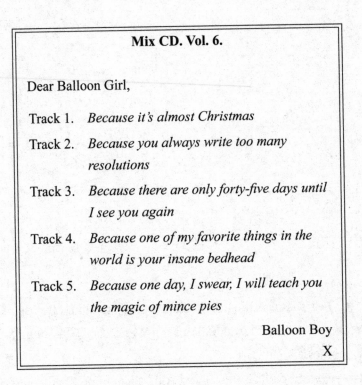

Mix CD. Vol. 6.

Dear Balloon Girl,

Track 1. *Because it's almost Christmas*

Track 2. *Because you always write too many resolutions*

Track 3. *Because there are only forty-five days until I see you again*

Track 4. *Because one of my favorite things in the world is your insane bedhead*

Track 5. *Because one day, I swear, I will teach you the magic of mince pies*

Balloon Boy

X

26

"**W**ell, that was the *worst*," I laugh down the line. "But thank you."

"*What?* It was 'Good King Wenceslas.' We—didn't you hear the harmonies?"

"I *knew* we should've sung Band Aid," sighs Eliot. "You could've murdered the Bono bit, live in Switzerland."

Luke laughs. "I don't murder it, dude. I *reinvent* it."

I smile, phone to ear, spiral wire stretched across my pajama top, a DVD paused on the TV. "And how *is* Switzerland?" I ask.

"Amazing," Lucas says, at the exact same time Eliot says, "Awesome."

"And seriously cold," adds Eliot. "Which I know is groundbreaking travel journalism, but it fuckin' is." The pair of them laugh, and I imagine them against the orange of the wood of a cabin in the Alps, the pair of them freshly showered and in shirts, ready for Christmas dinner in the five-star resort Jean and Amanda take them to every year, a fire flickering behind them, crowding round the hotel phone. I look around my flat. Tiny, cluttered but empty all at once, and feel a sinking, shameful feeling that this is where I am on Christmas Day.

"How's the head, Em?" says Lucas now.

"Hangover?" I hear Eliot inquire, and I shake my head pointlessly and say, "Migraine. I was up most of the night with it. But it's gone."

"Ah shit, that sucks. Take it easy today, yeah?"

"And hate to sound like my mum," adds Eliot, "but drink lots of water."

I smile, letting their concerns, their care, warm me through, like soup. "Probably because I ate a mince pie. Yesterday, when I went into Tesco, they had this charity table set up. Mince pies, chocolate logs—"

"You ate a *whole one*?" says Eliot.

"Yep."

"Ah," says Eliot, as if it's obvious. "You went too hard into Christmas cheer."

"You have to go easy," laughs Lucas. "Next you'll be saying you pulled a cracker."

I giggle, cheeks stinging, and hear Eliot answer someone in the background. His voice fades. "Dad's calling us," says Lucas, and I can tell by the change of volume, the closeness of his voice, that I am no longer on speakerphone, and he's holding the receiver to his ear. "You sure you're going to be okay, Em?"

" 'Course."

"I hate that you're on your own."

Me too, I want to say. Me too, and I wish I was with you. With Eliot. With your mum and her warm, tight cuddles, and your dad with his sensible and safe words. With the "Make sure you wrap up"s and the "What does everyone fancy for breakfast?" Instead I say, "I'm fine, honestly, Lucas. I'm having a really nice day."

We talk for five more minutes, until Eliot comes back and tells Lucas it's time to go for Christmas lunch. Lucas says goodbye, leaves the room to get ready, and Eliot takes the phone.

"Remember to stay hydrated," he says, smile in his voice.

"Yes, *Mum*," I joke. "I will."

"I mean it, though. Look after yourself, yeah?"

I swallow, feel small. "I will."

"And . . . Em?"

"Yeah?"

There is silence, and the only reason I know he is still there is the sigh that comes, eventually, on the line.

"Happy Christmas."

"Happy Christmas, Eliot."

Text Message from Marv:
> Dear Emmie, I'm sorry I
> haven't been in touch. I hope
> you understand, but I don't
> think now is the right time for
> me to tell my family. I will.
> Please trust I will. But just not
> right now. I'm sorry. X

The *EastEnders* special starts.

I want to take a photo—of the mince pie on Louise's tiny coffee table, with the TV on in the background, and the string of fairy lights around the frame—and send it to Eliot. But then I think of him in Luxembourg, with Ana, and I can't. Instead, I take the photo anyway, and go onto Instagram to upload it. I'll add a caption, like Rosie does, something like: *Cozy Christmas* or *Mince pie, TV, fairy lights, slippers on. Bliss!* But I can't do that either. Because the first thing I see is a photo of Lucas and Marie, arms punching the air, top-to-toe in skiing gear, eyes shielded by huge glasses, the sky behind them, a perfect Caribbean Sea–blue. And then I see Eliot's latest photo: a wintry sunset. A single glass of wine. In Luxembourg, I bet. Pathetic. That's how my Christmas feels. Truly pathetic.

I sit back on the sofa. My head is throbbing from a long, busy shift, and I have done nothing since I got home at nine, besides shower and sit on the edge of Louise's bed, the pair of us eating turkey club sandwiches the chefs made us with leftovers at work. Yet I barely feel like I've rested at all. I feel like I'm wading through treacle, and my head throbs, as if it's fit to burst with all that whirls through it tonight, like a tornado. Lucas. Eliot. Marv, and the message that feels like a boot to the stomach every time I read it.

I hold Eliot's gift in my lap. And slowly, in front of the TV, watching characters I don't recognize from the last time I watched, several years ago, scream at one another, kiss on the wet tarmac outside the famous Vic pub, I peel back the wrapping. I think of him. I think of Eliot's kind, strong hands passing the gift to me on that black, starry night. And once again, moving pictures of that moment on Louise's drive—the moment between us before he drove away—barges its way into my thoughts. Like clockwork, my insides flip over in my gut, like a fish.

A book. Blue. Hardback. Beautiful, and embossed with tiny boats. A padlock keeping it locked shut, and keys, dangling from string. A closed book. And handwritten in the inside cover, in neat handwriting:

Flower,

I support you and accept you, even though you're a wreck. (And even if your nose is ever a blighted tomato.)

Eliot

X

R osie straddles a bench in the small locker room of the Clarice, and
Fox lies with long legs along it, his head in Rosie's lap, his feet dangling over the edge and crossed at the ankle, his eyes closed. Rosie is doing
osteopathy on him. Something she learned on YouTube, and part of her
New Year's resolution to Learn Something New.

"How does that feel?"

"Fine."

"Just fine?"

Fox opens one eye. "Am I supposed to be feeling otherwise?"

Rosie looks at me, then back at Fox and shrugs. "Fuck knows. Just keep
still. I need to find your . . ." She looks over at her phone, bright and open
on a tutorial. "Your . . . *something.*"

The corner of Fox's mouth turns up. "I am in safe, safe hands," he mutters, and Rosie doesn't flinch, her eyes skyward as she tries to find whatever
"nodule" she is looking for in Fox's neck.

It has been six whole weeks since I said goodbye to Eliot on the drive
of Louise's, and I have spent every day of them revisiting, at least once, the
moment we said goodbye. The way he said he didn't have to leave. The way
he didn't let me go—the way *I* didn't let him go. How close our faces were.

Did he want to kiss me? Did I want to kiss *him?* Did I want to kiss *Eliot?* Lucas's brother. God. Did I misjudge it?

On Christmas Day, after opening his gift, I sent him a text. *Thank you for my closed book.* He replied: *You're welcome, Emmie xx.* That was it. And I haven't had a single text from him—apart from the ones in the STEN party group, which are all purely STEN-related, and mostly in response to "legend" Tom—but then, I haven't texted him either, so maybe it's an emotional standoff? Maybe he feels too awkward to text me, the way I do. We were so close, mouths inches apart, him mere seconds away from driving miles; to fly to fucking Luxembourg to celebrate Christmas with his girlfriend. *Girlfriend.* Of course he hasn't messaged me. Why would he?

"Out you come."

I look up. Rosie, hands still pummeling poor Fox's neck, is staring at me, the sort of look on her face that usually follows a tut.

"Step out of the vortex, Emmie. You're thinking about it again, aren't you?"

"A little."

"Not that I need to repeat this again for the seven hundredth time in almost five weeks—"

"Six."

"But (a) you did nothing wrong," says Rosie, running over my words, "and (b) he's backed off because of *course* he has. He asked you to tell him not to go. He put himself out there, basically told you he liked you. And he wanted to hear it from you. And you didn't say it. You literally told him to *go.*"

Fox makes a sound in the back of his throat. "Yes," he says. "As discussed at length, Eliot fancies you, Emmie. *Likes you.* Clearly. Very much so. And he has made it patently obvious in a number of ways—"

"Patently." Rosie smirks, still pummeling.

"And hasn't had much at all back from you. Why would he keep persisting? He's a gent. Am I wrong?"

I shrug. "But we're . . . friends."

Fox sighs, steepling his fingers together in front of his face. "But if you're friends, that must mean you can look at Eliot and feel absolutely nothing in that way of things. Not even an ounce of physical attraction—" Fox pauses, looks up at Rosie. "*What?*"

Rosie shakes her head, looks down at him. "Nothing," she says.

Fox raises an eyebrow and looks back to me, his head still in Rosie's lap. "And can you say that?"

I stare at him, groan, hide my face with my hands.

"She doesn't know," cuts in Rosie. "Because of—"

"*Lucas,*" they both say together, and I laugh from behind my hands and say, "Oh, piss off, with your good points and questions."

"Seriously though, Em. Can you say that you don't like him? At all?"

I drop my hands from my face. Rosie and Fox look at me, and I shake my head.

"No, I can't say that," I say. "I've missed him. Like, *really* missed him. And that surprises me because . . . well, I didn't expect to. Not really. I even called him on New Year's."

Rosie's eyes, the lids shimmering with glitter, widen. "You didn't tell me that."

"He didn't answer. Then he texted the next morning, asking if I was okay, and I told him it was a mistake."

Rosie groans. "*Emmie.*"

"I *know,*" I say. "But I dunno, I had this vision of him in Luxembourg with Ana . . . and I felt so embarrassed. But . . . I do miss him. I like having Eliot around. And he's really been there."

Rosie makes a sound like a horse, lips blowing out, and says, "Yes, he *has.*"

"And it's been nice having that. Someone there, when Lucas usually would be."

"Would he though?" Fox asks, hands one on top of the other on his stomach.

I look at Fox. "*Yes*. He's just busy at work and God, he *is* getting married, and there's so much to organize." I look up at them. "I'm a mess, aren't I?"

Rosie looks at me, smiles gently. "We're all a mess, Em."

"Speak for yourself, Kalwar," mumbles Fox, and Rosie looks down at him and raises her eyebrows. He smiles at her, and she giggles.

"Oh God, guys, I don't know."

"Well, I don't know what you're hanging about for, personally. He's fuckin' hot," adds Rosie, and when Fox croakily adds, his eyes closed as if he's sunbathing, "The *only* personality trait that matters," she does something that makes him flinch away from her amateur-osteopathic hands.

I poke at the pasta in the Tupperware box on my lap, leftovers from a pasta bake I cooked for Louise and myself last night, and Rosie continues kneading Fox's neck, while he grimaces. And *I don't know.* That is the truth. I don't know how I feel about Eliot. All I do know is that everything feels like it's a tower about to collapse on me. Marv. I've heard nothing from him. The wedding, now only two months away. The STEN party, merely two weeks. And there's Louise, who is really suffering lately. I can't help but worry about her when I close the door to her bedroom every night and come into work. She had a visitor last week—Steve, the ex-lodger, she said. The one who invited her for Christmas. She only told me because I inquired about the two mugs I found in the sink. And I miss Lucas. He texts, he calls, he FaceTimes, like he always has, but it's not the same. I can feel it slowly changing, like a breeze turning, only noticeable with hindsight. And I miss him. I really, really miss how it used to be.

"Isn't that right?" says Rosie. "I was just telling Fox this bloke I'm seeing, that who knows, he *could* be the one?"

"With a name like King-o?" Fox asks. "I doubt it."

"That's his nickname, you idiot. And yes. Why *couldn't* King-o be my one?"

I nod. "Exactly. He could well be."

Fox scoffs. "And I suppose, what, Lucas is your . . . *one?*"

I pause, face flushing. Because it feels like a huge thing to say out loud. I mean, I do think he's my one, don't I? Lucas Moreau. Balloon Boy. The one who found me, against all odds, when I needed a friend the most. When he needed home the most.

But I say nothing. Because there is no clarity right now. It all feels like a mad, confused jumble in my mind.

"Do you love him?" asks Rosie, and the words ring out, bold and brash, in the quiet.

"Yes," I say. "Of course I love Lucas."

"Yes, but . . . do you actually *love* Lucas. Do you wish it was you, picking out the white dress, watching him fall asleep, waking up to him every morning . . ."

"I . . ."

"Having a family with him," says Rosie, eyes fixed on me, hands beneath Fox's head unmoving now. "Washing *his* pants, post-stomach-bug," she carries on. "Sucking his *dick.*"

"Terrific," says Fox, getting up in one swift sit-up. "That certainly turned dark at breakneck speed."

"What I'm saying, Emmie," says Rosie, "is do you *love* Lucas? Really? Or do you just love the idea of him?"

Raindrops trail down Louise's window as I draw her curtains tonight. I turn back to see her smiling at me, her face lit amber by the pink bedside lamp.

"Miserable out there," I say, and she closes her papery eyelids for a moment.

"Oh, I don't know," she says. "I like the rain."

I raise an eyebrow and smile. "Really? I'm not sure I've met many people who like the rain."

Louise nods gently, pulling her duvet up to her chest so it fits snugly under her arms. "Makes you feel alive, I think. A reminder that the world is bigger than you. That's why I like storms especially."

I give a shudder and pull my face into a grimace. "We'll have to disagree on that one too, I think, Louise," I say, and she gives a sleepy chuckle.

Louise has been spending more and more time in bed lately, but she always tries, a couple of hours before nine, her bedtime these days, to be out of bed and out of her bedroom.

"I like to *go* to bed at night," she says, and I admit, helping her up and into bed has weirdly become one of my creature comforts. The both of us wish it wasn't this way—Louise being in pain, needing help to get into bed, to get comfortable, that sometimes, an hour out of this bedroom, in the conservatory downstairs, among her books and trinkets and plants, is as good as it gets—but if it has to be this way, then this is as nice as it can be. Me, drawing her curtains, shutting out the cold and the world, Louise, pulling her favorite bedsheets high, the room always smelling of the purple fabric conditioner she uses and her beloved patchouli oil. We drink herbal teas, in china cups bought from a shop in Brussels in the seventies, when Louise was young and supple and free. We read books and short stories together, the sound of rain our backdrop, and our soft and sleepy talks by lamplight, the last thing we do before she falls asleep.

I settle down, like I have done so often recently, in the wicker chair beside her bed. Eliot carried it up the stairs a few weeks before Christmas, from the conservatory, so I had somewhere to sit while I read to her. "Which book?" I ask now.

Louise shakes her head slowly, eyelids closing and opening, eyes cloudy, yellowy. "No book tonight, if that's quite all right," she says.

"Of course."

"Tell me something," she says softly.

I smile. "What about?"

"You," she says. "Tell me about Emmie Blue."

I lean to get the two cups of tea I set down on the bedside cabinet moments ago. "I think you know all there is to know about me, Louise. I'm thirty. I live here with you. I work at the Clarice. You really don't want me to go on, do you?"

"I don't mean that," she says, stretching, taking a mug from my hands shakily. "I mean . . . oh, I don't know." Her eyes rise to the ceiling, as if she is thinking, searching for something. "Happiness," she says. "What is that, to Emmie Blue?"

"Wow," I say with a smile, "that's a . . . big question."

"Is it?"

I bring my shoulders to my ears, look down into the green, minty tea in my hands. "I suppose when I was younger, a few years ago, I would have said . . . a family. A normal, safe family life."

Louise watches me, says nothing.

"You know," I say, "a home, with flowers in the window, a relationship with my mum where maybe she pops in for lunch now and then. Children, one day, maybe. Someone . . ." I swallow, words becoming increasingly difficult to say. "Someone to love. Someone to love me."

"Love," says Louise. "So you think love is happiness?"

I hesitate, laugh, nerves turning it into a high-pitched giggle. "I—don't know. Yes. Yes, I suppose it is. For me. Is it for you?"

"Love?" asks Louise.

"Yes," I say. "Have you ever . . . been in love?"

"Me?" Louise pauses. Her eyes close. She shakes her head. "No," she says. "No I have not." And before I can say anything else, she says, "So, a nice three-bed semi, a family, and someone to love you . . ."

I laugh again, my cheeks unabashedly burning red. "Yes," I say. "To me, that sounds perfect."

"Oh. And flowers in the window." She nods, knowingly. "I see," she says kindly. "Okay." Then she drinks.

"You think I'm mad, don't you?" I say. "Is this the part where you tell me I have my head up my arse for saying such a sugary, silly thing?"

"No," she says, lowering the mug to her lap. "Not even close, Emmie. Silly is something I would never use to describe you."

I smile. "Well, that's a little bit of a Louise Dutch compliment if ever I heard one."

"Take them where you can find them."

The rain pummels the window, and Louise changes her mind and asks me to read just a chapter from the historical romance we're midway through at the moment, and when I get to the word "member" she winces and says, "horrible things," which makes me spit out my tea.

It's almost ten when I stand to leave and go to turn out her light.

"Do you know why I like storms?" says Louise as my fingers reach for the switch. "They're a little reminder that we're not at all in charge, but Mother Nature is. And while the world might not look exactly how we'd prefer it to, it is enough, if we just stop and look. The whole sky lit up. The smell of the rain. Safe inside. What more could you need?"

29

Tom approaches me now, the way I imagine members of the RSPCA approach an agitated animal. With trepidation, his words careful, nervous. Almost the way the pharmacist's assistant spoke to Louise last week when I took her in the wheelchair to pick up her prescription. Polite enough, but with a hint of pity. And I thought as we'd walked away, "No wonder she never goes out."

"Happy with how it turned out, yeah, Emmie?" he says now, standing at the ballroom's long arc of a bar. "*Totally,*" I tell him. And I am. I really am. It's very Lucas and it's very Marie. White and shiny and modern and opulent. That's the word for this venue. *Opulent.* Huge chandeliers glitter from high ceilings, twists and delicate showers of fairy lights illuminate the room like tiny stars, and tuxedoed waitstaff flit wordlessly about the room. It looks more like a wedding than a joint stag and hen party. The only thing that takes it away from looking like a wedding is the lack of tables and chairs. There is a huge, shining dance floor, a DJ, and just two long banquet tables. One dressed in black and white, like a tuxedo, and the other donned with white fur and gems. One for the stags. One for the hens. I just don't know where I am supposed to sit . . .

"You've done an amazing job, Tom," I say, and he nods woodenly.

"And you too," he says. "Lucille's singer friend arrived awhile ago, by the way. She did a warm-up. Sounds good."

"And what about the pop-punk band? For Luke?"

"All here and counted for. They sound mega. Eliot's out back with them, going over their list. They have a set list of twelve, then it'll be the DJ. You might want to have a look over their list, just to be sure, but I've chosen mostly crowd-pleasers, and some songs I know Luke loves. Eliot's looking it over." He gives me a look that's an almost eye roll, as if to say, "I don't know what it's got to do with him." "Anyway. I'm just going to see where they are. Should be here soon."

I stand alone at the bar for a moment, my hand resting on the smooth counter. My stomach fizzes at the idea of seeing Eliot for the first time since that moment on Louise's drive. What if it's awkward? What if he's with Ana, and he told her about that moment on the drive—that I was so close to him, inches from his lips? What if that moment was all me—me reading it wrong—and now I've made him feel weird about us? But he asked me if I wanted him to stay, didn't he? God. You'd think after weeks and weeks of me asking myself (and Rosie and Fox, of course) these questions, I'd feel clearer about it all. But I don't. Not even close. A waiter places down an ice bucket beside me and I consider, for a moment, sinking my head into it.

I find Eliot where Tom said he would be: out back, hunched over a piece of paper. When Eliot sees me, he smiles warmly, and stands. Broad shoulders beneath a fitted dark shirt, open at the collar, straight-legged, black trousers. Strong. Tall. Unmistakable, this somersaulting in my stomach at the sight of him.

"Hi," I say.

"Hey you," he says, eyes flicking for a small second over my dress. "You look amazing."

"Do you think? I was iffy, about it being black, like maybe I was dressed for a wake or something, but—"

"Nailed it," he says, teeth grazing his lip. "Completely."

I can't bring myself to hold his gaze, so I look down at my feet. "You've nailed it yourself," I say. Because he has. He looks gorgeous.

"Thanks." He nods. "It's been a while."

"I know."

"What have I missed?" he asks softly.

"Not a lot, actually," I say. "Work. The usual. And you? How was Luxembourg?"

This feels like a dance, asking pointless, polite questions, avoiding the burning coals at our feet: that moment on Louise's drive. The weeks we've gone, barely speaking.

"Ah," he says, hand coming up to his chin, fingers on neat, dark stubble. "I didn't go to Luxembourg. I spent it in Le Touquet, at Mum's, alone." He gives an awkward grin that's almost a grimace. "Me and Ana, we . . . we're taking some time out. Well, that's the polite term for it, I suppose."

"Oh," I say, and silence stretches between us like elastic. "I'm sorry."

"Don't be," he says. "It's been a long time coming. Sometimes you don't realize how you feel till something shines a light on it. You know?"

"Yes," I say. "I get that."

Nobody says anything else, and I struggle to not blurt everything desperate to break free. I want to ask him why, and what taking some time means. I want to tell him I've missed him, and that I have typed out a text to him every single day, but not been able to send it. I want to ask him if he meant what he said, on the drive. If he'd have stayed with me, for Christmas, if I'd asked him to. But I don't. Instead I clear my throat, clap my hands together, and say, "So, expert opinion please. Do I sit at Marie's table, with all the girls, or do I sit at the black, tuxedo table among all the testosterone and man-spreading?"

And like the mood dispersed as my hands clamped together, Eliot laughs.

"Tough one, Em," he says, closing the gap between us. "I mean, if I have my way, you'll sit with me," he says ducking his head, eyes on mine. "I'm not getting stuck with Tom or that *ridiculous* boss of Lucas's with the eyebrows, who goes on about getting mistaken for Brad Pitt but actually looks like—"

"An armpit?"

"*Weak*," laughs Eliot, shaking his head. "So weak. But surprisingly accurate."

Tom, flustered, his cheeks the color of pomegranates, appears in the doorway. "They're here," he says. "Just pulled up."

Eliot turns to me. "Time to go greet the bride- and groom-to-be," he says. "You ready, Flower?"

The party is in full swing, the music loud, and tables littered with empty, sauce-smeared plates and half-full glasses.

Lucas and Marie were welcomed into the ballroom the way a bride and groom are when they enter the reception for the first time. And their joy was unmistakable as they walked in, both of them holding on to each other, gasping, gawping, their eyes traveling around the room in amazement.

Lucas grabbed Tom into a rough, tight, rugby hug when he arrived, then ran toward me—actually sprinted—and threw his arms around me, lifting me from the ground.

"Em, this is fucking *awesome*," he spoke into my ear. "The band. There's an actual *band*."

"I couldn't resist. Eliot helped me," I told him, and I think that was the moment I have loved more than anything, tonight, watching Eliot put his hand out to shake Lucas's, before Lucas pulled him in for a hug, and not like the one he gave Tom. This was a still, slow hug, ending with two rough fist-pats on the back. Two brothers. Too much time between them passed, for silly, drunken mistakes to have the clout they once had. Because so much time had passed since then. We have all changed; are still changing.

There was a warbling, rambling speech from Tom, who talked mostly, for some reason, about the women he and Lucas had hooked up with in their very short traveling days and the unexpected safety of the yurt they'd slept in; and then Marie stood up and did a quick toast, when she even mentioned me, holding her hand out to me across the table—the "girls" table, where I was swiftly put by Lucille, directly opposite Eliot, across the way on the boys' table. And who kept texting me from the other side of the room. During dinner, he'd sent:

> Eliot Barnes: Tom is talking about the day he pulled 21-year-old twins.

> Eliot Barnes: I sort of want to die.

Emmie: It's nice over here, although the subject derailed to balls a minute ago.

> Eliot Barnes: Of course it did.

Emmie: We're back on asparagus now, and a farmer Marie has made friends with for the deli. His name is Sven. Looks like Henry Winkler, apparently. Also, someone just mentioned conjunctivitis.

> Eliot: Very civilized. We're on to cars. Not cliché at all.

———————

And now he looks at me, slight smile on his pink lips, two men beside him in fast, passionate conversation, all hand gestures and deep nods. He mouths to me with a hand to his ear. "Phone."

———————

Eliot Barnes: So, Emmie. Closed
book. Flower.

Eliot: Dance with me?

———————

I look up at him, and he's already looking at me, smiling wider now. I shake my head.

———————

Emmie: I don't dance.

Emmie: I haven't danced in almost
fifteen years.

Eliot Barnes: Time to overwrite a shit
memory with a new
one?

———————

Across the room we hold each other's gaze. He knows. He remembers the last time I danced was the night of the Summer Ball. And I loved dancing. I remember the way Georgia and I danced that night, and I remember the song and the color of the light, and the way it painted her blue dress pink. I felt so free and young and excited that night. We were going into sixth form, and then it would be the next step; the next big step into the world. College. Then maybe even uni. Then: the rest of our lives. I remember the hope. I remember the excitement. Robert Morgan had found a Peter. A musician that could be my dad. Things were going to be okay—I wasn't going to be lonely anymore. And then, in one decision, in one moment, minutes later, the hope was sapped from everything. I was lonelier than I had ever been.

Emmie: Also, I can't dance.

Emmie: At all.

Eliot Barnes: Nobody can.

Eliot Barnes: Well, unless you're Nick Carter from the Backstreet Boys, and he isn't here.

I look up at him, head to one side, and shake my head, but he's getting up. He leans over, says something to the group of men he's sitting with, tosses down his napkin, and makes his way over to me.

"It's a slow song," he says into my ear. "You don't need to be able to dance, just . . . stand and *breathe*."

I laugh. And despite myself, despite not dancing since that night, despite my washing machine stomach and cold, shaky hands, I take his and stand up.

"One song," I say, as one slow song flows flawlessly into another. "Just this one."

He nods, looking down at me, brown eyes fixed on mine. "Just one."

We walk together to the dance floor, meandering in and out of dancing, swaying couples, his strong hand holding tightly on to mine. Ironically, Lucas and Marie, the bride- and groom-to-be, are at opposite ends of the dance floor, in quick, all-smiling conversations with people I don't recognize.

I stand in front of Eliot and look up to the lilac-and-blue strobes of disco lights. I remember. How Freddie, Georgia's date for the Summer Ball, was late, arriving two hours after everyone else, with his scruffy friends in tow, their shirts untucked, hair gelled, and he'd ignored her. When the slow song had kicked in, I'd taken her hand and said, "I'll dance with you," and she'd laughed and said, in a mock-posh accent, "I would be honored, Emmeline Blue." And we did. We danced in the middle of the floor, arms around each other, spinning each other in turn, all smiles, all laughs, all taut apples of cheeks and happy eyes. That was me and Georgia. Sisters, practically. Until he ruined that. He ruined dancing and discos and even dresses, for me, for a while. And I find my hands trembling, just a little, as I put my arms around Eliot's neck. The music. The lights. The bodies swaying around us; it's the same.

"Okay?" Eliot asks, arms around me.

"Fine," I say, looking up at him.

"Good. Only thing for it," he says, "hold on and hope for the best."

"And that's dancing, is it?"

"Well, yeah," Eliot says, then he leans in, and says into my ear, breath tickling my neck, "And everything else, too, Emmie Blue."

The longer we dance, the more relaxed I become, and one song turns into two, turns into three, and my head is against his chest now. I love the way he smells. Of a deep, woody aftershave and fresh laundry, and I can hear him singing along. And he can sing. I remember that now, about Eliot. The way he'd play guitar along to the Beatles, trying to work out chords, and I'd stand on the landing outside his room as I was passing, and listen. And he could hold a note. More than a hold a note.

The music changes, and I look up at him. *Somersault. Somersault. Do I like him? Is Rosie right? I do. I think I do.*

"Morning," he jokes as I straighten, the music changing into something more upbeat, slow dancers drifting back to the bar. "And look. *Three dances*, and you survived to tell the tale."

"I know," I say, "thank you."

Eliot scrunches up his brow. "Thank you?"

"For asking me to dance. For succeeding in overwriting a shit memory with a nice one."

Under the dim, smoky lights, I see Eliot's handsome face soften. "Anytime," he says.

And I don't know exactly how it happens and who leans into who, but Eliot is taking the side of my face in his hand, and our lips slowly collide. It's for just a second—a slow, soft press—and we pull away, inches apart, unmoving for a second, breath tickling my throat.

And I giggle. A delirious giggle that makes my cheeks burn, and I bury my face in his chest.

"I finally kissed Emmie Blue." Eliot bends, laughing into my ear. "My inner nineteen-year-old is *beside* himself right now."

30

When I answer the door of the guest cottage, I think Lucas is surprised to see me awake, dressed, made-up, and holding an almost empty mug of coffee.

"Who are you, and what have you done with my lazy-arse friend, Emmie," croaks Lucas, his sandy curls a giant bouffant of a mass on top of his head. He is wearing nothing but a pair of gray jogging shorts and a pair of sunglasses. His skin is tanned. His breath, enough to get you tipsy from just a sniff. "God, I'm gonna hurl."

"Good morning to you too," I say as he groans past me and throws himself facedown onto the guest cottage's soft gray sofa. "Nice night? I assume from the sunglasses in winter, the answer is yes."

He groans again into the cushions as I close the front door.

"Is that Lucas for 'yes, but I have thrown up into my dad's briefcase again and I need help blow-drying the checkbooks'?"

Lucas laughs into the cushion. "Who knows?" he moans, turning his head to face outward, his sunglasses wonky on his face.

I crouch. "Coffee?" I say, and he nods. "Also, you stink, Luke."

"Do I?"

"You smell like whiskey and garlic and . . . bed."

"Oh," he says sleepily. "Sounds quite nice."

"It isn't."

"Harsh," he says. "Just because you have a spring in your step. What happened? Were you in bed by ten with your best man book and one of Louise's hippy teas or something?"

"Nope. Although you could so do with one of her hippy teas right now."

"Coffee," he says. "I need a fuck-off, massive coffee. Nothing less."

I wondered the whole way home last night if anyone saw Eliot and me kiss. It was quick and it was dark, and when I'd pulled back from giggling in his chest like a giddy schoolgirl, all I could see was a sea of dancing bodies and chattering mouths. We didn't dance anymore, and after we kissed, we hadn't seen much more of each other. Amanda had taken Eliot off to see an uncle he hadn't seen in years, and I got lumbered with a paralytic Lucille, who fell asleep on my lap, on the ballroom carpet.

"What on earth are you doing down there?" Jean had asked, eyeing me as if I was a rough sleeper on his path.

"Stopping her choking on her own sick. You know. The usual," I said, and Jean had tutted and waffled, "But the carpet. Do not let her vomit on this floor. We do not want a cleaning bill."

I looked for Eliot for the rest of the night, but I also couldn't bear laying eyes on him for longer than a second when I caught glimpses of him between clusters of people on the dance floor, across the room, drink in his strong hand, smiling, chatting with that lovely mouth. The one that kissed me. That kiss. *That kiss.* Every time I think about it, the flurry of butterflies is so strong, I feel physically sick. His warm lips, the prickle of stubble, the brush of his thumb on my cheek, the tiny, slow touch of his tongue . . .

"Em?"

"Mm?"

"I said, what was up with Lucille?"

I push down the handle of the French press and take a cup off the mug-tree. "Same as you," I say distractedly. "Pissed as a fart. Bladdered."

He laughs croakily, still flat, stomach-down on the sofa, cheek pressed against the cushion. "She never drinks, though," he says, voice muffled.

"Makes sense," I say, holding out the steaming mug to him. "Come on. Up. Drink."

Lucas groans and turns, pulling himself messily up on the sofa. He lifts his glasses onto his head and takes the mug. "Thanks, Em." He sips. "Seriously," he says, looking up at me. "What's with you?"

"What?" I say, and laugh too easily. The way you do when you've been bottling up excitement, fighting off laughter, and finally get a chance to set some free.

Lucas's brow furrows. "Did you get off with someone?"

"No."

"Oh my God," he says, stretching his head around. "Are they here? Tom? Tom, are you in there, buddy, come—"

"No!" I say, and chuck a tiny scatter cushion at him. He winces as it bounces off his head. "Seriously," he laughs. "If he'd come out of there . . ."

"What?" I laugh. "What would you have done?"

"Well, smash his face in first and foremost, obviously," he says with a matter-of-fact smile.

"*Obviously*," I mimic, and he smiles.

"You all outdid yourselves last night, Em. And the band." He puts a hand on his chest. "I know you said you couldn't take all the credit, but that was so you. The band was an Emmie Blue move."

"Did you like the Busted one?

"Fucking *loved* it," he says, throwing his head back.

I smile. "I'm glad," I say, and he looks at me.

"Only one thing that sucked," he says.

"Go on."

"I know you don't like it but . . . I dunno," says Lucas softly, "I was sort of hoping I could get a dance out of you. It would've been nice."

Guilt trickles through my veins. I wonder, for a second, if he saw. It's hard to look at him, but I do. "You big sap," I say, and laugh, but Lucas doesn't. "There's always the wedding," I say.

He nods slowly, flyaway bedhead bobbing as he does. "Yeah," he says. "There's always the wedding."

WhatsApp from Rosie Kalwar:

oh my GOOD FUCKING GOD.

WhatsApp from Rosie Kalwar:

I AM DEAD.

WhatsApp from Rosie Kalwar:

He kissed you. YOU!!! KISSED BY THE GOD THAT IS THAT SEXY LIL CARPENTER WITH THE GIANT SCHLONG. (hearsay, but I believe it wholeheartedly to be true.)

WhatsApp from Rosie Kalwar:

He's been desperate to do that Emmie. I told you. He's probably been practicing on a potato or aubergine or whatever it is Shout magazine used to tell us to practice on to get it just right because why wouldn't he?

WhatsApp from Rosie Kalwar:

You're a queen. Seriously, I mean that Em. You stood under those disco lights and you did it. You danced. DANCED and kissed and let it all go.

WhatsApp from Rosie Kalwar:

The world is your lobster now.

WhatsApp from Fox Barclay:

Oyster.

WhatsApp from Rosie Kalwar:

Knew that'd get the fucker's attention.

31

Emmie: Hi Marv, it's been months
since we last spoke. If you
don't want to be in my
life, then I think it's only
kind you let me know. This
waiting is unfair on me. I
have waited long enough.
If I don't hear from you,
I hope you understand
that I will remove your
number and we can go
our separate ways. Be well.
Emmie.

Even when Eliot reads Louise the sad stories—the heartbreaking love stories in which some poor bastard always ends up dead—I hear laughter float from her bedroom, and tonight is no exception. It's just after nine, and I've not long finished washing up after dinner. Eliot cooked tonight, and it's the first time I've seen him since our kiss at the STEN party two weeks ago. I could hardly look at him when he first arrived armed with two Sainsbury's bags and a bunch of flowers for Louise. The butterflies in my stomach at the sight of him blindsided me.

"What's new, Emmie?" He smiled, coming into the kitchen. "All good?"

"Yeah. Great. Perfect." I'd pretended—and probably badly—to be struggling with the seal on a bottle of Louise's vitamins as he unpacked the shopping. "Good good," he said, and touched my waist as he passed. A brush of fingers against my skin.

"I thought I'd do some creamy, cheesy, bad-for-us bacon-y pasta thing with tagliatelle," said Eliot, tossing an onion in the air and moving to stand beside me at the counter. "Sound good?"

I nodded, glanced up at him. "So . . . a carbonara."

Eliot narrowed his eyes. "Um, I don't like to pigeonhole my cookery, thanks very much, Emmie Blue." Then he'd ducked his head and smiled at me, and whispered as if revealing a secret, tapping the side of my nose, "I totally just did pretend to invent carbonara. Keep it between us, yeah?"

Louise wasn't feeling well enough to come downstairs for dinner this evening, so Eliot took it up to her, and after going back up to collect her dinner plate, sat instead, as he has done a lot over the last couple of months, to read her a chapter of her book. It's amazing to me that this time last year, it was unusual for me to find Louise in bed for longer than six hours at a time, always rising before the sun came up. Now it's unusual to find her anywhere else.

I traipse up the stairs to ask if Louise wants a hot drink before bed, and can't help but smile at the sound of their low, chattering voices. It's become homely, climbing the stairs to the orangey lamplight spilling from Louise's bedroom. And tonight, with the additions of the lingering smell of someone else's recipes, the sound of Eliot's deep voice, his teasing tone, and Louise's raspy laughter, makes it feel even more cozy, and safer, than it usually feels. Because Fishers Way feels like home now. Something I never expected to happen, and something I'd hardly noticed happening at all. But it's home. I think I have finally found it.

I push open the door. Louise stuffs something in the beige tote bag she keeps all her belongings in—medication, essential oil, tissues, that sort of thing—and holds it on her lap, on top of the duvet, in a scrunched ball. Eliot is leaning forward in the low wicker chair, his strong forearms resting on his legs, and hands together between his knees. He looks up at me and smiles, eyes glinting in the lamplight.

"What are you two up to, eh?" I ask, smiling.

Eliot raises his shoulders. "Nothing. Just, uh, boring Louise about moons and meteors."

"Boring me? Enlightening me, I think you'll find," Louise says, smiling gently. "He's smart, this man."

"At least someone is interested."

"I *am* interested," I say to Eliot, "but I will be more interested when I actually see a shooting star that isn't an airplane."

Eliot shakes his head, gives me a wry smile. "You'll see tonight."

"Believe it when I see it," I say. "First though, who wants tea?"

Louise shakes her head immediately, her eyes dull and tired. "No thanks, Emmie, I'm exhausted," she says. "I'm going to turn in, I think." Then she laughs weakly and says, "Well, I'm already *in*, aren't I?"

Eliot stands, brushing his hands down his jeans, straightening his T-shirt. "You get some sleep, renegade," he says, and he leans to put his hand on hers. His strong and large, on her skinny, pale fingers. "And less shit said about my carbonara next time, okay? Go easy on me."

"I stand by it," says Louise. "More pepper next time."

Eliot touches two fingers to his forehead in a lazy salute. As he passes me in the doorway, he stops and touches my arm. "I'll see you outside," he says, and I tell him I won't be long. "I'll make the tea." He smiles.

I help Louise get comfortable in bed, adjusting her heavy feather pillows, and take away the throw at the bottom, which makes her legs too hot in the middle of the night.

"Your dessert was very nice."

I look over at Louise, folding the throw in four at the bottom of her bed. "It was, actually, wasn't it?"

"You sound surprised." Louise groans as she leans to pull the duvet to her neck. "You need to believe in yourself a bit more."

"I'll try." I cross the bedroom floor to the curtains and pull them closed, shutting out the pearly light of the moon. Full tonight, and glaring. And as large and as visible as it'll be all year apparently, according to Eliot. We used to look at the stars when we were kids, Lucas, Eliot, and I, and Eliot knew everything there was to know about meteor showers and planets and the position of the moon. I listened. Watched, hopefully, the black sky above, hanging on his every word. Never ever saw a shooting star, though.

"Would you leave them?" Louise asks.

"You want me to leave the curtains open?"

"Yes," says Louise. "I'd like to see the moon tonight, if I can. If it's going to be at its best, so Eliot says."

I nod. "Of course. He said it's a clear night, so you'll have a good view." I open the curtains wide and turn back to her. "There we are. Is that okay?"

She nods, but her eyes don't leave mine. I wait, thinking she's going to ask me to get her something before bed. "You should let him in," she says softly.

I pause. "Sorry?"

"Eliot," she says, and I feel my heart thump like a drum. "You asked me once if I was ever in love. Do you remember?"

I nod. "Yes."

"And I lied." Louise's hand grips the top of the duvet, knobbles where the knuckles should be. "The woman in the pictures downstairs you asked me about. The one with the shiny hair." Louise smiles to herself. "Martha."

I pause. "Yes?"

She says nothing.

"You were in love?" I ask. "You and Martha?"

Louise's eyelids close momentarily, and she nods once.

"Yes," she says. "And she was wonderful, Emmie. And I loved her the way that it sickens you." Louise smiles a watery smile. "I still remember the butterflies, the way my insides would feel as though they were turning over when she'd look at me. There is nothing like it. It's all-consuming, isn't it?"

I am frozen, feet on Louise's thin, seventies carpet. "What happened to her?"

Louise swallows then. "We . . . lost her young. She was thirty-seven."

My stomach aches as she speaks those words, and looking at Louise in this bed—frail, shrinking, her skin papery and lined—I can hardly believe she was once young, and in love. Young and grieving.

"I'm so sorry. That's so awful, Louise."

"Yes," she says, her voice quivering. "And my life was never the same after that. *I* was never the same. I shut myself off; never let anyone in after Martha, didn't want to depend on another soul because the pain of losing her was so great . . ." She stops, her shaky hand coming up to her mouth. I rush across the room then, sit on the side of her bed, beside her, close to her. "And it was a mistake, Emmie. Because I have spent my life alone. And I miss it. I miss being loved. Being held."

A lump sits in my throat. I want to say something, but I don't know what, so instead I lean forward and softly, lovingly, put my arms around her. I feel the boniness of her against me, the warmth. It's strange, but I love

Louise's smell. Patchouli, always, and that purple fabric softener she insists on using above all others. I always wanted a grandmother, years of wisdom behind her eyes, gentle hugs, the magic of real stories that took place when I didn't exist. And I feel like this is as close as I will ever get to one. And my heart fills with gratitude that I have met her.

I draw back, and she smiles at me, tears in her eyes, the moonlight lighting her old, beautiful face.

"Eliot is here, isn't he, Emmie?" she says, holding my hand. "He's always here. That can't be said about the other one. Let it be. Let him love you."

My throat feels as though it is stuffed with cotton wool. I nod. It's all I can do because the words are trapped.

"Thank you, Louise," I say softly, clearing my throat. "D-Do you need anything else?"

She shakes her head. "I have all I need here." Then she looks through the window at the moon, and instead of heading straight out the bedroom door, I lean in and kiss her warm, pale cheek.

"And you're not alone," I tell her. "And you are loved. You have me. You have us."

Louise looks at me, her eyes wet. "And I am very glad," she whispers.

"And of course," I add, "you have under-seasoned carbonara."

Louise laughs, reaches a hand behind my neck and puts her cold lips to my forehead. "Thank you," she whispers. "And remind me in the morning. I have something to give you that I think you need."

I leave, closing the door, leaving her to watch the moon and the stars dance in the sky.

I find Eliot in Louise's overgrown back garden, black jacket on but open, and beside him, two steaming cups of tea. When he sees me, he holds out a mug and smiles.

I take it, sitting beside him. "Thanks." I smile.

"Louise okay?"

I nod, lump still sitting in my throat. "Fine," I say. "She wanted to see the moon. Asked for her curtains to be left open."

Eliot smiles gently, his face lit just enough by the moon to see those crinkles at the side of his eyes as he smiles, and I feel it. That turning over in my stomach that Louise spoke about.

"So," he says, leaning back on the bench, long legs stretched out in front of him. "Here's to Emmie Blue seeing her first shooting star."

"Such confidence," I say. "And remember, I want proof it isn't a Boeing 747."

We're squashed together on this bench, arms, legs pressed together, and so close, I can smell the aftershave on his skin, the fresh smell of his clean clothes. Twice I thought he was going to kiss me this evening. Once when I stood beside him as he cooked, and a second time as I handed him the tray to take up to Louise. But it's me holding back, I know it is. Standing forever behind a barrier I can shrink back behind if I need to.

"*Seduce him*," Rosie had sung this morning. "Seriously, he is smoking hot, I don't even know how you'll even manage to refrain from taking him right there, in that musky ol' conservatory."

"Rosie, I don't even know if it's even—"

"Oh my God, the truck," she said, as if a lightbulb had pinged on above her head. "Fuck in the truck. Him in nothing but his little carpentry belt of tools."

"Dangerous," Fox had muttered. "All those sharp implements."

"And *them arms*." She had grinned at me. "I've seen them. Chuck you all over the place, they would. Get to it. Climb him like a fucking lamppost."

I'd burst out laughing at that, and Fox had smirked at her. "That how it's done, is it, Rosie?"

"Wouldn't you like to know, Fox?" she said.

And Fox's cheeks had pinkened, but not looking away, he'd said quietly, "Perhaps."

Eliot stretches an arm behind me, across the back of the bench, his hand resting on my shoulder. The air is sharp with February chill, the steam from our teas dancing and wisping wildly from our laps. "You won't need proof," he says. "Shooting stars are different. You'll know when you see it. It's like this . . . spark. This small but powerful little spark. Unmistakable."

"Fine," I say, looking up at the sky. "Eyes are officially peeled."

"And I promise," he says, "if worse comes to worst, Emmie Blue, and we don't see one this time, we will on the night of the Eta Aquariids."

I pause. "In English, please?"

He laughs. "A meteor shower. In May. You've got to stay up to an ungodly hour, but it's worth it. Trust me."

"I see." I nod. "Well, it's a date."

Eliot smiles. "It definitely is."

We drink our tea, talking in the low voices we'd use when we were kids and Jean and Amanda were asleep, our eyes fixed on the skies above, both of us silent for moments after Eliot points out certain stars or constellations. We did this all the time in Le Touquet. I must have been seventeen. Lucas, Eliot, and me, in Jean and Amanda's garden, on blankets on the neat lawn, me in the middle of them both. I can see it now, so vividly. Lucas was yawning, saying to Eliot, "Is the aim to fall asleep? Because I am almost there," and Eliot laughing and saying, "No, you dick. The aim is to not focus on anything. Just look at the sky as a big picture. And you'll catch one."

"There!" I'd squeal, and Eliot would groan from beside me, lean in and say, "Still a plane, Emmie."

"Can we just pretend it was a star and go in and watch TV now?" Lucas would tease, and Eliot would sigh and say, "The sky *is* one big TV."

We'd call him a knob then, but we wouldn't move. All of us facing the blackness of the sky, bats swooping overhead, birds, late home, but otherwise, the night silent and calm. I think of Lucas now. I wonder what he'd do if he could see us now, doing what we used to. He wouldn't like it. I know he wouldn't. He'd probably say something about looking out for me again. Maybe he'd even bring up the party itself. Our nineteenth. He'd bring up the fact Eliot spilled my secret just to impress a girl. He'd bring up that drinking game that derailed my whole life momentarily—dropping out of college, triggering the migraines again—if it wasn't for him, for Amanda, helping me get it back on track.

"Do you remember that night?" The words tumble from my mouth before I have even given it a thought.

Eliot doesn't move, but I feel him tense. He takes a noisy inward breath. "You're talking about you and Lucas. Your party."

I nod in the darkness. "Our nineteenth."

"What made you bring it up?" he asks calmly.

"I was just thinking of us. Of me, you, Luke, and lying in your mum's garden, you pointing out all the stars and constellations, and how much fun we used to have, how close we were . . . and that night, it all changed."

"I know." Eliot looks down at his lap. My heart thumps in my chest. "It was a long time ago," says Eliot. "But I'm still really fucking sorry it happened to you."

"I didn't bring it up to make you apologize."

"I know that, Emmie," he says. "But I am. Stacey had no right to do what she did."

"I didn't really care so much about her. It was more you. That you'd thought that of me. That . . . that what happened to me was my fault."

"*No*. God, no, Emmie." Eliot sits forward, shifting, turning, ducking to look at me under thick lashes. "Of course I didn't think that, not for a minute. I hated that what happened to you, did. I hate that you ever thought that I thought that of you—"

"But she was your girlfriend, Eliot. And in front of a garden full of people, she told everyone. And not that I was a victim—that I had lied, made it up, *teased* him, brought it on myself, and she knew *everything.* And only you knew everything. Only Luke did—"

"Emmie, no," he cuts in, looking at me pleadingly. "Just—I had no idea. I had no idea she knew."

"But . . . then how did—"

"I had no idea," he says again, long spaces between his words, and when I look up at him, I recognize that look—the dark, narrowed eyes, pink lips parted. The "judgmental" look he had on his face at the bar after I pushed Tom. The night of the party, as Stacey said those words, and I stood up, slowly, before walking away and crumbling in Lucas's bedroom. But it isn't judgment. It's worry. I know now that it's care. He cares.

"Let's not," I say, looking down at my lap.

"I think you should speak to Lucas—"

"It's done," I say. His hand reaches out, touches my chin, tips my face to look at him.

"Things, Emmie, aren't always how they appear. I did what I thought was best back then. For you."

He looks at me intently. I don't ask any more questions. I want to. I want to ask him what he means. I want to ask him why he thinks I should speak to Lucas; something that feels like a sting, stuck in the skin, since he said it. I don't want to ruin this beautiful, starlit evening. So I ignore the slow simmering in my stomach, and instead I say, "Let's get back to the shooting stars, shall we?"

Eliot hesitates, then smiles, his eyes still sad and glassy. "Sure." He settles back onto the bench beside me, arm back around me, but tighter this time, his hand stroking the top of my arm, and we sit for a while, gazing at the black sky. I feel as though we have popped a bubble that has been threatening to burst over us. This huge, unsaid thing that was never resolved. And although it isn't perfect, or neatly tied up with a bow, it is done. Louise is right. He is here. He's always here.

Eliot's arm suddenly shoots out, a finger pointing to the sky. "*Now*," he says. "See, see, look." And I catch it. For the first time in my whole life, I see it; a small spark, like the tapering of a firework, shooting across the sky, disappearing into nothing.

"Oh my God," I say, turning to him. "I saw it! It wasn't a plane!"

"It definitely wasn't," Eliot laughs. I snuggle into him, resting my head on his shoulder. And I wish so much, he would kiss me again. Because I think I would kiss him back this time. Properly.

Instead, Eliot leans in, and softly, lips against my hair, says, "Eyes on the sky, Flower. There are more to see."

A spark in my belly. A small, powerful spark. Unmistakable.

Eliot waits downstairs, making more tea as I go up to use the toilet. Louise's door is still ajar, and I don't know why, but I stop outside. Still. Everything is so still. Silent. And I think I know. I think that's why I push open the door, why I walk steadily across the floor to Louise's bed. That's when I see the mug of tea, on its side, its contents spread across the duvet like an ink spill. I reach out to touch her face.

I shout. I shout loud, so loud I don't even sound like myself. "Oh my God," I'm saying. "Oh no, please. Oh my God, oh my God."

I hear fast feet pummeling the stairs.

"Emmie?" Eliot says breathlessly, then I see his eyes travel over her. His face falls. His hand goes to his lips, gripping his mouth, his chin. Then he's by my side as I crumple to the floor and sink beside her bed, my face buried into her duvet. Patchouli. Purple fabric softener.

Louise is gone. Louise fell asleep and never woke up. The curtains still open, the moon watching over her.

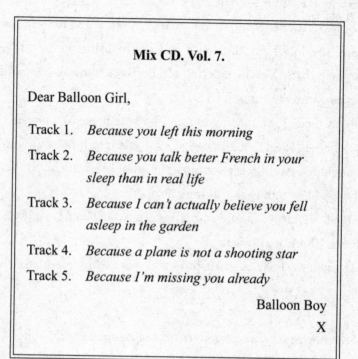

Mix CD. Vol. 7.

Dear Balloon Girl,

Track 1.   *Because you left this morning*

Track 2.   *Because you talk better French in your sleep than in real life*

Track 3.   *Because I can't actually believe you fell asleep in the garden*

Track 4.   *Because a plane is not a shooting star*

Track 5.   *Because I'm missing you already*

Balloon Boy

X

32

I remember when I was younger, three weeks felt like a lifetime. The two weeks following the Summer Ball were the longest two weeks of my life. Mum came home for two days, where she took baths and talked on the phone and made us one meal—a casserole—then she left again, and I was alone. I'd told her about Robert Morgan, but I don't think she really believed me anyway. She batted it away, the way she would when I fell over and grazed my knee.

"Oh, stop being so dramatic, Emmeline, there are far more worse off than you."

Two weeks now, though, pass like a gust of wind. That's how long it's been since Louise passed away, in her bed, watching the moon. The funeral was last week, and wasn't like normal funerals, with shiny coffins and drawling eulogies. It was a woodland burial; quiet, understated, simple. Like her.

Eliot and I went together. We were the only attendees, and that was by Louise's request, although later that day we had a visit from the next-door neighbors, Harry and Eve, with a printout of a charity donation in her name, and three tiger tomato plants Louise had loved. It was a small and beautiful affair among huge, old trees and wildflowers the color of coral.

Louise had planned it herself, just days after she was diagnosed with stage four cancer two years ago. She refused treatment because it would never cure her and she was petrified of hospitals. We only know that because Harry and Eve told us.

"Martha spent a lot of time in hospital. Died there," they told us. "And I think because of that, she wanted to be at home, with her things. I get that, I think," and Eliot and I had nodded in the doorway and said we did too.

The sound of the harsh ring of the doorbell interrupts me, mid-seal of a box of Louise's paperweights. When I get to the front door, it takes me a couple of seconds to realize it's Lucas's gray eyes peering over the brown paper bag in his arms.

"Whoppers for two?" he says, eyebrows raising behind his sunglasses.

"Oh my God." I throw my arms around him, the paper bag rustling between us. "What are you *doing* here?" My blood rushes with warmth at the sight of him; my best friend.

"You're squashing our Whoppers, love," he laughs into my ear. And then, "And you, obviously. You're what I'm doing here. How are you, Em?"

Ten minutes later, Lucas and I are sitting on Louise's floral sofa, burgers on our laps on square wrappers. "Fuck, I love a good Burger King," says Lucas.

"Do you *really*, though?" I laugh.

"What?" asks Lucas, mouth full.

"Just a surprising comment coming from the man who made a mushroom look like a burger bun last week and posted it on Instagram with the hashtag *can't tell the difference.*"

Lucas puts a fist to his mouth and laughs.

"A comment like that should get you hanged," I say. "It would if I were queen."

"If you were queen, you'd imprison poor Bon Jovi and force him to sing and caress you inappropriately."

"Correct. And it's—"

"*Jon*, yeah, yeah, eat your bloody burger, you."

Lucas and I eat in silence. I've been distant with him, I know, since the night we lost Louise. And not just because death has a way of throwing a dark blanket over everything—all the normal things you usually do, or pay a lot of mind to; all the trivial things, like what to make for dinner, and that slightly bitchy thing someone said about you at work. But because of the conversation Eliot and I had the night of the shooting star. About the night of our nineteenth. About Stacey. About Lucas. It set me off-balance, a little, and I've drawn back just slightly, because I wonder something I haven't wondered ever before in our friendship. If Lucas knows something I don't. "It's a beautiful house," he says. "Rickety, needs work. Updating. But it's beautiful."

I nod. "Victorian," I say. "I know that much."

Lucas smiles. "It may still have original tiles under here." He taps a foot on the carpet. "Or at best, floorboards."

"It'll make a nice family home," I say. "For whoever buys it."

"And what's happening with all that?"

"Solicitor is coming next week," I tell him. "Then I suppose it'll go on the market and—"

"And where will you go?"

I look at him, raise my shoulders. "I'll find somewhere else. Get another room somewhere, maybe even a flat on my own, but that's all down to money."

"Well, have you applied for any more jobs?"

It makes me wince. I know he has my best interests at heart—so pragmatic, sometimes, in the pursuit of what he wants—but I haven't thought much more about a new job in the last few weeks. I was concentrating on caring for Louise before she left us. Now I'm concentrating on missing her, of living in her home without her in it. On grieving her.

"No," I say. "I've been busy, obviously. Sorting Louise's house and going through her things is all I've really been thinking about."

"No, of course," says Lucas quickly. Then he puts down his burger, looks at me. "Em, I only mention the job stuff because I know deep down you want something else. I don't say it because I think anything is below you, or I'm measuring you against something. I say it because I want to help."

I swallow the food in my mouth, look up at him. "I know," I say.

"You studied, you worked hard and—"

"Luke, I know. And I'll get there. In my own time."

We eat, the TV on but the volume low, neither of us speaking. Until Lucas finishes his burger and screws up the wrapper. He wipes his hands on a napkin and looks around the room, then at me. "I know I should have come sooner, Em. I wanted to. But work. They're dicks. You have to give at least a fortnight's notice before you book off holiday, but I sorted it as soon as I could. I didn't want you to be alone."

"I haven't been," I say. "And you're here now."

"I am." Lucas smiles. "Yours until at least tomorrow night. Now. We need tea. Then it's up to you to put these muscles to work. Packing, lifting?" He flexes, kisses his bicep. "I'm your man."

I laugh. "You're a *knob*."

Lucas swoops off to the kitchen, taking the bag of rubbish with him from my hands. I hear him opening and shutting cupboards, trying to find mugs, and he starts singing to himself badly. I pass him on my way to the toilet and find him with my red polka-dot apron on. "You still have this," he laughs. "You used to wear this when manning the old lady fryer. It's like seeing an old friend." I am on the landing when I hear the doorbell sound. Before I can get there, Lucas is already scooting down the hallway, into the porch, and opening the front door.

"Oh," he says, teaspoon in hand. "*Hey*, dude. Nice surprise."

"Oh. Hiya, mate."

I rush to Lucas's side. Eliot stands there, tall, the breeze bristling his hair, rucksack over one shoulder, and square, paper-handled bag in his hand at his side.

"Nice . . . pinny." Eliot smiles at Lucas. "Hey, Em."

"Hey you." I smile, and I can already feel my skin heating at the sight of him.

"I carry anything off, you know that, big bro." Lucas looks down at the apron and brushes it with a hand. He puts his arm around me. "Fancy tea, El?" he says. "I just put the kettle on."

"Uh, actually, you two carry on."

"Don't be daft," I jump in. "You're not interrupting anything important, we're just—"

"Hanging out in pretty pinnies, eating burgers on the sofa, plotting hangings and Bon Jovi imprisonment—"

Lucas and I laugh at the same time, and Eliot smirks. "I'm intrigued, I can't lie," he says. "But actually, I was just passing by to give you these." He swings his bag off his shoulder, reaches into it, pulls out a fan of papers. "These are for Rosie. Drawings of the screen thing she wants, for the event next weekend."

"The blog-ference," I say.

And he smiles gently at me. "I mean, I've done some jobs, but this'll be my first ever *blog-ference.*"

"She'll probably have you dressed up à la Diet Coke Break."

Eliot laughs. "Yeah, she has a thing for the tool belt, doesn't she?" he says. "I told her I'd bring it but I am not taking my shirt off for less than fifty quid."

"Bit steep," I say, and Eliot raises his eyebrows. "What do you want, then, Emmie? Mates' rates?"

Lucas straightens next to me. "Right, well, I'll erm, go make the tea, shall I?"

"Little bro," Eliot says, reaching forward, and Lucas takes his hand; they do that rough, squeezing thing men do, when it looks like they're declaring a thumb war. "Should catch you at Mum's, at the weekend."

"Cool," says Lucas, and he walks off into the house.

"Are you sure you don't want to come in?"

Eliot smiles gently. "I'm sure," he says. "Plus, I've got a transatlantic phone call to take. So, no time for tea."

I raise an eyebrow. "Is this what happens when carpenters get head-hunted for blog-ferences? Transatlantic gigs, no time for your brother, or for boring old Emmie Blue?"

"Cabinetmaker, thanks," he says with a smirk. "And I'll explain what it's about. When I see you. I'll know more by then."

"You can tell me Saturday," I say.

"Pick you up at eight?"

"Perfect," I say. "Don't forget your tool belt."

Eliot gives a wink. "Wouldn't dare."

I find Lucas in the kitchen, squeezing tea bags against the sides of two mugs, still dressed in my red apron.

"So," I say. "Tea."

Lucas looks to his side at me, eyebrows raised.

"What?"

He shrugs. "Nothing."

"No, come on, what?"

He shakes his head, hesitates. "*Do* you want mates' rates?"

I laugh. Lucas doesn't. He just looks at me, stirring now, waiting for an answer.

"You do, don't you?"

I hesitate.

"Well, if you don't you better tell him that, then," says Lucas. "Poor dude's got it bad."

Lucas reaches across, touches a finger to the tip of my nose, smiles, and picks up his tea. It's later that I realized the bag Eliot was carrying at his side was a bag from Askew's. The bakery on the seafront he bought us lunch from twice last week. Eliot had planned to stay. Until he saw Lucas here.

33

WhatsApp from Lucas Moreau:

> Em, I need you.

WhatsApp from Lucas Moreau:

> Please please pick up.

WhatsApp from Lucas Moreau:

> I need to talk to you.

WhatsApp from Lucas Moreau:

> It's fucked. Everything is
> fucked.

I pack quickly, throwing two outfits and a pair of pajamas into an overnight bag. He'd sounded exhausted, drained, when he'd called last night. A child-like wobble in his voice, all sighs and disjointed sentences.

"I . . . I don't know what's going on, Em. We had this huge fight and I don't know what's going on—what . . . what am I going to do? I don't know if it's even happening. She—she's with her parents and I'm—God, I'm going fucking nuts here."

"I'll come," I said. "First thing."

And I meant to pack last night, too, but exhausted from a day of organizing barely a fifth of Fishers Way, I fell asleep on top of the sheets, in my clothes.

The doorbell cuts through my thoughts, and it's not until I see Eliot on the other side of the door, a grin on his face, that I realize I forgot to text him last night. I'd texted Rosie late, at about ten, and apologized for not being able to be there today, and . . . *shit*. I remember my finger on the screen, hovering above his name, to tell him, to text him and tell him I couldn't go. And I fell asleep. *I fell asleep.*

His smile fades when he takes in my face. "What's up? Am I too early? You said eight, didn't you?"

"I'm so sorry," I say, bringing my hands to my head. "I—I meant to text you."

"It's off?" he says. Then he laughs and says, "Oh well. Probably best. Wouldn't want to shame all those other carpenters being forced along to *blog-ference* under false pretenses when, really, it's all about objectification of our—"

"It's on," I cut in, cheeks burning now with embarrassment at bringing him here pointlessly. "At noon. As organized, but—I can't go."

Eliot nods, eyebrows knitting together. "Is everything okay?"

"Lucas," I say, and Eliot's face freezes, eyebrows still knitted, lips still slightly apart.

"Lucas?" he repeats.

"We spoke last night. He's—God, I don't know, Eliot, but he sounds terrible. Said he needed me, needed to talk, and . . ." I stop when I take in his face. Mouth now a hard line, sharp jaw, tense, eyes unblinking, as if listening to a story he doesn't buy for a second.

"What is it?" I ask.

Eliot takes a deep breath. "So, what, you're dropping everything and going over? *Now?* Just like that."

I nod slowly. "I'm getting the 11:00 a.m."

"And what about Rosie?"

"She was fine."

"And you are too?"

"Am I what?" I ask, face scrunching up, face burning even hotter now.

"Fine with that. Fine with not going to see Rosie today, at something really important to her. Fine with dropping everything—"

"Of course not, but he—he needs me. I'm his best friend, Eliot. He sounded really upset."

He looks down at the floor, runs his hand through his hair. "Okay," he says, looking up at me. "Okay."

"Eliot." I step forward, out onto the doorstep toward him, remembering our conversation before he left Fishers Way, when Lucas was here. "What did you want to tell me about?"

"What?"

"When you left last week. You said you had a phone call you'd talk to me about. You said you'd explain."

He pauses, mouth still a tight line. "It was with Mark. He's launched his business. He needs a hand. And he's asked if I'd consider going back for a while. To Canada. To help him. Like I'd planned last year."

My stomach aches at those words. *Canada.* That's miles away. "Wow," I manage. "That's—that's a big deal. Will you—will you go?"

He shrugs. "I don't know."

I step forward, closing the gap between us even more. "Eliot. Are we all right?"

He nods. "Text me the address of the place," he says shortly. "I'll head over there."

"Are you sure?"

"I can't let her down, can I?" He stares at me then for a second, jaw tight.

"Take photos," I say as he gives a nod and takes a step back, hand on his chin, eyes on the floor for a fleeting moment, as if considering something else, then he opens his truck door, gets inside, and drives away.

WhatsApp from Rosie Kalwar:

> OMG ELIOT FOR PRESIDENT.
> Look at my display! It's been
> Insta'd to shit!

WhatsApp from Rosie Kalwar:

> Also Fox is practically
> wanking because Eliot is
> interested in all his traveling
> stories, and they are both
> sitting there talking about
> Canada and some place I've
> never heard of that sounds
> totally made-up.

WhatsApp from Rosie Kalwar:

> Seriously, Fox is practically
> climaxing at the stories. Eliot
> said his friend has offered him
> work and he might go back
> though. WTF? You did not
> mention this?

WhatsApp from Rosie Kalwar:

Almost straddled him myself and shouted in his face "YOU CAN'T LEAVE, YOU HAVE TO FALL IN LOVE WITH MY EMMIE AND MAKE LOTS OF WOOD-CUTTING BABIES!"

WhatsApp from Rosie Kalwar:

Also, that belt. So hot. Utilize it. Role-play is your friend.

34

"Keep them closed."

"You want me to keep my eyes closed while I go *up* stairs?"

Lucas chuckles from behind me, his hands on my waist. "Just trust me."

"I do. But also, try not to let me break my spine."

"I won't, I promise."

I got into Calais an hour ago, and Lucas seemed so much happier than I expected him to be. He was grinning, eyes bright, dressed for the frosty weather, in a black overcoat and a gray jumper beneath. Smart and as waspy as ever. He greeted me with a giant coffee and hugged me, groaning into my ear as he lifted me, raising me onto my tiptoes. "God, it's *so* good to see you, Em." Then he said he had somewhere to show me, and before I knew it, we were on the motorway, on our way to Honfleur, like we used to, on our Dream House Drives, the winter sun high in the sky, the in-car heating on full.

"You're going to get lost again," I said as large dual carriageways turned into meandering country lanes, and he'd laughed and said, "With any luck, eh?"

We stopped at a tiny café, where, dominated by hunger, we ordered far too much food to take away and eat in the car with us. Sticky buns, toasted sandwiches, crisps, and two boxes of macarons, and like the old days, we slowed by huge mansions, and Lucas, now armed with several years' experience in architecture, pointed out things that were mostly lost on me.

"It's to give the illusion of no seams at all, you see."

"I do."

"Do you?"

"*Sort* of."

"Close enough, Em."

Then we pulled up here—the house in which I am currently being led blindly around. An ultramodern detached, three-story house—perhaps too white and modern for my tastes—with a stone driveway, a double garage, and a gate with touchscreen access. It is one of three houses in a row, in what feels like the absolute middle of nowhere. All three of them stark and brash among the green, soft surroundings.

"Why are you pulling up? Say if the owners come out," I'd flapped.

"She doesn't move in until next week. This," he said, clicking open the car door and nodding toward the house, "is my latest baby."

I followed him, stepping out of the car, and laughed, looking up at the vastness of it; the pure *Grand Designs*-ness of it. "This? You—you designed this?"

"Certainly did. Well. My firm did. I was the lead."

I stood back, gawping, my chest puffing up. "*Luke.* This is . . . amazing. You used to *draw* shit like this on envelopes when we were kids."

Lucas laughed, coming to stand beside me, muscular arms folded. "I know, right?"

"And here it is. In real life."

The pride I felt for him surged through my body, like sunlight. He dreamed of this. Of this job and of houses like this, and here he is, before it, within it, something he imagined, brought into existence. Nothing but fields and dust had been here before, and now, it was a house that is someone's to-be home. I've only seen the hallway so far though, a huge, sweeping staircase dominating the center of it, winding up to a mezzanine balcony. Doors, white and rectangular, with huge panes of glass inside. Modern. Much too modern for me, but beautiful. It's things like the clock: a clock that's just a shadow on one of the walls, that screams Lucas to me. It's all so him. "You're so Austin Powers," I'd said to him once as he'd fawned over gadgets—things with buttons and codes and contraptions appearing from kitchen counters with the click of a switch.

We reach the top step now. Lucas moves so he is beside me, but he doesn't take his hands from around my waist. I hear the squeak of a door handle. The air smells like wet paint and new wood, but swiftly, I am hit with fresh, late-winter air.

"Are we outside?"

"Wow. All that *Diagnosis Murder* certainly paid off."

"Fuck you," I say, and Lucas laughs. "Remember, I'm your eyes right now, Em. Don't bite the hand that feeds."

He takes my hand in his now and says, "Keep coming, keep coming." Then he lets go. "Hold your hands out," he says, and he places them to grasp what feels like a cool, steel pole, his warm hands on top of mine. I feel him beside me, my eyes still scrunched shut as I promised.

"There better not be a dungeon on the other side of my eyelids."

"You wish," he says, amused.

"I would run so fast . . ."

"Go on. Open 'em up."

And when I do, I am winded at the sight of the view. Stretches of noth-ingness, of heathy grass, and just at its edge, the sea. Turquoise, glittering with winter sunlight.

"That's the port," he says. "Remember? Where we'd walk and talk, when we were kids."

"Oh my God, *I do*. Way back, when for a while we thought my dad lived around here."

"In a house like this." Lucas smiles.

"A bed shaped like a drum set."

"Roadies guarding the gates like trolls," Lucas says, and we both laugh. We stand close. Arm to arm, the fabric of our jackets touching.

"Reality is a bit different," I say, gazing out to the port.

"But at least you know the reality," says Lucas gently, and I nod and tell him he's right. Gulls swoop overheard, and we watch tiny boats bob, like in souvenir pens, on the horizon. It's quiet up here. Calm.

"I really miss it," I say. "The surmising. The *dreaming*."

Lucas leans, forearms moving to rest on the balcony. "We still can, can't we?"

"Hard to dream up drumming, cool fathers when you know your real father is probably a hack."

Lucas nudges me and says softly, "It's his loss, Em. Totally. He has no idea what he's missing."

"I know," I say.

We stand, looking out to the sea, side by side, and I look up at the sun; the same sun that shone down on us, all those years ago, as we planned and dreamed out loud, speculating where we'd end up, never once doubting that we wouldn't be there together.

"You made this," I say after awhile, looking behind me at this beautiful house—this *design*—and back to the view; the blue distant sea, the blankets of green, the tufts of pure white cloud.

"And there's many more where that came from." He smiles at me, and moves closer again, the tops of our arms pressing together.

"You did it," I say, and he presses a cheek to mine, our skin warm from the sun.

"Just the Lamborghini left to get now, eh? Oh, and to actually *own* a place like this. It's Ana's, you know."

"Ana? As in Eliot's Ana?"

Lucas nods, gives a heavy shrug. "Well, she isn't Eliot's anymore, but yeah. That Ana. She's not due to move in for a week or so. We've got some stuff to straighten out before she does."

I nod, unconvinced, and can't help but think she would rather anyone here but me. "What happened with her and Eliot?"

Lucas brings his hands together, eyes on the horizon. "He ended it. And to be honest, I'm not surprised. He's not been happy for a while."

"Really?"

"Yeah, but then . . . he reached his scary age, you know?" he says, as if it's fact, as if it's common knowledge. "The same age as his dad was, when he died. And I think El's thinking life's short. If it doesn't make him happy . . ."

"And she didn't? Make him happy, I mean."

Lucas looks at me again. "I'm not sure anyone's ever made Eliot completely happy." Lucas looks over at me then. "What? You thinking you *do* want mates' rates after all?"

I clear my throat. "Actually, I was just thinking that I can see you and Marie here, in a place like this." I change the subject. Because now I can't get Eliot's face out of my head. The disappointment—the hurt—in his face when I told him I was coming here, instead. And Canada. He told Rosie about Canada. He might go back. How would I feel if he went back? If I didn't see Eliot again for . . . I don't know how long. "Yeah, I can see you raising a couple of kids in a place like this," I carry on. "Couple of dogs. Or horses. Marie strikes me a horse type."

"Really?"

I look at him. "Yeah. I mean, in my opinion, if you want all those kids Marie keeps going on about, you might need a few more carpets. Make it a bit more kid-friendly. But apart from that. Looks like your perfect marital home, if you ask me. Very *you two*."

His face falls a little and he looks down at his hands gripping the bar of the balcony. "Marital home," he repeats. "Can you *really* see that, Em?" It isn't a question, it's more of a scoff.

"Why do you say that?"

He sighs, doesn't answer, and looks up to the sky.

"What happened, Luke?" I ask then. "When you called, you said you'd had a big fight. Is everything okay now? I didn't want to pry straightaway but . . ." I trail off. "It's why you called me in the first place."

Lucas groans, rubs his face with his hand. "Ah, man, it was stupid. We were a bit drunk and talking about exes and . . . I told her about Holly. Do you remember Holly? At uni? It was like a million years ago."

"I remember."

"It just came out, that we were engaged, and she was—gutted."

I think of Marie, at that table, in that café, telling me how scared she was to be happy, that Lucas chose her to propose to, and I can see why something small like that would feel like a mountain to her.

"It just got stupid, got out of hand," he says. "You know what it's like, after too much wine, and yeah, okay, maybe I should have told her at some point, but everything was so good, Emmie, and—I dunno. I was a kid then. It didn't matter. But Marie said it's because she asked me to my face, if I'd ever proposed before, and I'd said no countless times."

I pull my mouth into a grimace. "Ugh. So a bit of a mess then."

"Totally. And I mean, I get it. She's been hurt before, and she gets insecure and . . . I haven't exactly helped things in the past, what with that business trip to Belgium last year, when we last broke up. You know, when I texted that girl from the Oz office, like a dick. But it all just sort of went to shit last night. Mountain and molehill, you know?"

I hesitate, then stand a little straighter. "You texted her?"

"What?"

"You texted Ivy?"

Lucas's brow furrows, gray eyes narrowing, the sun catching on his lashes. "Um, no, not now, I'm talking about like, two Novembers ago. When we broke up. The last time. You remember."

"I do," I say. "But you told me you didn't text Ivy. You told me *she* texted you and you didn't reply and that is why Marie and you split up. Because Marie was paranoid."

Pinkness spreads across the freckles on his nose. "Did I?"

"*Yes.*"

Lucas sighs, hands stretched out in front of him, as if about to clap. "Look, it was nothing, Em, it was a stupid flirty text that I shouldn't have sent, and I wanted it to go away. Forget it happened."

"But why did you lie to me?"

Lucas laughs, then stops at the sight of me, drawing back. "Are you serious?"

"Yes. Yes, I am. Why lie to *me* when you know I would be there anyway."

He shrugs heavily, standing, stuffing his hands in his pockets, shoulders square. "Because I was probably ashamed. I didn't realize I lied to you. I thought you knew."

"Well, you must've realized at the time."

"Emmie, *come on.*" He ducks then, to meet my eye, an almost amused "you're making a big deal out of nothing" smile on his face. "I'm marrying Marie in two weeks. We sorted it. And Ivy is water under the bridge—"

"Oh, you are marrying Marie, then?"

He looks at me, jolts back as if he's been slapped. "What do you mean?"

And suddenly I feel like a fool. I came here to help him. I thought he needed me, and that he needed *help*. Like he did when he was backpacking. Like so many times before.

"I was worried it might be called off or—your voice on the phone, Lucas, you sounded—"

"I know, I know. Look, I admit, I was nuts with worry. I thought that was it. That's why I called you. But Marie and I talked this morning, before I picked you up. We talked through it and—I'm sorry, I didn't mean to worry you." He takes his hands out of his pockets, holds my shoulders. "It means the world to me that you're here."

I look at him, and wonder how much of this is calling me, asking me to come, just to see if I still would. And I think of Ivy. A small thing, yes, but I defended him fiercely after that breakup, thought Marie to be jealous and unreasonable. And I think of Eliot. Lovely, reliable, gorgeous Eliot, turning up always when I needed him, for Louise, for Rosie, for me, beside me on that bench, beneath shooting stars. And his face when I brought up that night. The sadness in his deep brown eyes. The regret. What he said. About things not being how they appear.

"Lucas," I say. The winter chill swirls around us, goose bumps prickling my neck. "Can I ask you something?"

"Of course."

"That night. Of our nineteenth. Never Have I Ever."

Lucas looks at me and nods, quickly. Color draining.

"What don't I know about it?"

"W-What?"

I swallow. "It was you, wasn't it?" I ask again. Because I know now, looking at his face, at his body language, the way his shoulders have gone rigid and his jaw tight, that there is something. He looks the same as he did when I asked about Ivy. I know. I have known, really, since the night of the shooting star. But I've been too frightened to look it in the eye. To say it aloud. And any shred of doubt I've had, that the night of our nineteenth was all down to Lucas, I've watered with every kind thing he's done, every nice thing he's ever said, until denial felt easy. And I want him to say it, here, in front of me, in front of the port we'd walk along, dreaming up our futures.

"Emmie, I don't know what you—"

"Stop," I say calmly. "I want you to tell me."

Lucas stares at me, his chest rising and falling, lips parted. "I . . . Em, you need to remember that I was young and stupid—"

I remember the music playing that dusky summer's evening. A fast, soulless dance track that Eliot kept complaining about. I remember the way Stacey, from under Eliot's arm, giggled as she stood, her drink in hand, raising high above her head. The way her belly button was pierced with a rose-colored stud, and the way Lucas kept eyeing it, his eyes traveling over her body, laughing at everything she said.

"My turn," she'd said, and Eliot had held on to her hand, trying to pull her back down onto the sun-lounger with him. "Never have I ever . . ." she started, a grin on her face.

My heart speeds up now, pulsating in my throat, at Lucas, biting his lip.

"And Stacey, she was a bitch, Em, she was. I didn't realize that at the time, I was so stupid, but . . . but I was—I liked her. And she wasn't Eliot's girlfriend, not really. They'd had a couple of dates, and—Emmie, please, please look at me . . ."

"Never have I ever . . ." Stacey had giggled. Then she looked at me and I'd smiled, held up my drink, ready, because I thought she was my friend. I thought that whole group were my friends. Not like the kids back home. A new start, with friends like Lucas and Eliot. Friends who didn't know me as "that girl." Friends who saw me like them.

"And earlier that night, she asked if you and I were an item and—Emmie, please, don't."

I stride away from him, toward the exit of this clinical, encompassing balcony. I know. I know now. I don't even need him to finish the sentence.

"You told her," I say, voice wobbling. "About the assault. About Robert Morgan. Those were your words. 'No of course I'm not dating that *tease*; she tried to shag her teacher.' Is that what you said?"

"*No*. No, she said them, not me. I don't think that. I have *never* thought that." He speaks urgently, rushing his words out, striding to close the gap between us, hand outstretched, but I step back again. "I told her the truth. That I wouldn't get with you because you . . . you'd been through this thing with a teacher . . ." He stops, eyes closing. "God, I don't know what to say to you." Lucas's voice croaks now. "Besides, I was nineteen and stupid and a dick and trying to impress some idiot girl. Em, you are everything to me, you know that."

"But Eliot. You let him take the blame for that. Why?"

"I didn't want to lose you. It was a stupid, drunken mistake, and I have regretted it every single day."

The night rushes through my head now, and I want to remember everything about it. *How did I miss it?* And why didn't Eliot tell me? Why would he let me walk this earth for so many years believing it was him that threw me off track, when it was Lucas. When it was the only person I had relied on for practically my whole life.

"A prick tease." I remember her smirking mouth as she said those words. "Never have I ever been *a prick tease* and fucked a teacher's life up."

Those words hurt just as much now as they echo through my brain, as they did that evening, in the new dress I'd saved up for, excited for another year of college, sitting among a group of people who saw me for me. Emmie Blue. One of them.

"Emmie." Lucas reaches for my hands now and takes them, his gray eyes desperately pleading. "You are *everything* to me. Please don't let this ruin us."

He holds my cheek, face inches from mine. "Me and you. You and me. It's all that matters to me." I look up at him, and I am winded by how much I longed for this moment, him looking into my eyes, beautiful pink lips inches from mine, strong hand holding my face as if it's the most precious thing in the world. And he leans in. I freeze, feel his breath on my mouth. He kisses me. Lucas pushes his lips to mine. I reach up, a hand around his neck, and when his lips part, that is when I fall away from him—a huge lunge backward, freeing myself from his arms.

"Oh my God."

We stare at each other.

"What are you—what are *we doing?*"

He looks shocked. "I don't—I don't know—"

"You're getting married, Lucas," I say. "To Marie. To beautiful, kind Marie. I don't want this. I don't."

And he says nothing. He just stares at me. He doesn't say he isn't; he doesn't say he's made a mistake and that it's me. And when I say, "I need to go home," all he does is nod, and I watch the Adam's apple contract in his neck.

"Okay. Okay, Emmie," he says.

On the way down the stairs, neither of us speaks. "The car," he says. "I don't recognize that car," he says, motioning to the empty, white, parked Corsa on the drive. I say nothing. "Probably a neighbor," he says. "Was it here when we pulled up?" But again, I say nothing.

By four o'clock I'm on the ferry home, on that same ocean I had stared out at beside Lucas mere hours before.

I watch France disappear into the horizon.

35

Me: I know it wasn't you. I wish
you'd have told me sooner.

Eliot Barnes: What good would it
have done?

I am carrying a tray of empty breakfast plates when Rosie bursts into the kitchen, breathless, cheeks flushed, eyes wide.

"Emmie!"

I freeze, tray to my chest. "What? What's wrong?"

"You need to come into reception," she says. "Right now."

"What?"

"Now. Immediately."

I look over my shoulder at the busy, bustling kitchen, at the chefs, shouting to one another over the sizzle of pans, over the whoosh of open ovens, the scooting of waitstaff in and out of the kitchen door.

"Rosie, we're so busy—"

"*Emmie.* Seriously. Dump that and come. Now." Rosie turns and dashes out again, and by the time I get to the reception area, I'm not sure what I'm expecting. Mum glimmers into my mind for a second, for some reason. Lucas, fleetingly. And then of course Eliot, whom I haven't been able to stop thinking about.

But there is only one person in reception apart from Rosie, and it's a woman. Short, with bobbed blond hair, in a black furry coat, a black leather handbag on her shoulder, and she's looking around the room as if she's never stepped foot into the hotel before. I don't recognize her. I wait for her face to register—a disgruntled customer, perhaps, from this morning, but I recognize nothing. I have never seen her before.

"Excuse me." Rosie leans forward. "This is Emmie." And as the woman turns to me, Rosie sits down at her desk and busies herself, typing.

I look at the woman. "Hi?" I say.

"Gosh," she says, laughing, eyes shining. "You're Emmie."

"I am."

"Of course you are." She smiles nervously. "It—it's unmistakable."

I look at Rosie, but she's staring at her screen, purposefully avoiding my gaze.

"Sorry, I—who are you?"

She steps forward then, and I see that her green eyes are watery and her hands are shaky as she holds one of them out. I take it.

"Carol," she says, voice wobbling. "Marv's wife. Your . . . your dad's wife."

———————

"He told me last week," Carol tells me, the both of us sitting on a small two-seater in the quiet reception. "It was a shock. Ever such a shock. And of course my first reaction was a negative one. Shamefully."

I shake my head. "I understand."

"But then I thought of you, and our Cadie, and . . . I thought there is no way you should be punished for something you had no part in." Carol swallows, a tissue balled in her hand.

"And I went up the next day; visited Cadie. Who . . ." She laughs to herself, eyes skyward, shoulders rising and falling. "Well, it was like she'd had a win on the pools."

I smile, warmth spreading through me. *"Really?"*

"She's wanted a brother or a sister her whole life." She stops, looks at me. "But that was never to be. But. Well. Half is just as good as, isn't it?"

I nod, warmth spreading through my bloodstream like wine. "I—I think so."

"So, I told Marv he was to ring you. Invite you round. That we could work through it as a family, and if we could just meet you—" She stops, shaking her head and bringing her hand to her mouth. "Gosh, you do look like Cadie. When you do that. See, that." She laughs. "Those eyebrows going up. That's her, that is."

I laugh, tears caught in my throat. "I love that you say that," I tell her, my words barely there. Carol has a warm face. Glowy and welcoming and like every smiley, motherly dinner lady I'd chat with, sometimes, in the lunch queue.

"Did you block his telephone?" she asks.

I nod, look down at my lap. "I did. The waiting and checking my messages—I couldn't do it. I've waited my whole life, and waiting any longer, having it so close . . . it was just too tough."

Carol nods slowly, golden teardrop earrings swinging. "Of course," she says. "But anyway, that's why I'm here. He's at home. I didn't know if you wanted to see him."

"I do," I say.

Carol smiles, a gap in her front teeth, like Brigitte Bardot. "I wondered if you had plans for Easter. We're going up to see friends on Good Friday, but on Easter Sunday, I'd like to do a dinner. A nice lunch. Just us. Cadie. You. Me and . . . your dad."

Tears tumble now, suddenly, uncontrollably. I nod, can't speak.

"Oh my love," says Carol. Then after a while, she rubs my hand and says, "So dinner. Do you eat meat?"

I smile. "Yes."

"Oh, good," Carol says, hands squeezing the tissue at her lap. "Marv can do his lamb. One bloody thing he is good at."

Carol cuddles me when she leaves, and I wait, watching her walk away, block heels clopping on the tarmac, the tissue pressed under her eye. She stops at the corner, takes out her phone, and smiles as she speaks into it. I imagine it's to tell Marv that I'll speak to him. Or to tell Cadie that she's seen me. Cadie. My sister. I have a sister. I have a family.

A few nights later, Rosie sits at the kitchen table at Fishers Way, looking down into the silver-and-white gift box on the tablecloth.

"I only ever got one mix CD when I was fourteen. And that was from a boy who used to eat his own face."

I look blankly at Rosie, from the stove, stirring chicken around a wok.

"You know, his own dry skin."

"Lovely," I say. "Really looking forward to this pad Thai now."

"Sorry," she laughs. "Fox said to me yesterday that there isn't a tone I won't lower, and I think he meant it as a compliment."

"And even if he didn't, I think you need to take it as one."

"Oh, I already have." Rosie smiles. Then she takes out one of the CDs and turns it over in her hand. "God, look at this one. *Because I should've asked you to dance.* That's what he's put here."

"I know."

"Romantic teenager or what?" she says, putting it back down. "So, eight of them."

The pan sizzles as I stir, and I nod over at Rosie. "There should've been nine," I tell her. "I was owed another, but—"

"He forgot?" Rosie puts the lid back on the gift box. "I hate when things like that suddenly fizzle, because while you're doing them, you're so bloody sure and determined that they never will, you know? You can't picture it stopping."

"You're right," I say. "And really, I think things just changed after that night. They were just one of many things that stopped. And now, as an adult, I can see it as a nasty comment from some clueless girl."

"But at the time . . ."

"At the time it was catastrophic, really. It had taken me such a long time to accept I was a victim. And her saying what she did . . . I spiraled. I felt like I could never escape it. And that I couldn't even trust Eliot. And nothing really mattered anymore. Not college. Not anything. Especially not the CDs."

Rosie nods gently and picks up her glass of wine.

"Well, I think this is good," she says, gesturing toward the gift box of CDs on the table. "It's closure, in a way. On that part of your life."

"I think so," I say. "That's how it feels."

It's been almost a fortnight since Lucas kissed me on that balcony. Almost a fortnight since we said nothing to each other on the way home. We haven't spoken either. I got a text message from him that night, saying he was so sorry, that I was his best friend and his life would not have been the one it's been without me. But I didn't reply. Plainly because I didn't know how I felt. I wanted to. So much, but I just didn't know where to begin. I haven't spoken to Eliot either, except for the one text, which I sent on the ferry back.

That was it. And it's been hard, rattling about in Louise's huge house without them both on the end of a phone, without Eliot popping by. But I've needed it, I think. To be away from them. It's helped me get here. It's helped me realize what I need to do.

"You are incredible, do you know that?" Rosie says. "Like, you are fucking incredible. And I know you think everything is a mess, Em, but it isn't. You are out the other side of something, and not only are you standing, but you're standing *strong*."

"Do you think?"

"Fuck yeah, you *are*," says Rosie, putting her hand on mine.

You've had a lot to deal with, not just then, but recently. And look. You're strong, you're caring, and . . . I can't even begin, Emmie." She passes me my wine and dips her head, as if to say, "Go on. Down it." "Listen, you were in love with a man who is getting married, and where I would be turning up on his doorstep in nothing but a trench coat and high heels, you're fuckin' suit shopping with him, spending time with his fiancée, not to mention you've just found out that he lied to you and yet, you've written this incredible speech, and this gift . . ." She looks down at the box on the table. "You're brave. You're selfless and brave and moral and God, there are so many people out there that need that shit in their lives. Including me." Then she looks up at me, tears in her brown eyes. "I am *gassed* to have a friend like you."

And I laugh. "Me too, Rosie."

"And Eliot," Rosie carries on, cocking her head. "I know how he'd feel about that trench coat and heels."

"I don't know," I laugh, and Rosie smiles and says, "I do. *Gassed*."

I serve up dinner for Rosie and me and move the box to the kitchen counter. Lucas's wedding present. Every mix CD he sent me. His first email. The tag from my balloon: my mini confession. Our history, in objects, in a box I'll give away, to him, on his wedding day. The day he starts a new life as someone's husband. Lucas Moreau. My Balloon Boy. A grown man now. And soon to be, Marie's husband.

"So," chomps Rosie. "I've got news."

I put down my fork. "Go on."

"The other night, Fox and I went out to a pub after work. And . . . well we sort of . . . well, I shagged him," she says triumphantly.

I am glad I have just swallowed or I would have definitely choked. "*What?*"

"Yup. Twice. Two nights ago. Can you believe it?"

I stare at her. My mouth falls open, and then I burst into laughter. "Are you serious?"

"One hundred percent."

"I'm going to need details, Rosie. So much more than just that."

Then she grins, straight white teeth and lips the color of rubies, holds her glass up, and says, "Oh you can have them all. And they're hot. Believe Auntie Rosie." She giggles, and I am smiling so much my cheeks ache. "But first! Let's toast. Here's to you, Ms. Emmie Blue, the brave. And here is to me, Dame Rosie Kalwar, for I, just two days ago, had the best sex of my life—"

"Of your *life?*"

"Of my life, I swear!"

"With Fox?" I ask, still gawping

"*With Fox,*" says Rosie, clinking my glass. "Fastidious Fox."

We clink glasses and drink.

Mix CD. Vol. 8.

Dear Balloon Girl,

Track 1   *Because I worry this makes me a coward*

Track 2.   *Because for now, these CDs will have to do*

Track 3.   *Because sometimes I just want to send a letter*

Track 4.   *Because sometimes I lay awake wondering what you're doing*

Track 5.   *Because I wonder if you're awake, doing the same too*

Love,
Balloon Boy
X

37

Lucas throws his arms around me when I show up at the cottage, the morning before the wedding, his face melting with relief.

"You're here," he says. "God, Em, I'm so happy you're here."

Amanda looks relieved at the sight of me too, and Jean, although mostly constantly unreadable, gives me an unexpected long hug and says, "My boy can now relax, no?"

I don't know if Lucas told them. I don't know if they know we argued, or that he told me the truth, or kissed me. But I got on the ferry and researched buses in advance, to make sure I made it without anyone's help. And I know, from now on, that things won't ever be the same again with Lucas and me. Even if we put everything that happened that fortnight ago on the balcony behind us, which I'm sure in time we will, he's about to get married. Something that will undoubtedly change the dynamic of everything between us forever. I might have loved him—and I still love him— but after finding out about Stacey, about Ivy and that text, and especially, more than anything, after that kiss on the balcony and how *wrong* it felt, it is what Rosie said. It is the idea of him, I am sure, that I am in love with. And I am ready to let that idea go. He is my best friend. That is everything. That is all.

The ceremony is being held in a classically beautiful room on the first floor of the hotel, with high ceilings and large windows. It is simple and elegant: everything Marie set out to do. Hydrangeas and sprigs of baby's breath are wrapped in cream ribbon and pinned to the end of each line of chairs, and there is a play list of modern love songs playing quietly as we wait for the bride. Lucas and I stand beside each other at the front of the room as guests file in.

So nervous, he mouths, and I shake my head.

"No need," I tell him. "It's going to be amazing," and he looks at me and smiles.

I thought I would feel devastation in this moment. The Emmie Blue on the veranda of Le Rivage would have sworn that right now, I would be swamped with crippling heartbreak. But I'm not. The only sort of negative emotion I feel is slightly sad, but it isn't a jealous sort of sad, it's that end of an era feeling; the sort of feeling you have when you're leaving a job and you know so much that it's for the best, but you'll miss it. The familiarity. The routine of it.

I glance over my shoulder again. The room is filling up now, almost every seat full, a sea of hats and stiff, pressed suits. And that's when I see him. Eliot, walking in beside Jean, who popped out for a cigarette some moments ago. *Somersault. Somersault.* My stomach reacts before my brain has fully acknowledged that he's here. He walks slowly, nodding as Jean talks, and the sight of him, so tall, a smattering of dark stubble on his face, the sharp, dark gray suit he's wearing, makes my chest ache. I look away, and even when he approaches the chairs reserved for Lucas's family, in the rows behind me, I pretend I haven't seen him; but from the corner of my eye, I can see he is staring at me. When I turn, he smiles gently, then looks away, striking up a conversation with his mum, beside him.

The ceremony is being translated from French into English, and although it is being done tastefully, it is taking twice as long. But now, the registrar, the British one who has a head like an egg, turns to us, and asks us if we know of any reason why Marie and Lucas shouldn't marry.

I remember a conversation Fox and Rosie and I had once, when Fox jokingly said I should stand up in the ceremony and tell Lucas that I love him; that it should be me, and be carted off, like a classic Peggy Mitchell. My mouth lifts at the corner, just slightly, at the memory, but I say nothing now, of course. Lucas looks at me fleetingly, and smiles as nervous laughter echoes down the pews.

Moments later, Lucas says "I do" in French.

"I do," says Marie in English.

And that, is that.

I'm not sure who taps the wineglass to get everyone's attention, but all I know is that it is mere seconds before the entire room has turned to face me, standing at the top table beside Amanda.

The box is in front of me, on the table, and I am passed a microphone, and it is only now that my hands begin to shake. I swallow, clear my throat, bringing the mic to my lips. The speech I have written, and learned by heart, is on the table in front of me, in case I fluff my lines or forget what I'm going to say.

"Hello, everyone," I say. "I hope you'll forgive me for speaking entirely in English, selfishly, but also selflessly, because I speak French so horribly that I'm actually doing you all a favor."

Laughter. A titter. Nothing like Rosie's hysterical laughter when I practiced it on her last week. She acted like I was Lee Evans, live in her living room.

I take a big deep breath. Here goes nothing.

"My name is Emmie, and I am Lucas's best woman. Yes, very twenty-first century, very millennial, so I am told, but something I am honored to be today, for one of my oldest friends.

"Lucas, I struggle to remember my life without you in it. We were sixteen when we met, and we met in a way people hardly believe when I tell them how. I let go of a balloon on my school field, and Lucas found it, miles away on a beach in Boulogne. He emailed me, and a friendship was born from that one singular hello across the ocean, of even more emails, letters, parcels, and eventually, real-life meetings. I also once sent him my French exam tape, which I am not entirely sure helped, considering the last time I asked for directions, I asked if the man I'd stopped had a complicated horse I could borrow."

More laughter. *Good.* I look up to my audience and I see Eliot, on the table opposite. He's sitting back on his chair, arms crossed at his chest, finger and thumb holding his chin. He watches me, a small, encouraging smile on his lips.

"If you get nervous," Fox had said last week, "pretend you're saying it in front of just Eliot. It'll help."

"Just don't imagine him naked," said Rosie. "Unless you want your vagina all aflame at the top table, because I'd bet my dad's car on it that he's hung. What? Don't look at me like that, Fox, I don't make the rules."

"Some of you may know," I continue now, to the sea of watchful faces, "but Lucas and I share a birthday, and through that, have shared every year, on our birthdays, together. Lucas is a bad and sickly drunk. Sorry, Jean, but your lost silk tie, the purple one, with the diamonds on it, is buried deep in a pot in your beautiful garden somewhere. I buried it. It was me. Sorry, Luke. Marriage voids the nondisclosure agreement."

Jean bursts out laughing and points at Lucas, and Lucas hides his face as laughter fills the room.

"So, Marie, I guess you should take this as a warning to never lend clothing to your husband on a night out." I look at Lucas. "I won't be there to bury it next time."

Lucas smiles up at me.

"Not to sound like I am reciting Lucas's CV, here, but truly, really, Lucas, for all his faults, is a spontaneous, passionate, and driven man, the type that throws their heart out in front of them and runs after it. I stole that, by the way, I am definitely not that poetic."

Amanda, beside me, pulls tissue from her clutch bag. "And Marie. If he keeps his marriage the way he keeps his friendships, protecting them with care, and loyalty, and love, and the guts to hold his hands up when he is wrong . . ." I look at Tom now, who is very drunk already, and crying like a baby, his arm stretched out patting Lucas's back. "Then, I am positive you are in the safest of hands."

I bend and pick up the box. I lean over and hand it to Lucas. I see, when he smiles, a glimmer of that sixteen-year-old boy who'd flicker onto the library computer screen from his Webcam, raise a hand in a wave. The sixteen-year-old boy who'd text me until I fell asleep, who'd steal his dad's mobile to call me when he knew I was alone on a Saturday night, because he would be too.

"In this box is the very first email Lucas sent to me," I say, "and I cannot tell you how much I needed that email on that day during that particular time of my life. It was a life jacket more than an email. A lifeline." I swallow, tears filling my eyes. "Then there is the card that was attached to the balloon that he found, and even a jar of Marmite. The first gift I ever sent Lucas. I also sent him a DVD of *Footballers' Wives*, for those that remember, and I can't put that in the box because I know that still lives in his bedroom now, fourteen years on. He still watches it too. Pauses too much on the sex scenes. The one on the snooker table even jumps, it's been watched that many times."

Laughter again, Marie all grins, her hands to her chest, wedding band glinting.

"You'll also find in the box the eight CDs that Lucas sent me when we were kids. He said I had terrible taste in music, but it wasn't until I saw his own CD collection one day that I realized that was just another thing we had in common. I don't know how he pulled eight decent CDs out of the bag, but he did. Also, Luke, I sent you some Branston pickle twelve years ago. Where's my ninth tape?"

A titter of laughter, and Lucas looks to the table now, and won't meet my eye. And I'm glad this is coming to an end, because any longer and I would cry, I think. In front of this room of people.

"And Marie. Beautiful, kind Marie." Marie dabs the corners of her eyes and reaches her slender hand to me. I hold it, and bend to my feet, pulling from under the table, a white heart-shaped balloon. "I know it's super crap for the environment." I sniff. "But there's a card attached to this and you can write your wish on it. A wish for you. For your marriage. For your future. For *avocados*." Marie and I giggle through our tears. "Because last time I let go of a balloon, I wished for a friend. And I got just that. So I reckon this'll be good luck."

Lucas is looking down at the tablecloth. He brings a knuckle to his cheek, and when he looks up, the light reflects in his eyes.

"To Lucas. My best friend," I say, tears freefalling now. "To Marie. To Mr. and Mrs. Moreau. To your future together."

The room erupts into applause.

And just like that, I let him go.

It isn't until an hour later, the dance floor beginning to fill out, that Eliot and I speak for the very first time since we spoke on the doorstep, and I left him to go to France. Half an hour ago the evening guests arrived, of which one is Ana. I watched her, a knot in my stomach, as she walked straight up to Eliot, all glittering eyes and shining smile. They'd spoken, very briefly, and she had walked off, face like thunder.

Now I sit at the top table, nursing a large glass of red wine, listening to Amanda tell me, tearfully, how much my speech was her favorite part of the evening. (For the seventh time in an hour. She went a bit mad on the champagne, and started, as Amanda always does when drunk, oversharing about Jean's physique—"shockingly supple for a sixty-four-year-old.")

"That box shocked me," she says again, her hand on mine. "I mean, my boy and music. I thought he had the most dreadful taste, but *eight* CDs. I wouldn't have thought he knew enough for such a thing, let alone, *eight.*"

I look at Lucas now, arms around Marie, both of them singing into each other's faces, eyes locked, smiles taut, and I know that he is exactly where he is meant to be in this moment. That kiss on that balcony was a mistake. A blip. Life isn't black and white, is it, sometimes? Sometimes what something should be—a friendship—has areas that blur into the edges. We have loved each other for so many years, and come close so many times to that kiss, in the past, that it was something that came too late, or shouldn't have come at all. And I knew that the second his lips touched mine.

"Gosh, I need the loo *again,*" says Amanda, breathing tearful, wine-drenched breath over me as she stands.

My phone vibrates on the table.

Eliot: Dance with me?

I look up. Eliot is standing just a few feet away, hands in pockets, a small smile on his face. I get up, cross the floor to meet him. I don't put up a fight, or search for excuses. I want to dance. I want to dance with him.

"You look . . ."

"Don't say bangin'."

He raises an eyebrow. "I don't ever say bangin'."

"You did," I say. "About the cheesecake."

Eliot laughs, and shakes his head. "Well, that's cheesecake, and this is you," he says. Then, "I was going to say beautiful."

"Thank you." I put my arms around his neck. "And you—you look bangin'."

"God, yeah, I do," he says with a smile, slipping his arms around my back and pulling me toward him. And we dance, bodies closer than they've ever been, butterflies breaking free in my stomach.

"Why didn't you ever tell me? About that night?"

Eliot shakes his head, talks into my ear. Goose bumps pepper my arms.

"He was all you had, Em. The only person you depended on, and I knew how lonely you were, how much you relied on him and . . . I just thought, I have to take it on the chin. For you. Because you needed your friend. You didn't need to be let down anymore."

I swallow. "But why would you do that? For me?"

Eliot leans back to take a look at me, and smiles down at me. "Well, I reckon that's pretty obvious," he says. Then he leans in, brown eyes glinting, and kisses me. Slowly. Carefully. Hand holding the side of my face, his fingertips in my hair. I close my eyes, melt into his warm lips, the press of his body. And I forget Lucas. I forget Ana. I forget that night. I forget it all. And just feel this: safe. Happy.

The next morning I am woken by a knock at my hotel room door. Eliot had walked me to my room last night and it had taken so much, between us both, to not give in to him stepping over the threshold. We kissed, all over the dance floor, all over the corridors, and even the elevator, but it stopped outside my door, lips parting, bodies pressed together, the longing so strong, it felt physical, like a magnet, like electricity. Lucas, I think, saw us, and

Amanda definitely did. She froze on her way to being carted off by Jean to their room, his arm around her, and I think he'd have put it down to drunken drivel if he hadn't seen us for himself.

"It's like foreplay, that," Rosie had said once, about a guy she dated for a while. Someone she fancied but often said she "didn't actually like," which of course baffled Fox to the brink.

"You went to Pizza Express," Fox had said. "How is Pizza Express foreplay?"

"When you fancy someone, Fox, I mean *really* fancy," Rosie had explained, "then anything is foreplay. The way they lick their lips, drink their drink, the way they smile at you over their glass or the way your fingers brush theirs when you're passing them something, *God*, it's enough to kill you. The anticipation of it all."

And I get it. Now, I get it. That's how last night was between us—electricity every time his hand brushed my back, or took my hand, and every smile between us, secret. But I can hardly believe a smile like that on his face even exists, this morning. This Eliot in front of me on the other side of my door is pale. His eyes are narrow, his shoulders tense.

"Eliot," I say. "It—what time is it?" I laugh, looking down at my makeup-stained pajamas. "God, what must I look like? Am I full-blown Ozzy Osbourne?"

He doesn't move, and I feel my heart race with anxiety. "What? What is it, what's happened?"

He presses his lips together and looks at me. "Emmie, can I come in?"

"Of course," I say. "Of course, are you all right?"

He steps over into the dark, carpeted hallway of my room, but doesn't go any further. I close the door softly behind him.

He looks up at me. "Did you go to the house, in Honfleur?"

"House? Which house?"

"The one my brother's firm worked on." I go to answer, then stop when he says, "For Ana."

"Yes," I say. "But I didn't know it was hers. Not right away. Luke took me to see it. Wanted to show me his latest project and—" His face is completely unreadable. "I'm sorry, I had no idea it was hers. I wouldn't just go snooping round other people's properties." I laugh nervously. Eliot doesn't.

"So you did go there."

"Yes, I just said we went there, a couple of weeks back, you know, the day of Rosie's thing." I'm starting to panic and I don't know why. Eliot's face. The muscle pulsing in his neck, his tight jaw. He's angry. I know he is, and my bowels churn. "Lucas took me there, to show me the house, that's all. And—"

"Did something happen?"

"What?" My heart thumps now, in my chest, in my throat, and I can't breathe. Heat creeps up my body, to my neck, to my face.

"Did something happen?" Eliot asks again. "Between you both?"

I look at him, mouth open, no words obeying and coming forward, and he watches me. "Eliot, could you just . . . come inside, sit down, y-you're just standing by the door—"

"It's a simple question, Emmie. Is Ana telling me the truth when she says she saw you and Lucas kissing on the balcony."

I stare at him, breath trapped in my throat, my heart hammering like a trapped butterfly in my chest. "Eliot . . ."

He looks at me intently now, eyes pleading for me to say no. And for me to tell the truth. After all these years, we don't need another lie between us.

"A kiss," I say in a tiny voice. "We argued. About you and that night and . . . we were both upset and he—he kissed me and I for one second forgot what I was doing, and where I was . . . but it was not what we wanted—at all. Eliot, please . . ."

He closes his eyes, his face tipped to the ceiling. His chest rises and falls. He doesn't move.

"Eliot? Honestly, it was nothing."

Eliot's hand is on the door handle now, and he's biting his lip, shaking his head.

"So, let me get this straight. You missed Rosie's talk, her conference, you missed our day out together, so you could what, go to my ex-girlfriend's house and . . . what? Be together where nobody would find you?"

"*No*," I say desperately. "No, don't be silly. Nothing happened. Nothing at all. We were mortified, disgusted, because it was such a stupid thing to do and . . . I went straight home and . . ."

"Ana was there. She pulled up, with her parents, and there you were, on the balcony. She said you were both all over each other. They could see you, from the bedroom."

"No." I shake my head. "No, that is not the truth. It was a second and if she was telling the truth, she would tell you how much we were arguing, how angry, how upset I was . . ."

"But you were there. With him. And you did kiss."

I say nothing, because I was. And I don't know what to say. I am telling the truth. And perhaps I should have told him sooner, but what would it have done? It wasn't even a real kiss. It was nothing. Nothing.

"I was going to turn down Canada for you. The work, for Mark. To help my *friend*."

I stare at him, and he pulls open the door. "Eliot, please, don't walk out."

"I need some time," he says. "This whole thing. You, Luke, this wedding, me, you . . . I need some time. You do too."

And like that, Eliot walks away.

38

"Steve Fellows," says the man on the doorstep, stretching out a chubby, clammy hand. "We spoke on the phone. About Miss Louise Dutch."

Steve Fellows sits opposite me on the two-seater, and I sit in Louise's armchair, running my fingers over the armrest cover, embroidered with flowers she did herself before her eyesight got worse. The solicitor fiddles with a thick envelope and I bend my head, to put my nose to the arm. I can smell her still. Patchouli. Everything patchouli; on her pillows, in her bath, and on her skin, and I never figured out if it was pure, or a perfume she probably handmade herself. She burned incense in the conservatory of the same smell too. God, I miss her more than ever right now. I miss her cool hand on mine, her telling me off, rolling her eyes at me for thinking too much, for being too "wet." She'd know what to tell me. She'd know what to say to make things seem less hopeless.

"You are Ms. Emmeline Blue."

I nod. "I am."

"You have been Miss Dutch's lodger for the last two and a half years."

"Correct."

"Miss Dutch and I met several weeks ago, when she understood her time was very limited."

"She did?" I ask. "I mean. She knew?"

He swallows, adjusts the collar at his thick neck, red with what looks like a shaving rash. "She has always known, I am afraid." He pauses. "We sent flowers. My partner and me."

Three bouquets turned up at the house that morning of the funeral. One from the butchers in town. Another from the staff at a garden nursery. And another: purple gladioli with white daisies.

"Steve and Jude?" I say, and he nods, smiling. "They were beautiful. Thank you. Eliot—my friend. He took them to the woodland, to where she was laid to rest." Saying his name makes my stomach ache with longing. I miss him so much, I could cry. Hot, heavy tears. Tears I have been crying every single day, hoping that'll be the end of them, but it never seems to be. They are bottomless. It's been four weeks since the wedding and nothing much of anything has happened. And I mean that. I have become stagnant and sad. *Lost.* Lucas and Marie had jetted off on their two-week honeymoon three weeks after the wedding; and from Eliot, I have heard nothing from him. But then, he's about three thousand miles away. In Canada. I hadn't realized, although I had an inkling, but then Lucas called me from his honeymoon suite in Guadeloupe.

"Marie's bought you a hand-carved avocado," he laughed, and I admit, it did make me smile. Then he'd taken a breath down the line. "Anything?" is all he'd asked, and despite myself, despite promising myself I would try so hard to keep them dammed, I'd started crying, enveloped in my duvet, curtains closed, at past noon.

He'd sighed. "But we talked. And he was quiet, yeah, but he listened, and I thought—I thought once he cooled off, once he got there, to Mark's, he'd text. Call. I'm sorry, Em."

"He's not been online once," I'd said through the tears. "He's definitely there, right?"

"Yeah. I mean, I know he called Mum," he said. "And he *will* call,

Emmie. I know El, and I know he will. He's just getting his head together."

Eliot had left after he came to my hotel room, and I had been sure to grab Lucas, at the hotel breakfast buffet, moments later, on his own. The color had drained from his face and he'd whisked outside to call him. They'd talked. But he'd said he needed space. Then Amanda, unaware and oblivious, had told Lucas a few days later that he'd had flown out to Canada.

"Probably needs to get away from Ana, throw himself into his work," she'd said to Lucas. "For a therapist, she's acting frightfully scorned. Your dad reckons she'll boil the cats given half a chance."

And I can't bear to really think about it. Canada. I feel a surge of panic soar through my chest at the thought of being so many miles and oceans away from him. Perhaps that's why he hasn't been on WhatsApp or on Instagram. I remember what he'd said about Mark's place. About how after his divorce, he'd canceled all outstanding work over here and got on a plane.

"It's the sort of place you go to reset. Switch off from everything for a while. Mend."

And the thought of him needing to mend, because of me, breaks my heart.

Steve undoes a button on his blazer now, and sits back in the chair, shirt buttons stretching against a rounded tummy. "I stayed with Louise in my twenties. Lodged here, like you," he says. "And I came back a few years ago while Jude and I were renovating the house. He stayed with his mum."

"You invited her for Christmas," I say, and he smiles. "And she mentioned you visited. An old tenant, she said, and I teased her, pretended to die of shock at the sight of two mugs washed up, instead of one."

"Yes," he chuckles. "Louise kept to herself, that's one way of putting it. But she was fiercely strong and fiercely kind too."

"Yes," I say. "She really was."

He clears his throat and pulls out a handful of paper, stapled at the corner. I take it and look down at them in my hands. "Right," he says. "So, this is Louise's last will and testament. You'll see here that this is a document stating your name at the top."

"Okay."

"And then below, you'll see there is a sentence that begins that in the event of Louise's death, the property of Two Fishers Way . . ."

I blink to focus on the neat, typed words on the page.

"Why am I . . . why am I on this?"

He smiles, hands clasping together. He takes a breath. "She's left the house to you, Emmeline. It's yours."

"W-What? No," I say. "No, that's—that's . . . no—"

"*Yes*. Yes. It's yours."

I can't speak. I can't move. I am rigid in this chair, the blood flooding to my feet, the color I know, without even looking into a mirror, has drained from my face. This house. This beautiful Victorian house, with the gardens front and back. A house like those I would walk past on the way to school, dreaming I'd have one day, to raise a family inside, like Georgia's, like the kids at school, paddling pools in the garden, dinners eaten at kitchen tables. This three-bed house with flowers in the windows.

Steve talks again, but his voice sounds as though it's underwater.

"I understand this is a shock," he says, but he cannot hide his amusement at my reaction as he carries on with the formalities, about what will happen next, and I try desperately to take in the words so they feel real. But it still feels utterly unfeasible. I have a house. I have a house in my name. A house. *A home.* I look around the lounge, my eyes lingering on all of her things, and I cry, silently, on the armchair. Because I want to put my arms around her. I want to tell her thank you. I want to hear her raspy voice say, "That's quite all right, Emmie. Now, come on. No need to be so wet."

Steve explains the formalities to me, the processes, the things that will happen next, but I can hardly take it in, my hands shaking, my teeth chattering—the shock, Steve says—and in the end, he takes himself off to the kitchen and makes me a sugary tea, and stays, waiting to see that I finish it all.

"I'll call in a few days," he says as he unlocks his car. "Let it all sink in." Then he opens the car door. "Almost forgot," he says, reaching inside. He hands me a plain, white, sealed envelope. "This is for you," he says. Then he brandishes a plastic carrier bag. "And these are for an Eliot Barnes. From Louise. Her crossword books. She said he was always good at the obscure music ones."

Dear Emmie Blue,

A nice three-bed semi, a family, and someone to love you. You have all three now, if you just stop and look.

All my love,
Louise

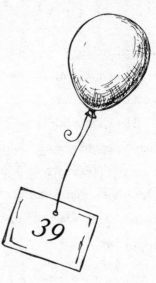

39

"It smells like a teenage boy in here."

"Great. Amazing. *Thanks.*"

"Like old washing and—"

"Disappointment," Fox adds, and his hand gently squeezes my shoulder from behind me as I stand in the doorway looking into Louise's dark, still-cluttered lounge. "I mean, I never thought I'd say this, Emmie, but even Rosie's place is cleaner than this."

I look up at him. "So, you've seen her place, now, have you?"

Fox clears his throat. "Never you mind the things I've seen. You need to turn your attention"—Fox grabs my head with two hands and angles it up and down the hallway, once into the living room again, then to the kitchen overflowing with dirty plates—"to your living quarters."

"I mean, he speaks like a dick, but he's right, Emmie," says Rosie, coming to stand next to me, rain mac still on. "It's a mess in here. I know you cleared a lot of Louise's stuff out, but this is a job bigger than you, I reckon. And it's time you let other people help. Like us. Your mates. Let us help you."

"Yes," says Fox. "But first, you need to go and get in that shower."

I am relieved to see them today, barging through the hallway, bags of groceries at their sides. I have been off work with a cold, but Rosie has diagnosed it a broken heart.

"But I can't breathe through my nose," I'd told her in protest on the phone this morning.

"Nose. Heart. It's all the same, Emmie. I got diarrhea when Alan dumped me. Shit my life away. And this is what this is. It's normal. But you've got to let us look after you. Can we come round later? Fox and me."

Instincts urged me to tell her I was fine, but instead I said, "Please," and I meant it.

I am emotionally floored. That's how I would describe myself at the moment. Floored and exhausted from living on a cocktail of such high emotions, and such low ones too. High, because Two Fishers Way is now mine. My home. And I am utterly staggered at the prospect of being a homeowner, overnight. The bills. The upkeep. And of course, the scope, the possibilities of everything this beautiful house could be. And the lows of missing Eliot. Of days and weeks passing since I've felt his strong arms around me, seen his face, heard his voice, watched the comforting sight of "typing" next to the gorgeous circle of a photo of him on WhatsApp, and waiting, smiling, for his next message.

"You're running on nothing but adrenaline," Rosie had said, packing me off upstairs with a towel. "Your amygdala is having a hoedown. We need to chill it out. Shower first. The rest, later."

And that's where I am now. Showering, at Fox and Rosie's request. My friends. My family. Two people I have realized I trust with everything, and two people who are clattering pots downstairs, and firing up vacuums and washing machines, all for me.

I wash my hair, and then blow-dry it. I open the curtains and throw up the windows in my bedroom and get dressed into proper clothes. Jeans. A tank top. It's turned warm since we entered April, and outside, new leaves the color of gooseberries begin to grow on the old oaks.

I tread downstairs, and already the house appears brighter. I can smell lemon disinfectant and hear Rosie shouting something to Fox from the kitchen to him in the living room, over the loud whoosh of the vacuum.

"Much better," says Rosie, rubber gloves on, wiping down the now clear sink. Everything washed up and put away.

"Thanks, Rosie," I say, and she nods to the table.

"Sit down. I'll make us a cuppa, then Fox is going to make lunch. And *then* you're gonna get your life in order. The moping cycle has officially ended."

Rosie and Fox stay for four hours, cleaning, scrubbing, helping me bag up some of Louise's things, which they take for the local charity shops when they leave. The kitchen and bathroom sparkle, and Fox has somehow made the cluttered, dusty living room cozy and warm-feeling. It smells like furniture polish, and before he leaves he lights some candles I didn't even know I had. Rosie has even made dinner for later—a curry that smells like coconuts. Something she said her dad makes when she's run-down or sad.

"It works. I give less of a shit once I've got a bowl of this baby. My nan's works the best, though. Fuck knows what she puts in hers. Men's souls, probably, and rightly so."

And I feel lighter having been with them. We laughed most of the afternoon, chatting, bundled on the sofa, over sandwiches and cups of tea, and it was nice seeing the little looks they threw each other, all sticky eyes and beaming smiles.

"You really like him," I'd whispered to Rosie, and she had put her fingers to her lips. "Shut up," she replied, wide-eyed, then we'd giggled when she said, "I think I fucking do, you know."

I sit now at the kitchen table, gazing out the window, the radio on as Louise always had it after dinner. I miss her, when I sit here, looking at the chair she'd sit in. I remember the way seeing her here, in the mornings, comforted me, made me feel less alone. So many meals we ate together at this table, and how much we'd laugh when Eliot joined us. I gaze now out of the window, up at the stars. The Eta Aquariids are soon. In two weeks, I think. There's a pull in my heart at the thought. It actually hurts. I just want to talk to him. Hear his voice. Say his name out loud.

I pick up my phone from the table and before I've even let myself mull it over, let my fear, my heart talk me out of it, I press a thumb to his name. Voice mail, as usual. Instantly voice mail, the way it is when a phone is switched off. I never leave voice mails. But this time, I can't bring myself to hang up.

The beep sounds.

"Hi, Eliot," I say, bright, breezy. "It's just me. I was just wondering how you're getting on down there. Or—up there. We definitely know geography isn't my strong point, eh? Ha. Yeah, um, it's no big deal. I just wondered how you were, how you're settling in. It's getting warmer here, and in true Brit style, I've already seen a few bare chests in the aisles of Tesco as if it's Saint Barts in August. Bet you're missing us over here now I've mentioned that!" I pause. Chuckle. Heart racing. "But yeah. Um. We haven't talked in weeks and . . . I just wanted to know you were okay. But listen, don't worry about calling back. It was just a quick call to check in, really. Anyway. Better go. Loads to do! Speak soon!"

My cheeks are raging hot when I hang up, and I feel sick. At the brightness. At the breeziness. I miss him. I miss him so much that it hurts, and the sadness in his face before he left that hotel room door replays in my mind. The way he was with Louise does too. With Marv. Everything he did for me. And I call him and practically sing down the phone? *What am I doing?*

I call again, cheeks burning even hotter now. Voice mail again, of course.

"Hi," I say this time. "I'm sorry. I—I rambled like an idiot and sounded like I really didn't care if you called me back or not, but . . . I do. I really do. And I forgot to tell you again that I'm sorry, Eliot. I'm sorry for the mess that I am, and . . . I miss you. I really miss you. And I wish you were here, actually. But. Canada deserves you. With all its . . . maple syrup and pretty blondes in furry hats and snow and . . . I hope you're well. I hope you're happy. Bye, Eliot."

I hang up. The house is silent, besides the soft mumble of the radio. I look around at the now glistening kitchen. *My* kitchen. I look at Louise's empty chair. I look at the pot of gingery, coconut curry on the hob.

Order. I need order in my life. Rosie's right. The wallowing cycle is up. It's time to find out who I am. Without Balloon Boy. Without the fear Robert Morgan planted within me, like an arrow I couldn't pull out, the night of the Summer Ball. Who am I, without the fear of that one night? Without Eliot. Without the need for anyone to complete me. Mum. Marv. A partner. Children. Eliot told me once I was enough, without all of that. And like the constellations and stars and obscure music facts, he is right.

I am enough.

I click open the padlock of the notebook Eliot bought me and turn to the first fresh page. And with Louise's golden pen, I make a list.

To: Emmie.Blue@gmail.co.uk
From: noreply@jobs.site.uk
Date: April 10, 2019

Dear Ms. Emmie Blue,

Thank you for expressing interest in the position of Junior Counselor for Fortescue Lane Secondary School. This email is to confirm that we have received your application and will be in touch shortly, should the employer wish to organize an interview.

40

I only remember one Easter in my life, and that was when I was seven. Den and I went to an egg hunt at the local park, and when we got home, we cooked messily, over multiple open recipe books, a roast dinner. Lamb. Potatoes. Peas that Den insisted we stirred mint sauce into. We all sat at the table that afternoon—Den, Mum, and me—and I remember staring out of the window as we ate, willing people to walk by, on their Sunday afternoon walks, and to look in, to see how much we looked like all those families on TV. To wish they could join us. Tomorrow will be the first Easter I've celebrated since then. And I'll be with my dad. I will be with my sister. I'll be with my family.

"What do eighteen-year-old law students even like?" I'd asked Rosie.

"It's Easter, Emmie. You don't need to take presents. You don't know them yet."

"But I feel I should. What about flowers for Carol?"

"How about you take dessert?" she suggested. "Louise must have loads of recipe books knocking about on those shelves of yours." And that's when I decided to make a cake. Something of Louise's; a recipe from the little homemade recipe book she kept in the tote bag that never left her side.

Some handwritten. Some handed down. Some cut from magazines. "It's full of recipes I've collected since I was about twenty-five," she'd told me once. "Everything in there works like a charm. As dependable as dogs, those recipes, every last one of them."

I don't often go into Louise's room. Her wardrobe is still stuffed with her clothes, but I'll get to it soon. One step at a time. Because that's what I'm doing now. One small step forward at a time, until I gather enough distance, that when I look over my shoulder, I can barely see those things in the past that held me back for so long.

I find Louise's tote bag down the side of her bed, where she always left it as she slept, Eliot or I placing it there gently, in reach when she was ready to sleep. It was her survival kit, she said, and she'd hang it over the backs of chairs she sat in, and on the handles of the Zimmer frame she used toward the end.

"You got the antidote to the future zombie virus in that thing?" Eliot used to say, and she'd laugh and reply, "If by zombie virus you mean indigestion, then yes, I do."

I pick it up, sit on the edge of her bed with it, and flick through the contents. Seed packets, lists and reminders scrawled on the back of receipts. Pens and packets of tissues and Rennies. Then I see it. A CD. A blank CD, I think at first, but when I pull it out, open the case and hold it in my hands, I see. I see the track listing on the inside sleeve. Five songs. I see the words. Not "Dear Balloon Girl." But "Dear Emmie Blue." And at the bottom, not "Balloon Boy X" but "Eliot X."

The ninth CD.

I am holding the ninth CD.

———

Mix CD. Vol. 9.

Dear Emmie Blue,

Track 1. *Because I wish I could tell you it was me
          (these songs)*

Track 2. *Because I wish I could tell you it wasn't me
          (that night)*

Track 3. *Because I miss you. Every single day.*

Track 4. *Because I loved you the moment I met you*

Track 5. *Because I always will*

Love,

Eliot

X

41

I can't believe I am here, in the walls of the place that broke me. The night I sat down to make my list, I opened a web browser and headed straight to the job sites. I checked the "education" box that I always leave blank, and could hardly believe the third job down.

School counselor, trainee position, at Fortescue Lane Secondary School. My school. The school in which my life fell apart. The fields of which I stood on and let go of the balloon that made its way to Lucas. The school I have been too frightened to even picture in my mind, let alone go to the same town it's in. But I hit apply. I hit upload and attached my CV. I spent a whole hour on a cover letter. A trainee school counselor. I studied education for this reason. Before I dropped out, I had started to study counseling and psychology alongside it for this reason. And I loved my job at the photo studio for this reason—yes, it was a completely different occupation, but talking to the kids, to families, learning their stories, was the best part of that job, for me.

Laura, Senior School Counselor, and the woman interviewing me today, smiles at me from across the desk, then looks down at my CV in front of her.

"And you are working at the Clarice in Shire Sands at the moment, is that correct?"

I nod. "Kitchen staff," I say. And she grins and says, "I have a soft spot for that place. I had my wedding reception there. Do they still do that sticky plum pudding thing?"

"Yes," I tell her. "I think there would be a revolution if we took it off the menu."

"Quite right," Laura chuckles. "I'd get sacked working there, I think. I'd eat it all."

I took the bus today, into Ramsgate, and saw it as the bus rumbled past it—my old flat. The flat Mum and I moved into when we got back from Cheshire. The flat I lived in until I was nineteen, and from age fourteen, mostly alone. I felt nothing really, other than the smallest of pangs at the sight of my old bedroom window. But that was it. Just a building. Just a window. Just a shell in which people make home with things and people; a shell which goes back to being just that, when those things and people are removed. And once I'd seen the flat, and once the bus had driven slowly down the old route Georgia and I would walk to school, past the chip shop, past the pet shop, and the weird hole-in-the-wall cobblers nobody ever seemed to use, my fear of walking into the school—into Fortescue Lane— had dissipated. From stomach-nauseating, leg-wobbling panic, to usual pre-interview nerves. It was another lifetime ago. I was a child. I am now an adult. He can't hurt me now.

"Emmie, why do you think," says Laura, who keeps on firing questions at me from a pre-typed list slipped in a folder on her lap, "that you, more perhaps than others, are suited to this role, as junior school counselor?"

I take a deep breath. I look Laura in the eye, and I finally say the words I was so afraid to tell the person on the other side of this desk fifteen years ago.

"I was sexually assaulted by a man who worked here at this school," I say. "And the worst part of it all was that I had nobody to talk to. I'd like to be, if I can, that someone to talk to for someone. It was the thing that saved me in the end."

I can hardly believe it's him, when I turn out of the school grounds. He leans against the car, keys in hand, his skin bronze. He looks taller, more grown-up. Maybe that's what happens when you're married, when you've pledged forever to someone—it shows in your face, in the way you carry yourself.

"Hey, Emmie Blue," he says, and a smile spreads across my face involuntarily at the sight of him. "You look like someone who has just smashed their interview."

"This is a nice surprise." I smile. He puts an arm around me as I approach, pulls me into him, kisses the top of my head. "Like, really, really nice."

Lucas pulls back, gives a smile. "Yeah, well, I actually wanted to drive you to your interview, make sure I was there when you walked in, but I couldn't get out of a conference call at work this morning."

"But you're here now," I say. "With . . . *potatoes?*"

Lucas laughs, and lifts the bag of potatoes he's carrying under his other arm the way a lawyer carries a heavy file. "I thought we could go back to yours and have chips and radioactive ketchup. Like old times. Celebrate."

"I don't have the job yet," I tell him.

"That's not what I'm celebrating, Em." Lucas squints up at the school behind me, and nods toward it. "I'm celebrating you walking in there."

I look over my shoulder. "I didn't know whether I would ever be able to."

"I did," says Lucas. I look up at him now, the sun turning his hair the color of spun sugar, the spatter of freckles on his nose, and all I see is the friend who was there when nobody else was. The only friend I had in the world, who showed me what it was to be loved. To have a family. Nothing else. Nothing more.

"Hey, remember all those times I'd say I wish I could be waiting for you at the school gates?" Lucas says. "Show those fuckers."

"I do," I say.

"Finally made it."

"But there're no fuckers to show anymore," I say, and Lucas lets go of me and says, "No. I suppose all the fuckers have moved on. Like us."

"Like us," I say.

When we get back to Fishers Way, we cook chips together, Lucas peeling and cutting the potatoes, and me turning off the gas every few seconds once the oil is boiling because I'm scared of setting fire to the house. My house. My home.

"Will you stop bloody turning it off?"

"Those chip pan fire demos on Blue Peter never left my memory, Luke, I'm only keeping us safe."

We talk nonstop at the dinner table. Lucas tells me about Guadeloupe. And I tell him about Marv, Carol, and Cadie. I tell him about the wonderful, warm, and cozy three-hour afternoon I spent with them.

"We had a roast dinner, crumble, and then played Trivial Pursuit," I tell him, and Lucas's eyes widen. "*Shit.* Family goals, or what? And Cadie. Was she nice?"

"Amazing, Luke. She cried when Marv introduced us. And so did I. She's really funny, and so intelligent. She looks like me. We have the same chin, the same shifty side-eye."

Lucas grins, shakes his head. "It's unbelievable, Em. You have a half sister. I have a half brother."

I smile. "Always meant to be."

We finish eating, and Lucas excuses himself to use the toilet, while I sip my beer. When he walks back in, he's holding the box I gave him on his wedding day. The box of CDs. The box of CDs Eliot made for me, all those years ago. He sits next to me at the table, places it down, and pushes the box toward me.

"These are yours, Emmie. Not mine." I see him swallow as he steels himself to speak.

"I know," I say. "I already know they were Eliot."

Lucas looks up at me, lips parted. "Did he—"

"I found a CD with Louise's things. I think he was gearing up to tell me and then didn't. Louise actually was going to, I think. She said she had something for me, before she died, and I kept wondering what it was . . ."

Lucas stares at me, nodding his head slowly.

"I called him, straightaway. Left some warbling mad voice mail, telling him I knew." I don't tell Lucas that I told him I was glad they were him. That I felt like I knew, on some level. That my heart knew before my head.

Lucas clears his throat, fiddles with the corner of the napkin in his hands. "You sent me the French tape, and . . . Eliot listened to it. He got a distinction in languages and I wanted to make sure you had the best feedback. And he said you talked about some *bad bands* and how I should send you a mixtape. The way brothers do, when sharing tips on impressing girls." Lucas laughs embarrassedly, the skin beneath his freckles going pink. "But I know shit all about music, really, compared to him, so he made me one, and I'd just posted it. You loved it so much that when you wanted another, I'd just ask him, and he'd hand it over, and I'd just send it, Em. I didn't even look inside. I just knew it made you happy."

And they did. Those CDs were proof I was loved. That someone cared enough to spend time making something for me.

"And then, in your room one day, I saw them. And . . . I was jealous, of all the shit he'd written inside. I knew he had feelings for you. So I stopped it. Then the stuff with Stacey happened at the party, and all three of us sort of . . . *broke up*—that was that, you know?"

The cold creeps in outside, the sky turning gray with heavy, black clouds, and the kitchen darkens.

"I wish I'd known," I say.

"I know," he says. "And I really wanted to tell you, Em. So many times. But I was so conscious of not upsetting you, or making you feel like you couldn't trust me as your friend. That is all I've ever cared about. And . . . I'm a coward. I am."

"Maybe you were." I smile. "But you're not so much now." I look down at the box of CDs. "Not even close."

"I thought you might throw me out."

I laugh. "No chance. You'd have to top previous Dick Moves to get thrown out, and that'd be quite a hard thing to do at this point."

Lucas laughs. He holds out his glass, and I clink it. We drink.

"When I spoke to him," Lucas says. "When we talked, after the wedding, about Ana's house and our stupid argument and . . ." The kiss, he wants to say, but he can't bring himself to. "I told him."

"Told him what?"

"That you belong together. And I should've never stood in the way. Even if I didn't realize I was at times."

I blink at him, my heart swelling behind my ribs. With happiness. With sadness. "Do you really believe that?"

Lucas nods, squeezes my hand across the table.

"I think if Emmie and Eliot doesn't happen, then there's no hope for the rest of us."

I smile, tears sting my eyes. I hide my face with my hand, and Lucas laughs. "Ah shit, she's getting all snively. Sort your life out, Emmie Blue, nobody likes a sap." But he squeezes my hand again and pulls me toward him. We hold each other across the table.

"You should call him," Lucas says as he pulls away.

"I have. Numerous times. Voice mail."

Lucas groans. "God, he's such a caveman. I mean, I know people talk about turning their phone off, having some downtime while they're away, but nobody really does it. They just tell Instagram they are."

"Except for Eliot," I say.

"Except for Eliot," Lucas repeats.

"Unless he's blocked me or something."

"Mm-mm," says Lucas, shaking his head. "Nah. Never. He'll come around. He'll be back."

"And if he doesn't?"

Lucas takes my hand again, balls his into a fist, like we're about to arm wrestle. "Then you'll get through it, Emmie Blue."

"I'm made of strong stuff," I say, and Lucas says, "Always have been."

Dear Emmie,

I hope my email finds you well, and I apologize for the delay in getting back to you. Things have been very busy in the run-up to exams here.

It was a pleasure meeting you and I feel, along with the rest of the team, that you would be a perfect fit for Fortescue Lane. I would therefore love to offer you the position of Junior School Counselor, starting on Tuesday, May 28.

I look forward to hearing from you and do so much hope that you accept.

Kind regards,
Laura Borne

43

WhatsApp from Rosie Kalwar:

Fox has got even posher since we got here to London. And OMG his dad is like a fucking royal or some shit. He has a mustache. Like a proper woolly mammoth mustache and keeps saying things I have only heard in Downton Abbey. I'm hiding in the loo texting this.

WhatsApp from Rosie Kalwar:

Also, Fox's brother told me that Fox was "agonizing" over telling me he liked me last year. HE LIKED ME LAST YEAR! Can you believe it? Fox literally choked on his bread at that point. Then choked again on his meringue when they started telling me all about his ex-girlfriend, Beatie. BEATIE. I asked if he dated her back in 1917.

WhatsApp from Rosie Kalwar:

(and also if I inherited his dad's house if he dies from all this choking.)

WhatsApp from Rosie Kalwar:

Anyway Em, see you at the hotel next week for your LAST WEEK. God. I am going to cry when you leave. I might stage a protest.

UK Stargazers Unite! In the early hours of May 6, keen star-spotters will be able to watch the incredible show of the Eta Aquariids: a meteor shower caused by the debris of Halley's Comet, and one that even the most unseasoned of astronomers will be able to enjoy, with up to thirty shooting stars an hour.

Eliot and I never really had plans. We'd barely got off the ground before he'd left for Canada, before it all unraveled messily and went wrong, but I knew the only way I'd get through today—the day we'd planned to watch the meteor shower—without that heavy, empty feeling in my chest, without the nauseous pull in my stomach of missing him, was keeping busy. I have been alone for the whole day, but I have spent it painting the hallway of Two Fishers Way, the stereo turned up loud, the windows and back doors open, pushing a fresh spring breeze through the house. I want to make every room here a clean slate, but decided to keep some of Louise's things—her handmade curtains, her framed traveling photos she took with Martha—so her stamp is always on it in some way. It's going to take awhile, but once it's completely clear and decluttered, I'll contact the charity Laura told me about during my interview. A charity organization that offers rooms to young teenagers escaping abuse or facing homelessness. I'd get some rent from the charity to help pay the utilities, and people that really need it, get a home. I feel good about it. It felt right the second she told me about it. And that way, the house will always be full. For them. For me. Like Louise and I were, really; an unconventional but functional family, in a way.

I stand back now, old jeans smeared with white paint, the smell of emulsion stuck in my nose, and smile. It looks bright and fresh; with new life breathed into it. I check the time on my phone. Almost six. I'll shower, have some toast, watch a film. Then I can go to bed, and when I wake up, our planned night with the shooting stars will be over, the sky no longer dark, but blue. And it'll be just another day. Missing him.

When I sit myself in front of the TV an hour later in fresh pajamas and my wet hair in a towel, a Tom Cruise film is the first thing that flashes onto the screen when I turn it on.

"Why is he always holding a gun?" I'd said to Eliot once. "It's so *boring.*"

"Well, you would say that. You've been spoiled with the groundbreaking likes of *Pucked.*"

"Exactly," I'd said. "*Pucked.* My now favorite movie of all time."

And my favorite only because I had watched it with him, snuggled up together on this sofa, watching and talking and laughing, hours ticking by. I miss him. And it doesn't seem to be getting easier. In fact, I miss him more every day, and it's physical. It hurts.

I take out my phone. I find his name. My thumb hovers above it. Should I? *Should I?*

I look at the television, then through the blinds to the darkening sky, preparing for its show. And before I talk myself out of it, I press his name. *Eliot.* And it rings. God. It's ringing. *It's ringing.* I don't breathe. My heart thumps in my throat like a drum. I feel sick. I wait. Wait for his voice. Wait for his lovely voice to say hello. But it keeps ringing, and voice mail, once again, clicks on.

I hang up before the beep.

If his phone is back online, he'd have heard the voice mails I have left, the texts. And he'll see. He'll see a missed call from me when he next looks at his phone. And if Eliot wants to talk to me, he will call me. He knows how to reach me. He knows I miss him.

I place my phone on the table, pull a blanket over my legs, and turn up the volume on the TV.

My phone vibrates; a buzzing on the coffee table, jolting me awake.

I didn't mean to fall asleep on the sofa, and for a moment, I am disorientated. The dark sky outside. The toast, half-eaten on the coffee table. The soap opera I started watching, now finished, and in its place a panel show, and audience laughter. I sit up, pushing my hair from my face, and feel like I'm still dreaming when I see Eliot's name on the screen.

I answer quickly, swallow. "Hey." My voice croaks with sleep.

"Hey you," he says on the other end, and my insides melt to jelly. I have missed him; missed his voice. "How's it going?"

"Good," I say, as if on autopilot. "Well, no. Not good. Not really."

Silence.

"I called you," I say pointlessly, reaching for words to fill the silence. "And I—I left you voice mails too, which I know you've probably already heard, God help you, and—"

"Emmie, I can't hear you."

"What?"

"You're in the living room, aren't you?" he says. "The signal in Louise's living room is always patchy—"

"Of course." I jump up. "Yes. Sorry. One sec." I rush into the hallway, practically running, head woozy with sleepiness, and I'm just glad he can't see me; how desperate I am to hear him, for him to hear me, to keep him on the phone. "How about now?"

"Hello?"

"God—really?" Now? I want to shout at my phone. You choose to do this *now?* "Hello? Hello, Eliot?"

"Hello," he says. "Have you moved yet?"

"Yes," I say, and I hear him laugh; a little chuckle. "You can hear me, then," I say.

"Sort of," he says, a smile in his voice.

Then there is silence again.

"I found your CD," I say. "I tried to call and I texted, too, but—"

"Louise was meant to give it to you. We spoke about it, the night of the full moon, and I told her. I wanted to give it to you, but I was . . . chicken-shit. She said you two talked a lot and she'd give it to you, so there was no pressure—in case, you know . . ."

"In case what?"

Eliot laughs again. "In case you were shocked. A bad shocked."

"I wasn't," I say. "I'm glad. I'm so glad it was you."

"Emmie? Hello?"

"Oh, you're kidding—hello? Eliot, can you hear me? Eliot?"

"Hello? Hello?"

"This is hellish," I say into the phone.

"Em, can't you just nip outside?"

Before he's even suggested it, I'm in the porch, and unlocking the front door. I step out, socks on gravel, and walk as if on hot coals, down the driveway. The tiny rocks sting the soles of my feet.

"How about now?" I wince.

"Better," he laughs.

"I thought it was 2019," I say. "We have robots, for God's sake, and Facebook and spiralizers, and yet our phones can't cope with a long-distance call."

"Well," says Eliot, smile in his voice. "It's not too long a distance."

I stop. "You're at home?"

"No," he says. "Not yet."

"France?"

"Could you keep going, Em? Little bit further?"

"Eliot, are you sure this isn't your phone?" I take my phone from my ear and look at the screen. "I have a full signal. Like, every bar."

"Little to the left," he says.

"Are you kidding? This isn't a game of Twister."

He laughs again. "Keep coming. Toward me."

I stop then, socks wet on the gravel. "What? What did you say?"

"Look up," he says. And his deep, warm voice doesn't just come from the phone.

I lift my face. And there he is. Eliot. *Eliot.* Standing at the top of the driveway, black jacket open, a smile on his lips, the breeze ruffling his hair. He slowly drops the phone down to his side.

"You can hang up now," he says, smiling.

And I freeze. I cannot move. And phone still to my ear, my socks sodden with water, I reach a hand out to him. He closes the gap between us, taking my hand, tucking hair behind my ear. He brings a warm hand to my cold face.

He smiles. "Hi," he says. "I've really missed you."

"And I've missed you," I say through tears. "Where have you been?"

"Pulling my head out my arse," he says, smiling weakly. "Hardest thing I ever had to do was leave you. But I needed that time, Emmie."

I nod. "I did too, I think."

"You did," he says softly. "We both did."

He pulls me into him then, arms tightening around me, strong hands against my back. Him. Him. It was always him.

He draws back and looks down at me with dark, playful eyes. "You've been painting," he says, bringing a curl of hair to my face, the tip white.

"I did shower. I missed a bit."

He nods, scrunches up his face, and looks down on the top of my head. "You've missed lots of bits."

"Have I?"

He looks down at me and laughs. "Just kidding. You look bangin', Flower. Painted hair and all."

"Ozzy eyes and all."

"Especially Ozzy eyes." He smiles. "I just hope you're not too knackered after all that painting." He looks up at the sky. "Meteors are best seen at the most ungodliest of hours, remember."

"I'm wide-awake," I say, and I look up at him, run a finger down his stubbly cheek and onto his soft lips. He kisses the tip of my finger. "You're really here," I whisper. "In front of me."

"I am, Emmie Blue," he says. "And I always have been."

He kisses me then, lifting me from the cold, wet ground with strong arms. The barriers are gone. There is nothing between us.

It's just us.

Us and the stars in the sky.

Epilogue

The French sun beats down, and Lucas Moreau ignores his mother calling after him from the beachside café. He doesn't want to be here, in France. He doesn't want to be on this beach, with his brother, with his parents. He wants to be at home, with Tom, with his school friends. He wants his old bedroom. He wants those chips he always gets from the café by the public pool he and Tom go to on Saturdays. He misses home. *He wants home.*

"Luke?"

He hears his brother from behind him, voice wobbling as his feet pound the sand. He ignores him.

"Luke, dude, can you hear Mum?" He slows as he catches up to him, strolling next to him on the sand. "She wants to know if you want lunch."

"No," he snaps. "I don't want anything, Eliot. Tell her I don't want anything."

Eliot puts a hand to his brother's chest. They stop on the sand. "Look, I know it isn't ideal," says Eliot, "but you need to try."

"Try what? Living here? I don't want to *try*, Eliot, I want to—what?"

Eliot looks past his brother, eyes focused on something in the sand. He steps toward it. "What's that?"

"What's what?" asks Lucas.

"That," says Eliot. "That red thing. Is it a—? Ah shit—" Eliot's phone buzzes in his hand, interrupting his train of thought. "*Shit,*" he says again, looking at the screen. "I think it's about the job. The apprenticeship. Don't go anywhere, okay? Mum'll kill me if I lose you."

Lucas nods, gives a shrug. "I'll be here. Not exactly sailing home to London, am I?"

Eliot trudges away, across the sand, lifting his phone to his ear. Lucas steps toward the item Eliot found in the sand. He pulls at it, sand scattering. A balloon. A deflated red balloon, a tag attached.

Lucas picks it up.

Acknowledgments

*D*ear *Emmie Blue* exists thanks to so many people, and I feel so lucky to know that I have such a brilliant team of people behind me.

I owe so much to my amazing agent, Juliet Mushens. I have said this so many times, and will probably continue to, until I'm old and wrinkly—thank you for making my dreams come true. I would be lost without your advice, plot solving, anxiety extinguishing, and your friendship. (Oh, and the expert tips on when to insert topless tradesmen and when to remove round jaws, obvs.)

Thank you also to the whole Caskie Mushens dream team, and to the brilliant Jenny Bent at The Bent Agency, New York.

To Emily Bestler and Lara Jones at the wonderful Simon & Schuster, thank you from the bottom of my heart for your passion, excitement, and hard work. It's a dream to have you as a publisher.

Katie Brown, working with you is pure joy. I live for your hilarious notes in tracked changes and you always work with such heart. Thank you to the whole lovely, hard-working team at Trapeze, and all my wonderful publishers around the world for your belief in this book. (OMG. I can't believe I even get to *say* such a sentence. Let me just pinch myself.)

To the many talented writer-friends I am fortunate enough to have; you are the best faraway work colleagues I could ever ask for. Thank you Gilly McAllister, L. D. Lapinski, Lynsey James, Lindsey Kelk, Hayley Webster, Laura Pearson, Stephie Chapman, Rebecca Williams, Nikki Smith, Holly Seddon, Hina Malik, and so many of you who are at the proverbial water cooler in my phone. Your words make the world a better place.

To my lovely, beautiful friends who accept and love me for the old-before-my-time, Friday-nights-in-my-pajamas hermit that I am. Thank you.

Bubs. Thank you for being the best brother and the best friend. Sparkle, next. It's written in stone (well, ink) now. I can't go back on it.

Mum and Steve, Dad and Sue, Nan and Grandad, and Alan. You are the warmest, proudest, funniest family of all. I'd be lost without you.

And lastly (because everyone knows you always save the best until last), to my beautiful babies, and my Ben. You are home and safety. Wherever you are, is my favorite place to be.